Grace & The Ghost

Estelle Maher

Grace & The Ghost

First published in 2017
Estelle Maher

Copyright © Estelle Maher 2017

The rights of the author has been asserted in accordance with
Sections 77 and 78 of the Copyright Designs and Patents Act,
1988.

ISBN 978-1542580168

This book is a work of fiction. Names, characters, businesses,
organisations, places and events other than those clearly in the
public domain, are either the product of the author's
imagination or are used fictitiously. Any resemblance to actual
persons, living or dead, events or locales is entirely
coincidental.

DEDICATION

To Pete
Thank you for your unfathomable love and support.

ACKNOWLEDGEMENTS

This book would never be here without the help and support of some wonderful people in my life.

My sincere thanks go to my incredible editor Sue Miller, for her guidance and Fairy Godmother approach in getting my book to the ball.

To Alan Jones, for creating my wonderful book cover and designing something that was not only better than I imagined, but he even managed to incorporate my two main characters' names in the design. (Can you spot them?)

To Phil Burrows at Team Author UK, for his support in morphing me into an author.

To my great friends, Jay Churchill and Carina Clarke, for reading the book before I sent it out into the big wide world with their enthusiastic stamp of approval.

To my beautiful children, Chloé and Zack, for listening to me witter on about characters they were yet to read and when they did, make them part of the family.

To my dogs, Levi and Souki, for keeping me company on those long, lonely days when Grace didn't want to talk to me.

And finally, to my husband Mr M, for keeping me sane and the wine glass full.

CONTENTS

It is impossible to see the angel unless you first have a notion for it.

James Hillman

CHAPTER 1

As she sat on the damp and musky bus on the way home, she started to make a mental list for the weekend ahead. She wanted to make sure that no one or no thing was going to remove her from the sofa until Monday when she had to hitch a ride on the soggy bus back to work. She often thought the bus was so damp that a shaft of light from someone's phone could probably produce a rainbow. Her mental list mainly consisted of wine and chocolate. She was not an alcoholic, just someone who was very thirsty at the weekends, she often told herself.

Every promise went out the window at the weekends. After a week of semi committed abstinence in the alcohol, sugar and carb department she always made it to the weekend and gave in. No one noticed she denied herself through the week and no one noticed the amount of wine and pizza she packed away at the weekend, except maybe the bin man. Like most girls, even though she was thin, she wanted to be thinner.

She pulled out her phone and started to tap away creating the list. As she popped the phone back into her pocket with headphones still furnishing her ears she continued to watch the world go by outside the steamy bus. The landscape would change dramatically from work to home. The office she worked in was buried in a huge Georgian building among other companies that were all equally impressed with the building's post code and iconic status. But after a while of working there it just felt like everywhere else and she was certain its inhabitants felt the same as they trudged in just before nine a.m. as well. She had left the tallness of the town behind and the suburbs where the buildings were somewhat shorter but just as dense. She was not far from home now and the landscape now illustrated fields cloaked in the night-time black with the occasional twinkle of streetlights in the distance. The odd hamlet would quickly disappear as soon as you realised you were in it and then the view would turn back to the black fields.

The small humpback bridge was her marker and she always waited until the driver had driven over it. She made the mistake once of standing 'mid-hump' and was flung backwards and forwards as if on an invisible horizontal bungee wire. The patrons of 'Cumfee Bus' watched in silent amusement but in her head she could hear their laughter and it was deafening. The natural marker came and went and she stood up to depart the bus. As the driver slowed down, she continued to look out of the window as she didn't want to engage with idle chit chat with him. Fridays, in particular, was the driver's favourite day to engage. He would ask the usual questions of what she was up to at the weekend. The first and only time she answered was that she was going back to the town for drinks, in which he enquired further as to why and with whom. Of course, she felt it was only polite to answer him but as she did she could feel the heat behind her. The tutting became louder and the frowns were more evident on the passengers who were clearly not interested in her social life and simply wanted to get home. The only reason they were not on their way home was due to her babbling on inanely about Vera retiring and what a good worker she was. Since then she had learned her lesson and would not dare to look at the bus driver, never mind give him a courteous nod for fear of engagement. She also kept the head phones in as a back-up deterrent in case he felt particularly sociable.

But as she looked out of the window she quickly noticed a black figure disappear from the top of the bridge as if climbing or, God forbid, jumping. She looked around at the four remaining passengers to see if they too had witnessed the sight. Two were asleep, one was on his phone and the other was reading. She carried on squinting in the distance but the darkness defeated her.

As the bus came to a halt, she hastily thanked the driver and jumped off still looking in the direction of the bridge. The bus drove off and left her standing on the edge of the pavement. It felt eerie just standing there in the semi darkness and she recalled the image back in her mind. The more she scrutinised the memory the more she was sure that it was a person that had climbed over the bridge.

'What if it was a kid?' she thought. 'What if it was some old person with dementia?' She took a few tentative steps towards the hump back bridge. 'What the bloody hell am I doing? What if it's some huge nutter waiting to pounce?' She was now hoping for a dementia victim, with malnutrition and cataracts to ensure her victory in persuading the person off the bridge. 'What if I'm too late? Oh God, who do I call if there is a body in the river? The police? What will they do? It's not as if they can arrest him. It will be too late for an ambulance and I'm not sure paramedics carry snorkels?'

She was nearly at the bridge. She could only hear the river running and her own Darth Vader style breathing. She looked behind her to see if she could pass the responsibility of the task on or at least share it, but no one was there. It was Friday night and she knew everyone in the village was either at The Blacksmith Arms – The Blacky, or settling down for the night to watch television. Except Nell, who was in the shop of course.

She was now at the bridge and the street light above offered her a little comfort. She looked around one final time but still no one was there.

'Hello....'

Nothing. Just the sound of the moving water beneath her. She walked towards the edge of the sandstone wall and stretched her neck as much as she could without actually looking over. With the lighting she gave a good impression of E.T.

'Hello...' a little louder.

Then she heard a rustle. 'What the....' she thought. She stepped forward towards the wall and plucked up the courage to peer over into the inky water.

'Is there anybody there?' From what she could see, the water was clearly devoid of any dead bodies. She felt some relief but only on a minuscule level. She then heard the rustle again and this time it sounded close. It sounded just beyond her fingertips. She mustered her courage and moved forward again. She was now so close the front of her coat was snagging the wall as she bravely bent over to get a good look.

'BOO!'

His face was inches away from hers and she jolted back, stumbled off the kerb and landed straight onto her backside in the middle of the road. His laughter ripped through the silence and as she watched him in his amusement she could feel her anger rising up like a newly shaken bottle of pop. The tears were now streaming down his face which he attempted to wipe away with one hand while still clinging to the bridge wall from the river side.

'You'll get piles if you keep your little bottom on that cold floor you know!' This statement seemed to reignite his laughing and he watched her quickly pick herself up and try to compose herself. He could see she was angry but he didn't care. He found the whole scenario highly amusing and he wanted to savour this moment as much as he could as they were very few and far between.

'Well, I'm glad you think all this is funny. You gave me the fright of my bloody life, you stupid idiot!' she bellowed.

'Are you Welsh?' he interjected with a look of bemusement which also ceased his laughter.

'What?' This totally confused her. 'Yes, I'm Welsh!'

Her anger was rising further. With the little light that was offered from the street lamp she studied his appearance. She noticed his huge overcoat and even in the contrasts of light and shadow she could see it was ingrained with dirt. His hand that was gripping the sandstone wall was so filthy it looked like he washed them with Cherry Blossom boot polish. She also knew that the hand and rest of the body that it was attached to had also not had a wash in quite some time. He was a tramp.

'What the devil are you doing round here then?' he enquired. She noticed his accent was very different to hers. He sounded posh. If the truth be told he sounded like Lord Grantham after a 'very satisfying party'.

'Can't Welsh people move away from Wales?' she spat. 'Never mind, what I'm doing here, what the hell are you doing hanging off a ledge,' her voice was getting louder and she started towards him, 'in the pitch black, with a river underneath you and no one around for bloody miles?!'

His face then became relaxed and he hunched over the wall on his forearms to find a more comfortable positon as if it was the most natural thing to do.

'I was not intending to hang off a ledge, as you put it. I was going to venture to the edge of the river and look for shelter. It is not pitch black,' he gesticulated towards the overhead street light, 'and you are here so I am not alone,' he finished calmly.

'Well, not for bloody much longer.' She grabbed her bag off the ground and started to stomp towards civilisation, or the village as everyone else called it. As she marched on, she heard him call behind her.

'I'm sorry I frightened you, Daff!' She stopped suddenly and turned around, her face seething.

'Daff? My name is Grace, you bloody cretin!'

'But I'm going to call you Daff, after the Daffodil, the national symbol of Wales. Don't you like it?' he shouted. But Grace turned on her heel and as she headed towards Nell's she began muttering under her breath.

She marched the whole way to the shop with the stance of a bull in a bullfight, with the glass door of the shop symbolizing the matador's red cloak. She flew into the shop, snatched up a basket and proceeded to pluck the items off the shelves while her gaze remained focused on the wine section. It was hardly a wine section to be fair. It was three bottles (red, white and rosé) nestled in between an old Baby Cham box and an unwanted bottle of Ouzo that Nell had been trying to flog since her sister brought it back from her travels in Greece. It should be noted that her sister had died thirteen years ago. Grace slammed the basket down on the counter and pointed to the top shelf.

'Do you have any more white Nell, or is that your lot?' Grace began to stare at Nell in the hope that the answer would come quicker than Nell's usual delivery. Nell began to feel nervous and she wasn't sure if it was because Grace was in a particularly bad mood or that she was struggling to recall if there was any more wine in the back.

'Let me go and check, Grace. I shan't be a minute, pet.' Nell went to shuffle off.

'Don't bother! Just give me all three bottles you have up there. That'll do for now.' Nell raised her eyebrows but was too scared to say any more. Grace looked at Nell, frustrated at her lack of speed in retrieving her plastic step to aid her in reaching the bottles. Her impatience rose further as she silently watched Nell climb onto the stool, take one bottle, shuffle to the counter, place it down, shuffle back to the step and repeat the same thing again. And again! Nell's hand began to shake as she punched the prices into the till under Grace's judgemental gaze.

'Everything all right, my dear?' Nell asked meekly.

'I'm fine! I just want to get home. How much is it?' Grace snapped.

'With all the other bits and bobs,' she said softly, 'that'll be £21.91.' Grace counted the money out, banged it on the counter, snatched the bag from poor Nell and marched out of the shop. Nell was exhausted with the short but very intense episode.

As Grace left the shop she gave a momentary glance in the direction of the bridge and quickly concluded that it was too dark to see anything and quite frankly, she didn't care. She headed for home and soon walked most of her anger out by the time she reached her own front door.

Grace lived in a small cottage off the main road through the village. To call it a main road was ambitious as the only traffic was the Cumfee Bus which ran every two hours, the occasional car owner in the village driving off to buy something more exotic than boiled ham and the milk float whose appearance was touch and go if it was raining. To describe the village sleepy would give the impression of a slow paced environment when truth be told it was reminiscent of a coma ward, on sleeping tablets. Sometimes it suited Grace and sometimes not. Working in town, which was by far a deep contrast, was sometimes enough life for her and she welcomed the snail pace of home.

As soon as she walked through the door and into the darkness of her living room she could feel the gentle nuzzling at her feet and the excited sniffing that accompanied it. She groped for the lamp and switched the light on to reveal Flynn. As soon as he could see her, Flynn became more animated at his owner finally being home and he wagged his tail accordingly. Grace bent down, scooped up Flynn with one arm and with the other carried the shopping bag through to the kitchen. By the time Grace arrived in the kitchen, she was aware that the last remaining odour of her perfume was now obliterated by Pedigree Chum mixed with dog saliva that Flynn had haphazardly painted all over her face. Grace didn't care though as she loved Flynn dearly. He was not the most handsome of dogs and it was hard to tell even what mix of breeds he was sporting. In his first week of moving into the village Flynn had caused a great debate in The Blacky as to his breed. Most concurred that there was Scottish Terrier in him but then the mix ranged widely from Jack Russell to a small donkey. Flynn was indeed small with a multi-coloured coat to rival Joseph's. He also had feet that could be sized by Clarks but he had the temperament of a grateful orphan and he loved Grace dearly.

Once in her pyjamas, Grace settled on the settee with a large glass of wine, the remote control and Flynn and she hoped to remain like this until Monday morning. What else could she wish for? She had grown tired of each weekend spent hoping that 'he' was just around the corner somewhere. She had grown tired of dressing up in her finest and walking into The Blacky in the hope that someone in the village had a visitor that was on the lookout for a 5 foot 7 inch, size 10 wine-guzzling blonde.

She had also grown tired of the 'falling over in the mud dream'. That was a dream of walking Flynn and not only did she fall but she was caught mid-air by 'him'. And in each one they lived happily-ever-after.

The dream would never come true as she would not be falling into any mud as the furthest she tended to take Flynn was to the bridge and back. That suited Flynn as Grace had conditioned him to think that it was perfectly acceptable to lie around all day and to only move out of necessity or guilt. The only fields Flynn saw were on various TV shows such as Countryfile and Escape to the Country. Grace noted that Flynn did not look upon the screen as if this green place was some sort of unobtainable paradise so would continue with her viewing without fear of the dog turning gangster on her.

And so the dreaming of 'him' stopped. Grace now dreamed of winning the lottery, buying a car and moving from Pelsby. 'The usual dreams everyone has,' she supposed. But until then she was content to ride with this life of routine, predictability and self-inflicted isolation.

Her night plodded by as uneventful as her week and once suitably inebriated she weaved and stumbled up the stairs to bed.

The next morning, Grace tried squinting from her pillow into whatever was in front of her without moving her eyeballs or actually opening her eyes. Her mouth felt like she had been chewing cotton wool all night and her head felt like it was nailed to the bed. She could see through the crack in the curtains it was morning and judging by the light it was late morning. As she lay there, she recalled that she had drunk the white and the rosé but couldn't recall the red if indeed she had drank it. As Grace tried to move her tongue, she noted that somewhere in the evening chives had been on the menu. If she moved her body she feared she would die so remained still and prayed to the Patron Saint of Hangovers, probably called St Ozzy or St Betty Ford, that her penance would be short. Flynn jumped off the bed with the resonance of a civil war cannon and she concluded the only way to speed up the cessation of this agony was not by divine intervention, this was a job for science. Namely paracetamol, ibuprofen, Alka Seltzer and Tropicana; the humanising cocktail known to all heavy wine drinkers and mixers of alcohol from the night before.

After a painful sitting up process, Grace tried to float downstairs to deceive her head into thinking it was still on the pillow. However, her head had other ideas and decided to give Grace a strobe-like feeling with each descending step. While Grace's body continued downstairs, her head decided to stay three steps back like the Duke of Edinburgh following the Queen, which only heightened the head crushing agony further.

After letting Flynn out, she began the treasure hunt of finding tablets. Her old ice cream tub had enough tablets to cure ailments ranging from constipation to a nasty fungal infection that she once inherited from wearing her Grandad's slippers years ago. However, there were no painkillers suitable for her current predicament and she pondered over the notion of applying a deep heat patch intended for back pain to her forehead, trying to convince herself the 'drawing out pain' qualities could be beneficial in this case. She quickly dismissed the idea when she remembered she once applied a muslin face mask and her colleagues in work thought she had been for a recent chemical peel. After a frantic root through her handbag she came to the conclusion she would need to get herself dressed and venture to the shop.

Grace opened the front door to retrieve Flynn and glanced up the street to ascertain if she could get away with her shopping expedition in her pyjamas and puffa jacket. However, to her surprise, the horizon was filled with 2 police cars, an ambulance and lots of strangers.

'What the hell is going on?' Grace thought.

CHAPTER 2

'Have you seen all the commotion?' Grace heard from her right. She turned and Big Mick was now stood at her gate with a tray full of steaming mugs.

'I just let Flynn out and noticed all the cars down there,' she said nodding towards the bridge. 'Is everything all right?'

'Mrs Mortimer took her Benji out this morning for a walk and decided to walk along the river bank,' said Mick.

Grace looked towards the bridge. She liked Mrs Mortimer, a lot. She was a cantankerous old goat but in this sleepy village she was the liveliest of them all. Grace would often look in on her or ask her to look in on Flynn if she stayed overnight at her parents' house. Flynn was not welcome at her parents' house. Her mother feared that Flynn would 'leave his mark' on her cream carpet so would not take the unnecessary risk. While Grace was initially put out by this barring of her dog, she soon realised that Flynn became a great reason to leave her parents when she wanted and not when her parents dictated, so every cloud and all.

'Is Mrs Mortimer okay?' Grace asked tentatively.

'Oh, it's not her Grace,' Big Mick moved forward towards the gate. He could see Grace's concern for the old lady. 'She found a body,' he whispered.

'What?!' Grace was relieved and stunned at the same time. 'Here? In Pelsby? By Mrs Mortimer? And Benji? Over there? Who? Is she all right? Is that what the tea is for?' Grace's confusion mixed with her hangover without the aid of pain killer intervention was starting to make her sweat.

'Mrs Mortimer is fine. She's a bit shook up but she's okay. The tea is for all the bobbies down there while they do their thing, investigations I s'pose. They're just waiting for the coroner to come and collect the body.' Big Mick looked at Grace who continued to look toward the activity at the bridge.

'They have no idea who it is,' he revealed. Grace shot Big Mick a look.

'Oh God, is it...mutilated?' she whispered. Big Mick started to laugh, then quickly realised it was inappropriate.

'No love, it's not anyone that Mrs Mortimer recognised. She thought it was someone asleep on the bank. But Benji started barking at them and because the body didn't move she thought it was a bit strange. That's when she realised. Poor thing.' Grace just continued to look down the street.

'Well, I'd best get this tea over to them before it gets cold. You get yourself in love. It's cold out here. Most of these will be off soon I imagine when the coroner turns up.' Big Mick looked at Grace expectantly and she realised that he was waiting for a response.

'Oh, yes.' Grace started to walk backwards, still

continuing to look up the road and thinking of poor Mrs Mortimer poking a dead body with a stick.

'I need to get dressed and erm…go to Nell's.' Grace quickly looked for Flynn who now took her walking backwards as a cue to go back into the house.

'I'll see you later, Mick.' Big Mick nodded and headed off towards the throng of activity while Grace shut the door.

Grace began to think of all the people in the village who might be dead. There were a couple of people she hoped it may be. Mr Cousins from Pool Farm would be high on the list. Not only was her landlord the rudest, vilest creature ever put on the Earth but there were rumours of him hanging around the local school in his younger years for no reason. He was also partial to picking up hitchhikers and taking them back to the farm. Those in the village that knew Mr Cousins knew him to be the most inhospitable man and refused to believe he took people back simply for Battenberg and ginger beer. There wasn't any concrete evidence of it, but most, if not all the hitchhikers were never seen leaving the farm and a lot of adults in the village remember when he hung around the playground when they were young and all were terrified of him. He would not be missed if the body was his. The other plus point of Mr Cousins dying was the fact nobody knew if there was a next of kin to inherit Pool Farm. Grace had always hoped the land would end up with developers and the new homes built would bring 'him'. Knowing her luck though, with 'him' would be 'her' with her swollen pregnant belly, beautiful face and fabulous hair. However, if it was Mr Cousins, Mrs Mortimer would have recognised him and it would be all over the village by now.

Even with her hangover Grace decided she still needed

to go to Nell's and the bonus was she would find out what was going on. She also had some genuine concern for Mrs Mortimer as well. She could be a tough old boot but she was still an old lady and she must have had a nasty shock. She decided to visit her friend later that day.

After Grace washed (a bit) and dressed (bottom half only), she fetched her coat and lead for Flynn.

'Come on Flynn; let's see what all the fuss is about, eh? We may even see Benji,' she said encouragingly.

Grace stepped out and immediately looked up the street. The scene was still the same except for a long black vehicle that reminded her of the car from Ghostbusters. It added a sombre note to the whole affair. So much so, Grace thought a media truck should be included in the scene as well. This was big news in Pelsby.

Flynn trotted quite happily at Grace's heel towards Nell's and as Grace drew nearer she wondered if it was a good idea to continue further on to the bridge to see what was going on for herself. Her head reminded her some things needed attending to first.

As Grace arrived at Nell's she instructed Flynn to sit and stay while she went to fetch her much needed medication. The shop was deserted but she could hear a faint conversation from the back room and concluded that it was from a television.

'Hello? Nell?' Silence. 'Nell, are you there?'

'She's outside with everyone else,' came the voice from the back room. Without investigating Grace knew it to be Roger. Roger was Nell's invalid brother. He had lived with Nell all his life and would do for the remainder. Their parents had died long since and Nell had taken over the family business, being the shop, while becoming Roger's sole carer. Roger had been paralysed since 1982 where he served as a cook in the Royal Navy. His ship has been hit by an Exocet missile that he was serving on in the Falkland Islands. During the blast, some of the heavy kitchen machinery had buckled from the floor and toppled on top of Roger's legs and he had never walked since. The ship and Roger were crippled. The ship was mended but Roger was not. He would make rare appearances now and again, namely New Year or a special birthday.

'Is that you, Grace?' Roger enquired.

'Yes, hi Roger. I'm just going to take some paracetamol and a bottle of water. I'll leave the money on the shelf by the till but I'll see if I can find Nell outside and tell her.' Grace stared in the direction of the back room.

'Okay, and if you see her can you tell her that the bread is still in the oven and I'm hungry.' Grace found the tablets and water and put the money on the shelf as promised.

'Will do, see you later.' She hadn't actually seen Roger since Patsy's 60th birthday party in The Blacky, which was 9 months ago.

Back in the street, Grace snapped the tablets out of their cosy cocoons, washed them down with the entire contents of the water bottle and slowly walked towards the hive of activity by the river with Flynn at her heel.

As she approached, she could not tear her eyes from the trolley carrying what was clearly a dead body zipped in a black bag. From the size it, Grace guessed a man was inside. The two men pushing the trolley did not speak as they slid the body into the Ghostbusters' car. As they started to remove their gloves, one walked to the driver's seat of the car and the other quickly spoke to one of the police officers. Within minutes, the car was over the hump backed bridge and was heading out of the village towards Lanson.

Some of the villagers started to disperse and silently made their way to their homes. The removal of the body was clearly the highlight of the whole episode. Grace spotted Nell who looked worried and slightly distressed so she made her way towards her.

'You okay, Nell?' Grace was now stood next to her and she felt genuinely concerned for the woman.

'Oh hello, Grace. What a to-do it's all been.' Nell seemed slightly relieved that Grace was now in her company.

'Listen Nell, sorry about snapping at you last night. Long week and all,' Grace sighed.

'Oh, don't worry, Grace,' Nell accepted her apology and continued, 'poor Mrs Mortimer found him this morning. He was right there,' she pointed to the edge of the river, 'on the bank. She thought he was asleep but when he didn't wake with Benji's barking she knew something wasn't right. She said she knew the minute she saw his face that he was a goner.' Nell's expression changed slightly with a more upbeat tone. 'It's not anyone from the village; she thinks it might have been a jumper that missed the water.'

Grace looked at the bridge and water in quick succession. 'A jumper? But the water at most is three feet deep!'

'He may have landed in the water and the tide tossed him on the river bank,' supposed Nell. Grace concluded that Nell had clearly been watching too much Bergerac.

'Nell, the current couldn't wash mud from my boots the other day. I doubt very much if it could wash a full grown man, completely dressed I might add, on to the bank.'

'Who are we to argue with force of nature, Grace?' Nell clearly wanted Grace to respect the awe of the River

Ince. If anyone else had said such an absurd thing Grace would have argued the point or at least laughed in their face, but as it was Nell there was no point.

'I went into the shop earlier. I picked up some paracetamol and water,' she waved the empty bottle at Nell. 'I left the money on the shelf. Roger said he wants you back as you've left bread or something in the oven.'

'I know his legs don't work, but his wheels aren't rusty as well. Lazy little shit,' Nell muttered. She nodded to Grace as if satisfied she had made her point and bid her goodbye.

Grace looked around and saw most of the familiar faces had now gone. She could see the back of Big Mick walking back towards The Blacky.

'Mick!' she shouted after him. 'Wait up.'

Big Mick waited in the street with his tray of empty cups until Grace and Flynn caught up.

'Mick, did Mrs Mortimer go home do you know?'

'I think so. The police spoke to her for a bit but I'm sure I saw her leave with Benji about fifteen minutes ago.' He looked in the direction of the Flower Cottages and then turned to look at Grace.

'I take it you will be popping in to see her?' asked Big Mick. Grace nodded. 'Pop in the pub on the way back and let me know how she is, eh?'

'Of course, I'll go up there now and make sure she's settled down a bit.' Grace tried to give Mick a reassuring smile.

'That would be great. I'm sure a few of the regulars wouldn't mind knowing that she was all right.'

Grace went to walk in the direction of Mrs Mortimer's cottage when she heard Big Mick shout.

'Shall I have a bacon butty ready for you? You look like

you need a bit of a kick start this morning.' Big Mick thought himself very amusing and continued up the street looking like a clumsy waiter with his tray of mugs.

Grace realised that she was only supposed to run to the shop and go home. She didn't exactly dress for visiting old people. She gave her hair a bit of a smooth, zipped up her coat further to hide the panda pyjama top and popped the empty water bottle in her pocket, clear evidence of a hangover at this time of the morning.

The Flower Cottages were not far and when she reached them Grace braced herself slightly. She was not sure what to expect. I mean, how often do you feel the need to console someone who has just discovered a dead body.

Benji started barking as soon as Grace knocked on the door of Primrose Cottage and Flynn jumped on his hind legs and started wagging his tail.

'Is that Benji?' Grace looked at Flynn and tried to act as animated as he.

The door opened and there stood Mrs Mortimer. She was all of five foot one in her eighty-two-year-old body and was as slight as an arrow. She was starting to look frail these days and though she had fought age for the last ten years or so it was starting to defeat her. Now on the odd days she had to succumb and rest a lot more than she would have liked.

'Oh hi, Grace,' she turned and walked back into the cottage toward the lounge and obviously expected Grace to follow. Benji wagged his tail and waited for them both to step in before turning back to his master. Grace walked through the cottage and found Mrs Mortimer sat at the dining table littered with cups and an over-flowing ashtray. The room was filled with smoke and

Grace squinted when she entered the room.

'You really should open a window in here.' Grace walked towards the window and groped for the handle through the yellowing net curtain and flung it open.

'You'll let all the goddamn heat out!' Her American accent became more pronounced when Mrs Mortimer was in one of her more irritable moods.

'Only for five minutes to air the room a bit,' Grace insisted. She looked at the ashtray, marched over and swooped it up. Mrs Mortimer noticed Grace's panda adorned cuff as she watched her take the ashtray to the kitchen to empty it. While in there Grace popped the kettle on to make some tea.

'Good night last night? I take it you are still drunk seeing as you haven't managed to dress the top half of your body.' Grace returned from the kitchen and banged the empty ashtray down in front of a smug looking Mrs Mortimer.

'I'll make some tea,' Grace muttered and returned to the kitchen. Once the tea was made she set everything on a tray, walked back into the lounge and placed it in front of the old lady to pour.

'Anyway, last night was okay. I stayed in,' said Grace.

Mrs Mortimer paused pouring the tea. 'Jeez Grace, how old are you? Thirty? Thirty-five?'

'Thirty-two,' Grace muttered.

'Thirty-goddamn-two.' She shook her head and then continued with pouring the tea. 'I've seen more life this morning than you have in your whole goddamn life!'

'The guy was dead!' Grace started.

'Exactly!' The old lady shrugged her shoulders and passed the cup to Grace.

'I actually came to see how you were. But clearly the

shock has not dampened your spirits has it?' Grace sniped.

'Look sweetheart, when you get to my age, seeing dead bodies is an occupational hazard and I've seen plenty. But my poor Benji hasn't. Look at him. He looks…different.' Benji was running around the sofa in hot pursuit of Flynn and his flapping tongue. Both dogs were clearly having a ball.

'He looks fine, Mrs Mortimer,' said Grace in an exasperated tone.

'Yeah, you're probably right, he's seen you looking half dead enough to desensitise him,' she said in amusement while sipping her tea. Grace wanted to change the subject of Benji's handling of Dead-body-gate and see if his owner was really all right.

'Anyway, he's running around happy as Larry,' said Grace.

'He's fucking running around to keep warm! It's freezing in here! Shut the goddamn window!' Mrs Mortimer bellowed.

Grace jumped off the seat like a scalded cat and shut the window as instructed. She looked at Mrs Mortimer who was slightly hunched over the table clutching at her cup at the far end of the room. The lounge was littered with memories and everywhere you looked there were hundreds of photographs, old letters and dusty ornaments, each of them holding a story. Grace knew a lot of her stories but she was sure there were a million more. Mrs Mortimer liked to talk, especially with a Jack Daniels in her hand. Grace tentatively walked back to the table and sat down and looked at her friend.

'I don't care if you've seen a million bodies before, you didn't expect to see one this morning, I'm sure. Just tell me what happened, eh?' Grace's tone was soft and concerned.

Mrs Mortimer pulled a cigarette from its packet, lit it, took a deep drag and exhaled. All the while she was gathering her thoughts and preparing to tell the tale.

'I got up, got dressed, top half as well,' she looked at Grace and smiled, 'then went outside to give Benji his walk. I went down to the river path as usual and then I saw him. I thought he was a man just asleep.' She waved her hand dismissively. 'You know, drunk like. But he didn't move, Grace. Benji started yapping and yapping and I shouted at him to leave the man but he kept yapping and yapping and that's when I knew. I walked straight over and looked at the guy's face. He looked cold Grace, and I mean real cold. Like a proper stiff.' Grace winced at her description but Mrs Mortimer didn't notice. 'I've seen dead bodies but in places where you expect them. Care homes, coffins, beds, airplanes…' The last one threw Grace a bit but she didn't want to interrupt the old lady. 'But not by the river! I know they say that dog walkers have more chance of finding a dead body than anyone else but in all the years I've been walking dogs I can't say I ever came across one before. Have you?' She genuinely asked the question and looked at Grace expectantly.

'Er…no. But half the time when I'm walking Flynn I'm looking at my phone. I've probably tripped over hundreds of dead bodies and not realised to be honest, especially where I lived in Wales. Half the town were on anti-depressants!' Grace thought this might amuse her and the old lady gave a chuckle.

'Well, I went straight to Nell's and we called the police together. They came and I told them what happened. Then some other car came and an ambulance came and they looked at him and left him there for ages!' Grace didn't interrupt.

'Then the police had a good look around and then I came home. Nell just called to say some other men picked him up, put him in a black bag and shoved him in the back of a car. And that's it.'

'What did the police say to you?' Grace asked.

'Police! Did you see how old they were? I have a boil on my ass that's been around longer than the snot who took my story.' She pulled on the cigarette again. 'He said it looked like the man had lay down and fell asleep on the bank but had died in the night, probably of hyperthermia. The police-boy said it looked like he was a tramp. I didn't know we had tramps around here.'

Mrs Mortimer was still talking but Grace wasn't listening anymore. Her mind was taken right back to the night before when she had jumped off the bus from work. The posh tramp! Oh God, was it him? It must have been.

'Was he wearing a huge overcoat?' Grace asked turning to face her.

'He could still die from the cold Grace, whether he was wearing a goddamn coat or not!' she spat.

'I know! It's just I think I may have saw him last night!'

'Were you looking at that freakin' phone again? You probably walked right past him. For God's sake Grace, the whole world is living and dying right under your fucking nose and you spend your whole life on Booble!'

'Google,' Grace corrected.

'Who gives a fuck? Booble. Google. The guy might have been alive last night and you could have saved him.' Mrs Mortimer was now shouting.

'Hey! Hang on! He was alive and well when I saw him. He was talking to me by the bridge. Taking the piss out of me he was, because I'm Welsh. He didn't complain about being cold to me and if he had I would have told him to button up his filthy coat! He gave me the fright of my life. I thought he was jumping off the bridge and I went over, actually, to see if there was anything I could do.'

'Like push him?' Mrs Mortimer was now smirking. Her previous high temper now dissipating.

'No, not bloody push him. I thought I might be able to help. But he just went on about it strange me being here in Pelsby and not in Wales and called me Daff.' Grace now looked at Mrs Mortimer and waited for her response. She hoped that the lady would say the man was an arse and should have known better than to walk along the river in the dark.

'Daff? Do you mean daft?' asked the old lady confused.

'Daffffff! Like the bloody daffodil!' she corrected.

'Daffodil?' The old lady was now totally baffled. Grace, now remembering the old lady's heritage, embellished further. 'It's the national flower of Wales.'

'Oh,' Mrs Mortimer wasn't sure whether to probe further with the botanical point but then realised she wasn't interested, so didn't. 'Well, you may need to tell the police-boy then. You were probably the last to see him alive and that will make you a suspect.'

'A suspect of what? Having the ability to manipulate the weather into just below freezing? A suspicious state of weather for December is it?' said Grace.

'Well, you still need to see the cops and tell them that you saw him. They can determine time of death and what he was likely to be doing and who may have been around the village that time of night.' Grace looked at Mrs Mortimer quizzically. 'I watch old Kojak re-runs on one of those crime channels, makes me feel at home,' she said while stubbing her cigarette. 'For New York, not Police Departments,' she interjected.

Grace thought for a moment and concluded that Mrs Mortimer was probably right and she should tell the police that if indeed it was the same fellow that he was alive and relatively well at six p.m. last night.

'You're right. I think I'll go home and get dressed, properly,' she smiled at Mrs Mortimer, 'and go to the police and tell them what I know. But anyway, is there anything I can get you? Are you sure you're all right?' Grace's concern was genuine.

'I'm fine. Especially, now you've closed the window,' she grinned.

Grace took one last mouthful of tea and took her cup and saucer out to the kitchen and placed it on the draining board to be washed when Mrs Mortimer saw fit to do it. As she walked back into the lounge she called Flynn who knew immediately that was the call to go and trotted to Grace's feet and sat down ready for his lead to be attached to his collar.

'I'll call you later, eh?' offered Grace.

Mrs Mortimer nodded in agreement and sat still while Grace placed a gentle kiss on top of her head. She watched the young woman walk out and noted Benji sat unhappily as Flynn also departed. They continued to sit still and look in the direction in which they left long after the front door was heard shutting.

'I can't believe I'm having to do this,' muttered Grace to Flynn, who now felt as miserable as a vegetarian Doberman at leaving Benji. Even though the tramp was dead, Grace was still annoyed that he was having an effect on her weekend. Then she was annoyed with herself for being so unfeeling. Should she have feelings about the no-named tramp? Of course not, but she still felt guilty. Bloody Catholic upbringing, made you feel guilty about everything.

She once had a dream that she was kissing Big Mick in the most unsexy dream she had ever had but still managed to feel guilty every time she saw Patsy, Big Mick's wife. Patsy was only 5ft 3inches but next to Big Mick she looked smaller. But what she lacked for in height she made up for in personality. Everyone was terrified of her in some way, especially her husband. But she was one of the most respected members of the community and was loyal to all its inhabitants. No one crossed Patsy but you could count her as one of your friends and knew she had your back.

Grace reached her house and began to get ready. Using the entire contents of her make-up bag and downing a bottle of lemonade, she felt ninety percent humanised.

She bid Flynn goodbye, shut the front door behind her and walked towards The Blacky to call a cab and give Big Mick an update on Mrs Mortimer.

The whole village consisted of cottages, one pub, a post office, a garage (not petrol), a tea room and various shops peppered here and there which included a bakery, a butchers' and a takeaway. Nell's shop was the shop that held everything else from booze to light bulbs. Anything unusual required a trip to Lanson, the nearest major town or a substitution would be called for. Grace had once been invited to dinner at Amos's house a few months back. She was presented with a fish pie and when Grace enquired as to what the orange crunchy bits were amongst the fish, she was told that as the village didn't have any fresh fish then fish fingers had to be used. The chef deemed the dish a success but Grace's taste buds wanted to argue the point. She had eaten as much as she could and had dropped an awful lot, without being noticed, on the floor much to Amos's cat's delight.

Most of the buildings within the village had all been built of the same material. A soft dove grey stone that deepened with the damp but still remained soft and inviting. The village, without a doubt, was beautiful and even though most of the time it bored her silly the occupants gave her a sense of belonging.

She walked into The Blacky and spotted Big Mick straight away. He folded up his newspaper as if caught skiving.

'Hello Grace, did you see her?' Mick enquired after Mrs Mortimer.

'I did. She's fine Mick, to be honest. Still having a go at me and smoking like a chimney.' Grace plonked her handbag on the bar and sat herself down on a nearby barstool.

'Drink?' he asked.

'Can I have an orange juice please, Mick? I'm just going to call a taxi. I think I may have seen the man who died last night when I got off the bus from work.' Patsy appeared from the side bar at this new bit of information. 'You all right Patsy?' asked Grace.

'So, you saw the fella that died, eh? Did he say he was going to jump? Or was he already dead when you saw him?' Patsy scrutinised Grace's face wondering if she had left him for dead.

'Why do people think I'd be so horrible as to leave a man for dead on the river bank in freezing temperatures? I told Mrs Mortimer, as I'm telling you, he was fine when I saw him and looked as far from suicide as you or me.' Mick placed the juice in front of Grace and noted that she was either wound up from defending herself or was still suffering from the hangover he witnessed that morning.

'Kojak, up there,' she nodded toward Primrose Cottage, 'thinks I should tell the police to aid their investigation. Something about determining time of death or something or other. He was a tramp, by all accounts, that looked like he had lain down and maybe died of hyperthermia.' The last point was directed at Patsy to set the record straight. The rumour was still in force about him jumping. No one seemed to question the fact that he would have broken his legs or simply ended up with wet socks at best. Grace took a large swig of her orange juice and pulled out her phone to call for a taxi. Big Mick second-guessed what she was doing.

'You calling a cab? I can run you over there. I've a few things I need to do in Lanson anyway. I'll just put a sweater on. Won't be a tick.' He didn't wait for Grace to respond and he disappeared through a door behind the bar to retrieve a sweater. Patsy continued surveying the fridges for obvious depletions of certain items. She made a list of what was necessary and turned to Grace.

'Do us a favour sweetheart? Watch the bar a sec. I need to see if we have any tonics out back. If not, he can pick some up in Lanson when he's getting his 'bits and bobs''. She rolled her eyes at the end with an air of cynicism which was lost on Grace. Patsy disappeared to the right of the bar as soon as Big Mick appeared through the open door to the left. He looked left to right as if he was about to cross a main road.

'Where she gone?' he seemed to be whispering.

'Checking tonic. She said she might want you to pick some up in Lanson. Everything all right?' quizzed Grace.

Grace wondered if she had either walked in on a

domestic of theirs or if tonic was a contentious issue. How tonic could generate such emotion was absurd, but this was Patsy and Big Mick we were talking about. Grace had once witnessed them have a public spat behind the bar about how loud he walked across the floor in their flat upstairs. It escalated to the point where she was screaming, 'Are you practising to be a bloody Nazi, it sounds like you are goose-stepping up there!'

He retorted with, 'They call me Big Mick for a reason, you stupid cow, I'm not a fucking ballet dancer!' She continued with telling him that he did it on purpose simply to wind her up and that he should, 'Go on a diet then, you fat bastard!' The patrons of the pub were quite used to these public rows and were the nearest thing they could get to live entertainment seeing as Patsy refused to ever get the karaoke machine back into the bar.

'Shall we go now, Grace?' he whispered expectantly.

'Patsy said to watch the bar. Go and tell her you want to go.' Grace found she was whispering back and wasn't sure why but just knew that it was probably best.

'It's fine. Come on.' He grabbed his keys from the counter and lifted the hatch, 'she'll text me if she wants some tonic.' Big Mick clearly wanted to make a run for it.

'Hold up,' Grace started to guzzle the orange juice and once she picked up her bag Patsy appeared.

'Thanks love, for that,' Patsy's appreciative tone soon changed when she spied through one of the front windows of the pub her husband getting into his car.

'You tell that mountain getting into his car,' she was prodding her finger in the air in her husband's direction, 'that I need six bottles of tonic water and if he so much as goes near a bookie I'll find out and hang his balls on this year's Christmas tree.' She turned and looked at Grace to satisfy herself that Grace had understood the message and would deliver it accordingly. Grace was too busy envisaging Patsy hanging his balls on the tree and letting the customers of the pub have a good gander at the hairy offerings. She presumed they were hairy as Big Mick did not seem the type to know that razors were not just for chins and wax was not just for candles, or ears.

'I'll tell him, Pats,' said Grace with a smirk that was not lost on Patsy.

'Good luck with the police, don't let them make you say anything you don't want to. Sneaky bastards they are. Nothing goes on around here so wouldn't surprise me if they make a big story out of this one....'

'Bye, Patsy.' Grace continued to walk out of the pub with Patsy wittering on in the background and shut the door behind her.

She made her way to Big Mick's old navy blue Volvo that reminded Grace of a huge Lego piece. She had never known Mick to drive anything else and he had been clearly driving this one for some time as even when he was not in the motor it still leaned on the driver's side. Grace climbed into the car which smelled similar to the pub, or that could have been Big Mick, she wasn't sure.

'She collared you didn't she?' Big Mick looked at Grace with the look of a disappointed parent.

'Don't blame me! You ran out of that pub like Daley bloody Thompson. She wants six bottles of tonic and gave a warning about the bookies. I take it you know what's that all about and I don't want to know. But if you know what's good for you, you'll do as you're told.' Grace looked out of the window while she delivered the message. Big Mick looked out of the windscreen while he processed and digested this message. He then started the car and made his way toward the bridge and out of town.

It was quiet for a while. Grace was anticipating what the police would ask her and wondered if the police were as thick as some of the residents in the village. Would they steer toward the conclusion that Mick had jumped to?

Big Mick was thinking he needed to be discreet and make sure no one saw him going into Sid's the bookies. He glanced at the clock and was happy that he had plenty of time to act nonchalant around Lanson to throw people off the scent. Who these people were he was not sure, but Patsy either had a sixth sense or she had spies planted around the town. Either way he knew he had to be clever about it. Grace noticed him looking at the clock.

'So Mick,' she drawled trying to make it sound casual, 'you got an appointment somewhere?' Grace continued looking out at the passing scenery.

'No, just getting some tonics.' Mick tried to sound jovial but Grace interpreted it as nervous especially when he shifted in his car seat.

'You wanted to go to Lanson before Patsy mentioned the tonics.' Grace now looked at Big Mick who continued to look through the windscreen.

'I did?'

'You did,' she continued.

'I erm, want to look for some ideas for Christmas presents. But don't tell Patsy,' he now turned and looked at Grace who raised an eyebrow accusingly.

'I don't give a hoot if you go to the bookies, Mick; you take your life in your own hands.' Grace turned back to looking out of the window and Mick realised she wasn't bothered at all and more importantly wouldn't grass him up to his irascible wife.

'Thanks Grace, it's only a little flutter. She won't even

know. I'll get the tonics and a Dairy Box for her and she'll be right as rain. There's a programme on tonight and they've all got long dresses on. She likes watching stuff like that so she'll be happy with the chocolates.' He was clearly trying to calm himself down as he realised that his secret was not so secret as two women knew of his actions already and he had barely left Pelsby.

The car trundled on through the fields and hamlets to Lanson which was six miles from Pelsby. There was no denying that this part of the country was beautiful. A lot of it reminded Grace of home. Moving here gave her the comfort of familiarity and enough distance between her and her parents that they couldn't just pop in for coffee and criticism. Grace had moved here from Wales three years ago; the plan always being she would stay for the initial six month lease and then move to Lanson near her job. But to afford anything in Lanson that had a garden would mean her looking for a better paid job or finding an affordable flat and getting rid of Flynn. The first point required effort which Grace couldn't muster at the moment and the second was unthinkable. Flynn, after all, was her best friend.

'So Grace, you looked a bit worse for wear this morning. Big night last night with the girls, eh?' Big Mick felt it was necessary to fill the silence as it was making him uncomfortable. Living in a pub did that to you. The constant din became the unnoticed background noise to your life. When he was out of the pub, the silence was deafening and made him feel uneasy.

'No Mick, I stayed in and just had a couple of bottles of wine. I don't go out much these days to be honest,' Grace said with resignation.

'You're a young woman, Grace, you should

be going out more. How're you gonna meet the love of your life, eh? While you're sat watching TV someone out there is snogging your man.' He turned to intensify his point. 'You want that? No of course you don't. Which is why you should be putting your glad rags on and getting out there,' he waved to the fields around him. 'He's not gonna land on your doorstep like they do in the movies.' Grace tried to think of a movie where the main star was delivered to someone's doorstep. If only you could rummage to the last pages of the Argos catalogue and pick a man with the option of next day delivery for a further £3.95.

'When did you adopt me Mick, and become my dad?' Grace was not in the mood for the lecture, advice, words of wisdom, blah blah blah.

'I'm only trying to be nice, love. You're a very attractive woman, especially when you do your hair and put your slap on.' Coming from Big Mick this was like being told you could run for America's Next Top Model.

'Cheers Mick, but honestly I'm fine. Once I get Christmas out of the way I'm going to make more of an effort with myself and stuff. But at the moment I'm quite happy just being on my own.'

'I think you've got SAD,' Mick decided.

'I'm not sad, I'm just bone idle.'

Mick noted her Welsh accent becoming more prominent which meant she was getting wound up. Mrs Mortimer was the same with her accent and watching Grace and Mrs Mortimer on issues that they didn't agree on was like watching Taylor and Burton.

'No, I don't mean you're sad, I mean that you have that SAD disorder thingy.' He felt that saying this was better than her thinking he called her miserable.

'Jesus, Mick. What is it, when you stay in for a bit then people think you have a medical condition? There's nothing wrong with me that a decent pay rise and a day in a beauty salon wouldn't sort out. Honestly!'

'You get so Welsh when you are wound up, don't you?' Grace was reminded of the tramp last night. She thought for a moment and replayed the last sentence in her head.

'I s'pose I do,' she agreed. 'Don't worry about me though Mick, you worry about the plans Patsy has for your knackers if she finds out you went to visit Sid.'

The last couple of minutes of the journey as they approached Lanson were continued in silence until the debate of where to park broke it. Once they had found somewhere they made arrangements to meet in the police station or Sid's; whoever finished first was to look for the other.

The police station was only over the road from where Big Mick had parked. She crossed over the fairly busy main road that ran through the centre of the town and glanced behind her to see Big Mick disappearing into a Tesco Metro to fetch the tonics and a Dairy Box. He was a good man, Mick. Everyone loved him including his hot tempered wife.

The police station was a detached red bricked building with a car park that completely circled it like a moat. The nearest building on either side was at least 100m away. This could have been on purpose to make the building more imposing or simply because no other building wanted to be associated with it. Either way, the message was clear that the building held some importance and even if you didn't know the purpose of the place you'd never want to go in there unless you had to.

As Grace walked in, the desk sergeant raised his head and looked at her inquisitively. The room was painted in battleship grey and the perimeter walls were furnished with plastic chairs, low tables littered with leaflets and a drinking water dispenser. There was an old lady sat in one corner watching as Grace walked in and a young man who gave an uninterested glance and then continued playing a game on his phone.

'Can I help you?' the desk sergeant enquired. He was around fifty and what hair he didn't have on his face he made up for in various other areas, including his chin, eyebrows and what little was growing above his ears he allowed to flourish with abundance. Grace tentatively stepped forward.

'I erm, wanted to speak to someone about the body that was found in Pelsby this morning,' Grace glanced at the young man who had lost interest in his phone as Grace's offerings seemed more appealing. The desk sergeant noted the added interest, asked for her name and instructed Grace to take a seat while he fetched DC Kelly. Grace walked slowly to a chair, sat down and waited for someone to tell her what to do next. Being in a police station made her feel guilty even though she had nothing to feel guilty about. She distracted herself with posters warning of pickpockets in the area, car crime and pictures illustrating stats on crime in the UK. She decided to not read any more as some of the information was frightening her so she looked at her feet until her name was called.

'Grace Hammond?' She looked up and was relieved to see a very good-looking man looking at her expectantly. 'This isn't so bad,' she thought.

'Yes,' Grace stood and looked at him and fidgeted with her bag while she waited for his next move.

'Would you care to follow me?' The handsome man stretched an arm towards a double door and gave her a Hollywood smile.

'Jeez, would I.' Grace trotted behind him like an obedient lap dog while he guided her to an extremely small room. Once inside, Grace took a seat opposite DC Fabulous.

'This is cosy,' she declared. He looked slightly bemused and then continued.

'Right, Miss? Mrs?' he paused waiting for her confirmation.

'Miss. But call me Grace. If you want. I mean if it's appropriate.' She became more nervous. 'Not that I mean you're inappropriate. I mean if it's allowed. By people. Your people. Police people.' DC Fabulous was trying to resist laughing. 'I think I'll shut up now. Call me what you like. Except Mrs. I'm not married. Yes, I'll shut up.' Grace willed her mouth to stop moving.

'Well, Grace, I'm DC Kelly. I understand you wish to report something about the gentleman we found in Pelsby this morning. What do you know?'

Grace divulged as much of the story as she could from leaving work up to Mrs Mortimer advising Grace to come to the police station and telling them what she knew. DC Fabulous made a lot of notes and nodded throughout the story and occasionally asked a question for clarification. Once she was finished, he went over her personal details again and thanked her for coming in.

'Can you tell me anything about him?' Grace was genuinely interested. It was very likely, according to DC Fabulous, that she was indeed the last person to see him alive.

'CSI went over the area this morning and they are

confident in the conclusion that he simply went to sleep and didn't wake up due to hyperthermia. We don't suspect any foul play and could only see his footprints in the area. Good thing about this time of year is that everywhere is pretty muddy so it makes the CSI's life easier. Judging by his clothing and hygiene it looked like he had been sleeping rough for quite some time.' He switched off his computer and leant back in his chair. 'The hardest part is trying to identify who he was and seeing if we can find his next of kin,' he shrugged and gave the impression he was not holding out much hope of finding either.

'He was very well spoken, as I recall. I don't know if that would help. I couldn't place an accent but he sounded 'very well-to-do' shall we say.'

'That may help if we get some other pieces of the puzzle first. I'll make a note of it.' He stood up to make it clear that there was nothing further to discuss and she followed suit. He opened the door and gesticulated for her to leave the room and he followed behind her back to the main reception.

'Thank you for your statement. Like I said, if we need any more details we will be in touch.' He offered his hand to shake which Grace took and thanked him back. He then nodded, turned and as he walked away she watched DC Fabulous's bum a little longer than was appropriate. She then thanked the semi-hairy desk sergeant and walked back out onto the street. She quickly looked around and assumed as she hadn't been that long, that Big Mick was still in the bookies.

She soon found Sid's and went in. Big Mick was not hard to miss as he towered over everyone like Gulliver and made all the other patrons look positively Lilliputian. He didn't notice her walk in as he was completely engrossed in a horse race that was still yet to finish. He was gripping a slip tightly in his hand and was clearly suppressing any want of shouting.

'Hey Mick, any luck?' she sidled up beside him and felt safe enough to assess the rest of the clientele; most of them looked like they needed a win more than Big Mick.

'Not a bean Grace, not a bloody bean. You might bring me luck though.' Mick never took his eyes off the screen and started to jiggle more on the spot. He was now talking inarticulately under his breath as if in prayer. Grace took this as her cue to keep quiet until the race had finished. Mick's speech became more audible and it was clear that 'Seabank' needed to 'move his fucking legs' a lot faster for Big Mick to calm down. When the race had finished with Big Mick deciding that, 'a fucking donkey from Blackpool in callipers could have done better', Grace concluded that it was time to go. She made her way to the door knowing that Big Mick and his heavy heart to match his feet were following behind her.

'Never mind Mick, better luck next time, eh?' Grace was trying to brighten his mood. 'Did you get Patsy's Dairy Box?' trying to change the subject.

'I did.' Mick was clearly defeated while he rummaged for his keys in his jeans pocket.

'Well then, not all bad is it? Once Patsy's finished with her Mr Darcy she might be in the mood to cheer you up once you've locked up.' Grace was trying her best.

'You won't tell her, will you Grace?' he unlocked the car and looked at her with a face of a five-year-old that had just been caught nicking the last malted milk from the biscuit tin.

'Don't be daft,' she jumped into her seat and waited for him to shut his door. "Sides, I haven't got anything black that fits me for your funeral if Patsy ever found out. And she would probably have my guts for tinsel to go with your balls on her Christmas tree.' They looked at each other and burst out laughing at the thought.

Big Mick enquired about her visit to the police station and both began to wonder who the man was and how did he end up on the streets. Grace shared Big Mick's puzzlement as to how someone who sounded like he came from a privileged background could not have any family enquiring after him. They also pondered as to how the police would ever find out who he was. Grace shuddered at the thought of dying and no one actually missing her or at worse the thought of no one knowing that she was even dead. She was now envisaging lying dead on a threadbare rug somewhere with an Alsatian gnawing on her foot. Where the Alsatian came from was anyone's guess but abandoned people always seemed to have a dog eating them or a ton of cats defecating all over the room. She vowed not to buy an Alsatian to ensure the dream didn't come true, or a cat for that matter.

They soon arrived back in Pelsby and it was clear from her driver's face that she was more relieved to be home than he was. She was close to inviting him in and prepping his balls for any onslaught. She was sure she had a small bread tin somewhere and a roll of duct tape that would help protect Big Mick's nether regions and ruin any attempt by Patsy to adorn her Christmas tree with Mick's bodily parts.

After she had said goodbye to Mick she trotted back to her house and noticed that she felt much better coming back than she did when she left. Flynn was pleased to see her as soon as she opened the door and after removing her coat she called Mrs Mortimer and provided her with an update on her visit to the police station.

'Was the police boy there? Did he interview you?' she enquired.

'No. It was another man. He was lush. Totally out of my league but a highlight of my day nonetheless.'

'Sort that head out of yours and haul your ass back over there. Tell him you forgot something and flirt. And I mean properly. Like women are supposed to,' she growled.

'And what exactly am I supposed to have forgotten?' questioned Grace.

'How the hell am I supposed to know?' There was a pause. 'Tell him you forgot your goddamn sexuality.' Mrs Mortimer finished by coughing down the phone on her cigarette.

'You okay there, Doc Holliday? I wish you'd give up those fags,' said Grace.

'I'm fucking eighty-two-years-old! I've got no youth, osteoporosis, arthritis, a bladder that can't hold a spit, eyesight so bad I stroke the cushion thinking it's Benji and no one to hold me at night. None of that is killing me but I'm hoping that these goddamn cigarettes do, so I can be with my Mort!' She started coughing again down the phone and Grace felt guilty and stupid for lecturing a woman of her age.

'Do you need me to fetch you anything from Nell's?' Grace asked.

'No,' silence again. 'But thank you. Pop by tomorrow though I might need you to post something for me.' Mrs Mortimer had calmed down in temper and in her coughing fit.

'I'll see you tomorrow. Don't forget to lock up, now.' Mrs Mortimer hung up the phone before Grace, which was usual.

The rest of Saturday went by without any further fuss or fun. By the evening, Grace had enjoyed a bath and had popped back into her pyjamas and settled in to watch the National Lotto and then an old DVD if results from the first part hadn't made any changes to her evening plans. She toyed with the idea of having a drink in The Blacky. But, after Big Mick's bad luck today she didn't want to tempt fate further if Patsy started asking awkward questions. Grace supposed that Big Mick was probably secretly hoping that she wouldn't make an appearance either.

By the end of the night with no luck from the Lotto balls Grace declared it a night and chivvied Flynn up to the bedroom with her. She was goosed, even though she had not done an awful lot. Obviously still the affects from last night were taking their toll. It didn't take long for her to go to sleep. Or Flynn for that matter.

Grace was dreaming of being on a yacht, somewhere in the Mediterranean. She couldn't see the man of her dreams but he was there somewhere. Probably fetching her a glass of champagne and some exotic food. Judging by her body on the sun lounger though, Grace in dreams clearly didn't eat and went to the gym. A lot! She knew he was coming, she could hear his steps approaching her and she sat up on the sunbed in anticipation…

There was a loud crash from downstairs and Grace shot up in her bed and Flynn flew at the closed bedroom door and started to bark. She remained still trying to listen for anything more from downstairs. She stretched her hand over to Flynn to try and pacify him which worked and his barking ceased immediately. Grace sat still on the bed and Flynn stood still looking at the closed door. 'Did I really hear something? I must have done, otherwise why would Flynn have started barking? Where's my bloody phone? Shit, I left it on the arm of the chair. What if the tramp was killed? What if the killer has come back for me because I've snitched?'

Grace couldn't hear anymore from downstairs. It was deathly quiet. She remembered she had security lights on the front and back of the house. More so for Flynn when he went outside at night and Grace could see where he was. She gingerly peeled the quilt off herself and tiptoed to the window at the end of her bed. This window overlooked the front of her house and the window was directly above her front door. The light was off and as she looked up and down the street there wasn't a soul in sight. She looked behind her and could make out the clock said 3.10am. She scanned the street again and it was quieter than a graveyard. She still needed to look out of the back window which meant her opening the door. 'What if someone is just stood there? With a knife? With a mask? With a gun?' Grace could hear her mother's voice ringing in her head full of admonishment about 'why she didn't take the phone to bed' and 'why on earth did you decide to live in such a remote place as Pelsby'? How do you tell your mum that you would rather live in mortal danger than back home with her and Dad?

Grace looked around the room for a weapon. There was nothing shaped like a bat or a knife. She looked at the hairdryer and pondered for a moment if she could fool anyone into thinking it was a gun. Only if she left the lights off like they do in American thrillers. The only thing that she had to hand was the base of a bedside lamp. She quickly pulled the plug out and the shade and held the candlestick shaped base like a baton. 'Jesus,' she thought, 'is this what stands between me and certain death?' Flynn shot her a look as if to say, 'You're on your own with that.'

Grace tiptoed towards the door with an arm raised like the Statue of Liberty. Her heartbeat was like a mallet in her head.

'I'm gonna do this dead quick Flynn,' she whispered, 'ready?' The dog was fed up of waiting. Grace took a grasp of the doorknob and flung the door open with one hand and instead of waiting to see what was at the door and strike she just threw the lamp into the vacant space. The lamp hurtled across the landing and hit the wall with an almighty thump. Grace stood there breathing like a porn star while Flynn shot off downstairs barking and snarling all the way. She ran to retrieve the lamp and moved quickly to the top of the stairs.

Flynn had stopped barking now which was a good sign. If there was anyone down there then he would keep barking until she told him to be quiet. 'What if someone has done something to Flynn? Oh God!' Panic set in more.

'FLYNN!' She stood like a statue still holding the lamp aloft when she heard the pitter-patter of Flynn's footsteps bounding back up the stairs. The relief was incredible and she stooped down to pet him in the dark. She eventually switched the landing light on and looked down the stairwell. Some of the lounge was now illuminated as the stairs led straight into it. Still not completely relaxed she walked down the stairs but stayed against the wall as much as she could, straining her head to see before the rest of her body followed. Halfway down she could clearly see the rest of the lounge was empty and when she reached the bottom she turned the light on. Nothing looked out of place and it all looked as she left it. She spied the phone and plucked it from the arm of the chair. A lesson was learned already.

Even though the kitchen was still in darkness she could see enough to know that that too had not been disturbed. Flynn had followed her back down and ventured into the darkness of the kitchen. He soon came back and let out a small but audible whimper. Grace went over to the lounge window for one more look and concluded that whatever it was, it had not come from her house. Maybe, The Blacky had had a lock in and someone had crashed into something when they left the pub. Maybe Patsy had found the betting slip in Big Mick's pocket and she had thrown one of the many bottles around the pub.

Grace checked the door was still locked and looked around one last time before turning off the lounge light. The stairs were still illuminated and she walked upstairs to go back to her yacht. Flynn continued to stare through the opening to the black kitchen and was only snapped out of his trance when his master gave instruction for him to follow her. It wasn't long before Flynn had padded in a circle on his spot on the bed and curled up for the remainder of the night. Grace kept the lamp base on the bed and stuffed the phone under her pillow and tried to relax. Her mind started to wander as to what the gentleman looked like on the yacht. While she was waiting for sleep to come she manipulated the dream herself and inserted DC Fabulous complete with white pants and no shirt as her champagne server. The real dream had a lot to live up to.

However, downstairs in the kitchen, she hadn't noticed him in the dark.

CHAPTER 3

He didn't think he would make so much noise. He was still out of sorts and didn't know how to control physical contact. The dog had seen him. Flynn, she called him. He wasn't sure what he would have done if she had seen him. Or what would she have done, more to the point? He wasn't sure why he picked her in the first place. They simply said that he could make contact with one other person and he chose her. A positive affect, they said. What does that mean? He had argued that it was subjective as to the degree of positivity and how much effort was deemed to have made an affect. Apparently, both parties would know when this was accomplished.

He decided that three o'clock in the morning was not a good time to make contact with her and it was simply unfair to expect her to be engaging when he had just woken her up. Was he looking for excuses or did he just want to get back to a superb dinner party that he had just left? He was warned that while he could have fun he still had a duty to fulfil and the timescales on that would be up to him. All of his new friends that he had made were yet to complete their task and seemed no happier or unhappier than him. He was in no rush. In the dark he shrugged his shoulders, looked through the kitchen window at the moon and then he was gone. All that could be heard was a low satisfied moan from Grace who was clearly back on the yacht and the gentle snoring of a strange looking dog at her side. The house was now still and so was the street.

Sunday morning came and Grace awoke with a clearer head than she had done the day before. She lay in bed and recalled her night time to-do. She sat up slightly and looked at Flynn who was still curled up like dormouse at the foot of the bed. He opened one eye to see if she was making a move to actually get up. He soon decided that she didn't look that energetic just yet so closed the one eye and resumed his dream being fed meatballs by Grace. Grace grabbed the lamp base that was still on the bed and placed it back on the far bedside table deciding she would reassemble it later. She realised that she had never had a scare like that before and the lack of phone, weapon or man made her feel very vulnerable. She would need to get into the habit of remembering her phone at bedtime and remembered there was a huge knife in one of the drawers in the kitchen. She had never used the knife as it seemed too hazardous to use on the odd teacake or uncut bloomer. She decided she would keep it under the bed and hoped she would never have to use it and it would gather dust with all the other objects under there including hundreds of bobbles, an old Sunday paper and probably the odd sweet wrapper. The man on the 'need' list might never come but she could certainly address the first two on the list. She entertained the thought of maybe an alarm for night time only downstairs as Flynn stayed in her room all night anyway. She could ask Big Mick did he know anyone who came into The Blacky that might be able to help her.

She eventually rose from her bed and Flynn took the cue and jumped off. He waited for her to open the bedroom door while she put on her dressing gown. Grace followed him down the stairs to the kitchen where she took the back door key from its hook conveniently nailed into the frame and opened the door to let him out. She then popped the kettle on to make herself a hot drink.

It was then she noticed that the plate drainer was half hanging over the sink and the other half still on the draining board as if someone had pushed it aside. She looked behind her and recalled that she had just unlocked the back door. She looked back at the plate drainer. Above the sink was a window with an opening at the top but that was still shut, as was the one on the window next to the back door she had just let Flynn out of. 'Strange,' she thought. She walked to the front door and was relieved to see that it was still locked. If someone had moved the plate drainer then how the hell did they get in, she thought. She recalled that she hadn't entered the kitchen during her nocturnal investigations so wasn't sure when it happened. She could not think of a reason why she would push it to one side. It was like someone was trying to make room for something on the draining board.

The pop of the boiled kettle interrupted her thoughts and she continued to make herself a cup of coffee. 'Maybe, there was an earthquake tremor in the middle of the night and that was what the bang was that woke me up.' It was the only logical explanation. From the rest of the house she could see no evidence that anybody had been in and the only thing that was strange was the drainer. Maybe it just moved with the tremor. She would ask in the village had anyone else felt it.

She went to the back door and shouted for Flynn. The obedient dog soon returned and gave himself a shake while she put the key back into its rightful place. She then made her way to the sofa to finish her coffee and contemplate her day. Grace had decided it was time to dedicate some serious investigating into looking for a car. She had enough savings now to buy herself a little run-around. She didn't like relying on buses, cabs and the odd lift from friends. She was pretty self-sufficient when it came to all other aspects of her life so this semi dependence on others took some control away from her and it bothered her.

Grace had decided that she would never use the car for work. The parking plus petrol costs outweighed the cost of a monthly bus pass so it made more sense to continue with the Cumfee Bus, as much as this irked her. The car would be used for bigger shopping trips, taking Flynn for alternative walks somewhere and more importantly being able to say yes to more evenings out. Even though she would not be able to drink at these invites it would get her out of the house more. She was starting to feel that maybe Anne Frank had had a better social life than she was having at the moment. The only downside to her getting a job would be that her parents would no doubt expect more visits.

Visiting her parents was like spending a weekend with Miss Marple and Sherlock Holmes. They had now left Wales since they retired and moved to Cornwall a couple of years ago. They had bought an old dilapidated bungalow on the coast overlooking the Celtic Sea. The bungalow was no longer habitable so they razed it to the ground. Within a few agonising months, more for the builders putting up with Penny, Grace's mum, the build was finished. Now where the old bungalow stood stood a stunning contemporary home with as much glass as they could build without it looking like a greenhouse. But even with its stunning views of the ocean and gorgeous interiors, to Grace it was still Mum and Dad's house and with that came the questions. The questions, the questions. It was exhausting. While it was perfectly normal for parents to ask as to how their children are faring, it was a bit like Groundhog Day with each visit. The same questions would be dodged like bullets over a two day visit. Favourites included, have you met a boy yet, do you still like your job, are you due a pay rise, when are you buying a car, why don't you advertise for a lodger, are you still drinking, have you put on weight, when are you selling that dog, have you replaced the carpet in your lounge yet, do you have another coat/jumper/top/trousers/shoes/face?

During a visit they would both pull Grace to one side and reveal a secret that they didn't want her to disclose to the other parent. Nine times out of ten the other parent would also pull Grace to one side and say they knew something (usually the recently revealed secret) and add more detail for Grace to consider in her deliberation of taking a side. The details might change but Grace's attitude to these 'heart to hearts' was always the same, which was for them to talk to one another. She knew they wouldn't as it was the only bit of drama they had in their lives.

They occasionally embarked on hobbies sometimes when the boredom was too much for one of them. They tried the usual's such as golf but her dad was jealous when the men would flirt with her mum so he only really enjoyed going on his own now.

Her mum was a good looking woman and in her youth was stunning. Her hair was strawberry blonde, was cut short and accentuated her heart-shaped face even though her mum worried she might look like a lesbian. She had kept her figure after bearing two children and although there was a lot of assistance from the beauty counters and local hair salons she could still turn heads.

Grace took more after her father. He was now retired from public relations and had left his mark within the industry in some parts. He was extremely well-respected and was once described as a 'sensible risk taker.' In actual fact, her dad took risks all the time and they always turned out to be a sensible idea. The ideas never seemed risky, they just made common sense. Not something that is embraced much by today's population due to rules, guidelines, vision statements, mission statements, customer journeys and limited people. Her dad once told her that there are two types of limited people. Those that are limited by their own imagination which stunts their decisions in all manner of life and the other type is those that only consider and limit themselves to their own opinion which stunts their consciousness of humanity.

Grace loved her dad dearly and often went to him for sensible advice which often did not involve her mum. His life now was far more sedate; he even thought he would still be consulted about something from someone in his old firm or from an old colleague that valued his advice and opinion. Grace hoped that one day she would be as wise as him but as she got older that goal became more of a wish. Years of being wined and dined had left its mark on her dad much to his annoyance when he bought clothes. He would argue that the sizes in shops were getting smaller due to the countries that were making them had a smaller population in the physical sense. He once said that, 'someone large in the Philippines is probably only about 5'

2", so how in the world can they make clothes to fit someone of his stature when they have probably never seen anyone of his size'? Her mum had pointed out that his comment could be interpreted as racist. To which he then became quite energetic in delivering his opinion amongst the slacks in Marks & Spencer's about him not being racist and 'when was the last time you seen a man from the Philippines who was 6' 4"?' He had a point but it wasn't something her mum wanted to debate with him while trying to get him to try on 38 inch waist corduroys.

Her brother Gethin was extremely fit. He now lived in Australia and had been there for nearly two years. Grace missed him terribly as he was the only one who 'got' her parents as well and she sometimes needed him there just to have him smile when she rolled her eyes at them. They kept in touch through Skype often but the frequency of the calls were becoming longer in between. Time differences, social lives and work commitments all started to become regular excuses, but that's life. He was working as a sports massage therapist in Sydney and was loving life.

Another hobby of her parents was the excuse to throw a dinner party. They constantly invited people to stay and then would invite a few more friends for them to meet each other. To be fair, Grace thought, they did have a wide social circle but it was just a shame that a lot of them were bores who smelled of old leather and Steradent. Her dad entertained with 'stories from the city' and his childhood in Wales, while her mum would snake and smile her way around the room, much to the delight of her dad's old work buddies.

Grace toyed with the idea of texting Gethin for a catch up but decided to look for cars instead. Armed and ready to go with her iPad she soon realised after five minutes that this was the most boring shopping exercise she had ever encountered. All the cars she really liked were out of her price range and those that were in her price range were just plain ugly. She kept having a word with herself about it being an essential item not a luxury item. Things that are essential tend to be boring and ugly. Like warm coats and wellies. No one enjoys shopping for wellington boots do they, unless they're under five and like jumping in puddles. But Grace was not five and the rain turned her into short tempered witch so she tried not to venture out in any weather that even had an air of dampness about it.

Grace wasn't even sure what she was looking for. Most of the motoring abbreviations were lost on her. She looked at Flynn.

'What the hell are PAS, EW and this one keeps cropping up…FSH?' she looked at Flynn awaiting his answer but he rested his chin back on her feet and closed his eyes.

'How can you still be tired, you lazy bugger? You've only just got up!' she looked at her feet and he continued to feign sleep.

'PAS is power assisted steering. EW is electric windows and FSH is full service history.'

The man's voice came from her kitchen. Grace shot off the couch and turned to face the opening to the kitchen and there, larger than life, he stood.

At that moment Grace had never felt so scared in all her life. She stood looking at him for what felt like an age, not sure what to say to him. She was frozen to the spot. Flynn trotted over to the man, gave him a sniff then continued past him to the kitchen. The man turned his head to investigate where Flynn had gone and was amused by the dog's nonchalant demeanour. Grace was still unable to move and continued to stare at the strange man. He was still stood in the entrance of the kitchen and was continuing to chew on something in his mouth in such a casual manner that it made him look more sinister. He could see from her reaction that she was scared.

'If this was a game of musical statues then I would declare you the winner. You are very good at it, Grace.' He finished with a smile hoping that would lighten the mood. Grace was still too frightened to move. *'How the hell did he get in? I'm sure I locked that back door'.*

'Who are you? How did you get in? What do you want? I don't have anything. Oh fuck!' She was gabbling and her nerves were screaming so much in her body her skin was hurting. She had never felt fear like this in her life.

'How do you know my name?' she whispered.

She wasn't sure she wanted to know the answer now that she had asked the question. Someone must have told this man all about her and that she lived on her own. Her mum was right and she could hear her voice in her head saying, 'why in the hell would anyone want to live on their own is beyond me, unless they are widowed'?

'Grace, I'm not here to hurt you,' he said tenderly and moved towards her.

'STAY BACK!' she backed away from him. Her mind was now whirring with how to get him out or how she could get out and find help. She needed Big Mick. He would kick ten shades out of this fella. Her eyes were scanning the room for something but she didn't know what. That upstairs lamp would have come in handy again.

'Okay,' he raised his hand in agreement and stayed rooted to the spot in the entrance to the kitchen. 'Do you want me to answer all your questions or shall we start again, Daff?' he smiled.

Grace was taken aback by the name. She looked at him through squinted eyes and he started to beam at her. She remembered.

'You're the tramp from the bridge on Friday,' Grace was speaking like she was in a trance and was struggling to try and make sense of the last 36 hours. He clasped his hands together in front of him as if in a police line-up and waited for her to speak. He was enjoying this game.

'I thought it was you,' her voice becoming more monotone, 'they said a tramp and I thought it was you,' she carried on staring at him.

'Daff, I'm not here to hurt you. I just need to speak to you,' he looked at her imploring now. He was no longer grinning which Grace was a tiny bit grateful for as it took the menacing edge from him.

'Please?' he begged.

Obviously, Grace had never been in a situation like this before. Should she engage with him or just simply bolt for the door and let Big Mick sort him out. There was a reason why he was here and she had noted the fact that he had not moved since she asked him not to.

'Don't move, I mean it!' Grace tried her best to sound authoritative and raised her hand in a halt position, but wasn't quite sure if she had pulled it off.

'I promise, I'll stay here,' he assured her.

Grace noticed that he was actually wearing a tuxedo with a white shirt and a black bow tie undone but still in the collar. His brown curly hair had been washed and was shiny. His face was not only clean but he looked healthy. She gave him a thorough once over and took a guess that he had been to an all-night party. He looked very different from the last time she had seen him.

'Have you come straight from a party?' she cocked her

head to one side reminding him of a spaniel he once owned.

'Well, of all the questions I expected, that was not on my list.' He smiled again warmly after giving himself the once over. 'I have been, yes, a good one as well. I felt I needed a bit of Dutch courage to come and see you. Frank suggested it,' he stopped talking as if he said something he shouldn't have but then continued, 'I erm….thought it might be best if I saw you in the day. Less atmospheric, shall we say.'

Grace noticed that he seemed a bit nervous which was making her more nervous about what he was going to say or do next.

'Promise me you're not going to touch me?' she waited for a second, 'mind you if you were then you would still promise anyway wouldn't you?' She looked at him with an earnest gaze.

'Daff, if I was going to hurt you I wouldn't start the attack by enlightening you on motor abbreviations. And if I was going to rape you,' he noted her flinching, 'then I would not need to dress in a tuxedo for the occasion would I? Not the most suitable attire for a physical assault.' Grace gave a nervous laugh.

'No, I suppose not.' Her emotions were still at screaming level. 'So…you left your mate Frank to come here? Yes?' she was wringing her hands but was trying to sound casual. Her mind went back to the bridge on Friday. 'You were dressed like a tramp on Friday when I saw you, at the bridge.' In a matter of seconds she recalled Mrs Mortimer, DC Fabulous, the police station and all the nosey parkers yesterday at the bridge. She had not forgotten his laugh either when she fell over.

'Daff, may I please sit down?' he asked gently.

'Not until you tell me how the hell you got in. I know I locked that door. I always do. Have you got a key?' Grace didn't know what to think. She was trying to remember if there had ever been an opportunity for someone to copy her keys. She wondered if he had ever lived here in the cottage and wanted to come back for something and simply thought he could still walk in.

'I need to tell you a story first and then at the end you will understand how I got in. Please just let me sit and explain?' he stayed on the spot awaiting her permission. 'If it makes you feel any better, keep your phone on you and open the front door so you can run out if you feel at all threatened by me.' He seemed quite proud of this idea.

'In case I feel threatened? IN CASE I FEEL THREATENED? Are you stupid? Do I look RELAXED to you?' she was starting to shout.

'Now there's the Daff I met on the bridge!' he started to laugh, still finding much amusement in the whole scene. He decided that this stalemate situation could go on all day and felt he had waited long enough. He moved away from the spot in the kitchen doorway and walked toward the couch which sent Grace into a panic. He knew it would but pretended he didn't notice and sat down on the couch and crossed his legs casually.

'Well, go and open the door if you want.' He looked to his left and there on the couch was her mobile phone. She spotted it and he could see the desperate look on her face. He picked the phone up and passed it to her. 'You may want this.' This action totally confused her. Surely if he wanted to hurt her he wouldn't just take a seat and pass her the phone, just like that. She slowly reached out and took the phone from his hand. Her eyes never left his for one moment. Once she took the phone, he sat further back into the sofa to make himself more comfortable.

He looked up at her, 'Daff, please sit down dear. I feel like R2D2 talking to C3PO.' There was a pause and then she backed away from him into an armchair and watched him the whole time. She sat down with the phone firmly clutched in her hand. He noted that she had not opened the front door and took this as a good sign that she was relaxed or that she was now in shock. He wasn't quite sure which the better option was.

'Firstly, I would like to say sorry for laughing at you on the bridge on Friday when you fell over. It wasn't very gentlemanly of me and I offer my sincere apologies.' He looked at her expectantly. To her, he sounded even more upper class than he had on Friday. Maybe because posh people apologise a lot. All she could now hear in her head were a lot of posh people saying, 'Soway, soway, oh ever so soway.' He was still looking at her, clearly waiting for absolution.

'Erm…..okay,' said Grace slowly.

The man placed his elbows on his knees with his hands in front of him and he stared at them as if for guidance. Grace noted that he was still nervous and was struggling to say what he needed to say. She opened her mouth to hurry him up but something told her to be patient so she closed it and continued to stare at him.

'There's no easy way of saying this,' he carried on looking at his cupped hands, 'the man that they took away from the river bank yesterday…was me.' He looked up at her. Her expression had not changed since he had sat down and he wasn't sure she understood.

'I mean, it was me, but not all of me,' he carried on looking at her for some form of a spark. Nothing.

He tried to become more animated and his cupped

hands started to move to weakly illustrate his explanation. 'What I mean is, that when I saw you on the bridge on Friday, it was me and then on Saturday, I mean yesterday, it was me but not me, as it was only some of me. Part of me wasn't there, it was somewhere else and now it's here.' He arrived at the end of the sentence and very briefly had a look of triumph until he looked again at Grace. 'Do you understand any of this?' he quizzed. There was no denying that Grace was just as confused as to what he said as she was when she watched the season finale of Lost.

'I'm not sure I follow.' Her accent was more evident now. It became more pronounced when she was emotional or drunk apparently. He was running out of options. He didn't want to upset her or frighten her. He had only seen her for a few minutes and yet he felt emotionally responsible in some way.

'Grace,' he stared at her. He needed her full attention and she held his gaze. 'I'm dead!'

He continued to look at her and noted that she hadn't even blinked. Was she in shock? Did she hear him? Grace blinked all of a sudden and then burst out laughing. Maybe because of nerves, maybe because of adrenalin pumping through her. She laughed and couldn't stop. Her hysteria rose and she brought her knees up and clutched her side. The tears were now starting to roll down her cheeks. She started to calm down and then looked at him which then started the hysterical process all over again.

'My God, it's like sitting with Mutley the Dog,' he muttered under his breath starting to become impatient. Grace began to calm down, gulping some air to speed up the process. Once she felt composed, she turned to look at him.

'Dead? Really? How are you dead?' She tried to hide

the amusement from her voice but had failed miserably.

'I died on the bank. Remember? You told the police!' his voice sounded a little exasperated. Grace knew that she had not mentioned going to the police station.

'How do you know I went to the police? I never said.' Grace was becoming nervous and confused again.

'I know you didn't say. But...well...' he was struggling, 'I just know, okay?' he looked at her for acceptance.

'No, it's not bloody okay,' she was now on her feet. 'You walk in here and offer your feeble apology and then tell me you're a ghost.' She placed her hands on her hips as if chastising a child for fibbing. 'Of course you are! That's how you got into my bloody house without me hearing you...'

'Bingo,' he exhaled.

She stopped dead on her feet and looked through to the kitchen. She marched her way to the back door, took the handle and pulled. The door didn't give. It was still locked and the key was gently swinging on the hook to the side of it, on the architrave. Flynn was on his feet next to her thinking he was being let out again but was confused when the door didn't open. He was confused more when his master told him to lie back down. She watched Flynn return to his basket and glanced upwards at the drainer. She wondered and glanced back into the lounge. He was still seated on the couch with his back to her waiting for her return.

'Were you here last night?' she was tiptoeing back into the room and making her way to the vacant armchair. He looked at her and then glanced at the armchair and she understood the silent instruction. She calmly sat down and waited.

'Yes I was,' he confirmed and she gasped in horror.

'I'm sorry, truly I am. I'm still trying to get to grips with all this and realised that it probably wasn't a good idea to visit you at night. By the time I decided it was best to leave you were down here and I wasn't sure if you could see me so I stayed still. I was sat on that worktop thingy,' he pointed with his thumb behind him. 'When I 'arrived' shall we say I was a bit…well…,' he was again struggling for words.

'What?!' she shouted.

He looked embarrassed, 'I was at a party and Frank said that I should have a little drink before I make my first visit to you…' Grace interrupted.

'First visit? Look, Bob Marley, don't think you are coming back here again. One visit is enough. Christ, I'm not even related to you!'

'It's Jacob Marley.'

'What?'

'It's Jacob. You said Bob Marley. He's the reggae singer,' he corrected.

'I know who bloody Bob Marley is for chrissakes!' Grace looked away from him slightly mortified at her gaffe in what should be a very serious situation but was now feeling like she was in a scene from a Carry On film.

'So are you telling me that you turned up at my house, in the middle of the night, crashed into my dishes, scared me half to death and gave Flynn a heart attack,' she pushed the last one, 'because you were pissed?' She faced him accusingly and right on cue he hung his head in shame like a five-year-old child.

'I did, I was and I'm sorry,' he continued to look at his feet as she chastised him. There was a long pause as Grace tried to gather her thoughts and control her sense of disbelief.

'Did you see who found your body?' she asked this as more of a test.

'An old lady. American I think. With a dog called….,' he tried to recall, 'Benji!' he remembered victoriously. It was now starting to dawn on Grace that he could be telling the truth. She shifted in her chair and continued to look at him. He didn't look like a ghost. Not that she had any great experience of being with ghosts but she thought maybe a bit of transparency or a floating gait might add to his authenticity. He looked just like anybody else.

'Aren't ghosts supposed to be a bit older?' she enquired. He looked confused at this notion.

'I don't mean old old. I mean, well, you only died on Friday. You haven't been buried yet.'

'My dear, all this is new to me as well. One minute I was on the river bank about to have a little sleep and the next I was in an office.'

'An office? Whose office?' said Grace. He stared into space as he recollected the memory.

'It was all glass walls. But not glass you could see through. But the light outside the glass was the brightest light I have ever seen. But you could look at it. Very strange Daff, to be honest.' He was aware he had her full attention and continued with his story. 'There was a desk, white of course and behind the desk sat the most beautiful lady I think I've ever seen.' He paused and savoured the memory for a moment. 'Red hair, she had. I do like a red head, my dear,' he looked at Grace with amusement. 'To cut a long story short I have to make a positive effect on someone's life. Just one person.' He shifted and turned on the sofa and looked directly at Grace. 'And I picked you, Daff,' he concluded. Grace continued to look at him while she processed what he had just revealed. But still couldn't compute it entirely.

'Sorry, you picked me? What are you going to do to me?' Grace very quickly made a list of things she hoped he wouldn't say, including killing her, making her ghost like, something that involved money, anything that involved physical exercise or having to tell someone about this whole tale and trying to get them to believe her.

'Well this is it Daff, I'm not sure myself. All I have been told is that to earn my true place I have to make a positive effect on someone and I picked you.'

'But why me? You don't even know me?' Grace was becoming more confused.

'I know, so won't it be splendid getting to know each other now?'

'Just like that? They said pick one person and you can have your wings, Clarence. Nah, there's more to this tale than meets the eye and I want to know exactly why you're here, why you chose me and more importantly what the bleeding hell I have to do?' Grace prodded her finger on the arm of the chair as if her points needed illustrating.

'Well, you start by offering me cup of tea?!' he snorted.

'Tea? You're a bloody ghost. Ghosts don't drink tea!'

'Name me one ghost that doesn't drink tea?' he challenged.

Grace thought for a moment then with smugness answered, 'Patrick Swayze.' She looked at him for his look of defeat but was presented with a resounding laugh.

'Patrick Swayze! From the bloody film! I mean a ghost that you have met. Not some film star that likes pottery and a spot of dancing,' he chortled.

'But I don't know any other ghosts. Not proper ones!' she retorted.

'So how do you know we do not like tea?'

She stared at him blankly. She wasn't sure if it was more stupid to think ghosts drank tea or to give Patrick Swayze as a good example of a ghost.

'Look, I'll put the sodding kettle on when I get to the why-fors of you being here.' He relented. He had no idea she was this tenacious. He didn't know her at all. The redhead was quite persistent that he had to pick someone and quickly. He probably picked Daff because she was the first person that had actually spoken to him in quite some time. And he adored her lovely accent.

'My dear, this whole thing may take some time. I haven't got all the answers either.' Grace went to interrupt and he raised his hand to stop her. 'And yes, I have asked.' He paused for a moment and looked at the floor. 'Daff, there's a gentleman 'upstairs' shall we say,' he pointed upwards obviously to indicate he was talking of heaven, 'who has not fulfilled his task. He is having a marvellous time on the plane that we currently exist on and he is waiting for his wife. He said his wife would enjoy a good party and he wants to wait for her so they can have a drink together. He feels the 'pull' of something else but he will not go until he can leave with his wife. So whomever he is supposed to see and carry out the same task as I have been set for you are not even aware yet that there is a mission that involves them that is yet to be fulfilled.' He continued to look at the floor.

'Does the man know when his wife will join him?' Grace asked.

'No, my dear. Even though 'they' know, none of us know when our time is up. So he simply has to be patient and wait for her. Only then will he embark on his own personal mission.'

'It must be some party up there!'

'It's beyond your imagination my dear. But you cannot move on to the next plane until the task is complete.' He looked at Grace with almost a sad look in his eyes.

'I've never had love like that before. Imagine someone waiting for you for years just so they could have a drink with you,' she mused.

'There's a bit more than that, but you're getting the idea,' he said.

They sat in silence for a moment lost in their own thoughts unaware that their thoughts were similar. Both of love and the longing. The silence was interrupted by him standing on his feet.

'Well, I'm not going to get a drink around here so I will be off.' Grace jumped to her feet in surprise and then wondered how he 'went.'

'I'm sorry. Stay. Have some tea. I'll put the kettle on.' She went to run to the kitchen but he caught her hand. She looked at her hand in his. There was no coldness or warmth only pressure and a slight tingle. It felt bizarre. He looked at her and asked, 'What does it feel like to you?'

'It's weird. I can feel your hand but no temperature and it's like you're giving me pins and needles a bit,' she looked up at him. 'How about you?'

'You feel perfectly normal to me. Like I'm alive,' he smiled at her. 'My friends call me Crowley.' She looked back at her hand but his was gone. He had gone. She gasped. She stood in the middle of her lounge and looked around but it was empty.

CHAPTER 4

Grace's mind was whirring with questions. She had so much more to ask him. She didn't even know when he was coming back. What was this effect he was going to have on her? Could she tell anyone about him? Would anyone believe her? She was still stood in the middle of the lounge and was continuing to scan the room to see if he had appeared somewhere else. She wondered if she had just had a dream about him and standing up had woken her. She looked at the armchair and saw the phone on the arm. When she was looking at cars she was on the sofa. He was here.

She walked to the kitchen and Flynn raised his head slowly to make sure he was not being approached by anything or anyone that might require him to move. His master was shuffling towards him but he knew that walk was an indication that she had no intention of introducing herself to any fresh air today and that suited him fine.

Grace noted the plate drainer. It still wasn't sitting quite right, another indication that he had been there. She wandered back into the lounge, half expecting him to have returned as he realised that he had told her absolutely nothing. But no, he wasn't there.

She sat on the couch and stared at the same spot that he was looking at earlier. Grace started to go over the last half an hour. She had just been conversing with a ghost and it wasn't like at all she imagined. Even though she had used Patrick Swayze as an example she always thought of ghosts as scary or sinister and he was neither. Okay, yes, he gave her a fright last night but in the cold light of day he looked just like anybody else. All those haunting films and TV shows had it all wrong. They weren't howling and whooping in attics and cellars. They sat on couches and asked for tea! They partied and dressed well. What Crowley had told her was nothing like they portrayed on the telly. Even Flynn had not been a bit bothered by his presence. What happened to dogs being super psychic? She turned and looked at the strange looking beast on the kitchen floor. She rolled her eyes and concluded that maybe Flynn wasn't the best example of a sensitive dog. It had taken Flynn months to learn his own name and that the bowl on the kitchen floor contained food for him. He had mastered the basics now, but to push him into 'rolling over' or 'play dead' was like asking Nell's brother Roger to do the can-can.

She wondered more as to when he would return. Did she have to call him? How did she call him? Was there a spell of some sorts? Or a certain type of condition she had to be in to summon him. If she did call for him what was she supposed to say? What if she woke him up? Did he sleep? He must do if he eats and drinks and gets drunk. Surely all the other human traits would remain as well. She wondered if he went to the toilet and if he did, where did the flush go. *'Oh God, I hope that's not rain'* she thought.

Then realised that was ridiculous as there was no evidence as to number twos. Unless number twos were white in heaven. He said everything else is. *'Maybe our weather is heavenly sewage'*. She realised that she was being stupid but then her brain argued that a ghost had requested a cup of PG Tips so she shouldn't be hasty in dismissing anything.

She felt like her head was going to explode and realised she had a headache. She padded her way back to the kitchen and looked for tablets. She realised they were still in her coat pocket from yesterday. She retrieved the open packet, took the recommended dose and then lay on the couch trying to keep her head still and allow the tablets to do their job.

She soon realised she wanted to speak to him again. She had too many unanswered questions. She sat up and looked around to check he hadn't arrived just by simple will, but no, he wasn't there. In a way, she was kind of relieved that he hadn't just arrived with the power of her mind. To able to call upon an entity with your mind alone was quite a scary thought. Grace knew that she would have more success controlling her bladder after a night of drinking Prosecco than controlling her mind of any random thought.

She sat in the silence for a while thinking about Crowley. She wanted to ask about his family, if he had any and why he was living rough. She then remembered that DC Fabulous had said the hardest part of the investigation was to find out who he was. Maybe, next time Crowley came to visit she could get all the information and then pass it to the police. But then how would she explain knowing all that she did? The police would probably think that she knew him when he was alive and make some connection and think that she may have had something to do with his death. But if she didn't say anything then he might just be cremated or buried in an unmarked grave and if he had any family, they would never know that he was dead. Surely, someone in the world was interested in him. Surely someone had loved him once.

She wanted to tell someone about this but after deliberation realised there was no one she could tell and no one would believe her either. Big Mick would look at her like she was an imbecile, Patsy would recommend a doctor or a vodka and tonic and Mrs Mortimer would find the whole tale so amusing it was bound to induce a coughing fit and kill the old lady. She was best to keep this to herself for now. She thought some more about Crowley and it made her want to call home for some reason. She just needed a normal conversation to bring some realism back to her day. When she called home, her mum answered.

'3548,' her mum announced.

'Hi Mum,' Grace's tone could have been interpreted as disappointed or bored.

'Grace darling, Daddy and I were just talking about you. How are you?' her mother seemed pleased to hear from her.

'I'm okay. I was only phoning for a chat and to see how you all were. Is Daddy all right? Grace enquired.

'Daddy's fine. He was playing golf yesterday. I didn't go, Darling; I don't think he likes me to join him anymore. Plus it's far too cold, don't you think? Or is it warm by you?'

'No Mum, the weather here is pretty much the same as in Cornwall. I'm not that far away.'

'I know you keep saying that dear but you are. It's not as if I can just pop round to see you is it?' Grace had always wondered if she did live near her parents would they ever just pop round.

'Once I buy a car we can see each other more. We can meet half way and go shopping and have spa days. Wouldn't you like that?' Grace tried to sound upbeat. She wasn't sure if *she* would like it never mind her mum.

'Of course I would Darling,' her mum sounded just as enthusiastic. 'Have you seen a car yet?'

'No, I started looking this morning but then…erm…Mrs Mortimer called,' lied Grace.

'That woman relies on you far too much. Where are her family?'

'I've told you Mum, all her family is in New York or Ohio.'

'So, why isn't she?' her mum sounded irritated.

'I have told you Mum, her brother died and his wife is in a home in America somewhere. They've got kids, not sure how many. Think it might be two and they have their own lives. I don't think they hardly know Mrs Mortimer to be honest.'

'So why is she living in Pelsby?' her mum enquired.

'Something to do with her husband's job I think. They didn't have kids. I'm not sure why, I've never liked to ask to be honest. I think he came from a large family. I know he worked for the American Embassy in London and they bought Primrose Cottage years ago. It was like their holiday home. Anyway, when he retired they moved to Pelsby permanently.'

'So, what did she do with her life, just follow him around?' Grace picked up on her mum's sarcastic tone and felt defensive all of a sudden. Her mum didn't know Mrs Mortimer, and yes, the old lady did ask favours but Grace relied on her too and maybe she had been amiss not revealing this to her mum.

'She worked too as a photographer for the government, I think; they moved around a lot because of him. She was very supportive of his career which must have been hard for her. Not knowing anyone in a strange country.'

'Britain is not a third world country, Darling, I doubt it took too much of an adjustment.' Grace was slightly taken aback by this.

'Don't be callous, Mother!' The silence fell between them. Grace could tell that her mum was smarting at the other end of the phone and the only way the silence would cease would be if she broke it.

'Her life with him was very active. They went all over the world. He could fly planes I believe, and his family had a ranch when they were younger. If you met her, Mum you would probably find her very interesting.'

'I'm sure I would dear,' her mum said unconvincingly. The silence fell again.

'Have you heard from Gethin?' Grace enquired.

'No. Not for a couple of weeks now. I think he said Australia is having their school holidays at the moment so him and Jenna were planning to go away somewhere. It's too late to call him now I suppose. I'll probably try next weekend. Have you?'

'No,' Grace felt the conversation was starting to run dry now. 'Is Daddy there?' Grace asked hopefully.

'He is. I'm sure he can give you lots of advice on what kind of car you should be looking for. Call me through the week, Darling. It's my only way of knowing that you haven't been slaughtered in your bed by some English interbred.' She didn't wait for Grace to respond. Grace heard the muffle of a hand over the receiver and the faint shout of, 'Dai, telephone. It's Grace, dear.' More muffling. 'He's coming now. I'll speak to you in a few days. God

Bless, Darling.'

'Bye Mum.' Grace could hear the phone being passed and some faint whispering. Her mum always did this. She couldn't pass the phone to her dad without some instruction before he took the call. It wouldn't matter who was on the end of the phone it was something she simply felt compelled to do. Grace was imaging the instruction would be something inane as *'don't forget to tell Grace the difference between petrol and diesel'*, totally unnecessary but it was as if by saying this it would give her the power to relinquish the phone.

'Grace, my darling. How are you?' Her dad sounded jolly.

'Hey Dad,' Grace could hear her mum still muttering something in the background.

'Yes Penny, I will ask her.' This clearly was a response to her mum.

'What does she want you to ask me? She's just passed the phone over so why she couldn't just ask me before, I don't know.' Grace recalled the silences and knew there had been plenty of opportunities for her mum to say what she needed to say when she was speaking to her.

'Your mother is asking, have you had anyone to check your boiler as the weather is really taking hold now.' Dai looked at Penny to make sure he had said it correctly and if he had she could go away and leave him in peace to talk to his daughter properly. Penny nodded with satisfaction that it had been asked and noted that she was to leave him.

'Hold on dear,' Dai said to Grace.

Dai took his phone to his study to ensure some peace while Penny went off to busy herself in the kitchen. Dai's study was not a study in the traditional sense of the word. The room was large and two of the walls were entirely made of glass that looked out onto the sands that were currently being battered by the Celtic Sea. The centre of the room was sunken with a huge cream horseshoe-shaped sofa that faced a wall full of books from floor to ceiling. Some of the wall was partially obscured by a spiral staircase that rose to a mezzanine area that housed Dai's telescope, binoculars and battered leather chair. The chair matched nothing in the room except some of the old books and Dai, of course.

Dai walked over to a tub chair that was facing out to the sea and sat down to speak to his daughter.

'Have you gone to your man cave, Dad?' Grace could tell from his sigh that he sounded more relaxed.

'I have dear,' he sounded amused at her observation. 'The sea is dancing to an Argentinian Tango today!'

'As dramatic as that?' Grace loved the way her dad would describe the sea to her in the form of a dance. It conjured up the right image though.

'The sky is looking quite ominous as well. We may be in for a storm, with a bit of luck.'

'The only weather we have here is damp. Varying degrees of damp but still damp nonetheless.'

'How are things in Pelsby?'

'Well, the highlight of the whole weekend was old Mrs Mortimer, the American lady, found a dead body on the river bank yesterday.' Grace was quite chuffed that she actually had something juicy to tell him.

'Good grief! Who? Not a friend of yours is it, Darling?' Her dad seemed genuinely shocked. Grace smiled to herself as to how to answer his question. How should she describe Crowley now?

'No, it wasn't anyone from the village. It was a homeless guy who died from hyperthermia. The police don't know who he is. I saw the man on Friday night when I got off the bus from work. He gave me a bit of a fright...'

Dai interrupted, 'Did he touch you?'

'No! Nothing like that. I just didn't expect anyone to be on the bridge in the dark at that time of night. It looks like he went to sleep on the bank and the cold got the better of him and he died of hyperthermia.'

'Good God! The poor man.'

'I know. Anyway, I had to go to the police station yesterday as it seems I might have been the last person to see him alive. So I had to give a statement or something. They said they would let me know if they needed any more information but there's nothing else I can tell them really,' lied Grace.

'He must have family, or someone that needs to know.'

'But with no ID on him the police said it will be hard trying to find out.'

'Well, the police have lots of tools at their disposal. I am sure they will get to the bottom of it soon enough. It must have been quite a shock for Mrs Mortimer.'

'You think? She took it all in her stride, Dad. The woman is unshakeable. She reckons she's seen more dead bodies than the Grim Reaper, the way she talks.'

Dai laughed at the thought of the old lady giving Death a run for its money, with Death submitting to come back another time for her.

'Anyway, I've just stayed in since then. I need to look for a car.' Grace had decided not to tell her dad about Crowley. What was the point? Her parents wouldn't believe her or at best they would think she was insane.

'Oh, while we are on about that, I have put some money in your old Nat West account. I'm not sure if you use it anymore. But there's a little something in there to help you buy a car.'

'Dad! We talked about this and I said I was saving.'

'Yes, I know, Darling. But you can't save that much on your salary and I want you to get something fairly decent. Running backwards and forwards from Pelsby to Cornwall will take its toll on an old car. So just get something a wee bit newer and more comfortable and I'll be happy.'

'But Dad...'

'I won't take no for an answer. I would be worried sick every time you said you were coming up.' Grace picked up on the fact that they clearly expected to see her more often once she bought the car.

'Well, thanks Dad and thank Mum as well.'

'And I've cleared it with your mother that when you come up you can bring that dog of yours as well, if you want. I've told her, we finally have our dream house and it's full of people but none of them are family. She won't have her sister here and we all know why.' Penny's sister Flo was not as polished as Penny and liked to put Penny down at every opportunity. 'Gethin's on the other side of the bloody world and I've got no one on my side. There's only you and I'm not having you feeling like you can't visit because your mother can't cope with a little dog!' Dai was starting to become wound up and Grace could tell that they had obviously had words about this and recently too.

'You been fighting with Mum?'

'Not fighting,' he sighed, 'just putting her in her place and reminding her of a few things, that's all.' Dai looked at the sea and recalled the argument they had had. Penny was adamant that Flynn was not allowed in the house. Dai pointed out that most of the ground floor was uncarpeted anyway. He also pointed out that Flynn was not a puppy and was perfectly house trained. He finally won the argument by saying he refused to go through another year of not seeing his daughter more than three times. There was nothing they could do about Gethin, but Grace was a different matter and if Grace and the dog were not welcome at the house then they had no option but to visit her in Pelsby.

The final statement was the clincher. Penny did not relish the idea of visiting Pelsby again. She found Grace's cottage too small, too untidy and too public. Penny had difficulty sharing a bathroom, even though it was her daughter's home. She was not happy sleeping in Grace's bed as she knew that Flynn was allowed on there, even though the linen had been washed and Grace was giving up her bed and sleeping on the couch. But the best was when Grace took her parents to The Blacky. Dai soon acquainted himself and by the end of the night was telling jokes and embellishing stories of his life to a drunken captive audience. Big Mick loved Dai as he kept some of his early darters in the pub 'til closing time with his tales of one-up-manship and secrets of the city. Penny however, sat at a bar stool all night with a mouth like a bulldog's arsehole.

Patsy would watch her and become more wound up each time she looked and soon revealed to Big Mick, 'Only because I like Grace, I'll stop myself from slapping that snooty bitch off my bar stool. I don't think I've pulled a decent pint since she's been in. She's turning all the beer flat. Look at that mouth and how thin her lips are. A lipstick must last her years, I tell ya, years.' Big Mick would confidently ignore his wife. She had never slapped anyone off a barstool even though she said it nearly every day and judging by the pints filling all the tables in his pub he was assured the beer was fine.

'So, will you look for a decent motor and bring yourself and Flynn up in the next few weeks?' Dai asked.

'Of course I will. Thanks, Dad.' Grace was grateful and he had reminded her that their family unit was very small and more of an effort should be made by everyone including her.

'And will you get that boiler looked at?'

'Oh, I will. There's a man who drinks in the pub called Tom I think. I'm sure someone said he's a gas engineer. He's got a van.'

Dai started to laugh down the phone, 'Oh well, he must be good with boilers then if he has a van,' he continued to laugh.

'No, I don't mean that. I just meant he must have a job with tools and stuff if he has a van.' This set Dai off again. He loved his daughter's simplicity.

'Well, go and see the man and his van and see if there is a certificate anywhere in his van that qualifies him to service your boiler. He can send the bill to me and I'll pay for it. I don't want you calling me in the middle of the night saying your pipes have frozen.' How she would discover that her pipes were frozen in the middle of the night and not the morning when people are usually up she didn't know. Also, why on earth would she call her dad in Cornwall, more than a three hour drive away, to sort her pipes? If last night was anything to go by there were more interesting things that could happen in the small, wee hours.

'I'm not destitute Dad, I can pay for a boiler service,' said Grace.

'I know you can, but you don't need to. Let me look after you Grace, eh? For once can I feel needed?' his voice at the end became comically whiny and Grace relented.

'Okay, I'll see if Tom can have a look this week and I'll let you know what he says.'

'Not a word to your mother, mind.' Dai instructed. This was a given. Grace was not sure how much Dai told his wife about assisting her in some financial matters so she kept schtum about everything.

'Okay,' she said. Grace would much prefer if her mum knew, even though she knew she ran the risk of not having this financial support. But it kept her dad happy and to some extent kept Grace happy, so two out of three was better than none.

'So, any other news to tell me dear?' Dai sat back in his tub chair.

'No. Nothing else. Work is just as boring as ever. Still Christmas only a month away so that's something to look forward to.'

'You are still coming here aren't you? And you can bring Flynn now.'

'Of course, I'm looking forward to it. I can't fit a sparrow in my little oven, never mind a turkey. And 'sides, like you and Mum would be happy coming here for Christmas Day and eating off your knee! Noooo, I'll come to you and let Mum cook the dinner and I'll struggle on to eat it in your beautiful beach house.' The humorous sarcasm was not lost on Dai and he was relieved that she was still going to be there.

'Good, good,' he said. There was a natural pause and they both instinctively knew that the call was coming to an end.

'Right then Dad, I'll let you go and I'll call you as soon as I speak to Tom then, eh?'

'Splendid. Don't forget now, mind. I'll speak to you through the week.'

'Bye Dad. I love you.'

'Love you too, Gracey darling. Bye.'

Grace mulled over the conversation and shouted Flynn from the kitchen. He trotted over and she ruffled his coat while telling him he was now allowed at Chez Hammond and how privileged he was to be in Penny Hammond's company. Grace smiled at her recollection of Penny's face full of disdain when she first looked at Flynn. Her dad was very direct and said he was the strangest looking dog he had ever seen and drew a laugh when he concluded the dog's parents were a terrier and a sheep. Grace knew the dog was ugly but he was the most beautiful dog in other ways. Even the villagers now had a soft spot for him. Most villages had the village idiot, well Pelsby had the village idiot dog. Except he wasn't a complete idiot, he just looked like one.

Grace decided to return to her iPad and continue looking for a car. However, she wanted to know how much her dad had put in her account. She felt slightly guilty as she hoped he might have placed a couple of grand in the old account. This would help enormously and mean that she could move away from her selection being limited to cars that were beige. The last time she looked at the account it was in credit for £2.12 and that was a couple of years ago. She actually forgot about the account these days.

She opened the account details online and was aghast to see the balance was £10,002.18. Her dad had placed ten thousand pounds in her account and made it sound like he had just put in a few hundred. She knew her mum and dad had a few pennies put away and with Dad's investments and pension they were not short but this was an incredible amount to give for no reason.

She picked up the phone again and tried to call him on

his mobile. If she called the land line again her mum would answer and start questioning as to why she was calling back again so soon. His mobile went to answerphone. It was probably in a jacket somewhere and he forgot to pick it up. She left a message saying she had seen what he had deposited and it was too much and could he call her back.

Dai was still in his study when he heard his mobile ringing from the mezzanine. He saw the phone in time to answer and saw his daughter's name flashing on the screen. He knew why she was calling, so ignored the call. She had clearly seen the money in her account. The phone stopped and after a short time bleeped with a voicemail message.

'Dad, I've just opened the account. Ten grand! It's too much. Mum would go mad if she knew. Please call me back. I can't take this much. I mean it; call me back when you get this.'

'Typical Grace,' he thought. She was completely different from Gethin who took everything that was offered to him with thanks. With Grace however, there was always an element of protestation. She couldn't take a gift outside of her birthday or Christmas without fuss.

Grace didn't want to look at cars now. She felt guilty and greedy so put the iPad away and decided to have a shower instead. Her mind was still reeling from her eventful morning with her parents and more importantly Crowley. She remembered that on the other side of Lanson from her office was a large library. She decided she could look something up in there on the supernatural and how to summon spirits properly. Maybe she needed some ingredients to do this as well. She wasn't sure what but all the TV shows always had people mixing stuff in antique brass bowls and reciting spells to conjure something up. There was a strange shop in Clune, the next village on the road to Lanson. 'They were bound to sell spelly stuff,' she thought. There were some dusty dragon ornaments in the window, crystals and various items that always made you think, *'what the hell is that'?* which qualified the shop as strange and that was enough for Grace.

After her shower, she noticed a missed call and a voicemail on her phone. It was her dad.

'Grace, I've just got your message. My dear, I don't know how much you think a decent car costs these days but it's hardly an exorbitant amount. Your mother's last handbag probably cost more than that and I get no pleasure from that. This is money well spent in my book as I will see you more, so we will say no more about it. If you don't take the money I shall come to Pelsby and tell everyone in that pub you drink in that you wet the bed until you left university.' He laughed at his own untrue joke, 'so take the money and be assured that your brother has had just as much money out of me this year if not more. I love you, Gracey darling. Bye. And don't call me back about this.' His words at the end were warm and Grace was teary by the time she ended the message. With the three thousand pound she had saved as well she could get herself a really nice car. People in the village would think she had won the lottery.

After drying her hair and getting dressed, Grace remembered that she needed to call in to see Mrs Mortimer. She also decided to call at Tom's and see if he could look at the boiler. The boiler was actually the landlord's responsibility but seeing as her landlord was Mr Cousins from Pool Farm she didn't like to bother him. Mr Cousins had not increased Grace's rent since she moved in. He had never been to the house to make sure she hadn't trashed it or made changes he wouldn't approve of. The last time she spoke to him about the house was when she wanted to buy a dog and she stopped him in the village.

'I don't care if you buy a gorilla. It's you that's got to live with the bloody thing!' Mr Cousins growled when she asked would it be ok to have a pet in the cottage.

'I just thought it best to check,' Grace had replied meekly.

'Right,' he went to walk away, 'everything else okay with the cottage?' Grace felt like he had asked just to be courteous but wasn't interested at all.

'Fine, thank you. Only…can I ask?'

'What?' he snapped.

'Is it all right if I paint the lounge? It's a bit tired looking. I'll check the colours with you if you want or don't want. It's up to you,' she was nervous, 'or I can leave it. It's not that bad I s'pose.'

'You can do what you like. I don't bloody care. It's your house. You can tear the walls down and put a lift in and turn it into a nightclub. Just don't ask me for money. You want it, you pay for it. Yeah?' he squinted at her through one eye making his gnarly face more sinister.

'Yes, okay,' she giggled nervously, 'only I can't knock walls down as it's a listed building.' She paused for a slight change in his face bit he continued to scrutinise her.

'Like I said, do what you like. I'm never going to live in the cottage and as long as you keep paying the rent then I'll have no need to come to the door.'

Grace just stared at him unsure what to say next. His voice softened for a moment when he asked,

'You…erm…happy in the cottage? You like living there?' He seemed a bit unsure whether he wanted to ask this or not.

'I am. Thank you. I'd like to stay, for a while anyway.

If that's okay with you?'

He changed again back to his gruff demeanour, turned on his heel and shouted back, 'Like I said, do what you like. It's your bloody house.'

Since then Grace had done exactly what he had said. She bought the dog and decorated the whole house and not just the lounge as she had asked. She had replaced a couple of the cupboard doors in the kitchen and had asked Big Mick to remove the door from the lounge to the kitchen. The cottage was tiny and any valuable room could not be wasted allowing for doors to open. The kitchen door was now gathering dust in the spare bedroom in case she ever moved and needed to put it back on. Only for her monthly bank statement showing Mr Cousins' name, she frequently forgot that she was renting. Her dad had looked at rental prices in the area and knew that the rent was extremely low for Pelsby. This and the fact that the old farmer had never increased the rent in three years gave more reason to resist in bothering him with things like decorating, leaks, windows or boilers. Her dad had said in the long run she was probably financially better off to sort things out herself. The only exclusion to this unwritten rule, that Mr Cousins was not aware of, was roof problems and any major rewiring.

Grace called Flynn who obediently trotted to her and noted that she was putting her coat on. He became excited as he realised he was going for a walk. Flynn danced on his hind legs below the hook that housed his lead and sat down as soon as Grace removed it. She clipped it on and in a high pitched voice said, 'Benji.' Flynn's tail immediately wagged and Grace was happy that he was excited.

CHAPTER 5

Mrs Mortimer was padding around her house looking for parcel tape. She wasn't sure if she had any so went through the usual routine of opening drawers and cupboards like an incompetent burglar. She eventually found it in a random drawer and chastised herself for putting it there. She hoped Grace had remembered to call in and collect the parcel and take it to the post office. She was a good girl and knew that she would turn up eventually.

Once the parcel was wrapped, she walked over to the mantelpiece and picked up her favourite photo of her Mort. She gently caressed the mother of pearl frame and looked into her husband's eyes. The photograph was taken by her in 1963. Her husband was leaning on an old crop dusting plane that belonged to his Uncle Gary. Gary lived in Circleville, Ohio and grew corn while his younger brother Jake, Mort's daddy, bought himself a small ranch about ten miles away from Gary. The brothers were close and help was often switched between the two brothers to help make a success of their own enterprises. Gary had a large family and the last that Mrs Mortimer had heard was that one of his sons had taken over the farm in the early eighties after Gary had died of a heart attack. Jake had three children, Dotty, Paul and Jake Jr. but they called him Mort from a young age and it stuck. Mrs Mortimer could not think of an occasion, apart from when she called him at the Embassy, where she had ever called him Jake.

Dotty had died when she was a child from scarlet fever, so Paul inherited the ranch when Jake Snr died in 1971 of cancer. The ranch was substantially larger when Paul took over and he had taken it from strength to strength. Then Paul's son Todd had taken over when Paul retired and the last that Mrs Mortimer had heard was Todd and his brother Beau were still manning the ranch.

Mort had been the brains of the family and had been packed off to college to study agriculture at Washington State University in 1948. From there he had gained a position in the US Department of Agriculture where he worked for a number of years. It was when he was here he met Kate Barker, the love of his life. Kate worked as a photographer in Photograph Services Division of USDA. They were soon married and hoped to start a family. But the years rolled by and the spare bedrooms remained empty. And in the end they resigned themselves to the fact that the Lord would never bless them with children. So they took life by the boot straps and tried to ride as much life out of their existence as they possibly could.

They travelled all over the world with various posts in their careers with Mort's always taking the lead and Kate's fitting in around his. Kate wasn't always fortunate to find posts for photographers but she would keep busy either by volunteering at local children's homes or making money selling family portraits. But eventually the camera became a tool for a hobby and Kate devoted her time to Mort and supporting him.

They finally settled in London in 1981, not long after his Uncle Gary had died, where Mort had been transferred to working for the Foreign Agricultural Service in the American Embassy. They lived in London but also bought Primrose Cottage in Pelsby, a place where they could switch off and a stark contrast from life in the city. When Mort retired in 1995, they had already made the decision to stay in the UK. There was nothing for them to go back to the USA for. The family that was left were the new generation and they hardly knew Mort or Kate. Only for the odd visit over the years and Christmas cards, the younger members of the family didn't really know them. Mort was also aware that Kate had now settled in Pelsby and was teaching art at the local primary school and it would break her heart to move again.

They spent 10 wonderful years together in their retirement in Pelsby until Mort's death of a heart attack in 2005. He had been helping with the summer fete in the village setting up the bar with Big Mick, Amos and a few of The Blacky regulars. Mrs Mortimer recalled that it was a very hot day and Mort had been complaining of feeling tired. But no one thought anything of it, everyone was tired and hot and him more so at seventy-four-years-old. At the end of a lovely day at the fete, the old couple walked back to Primrose Cottage hand-in-hand with Kate's promise of a back rub and some toast with Marmite. Mort settled himself into his armchair and turned the TV on to watch his favourite comedy programmes while Kate busied herself in the kitchen. By the time she came back with his supper he had gone. She thought he was asleep at first but the hang of his head told her otherwise. She cried when she knew and also shouted at him for telling her to make him Marmite toast. Mort was still talked about to this day and missed by most.

Mrs Mortimer's thoughts were interrupted with Benji's barking and she was brought back to the present day. She was alone in her cottage with only her pictures and knickknacks to take her back in time. She shuffled her way to the front door and there stood Grace and Flynn.

'Hey Grace,' she said hoarsely and walked back into the lounge. Grace stepped in and pushed Flynn's lead into her pocket and followed the old lady to her usual spot at the dining table at the end of the room. Mrs Mortimer looked tired and looked like she needed to be in bed. Suggesting this to the cantankerous old woman would ignite a fight so Grace left her opinion to herself.

'How are we today, Mrs Mortimer? Full of the joys of spring?' Grace tried to sound upbeat. She spied Mrs Mortimer scrutinising her. 'Oh, here we go,' Grace thought. 'It'll be my hair or face or the fact I need to put on weight.'

'You okay?' asked Grace, waiting for the onslaught.

'You look different,' Mrs Mortimer said flatly.

'What do you mean, different?'

'I dunno,' she stared, 'you just seem different.' Grace started to feel self-conscious and frustrated.

'Do you mean my hair? My make-up? What?'

'I don't know!' she barked. 'No, it's not your hair, even though it could do with a good condition.' Grace rolled her eyes while Mrs Mortimer continued to look at her.

'Did you have sex last night?' the old lady asked bluntly.

'What? No! I was in on my own last night. What kind of question is that?' Grace was taken aback.

'It's like there's an air of something different about you. Like you finally lost your virginity,' she said dismissively.

'I'm not a bloody virgin!' protested Grace.

'Really? I'm surprised.' Mrs Mortimer pulled a cigarette from its carton and started to pat her pockets for a lighter.

'Stop winding me up, you old goat. You know very well I've had men in my life and in my bed.' Grace walked to the kitchen to put the kettle on. No doubt there would be round two to this conversation and she decided she needed a tea to cope with it. She took the teapot from the shelf and popped in the tea bags. Grace noticed the new tea that she had bought still sat there unopened.

'Flynn don't count as a man in your bed,' the old lady called through so Grace could hear her. Grace walked back into the lounge and picked up the ashtray to empty.

'I see you've not been drinking that chamomile tea I bought you. And there was me thinking that if you drank it, you might calm down.' Grace had bought the tea hoping it would turn her into a gentle and sweet old lady. Who was she trying to kid? Grace walked back out to the kitchen.

'You made me try it years ago. It was like drinking flower water. Felt like a fucking hippy. Take it back with you and you drink it.' Grace came back into the room and plonked the ashtray back in front of her.

'I'm surprised you can taste anything with all those bloody fags you smoke.'

'Oh change the record, sweetheart, I've danced this one to death,' Mrs Mortimer tried to sound bored.

Grace went back to the kitchen and set up a tray for the tea. Mrs Mortimer would drink out of a dirty mug all day and only rinse it through when she was going to bed. She had once confided to Grace that she liked tea from the pot as it was very British. So Grace had bought the pot when she went shopping in Lanson. The old lady had received the gift gratefully and now expected Grace to make all her tea from it. Not that Grace minded. It was the most used item in the house apart from the dirty mug, and the ashtray of course.

'Here we go,' Grace placed the tray on the table and Mrs Mortimer used her arm to sweep the stray ash onto the floor. As Grace poured the tea she enquired after the letter.

'It's a parcel,' Mrs Mortimer pointed to the package on the sideboard in the front window. Grace rose to her feet, picked up the parcel and brought it back to the table. The parcel was as big as a milk crate but not too heavy and she noted the address on it was Ohio.

'I won't be able to post this until tomorrow. I will have to go into the post office and get it weighed and stuff. Okay?' Grace said.

'Whatever you think is best, dear. Will it take forever to get there, you think?'

'No. I would imagine they would have it in a week,' Grace looked again at the addressee. It was addressed to Todd Mortimer.

'Who's Todd again?' asked Grace.

'Todd is Mort's nephew. Paul's son, Mort's older brother.' Mrs Mortimer nodded toward a photograph of a young man sat on the hearth of an open fire with a Christmas tree in the background. Grace turned to look at her good looking nephew.

'Oh yes, I remember. They still live on the ranch that Mort grew up on, right?

'That's right kiddo,' she leant back in her chair, 'tidying up a few affairs.' Grace didn't like it when she talked like this. It was something she talked about more and more and both girls knew that time was short. The only thing about life is you didn't know how short it was. There was a heavy silence in the room and they both felt they should respect it for some reason.

Mrs Mortimer started to stare again at Grace who was gazing into space. She definitely looked different. 'I think I'm having a fucking stroke,' she thought.

Grace finished her tea and enquired after Mrs Mortimer's health, expected visitors and any provisions that she may need. Once she cleared, washed and stored the teapot until her next visit she retrieved the lead from her pocket whereby Flynn trotted over and sat down before her.

'I'll get that parcel posted in my lunch hour tomorrow and I'll ask how long they think it will take,' she clipped the lead to her dog's collar then walked over to Mrs Mortimer.

'Make sure you take Benji out for a little run, even if it's just to the bridge and back. Yeah?' she looked at Mrs Mortimer for an acknowledgement.

'I'll take him, don't worry.' Grace knew she could take Benji herself and give him the run but she wanted the old lady to have an excuse to get out. Even if it was just for a fifteen minute walk with the dog. It was the one thing that Grace wouldn't do for her but it was with good intentions. Grace placed a kiss on top of the old lady's head and said she would call on her through the week.

As Grace shut the front door, Mrs Mortimer trundled her way to the window and pulled back the curtain to watch Grace, Flynn and her parcel walk down the road. She still had a feeling that there was a change in her friend and even though she had left, the cottage felt different somehow. Not in a bad way, just different and slightly alien to her. She brushed it off as being old and sensitive and dropped the curtain back.

'She's a good girl,' she said to Benji. Benji wagged his tail in agreement. He always enjoyed their visits.

Grace made her way to the bridge instead of going straight home. She thought about the contents of the box on the way and wondered what was in there. She didn't like to ask. She had learned that if Mrs Mortimer had not divulged certain details in a conversation then it was best to leave. She could only imagine the response she would have received if she had enquired what 'tidying a few affairs' meant.

As Grace arrived at the bridge she immediately recalled Crowley. It seemed a bit of a dream now and she started trying to rationalise it in her mind. Was it a dream? If it had been then surely she would have known at the time? Was he really a ghost? If he wasn't then how did he get in? And how did he disappear? She then went back to the question of the dream and her mind started to swirl again with the absurdity of it all. If it was true, who could she ever tell? She wasn't even sure her dad would believe her. She thought more about her parents' reaction and realised that all they would actually do would worry about her mental health. So what was the point of telling them and having them worry about something that wasn't the case?

She thought about telling Gethin. He would either laugh or play it cool, act interested for ten minutes and then go back to talking about himself, Jenna or how wonderful Oz was. She thought about telling Sean, her friend from her office in the next department to hers. He always described himself as sensitive but Grace thought he had this confused with feminine. Sean was more feminine than a five-year-old girl making daisy chains.

She had reached the bridge wall and was leaning on the very spot that she had first seen Crowley. She looked beyond to the spot where he had been found and beyond again to the quilted fields that stretched for miles and miles. Grace wasn't sure whether it was a good place to die or not. It was far better than dying on the streets in the city and she envisaged a bunch of kids poking at Crowley's dead body on a park bench and only stopping when he rolled off onto their feet. No, surely it was better that Mrs Mortimer and Benji found him. But even still, he had died on his own and from the cold and no one knew who he was and as far as she knew, missed him.

'Come on Flynn,' she called to the dog, who was sniffing at some reeds at the edge of the river bank, 'time to go.' Flynn obediently trotted back and stayed at her heel, without the lead, all the way home.

The rest of Grace's evening was dominated by looking for a new car and feeding herself and Flynn. She had whittled it down and decided to look at two cars that were within her price range and made a note of the numbers on her phone to call the following day. The freedom she would have once she had a car excited her, especially now she could afford something really nice that wasn't beige.

She switched everything off and as she climbed the stairs in the semi darkens she felt uneasy. She was halfway up the stairs but could still see all of her lounge and some of the kitchen.

'Please don't visit me tonight,' she called out to thin air, 'I have work tomorrow and could do with a decent night's sleep.' She waited for something; she wasn't sure what but something. But nothing happened. 'Well, I'm off to bed now.' She was still searching the room but it remained empty. 'Erm…good night.' Still nothing. She climbed the stairs where Flynn was waiting for her at the top. She looked at him and said, 'I'm a bloody lunatic, Flynn.' He wagged his tail and ran into the bedroom ready for her to join him. She followed him in and shut the door behind her into the quietness of the house.

Not a sound came from the cottage until the shrill beeping from her alarm clock that woke Grace at 6.30 am. Grace's body kicked in long before her brain did. She automatically went into her routine of letting Flynn out, putting the kettle on, letting Flynn in, showering, applying make-up, getting dressed, feeding Flynn and then hunting for her keys, phone, bus pass and handbag. The whole routine was done and dusted by 7.30am where she was found at the monument in the middle of the village.

Most of the village was still asleep or they were executing their own routines in the quietness of the morning. It was still dark and she stood under the dim light that was radiating from the bus stop sign. She looked around while waiting for the bus and noted that her morning scene was just as it always was. The Blacky was still in darkness, even from the flat upstairs. Big Mick and Patsy not rising for another half an hour yet. The tea room was illuminated at the back as Shelly would be baking her cakes and scones at this time of the morning ready for the day's trade ahead. Tom's van was still parked in front of the terrace of shops. His light was on in his flat above the takeaway and she made a mental note of seeing him later about her boiler. There were a few lights on here and there from various other villagers and Nell's shop could clearly be seen as her light was illuminating the street outside.

The Cumfee Bus came and the bus driver gave his usual nod of recognition as she climbed aboard and took her seat. She placed her handbag on the seat next to her with Mrs Mortimer's parcel to ensure a solo ride all the way to Lanson. Not that anyone would attempt to sit next to her anyway. The bus was only ever a third full by the time it reached its final destination.

By the time the bus reached Lanson, dawn had broken and Grace's brain finally kicked in with her body. The town was busy with people running to and fro to their various points of destination. Everyone looked lost in their own thoughts of the day or their own MP3 players. By the look of some of the faces she could only imagine that they were listening to sad ballads after another partner-free weekend.

As Grace walked into the office she was greeted immediately by Ellen who ran over in a fluster.

'Oh Grace, Mr Moore has been looking for you.' Ellen absentmindedly took Grace's parcel while Grace hung her coat up on the coat stand.

'Oh yeah,' Grace said calmly, 'wonder what he wants this time of the morning?' She took the parcel out of Ellen's hands and walked to her desk and popped the package in her in-tray.

'I'm not sure, but he didn't look happy. He said I was to tell you that you were to see him as soon as you came in.' Ellen was now breathless.

'Well, he can just wait until I've made myself a coffee,' Ellen was about to interrupt, 'then I'll go and see what he wants.' Ellen closed her mouth and returned to her desk but kept glancing at Grace to see if she was going to make a move.

Grace turned her computer on and checked her diary for reminders.

'Ellen, did you get hold of O'Keane's?'

'I was trying all Friday afternoon and this morning there's been no one answering the phone yet. I'll try again.' Ellen immediately picked up the phone and started punching at the buttons.

'If he gives you any flannel, tell him I'll be calling him later. He can't just turn up when he feels like it,' said Grace. After getting herself a coffee from the kitchen she returned to her desk and picked up her pen and notebook. She then gestured to Ellen that she was on her way to Moore's office.

His office was at the bottom end of the large open room. From where he sat, he could survey his whole workforce which made some of them nervous, especially Ellen. The office was tired and needed decorating badly. It hadn't been touched since the 70's and there had been a debate in the workforce as to what the original colour of the walls had been. The landlord of the building was frequently seen arguing with Bill Moore about having to do some work in the office. But Bill always managed to bark him back out the door with a 'this is a 24-hour business, sunshine, we can't stop so some painters can come in and disturb our finely-tuned process.' The fact of the matter was that Bill would have to stump up some of the costs as the landlord had pointed out that not all the repairs were due to 'wear and tear'. Some of the repairs had arisen from various office parties, Bill's temper and Bill was notoriously tight. Bill would only spend money on something that was originally double the price or if it was to invest then he expected double back. He didn't have a business by being lucky; it was all built on stinginess.

Grace walked into his office and found him on the telephone.

'I'll call you back,' he growled in his Cockney accent. He slammed the phone down to some poor listener and turned on Grace.

'What the fuck is happening with O'Keane's,' he

shouted.

'Morning, Bill. Yes, I had a lovely weekend, thank you for asking. How about you?' she smiled at him sarcastically.

'Grace, don't pull my chords this morning, I'm not in the mood. Well?'

Grace continued in her calm tone; she had learned not to rise to Bill's moods as it only made him worse which then sent shockwaves through to the rest of the office. Early on in her employment she had argued with Bill Moore over his decision of sending her to the Annual Hauliers' Ball. She didn't know anyone, let alone enough about the industry and felt it was a cop-out on Bill's behalf as he would have had to have bought a new suit. The argument dragged on and the atmosphere in the office became more and more tense. In the end, they both compromised that they would attend the ball together. This was the first and only time they had accompanied each other to an event. It wasn't as bad as Grace envisaged and she not only got drunk but managed to snog a very nice man from the North Region of KLF Hauliers. Bill had spent most of the night talking to tight-fisted business men in various suits from various decades. Two clearly had been wearing their wedding suits from thirty years before and one looked like he may have borrowed his son's as it was too modern and too small. All of them were terrified to finish the whisky in their glass as then it would be assumed that they would be the next to get the round in.

'I've told you about using O'Keane's. They clearly cannot manage the work that we give them and that isn't a lot these days. We had to give them this job as Denby's had no drivers to do the collection. What do you want me to do, Bill? Tell the client that there is no one to collect their shipment as we don't want to take a chance on O'Keane's?'

'What has Jim said about all this?' Bill enquired after the MD of O'Keane's.

'We can't get hold of him. Even the driver had his mobile turned off on Friday. Probably because Jim knew he was late and told him not to talk to us,' explained Grace. Bill shook his head. Taylors, the client, were not happy that their container had not been collected on time and therefore missed its slot for boarding the ship. The container was now at the dock and poor Bill was having to pay the quay costs until he could recoup the money from O'Keane's and God knows when that would be paid.

'I don't know, Grace. What am I supposed to do?' he said despairingly.

'I've told you Bill,' Grace leant forward in her chair over his desk, 'put his contract on notice. We can't look for another haulier until you're finished with O'Keane's. If you ask me, Denby's knew what they were doing when you signed that contract stating for no more than two hauliers on that patch. Our hands are tied Bill. Either get rid of O'Keane's or reduce your client base in the North East so we only have to go to Denby's.'

Grace had had this argument will Bill a number of times over the last few months. Bill had always been dismissive of the problems in the past but now he had to take notice. Craig Johnson, Head of Sales, Grace and Bill had worked hard to get Taylor's to use their haulage agency. They had not been in business with Moore Haulage that long and Bill was struggling for the client to stay with them as some of the service they had received had not been as promised. Grace had analysed some data and noted that any problems had only been with the O'Keane runs. So Ellen and Grace had tried to appoint Denby's on the account as much as they could.

'Keep trying O'Keane's. And I want you to take over trying to call. Take that bloody Mavis Riley off it. She'll swallow any flannel that they give her. They're not taking the piss out of me again. As soon as you get hold of them I wanna speak to them. And I don't wanna speak to no driver either I want the fucking organ grinder, you hear me?' he spat.

Grace stood up, gave him a nod and walked out of his office only to be interrupted by Sean as he sprang in front of her. Grace jumped in surprise. He was immaculately dressed, as always, and was one of the few in society who could carry off slim fit. His body was long and lean and covered in fake tan that had been expertly applied. His jet black quiffed hair only wobbled slightly with his energetic pounce.

'Grace, talk to me,' Grace continued to walk back to her desk. 'Is Bill being an arse?'

He didn't wait for her to answer; he bent his head towards Grace and talked out of the side of his mouth. Sean thought this was discreet but he still talked at the same volume akin to a Shakespearean actor.

'I saw him this morning. Oh my God,' Sean said camply. 'I was like, 'what's eating you, Bill'; clearly his wife has been out flexing his flexible friend, the tight bastard.'

They reached Grace's desk and Sean was still talking. 'You fancy lunch? My treat. I feel like I haven't spoken to you in an absolute age,' he drawled.

'I had lunch with you on Thursday,' Grace reminded him.

'Oh my, Gracey, so much has happened since then.' He was practically jumping up and down on the spot like a three-year-old that needed a wee.

'I can't today, Sean. I have to post a parcel for a friend of mine, go to the library and make some calls about a couple of cars,' she explained.

'I'll come with you and I can tell you my news while we are in the post office. The queue in there is always longer than Celine Dion's standing ovations anyway,' Grace smiled at his joke.

'Okay, but you have to let me make my calls as well,' she wagged a finger at him and he understood.

'See you at one,' and he pranced like a gazelle back to his own department. Grace turned to Ellen.

'Why does he have so much bloody energy at this time of the morning?' Ellen shrugged. 'Anyway, any luck with O'Keane's?'

'No, I've left a message with their receptionist,'

'Leave it with me Ellen, I'll keep chasing. You just crack on with all your other stuff.'

'Your delegation skills are very…general shall we say.' Perched at the end of her desk trying to look casual, was a very drunk Crowley.

CHAPTER 6

Grace looked around the rest of the office in a slight panic. Ellen was buried in her notebook and Kevin who normally sat behind her stood up and walked past Grace and Crowley to the printer.

'Morning, Grace,' said Kevin cheerfully.

'Morning,' she replied slowly still looking at Crowley. He looked back at her and then his leg slipped off the edge of the table causing him to fall on the floor in a heap. He quickly tried to compose himself and popped his head back up over the desk like Punch, complete with a grin. Again, Grace looked around and no one had flinched with the noise of his fall or even noticed. She looked back at Crowley who was struggling to get back onto his feet, which was amusing him no end.

'Are you pissed?' she said.

'Sorry Grace?' She heard someone answer but it wasn't Crowley. She turned and Ellen was looking at her expectantly. She looked back at Crowley who had now managed to find his feet and was standing bolt upright trying to hide his inebriation.

'Did you ask if I was pissed?' Ellen was confused.

'Eh? Erm…yeah…sorry. I mean...sorry...I wasn't talking to you.' Grace was starting to panic and opened her eyes wide to Crowley and nodded her head to a door behind him.

'I'll be back in a minute Ellen…erm…just going to the print room.' Grace walked towards the print room door and looked at Crowley for him to follow her. He saluted her and walked behind her as mutely instructed. Grace opened the door and in the room already was Crowley.

'Jesus!' she said aloud jumping back.

'You all right, Grace?' Ellen had heard her swear.

'Erm…yeah, I'm fine Ellen. Just the cold took me by surprise,' she called back. Grace walked into the empty print room, shut the door behind her and put her back against the door and looked at Crowley.

'What the bloody hell are you doing here? In my work for fuck's sake! I can't cope with you here. And you're pissed.'

'I'm not that pissed,' he protested.

'You can barely stand!' Grace was trying to shout at him and whisper at the same time.

'I'm fine,' he raised his arms in the style of Jesus on the cross.

'You're not,' she stepped closer to him, 'Why are you here? Why now? I can't talk to you here. It's totally inappropriate. You can't just come in here and expect me to drop everything and start talking to you.' Grace was aware her voice was starting to rise and tried to control her temper. 'I'm not some bloody Samaritan who's *always here*,' she said sarcastically. She kept looking over her shoulder at the door to make sure no one had come in. 'You'll have to come to the cottage later.' Crowley stooped over and tweaked her nose as he thought she looked cute when she was cross. It amused him no end.

'Sober!' she instructed.

'You're not much fun today. Oh well, later then,' he looked slightly peeved and then took a breath as if he was preparing to do something.

'Wait!' she shouted. 'How do I call you?' He held his breath and looked confused.

'I mean how do I...summon you?' she asked.

'Summon me?' He burst out laughing and Grace looked behind her at the door thinking someone would come in to investigate who was laughing. 'Would you like a little bell?' he mimed tinkling a bell in front of her face.

'Seriously Crowley, I need to know.' Grace wasn't sure if he could be serious at this moment. He straightened himself up to his full height which was quite imposing and pumped his chest out and gave the best Sir John Gielgud impression he could muster.

'You need to find a bowl and draw the blood of a gay, but still experimental, virgin. While stirring his blood you must sing Raspberry Beret by the artist formerly known as Prince.' His voice rising to a crescendo, 'Only then,' he peaked and pointed a finger to the sky, 'will I be able to appear in front of your very eyes.' He started to dance moving his fingers across his face like Lulu. Grace was not impressed and Crowley noticed that she was not enjoying his performance.

'Crowley will do,' he said exhaustedly.

'You ok, Grace?' The voice came from behind her and she turned to see Kevin poking his head around the door. She looked back in front of her but Crowley had gone. She felt the instant relief and told Kevin she was fine as she walked back out into the main office.

She sat back at her desk feeling out of sorts with Crowley's badly-timed appearance. Not only was it distressing enough that he turned up in her work but he was drunker than a New Year reveller. Grace found herself gazing at her screen and chastised herself for becoming distracted. Bill would maul her in front of the office if she didn't get her act together.

She called O'Keane's and was finally put through to Jim O'Keane, the head of the company. After listening to his pitiful excuses, Grace gave Jim cryptic clues as to what Bill was planning on saying to him. By the time Grace had finished, Jim was begging to be put through to Bill.

She trundled along with her morning, which went too slow, and watched the clock until lunch time. Sean came bounding over like an energetic puppy on the dot of one o'clock.

'Ready?' Grace looked up and he already had her coat over his arm. She clicked her computer off and grabbed the coat and her bag and they both made their way out of the building.

As soon as they were outside, Sean pulled a cigarette out of his pocket and lit it. He took a deep hard drag and then announced, 'I'm in love, Grace.' He delivered the message with a Tommy Steel sugariness. Grace rolled her eyes.

'What? Again?' Sean tried to look shocked and then gave her a friendly dig in the ribs.

'No, seriously, Grace. I think this is the one,' he looked to the sky.

'You said that last time when you met Paul and when you met John as well. Which one's this Ringo or George?' Sean was determined to make sure that Grace knew he was serious this time.

'His name is François,' said Sean dreamily. Grace burst

out laughing. It was not what she expected at all.

'You mean Frank!' Grace continued to laugh.

'No, not Frank, François,' he tried emphasising his name with a French accent.

'So, he's French then?' Grace enquired.

'His mother is French,' he bragged.

'Was he born in France? Does he talk French-like?' Grace probed further.

'I'm sure he does. I've not asked him to talk French. And even if he did I wouldn't know what he was saying would I?' Sean said.

'Yes, but you would know if he was talking proper French and not just some 'Allo 'Allo type French wouldn't you?'

Sean took another drag on his cigarette aware that they were getting closer to the post office. 'Of course I would. I just haven't asked him to talk French that's all.' He was starting to become disappointed in Grace's reaction to finding the love of his life.

'So how did you meet him then?' Grace asked reluctantly. She realised that Sean was deflating faster than a pricked balloon before her eyes and it was her fault.

'I met him at The Kasbah on Friday and we've been inseparable ever since,' Sean's enthusiasm had returned. 'He's still in the flat now. He's been texting me all morning saying how much he has missed me.' He turned and looked at Grace like an excited child. 'This is it Grace, I've finally met my Liberace.' Grace wanted to laugh again but managed to supress it.

'Is he not missing his job this morning or doesn't he have one of them?'

'He does, Miss Cynical. He works in logistical services.' Sean was clearly proud of his new beau of two days. Grace nodded with unimpressed approval to pacify Sean while she walked into the post office to mail Mrs Mortimer's parcel and he stayed outside finishing his cigarette.

When she returned, she informed Sean that she didn't need the library anymore but they needed to find a quiet spot to make the calls about the cars. They decided to go to the park and while they walked Sean continued to witter on about how attentive French men were and how he would never entertain another Englishman as long as he lived.

'I hope you're not turning into a racist. Having a Welsh mate and all,' Grace joked.

'Darling, if I wasn't as bent as an allen key I'm sure we would have made lots of babies by now.' Grace curled her lip at the thought. 'I hope that look is directed at motherhood and not at me!' he retorted. She didn't answer. Some things were best left unsaid for the sake of their friendship, she thought in amusement. 'Anyway, what sheds are we planning on looking at then?' Sean asked.

'My dad gave me ten grand towards a car,' Grace announced smugly. Sean clapped his hands on each cheek.

'Shut the actual front door! Honestly? Grace nodded in silence, savouring his reaction. 'You lucky bitch! My dad wouldn't give me his bloody name in case my mum ever went after him for maintenance. Can you believe that? Fucking scumbag. My mum didn't need his money. I used to wear all her 'hand-me-downs' anyway,' he started to laugh at his own joke and Grace joined in. That's what she loved about Sean. He was the eternal seeker of the bright side and he had never failed to find it yet. If you told him that your house had been robbed of all its furniture and you had no insurance, he was the type to turn up with a crate and a cushion and make you feel like it was a throne.

It was just the way he was. Plus, he was the biggest bitch in Lanson so to Grace he was a perfect friend.

Grace told him the details of the cars and she called them both up. One of them had sold but the other one was still available. After asking all the questions that every man in The Blacky had told her to ask, she was satisfied enough to tell the man at the garage that she would be there tomorrow night to give it a test drive.

'Why can't you go tonight?' asked Sean.

'I've got a visitor coming later.' Grace was aware she had been too vague and Sean's interest was now piqued.

'Oh yeah. A visitor. Who is the visitor then? Male or female?'

'Male…'

'Fit or fugly?'

'Neither. He's old,'

'Ew Grace. How old is he?' Sean said, slightly disgusted but still interested at the same time.

'It's not like that.' Grace was desperately trying to think of a back story. She didn't want to tell Sean, not yet anyway. 'Mrs Mortimer met him and then I managed to speak to him later on. He just wants to pop round to sort some things out and I said I would help.'

'What things?' he probed.

'Erm…communication things. You know how it is with that generation,' she said vaguely.

'How boring. I know what you mean though. My nan still looks at my mobile and thinks it's powered by witchcraft or something. I wind her up and put it on the table in front of her; you can see her recoiling from it waiting for it to pounce. It's hilarious.' Grace was relieved that he didn't see that her story had been edited heavily.

Sean looked at his watch and they both rose to their feet

and started to make their way back to the office.

'So, when am I going to meet Frank then?' Grace asked and Sean became excited again.

'I'll speak to him later and get him to check his diary. Apparently, the demands of his job mean that he has to work unsociable hours.'

'Well, while I'm not holding my breath, you just let me know when you are coming and I'll get Flynn to dig up a few snails in the backyard. Make Frank feel right at home, that will.'

They were still laughing when they walked into the office and then their mood became glum again. The rest of Grace's afternoon was spent talking to Mrs Patterson, their solicitor on how to end their contract with O'Keane's and what she was going to say to Crowley. She wondered if he had any more details on this task of his. How he was supposed to have a positive effect on anything was going to be a hard slog if his last two visits were anything to go by.

Later that evening, Grace jumped off the bus in the village instead of the bridge as she wanted to see if Tom was home. His van was parked in its usual place so she walked over to the small door next to the takeaway and rang the bell. His slightly thunderous steps could be heard running down the stairwell upon which he opened the door.

'Hi Grace,' he beamed. He was genuinely surprised and pleased to see her.

'Hey, Tom, I'm not disturbing you am I?'

'No, not at all, come in through. My mum's hanging on the phone. Come on up.' The space was small so he ventured up the stairs first while Grace shut the door and followed him.

She realised she had never been in Tom's flat before but then there never had been a need to until now. She walked into the lounge where his voice was coming from and waited at the room entrance for him to finish his call. He was clearly trying to get his mum off the phone but his mum obviously still had things to say before she hung up.

Tom was tall, dark and slender and was the same age as Grace. She knew very little about Tom even though he had been living in the village for over a year now. It was not long after he had moved in that he had been having a drink in The Blacky with some of the locals that Grace had been asked to join the table and was quite taken by Tom. He was the eye candy of the village and she remembered initially sitting by him and feeling really nervous. So she did what any girl would do in that situation and got drunk. Horribly drunk.

Over the next few days she was fed titbits of her behaviour that night. Highlights of the lost night had been repeated back to her where the questions she had interrogated poor Tom with were, why he was single, did he sleep in the nude and the best was revealing he was the man of her dreams simply because he had a pulse and lived above a chippy.

Since then she had kept any chat with him to the minimum as she knew when she was nervous her mouth was liable to run away with itself, again. However, standing in his lounge doorway did make her wonder again about his bed attire. He clearly had a manual job judging by his clingy t-shirt which she found very pleasant to look at and as he turned his back to her she found his backside just as pleasant also.

He put the phone down and spun around quicker than she felt she could raise her eyes to his and she could feel herself blush. He beamed at her with an incredible smile and clapped his hands together. 'I don't often see you in these parts,' he said. She could feel herself wanting to fidget.

'No, I s'pose not,' she smiled nervously, 'why would I ever need to be in your flat.' She looked around the small but cosy room and he became embarrassed by its state. He rushed to the sofa and started to tidy the magazines and newspapers that had been discarded there over the last few days and put them on the floor to the side of the same sofa out of view. He scratched the back of his neck trying to gauge her.

'Wasn't expecting visitors today,' he muttered shyly.

'Oh, I'm not stopping. Don't worry about the mess…I mean not that it's messy…just that I'm not here to look at your mess….I'm here to look at you…SEE YOU!' she was babbling. 'Sorry. Let me start again, eh? I'm here as I wondered if you knew anything about boilers.' *Please say no, please say no. I don't want to do this again*, she thought.

'Er, yeah.' He looked a bit taken aback. 'It's my job, I thought you knew.'

'I wasn't sure to be honest. Just knew you drove a van.' She was embarrassed by her lack of knowledge about her neighbour. She had often fantasised about Tom but in her fantasies he was usually a fireman. She never felt the need to shatter that illusion. He laughed slightly at her summarisation of him.

'I did tell you. When I first moved here. We were in The Blacky. Remember?' He waited for her to recollect the night. Grace began to fidget more as he was clearly waiting for her to say she could recall this basic piece of information about him.

'I was a bit drunk that night,' she tried to brush it off.

'It was ages ago,' she shrugged her shoulders. 'You probably did say but I'm a bit of Dory, see.' She felt that was the best case she could present in her defence.

'Dory?' he looked confused.

'Yeah, Dory, from Finding Nemo?' Her voice faltered at the end. She wanted to run. 'Well, I don't s'pose you're into kids films eh?' She was desperately trying to wrap this up.

There was an uneasy pause then Grace said, 'So, the boiler.' He was relieved she started to talk. 'There's nothing wrong with it. I just want it servicing that's all. My dad said he would pay if that's okay? I should have done it when the winter started but I just forgot, sorry,' she confessed.

'The really bad weather hasn't set in yet, so you're okay.' She was relieved. Why she felt she needed Tom's forgiveness for not getting him to look at the boiler sooner was absurd but yet she felt a compulsion to explain.

'I'm finishing my last job early tomorrow, so I could do it then if you like?' he asked.

'I'm not home until around this time,' she paused for thought. 'Tell you what, I'll give you my spare key and you can just let yourself in, if you like? Flynn will be in the kitchen so don't mind him. The boiler is in the cupboard under the stairs.' She looked at him expectantly.

'Well, if you don't mind me letting myself in to your house, then yes.' His tone was bright.

'Mind, the space under there is tiny and you're so big,' she stopped suddenly. She knew that her mouth was about to take her somewhere where her brain couldn't keep up. She took a breath, 'I just mean it's small, that's all.' Grace exhaled slowly.

'Don't worry, I'll be fine,' his voice was reassuring and

Estelle Maher

Grace found herself staring for a moment. She realised that she was gawping so snapped herself out of it by rummaging in her bag for her spare keys. She found them and passed them over to him, mumbled a quick thanks and walked out of the room. He jolted after her and walked behind down the dimly lit stair well. Once she stepped outside she turned to look at him.

'Thanks, Tom. And I'll see you tomorrow,' Grace smiled.

'I like Jungle Book,' he said. Her face was blank. 'Kids films?' he reminded.

'Oh, yes, yes.' Grace nodded and slowly turned on her heel toward home. She heard the door shut behind her. 'Why didn't I just look in the bloody Yellow Pages?' she thought. 'You're such an idiot, Grace Hammond! You talk like you're an imbecile.'

Tom had his back against the front door. 'Jungle Book! Why did I say that? She must think you're a right nerd.' He closed his eyes and wished that he could go over the last ten minutes of his life again. He liked Grace. She was very beautiful but didn't realise it and that made her more attractive. He liked her vulnerability but also he liked how independent she was. He had hoped that Grace would end up being a good friend of his as they were the same age but it wasn't meant to be. She clearly had her own life and own friends. He was strangely looking forward to the job in her cottage tomorrow. He wondered what her home looked like and would her decorating taste be as strange as her taste in dogs. He threw the keys up and immediately caught them, then ran up the stairs to head back to his usual routine.

Grace came home and kicked off her shoes as soon as she walked into the lounge. Flynn was pleased to see her and danced around her feet for a moment and then ran to the back door expectantly. Grace promptly let him out and then put the kettle on. She walked upstairs and changed out of her work clothes and came downstairs to cook her tea. Her tea comprised of two chicken legs and a boiled egg. She was hoping she may be able to stretch the meagre contents of her fridge and cupboard until she bought a car. Then she would be able to drive to Lanson and do a 'big shop'. The thought excited her.

Flynn sat and watched her the whole time as she was preparing her meal. She looked at him, 'Look mate, there's barely enough for me to eat never mind you. Anyway, you have a full bowl over there, you big scav!' Flynn glanced at his bowl with a look of disdain. He didn't know what was in the bowl but he knew it wasn't chicken. When he looked back she was already in the living room. If he was going to be sharing any of her chicken she would have thrown something by now. He reluctantly trotted over to his bowl.

Grace sat on the couch and she was immediately sat next to Crowley. She jumped back up again.

'DO YOU HAVE TO DO THAT?!' she bellowed.

'What?' he was clearly puzzled.

'That!' she pointed to him.

'Do you mean appear?' he asked.

'Yes!' she replied like he had asked a stupid question. She was still holding the plate of chicken.

'What the hell do you want me to do, Daff?'

'I don't know. It's just when you do...that...,' she pointed again, 'you scare me half to death.' She was rocking slightly from one foot to the other making her boiled egg roll around the plate. Flynn was now underneath the plate waiting for it to fall straight into his mouth. Crowley noticed the dog and then looked at his feet.

'When that dog dies they could use his paws to size skis,' he cocked his head to one side to look at him from another angle, 'he has feet like a shire horse.'

Grace looked at Flynn and realised her egg was tempting him. She sat back down next to Crowley in a huff. They both sat in silence for a moment. Crowley was clearly waiting for her to speak first and Grace didn't know how to start.

'Look,' she said, 'we need to make some ground rules.' She put the plate on the coffee table in front of them both. 'Is there another way that you could come in?' she asked. She placed a hand on each knee and turned to him. He didn't move to look at her but just continued to look straight ahead. She wasn't sure if he was thinking or if he was asleep with his eyes open. Either way he looked catatonic.

'Do you want me to knock on the door?' he asked looking at her. It was his only shot. If she said no, he would have to admit that he had nothing else to suggest.

'Back door?' she asked.

'Whatever door you want my dear. I just can't cope with the analysis and critique each and every time I visit,' he said despondingly.

Grace immediately felt guilty. It was true. Each time he arrived she had scolded him like she was his mum. 'I'm sorry,' she said, 'it's a bit strange for both of us I s'pose.' Crowley turned and smiled at her.

'Let's start again then, shall we,' he said with relief. 'How was your day?' She half smiled at the bizarreness of it all, but thought it only polite to play along.

'Very well, thank you. And you?' she replied.

'Oh, I've had a marvellous day. Noel had a grand dinner party and I've spent most of it next to the lovely Norma Jean,' he started to daydream.

'Baker?' Grace asked and he nodded at her question. 'Marilyn Monroe? Are you kidding me?' she said flatly.

'The one and only,' he said with an air of satisfaction, 'but she likes to be called Norma, where we are,' he raised a knowing eyebrow.

'Is that why you were drunk this morning, because you were at a party?' she asked.

'Daff, I'll be merry most of the time, so you had better get used to it. I'm in heaven for God's sake. Well, not quite heaven. But where I am has most of the perks shall we say,' said Crowley with a grin.

'So, where are you then? Like a half-way house or something?' He wondered how best to explain to her where he was on the astral plain. Then he had an idea.

'If you imagine that you visit your local supermarket and you go to the lovely meat counter,' he paused and looked at her.

'Yes,' she said slowly. She had no idea where he was going with this.

'And it's the kind of meat counter where you pull one of those little tickets out of the machines to wait your turn, the red ones that look like they're pulling tongues.'

'Yes,' she was still confused.

'Well, the supermarket is where I am, but once you have pulled the ticket you know that there is no going back. You need to stay and do what you need to do and only until you have fulfilled that, then you know you can go.'

'But where do you go?'

'Well, you would go outside with your two chicken legs,' he pointed to her plate, 'and make your way home. But for me I'll go to heaven with my chicken legs.'

'That must be some bloody chicken,' and they both roared laughing imagining the scene. They continued to fuel their laughter describing Crowley on a cloud with wings and a Bargain Bucket.

'So you all know you are supposed to be somewhere else, because of this pull thing?' She was trying to make sense of it all. 'But your number won't be called until you do whatever it is you're supposed to do that involves me.' She looked at him.

'That's about this gist of it, yes,' he confirmed.

'But you don't know what it is that you need to do,' she reiterated.

'Not yet. But that may change,' Crowley revealed.

'How?' she asked.

'Well, there are some people, 'up there',' again he pointed to the ceiling, 'that know what their task is and for various reasons haven't completed it yet. There are some who simply are too afraid to move on and want to stay on the plain that we are on at the moment.'

'So do you spend all your time at parties?' She was trying to conjure images up in her mind.

'Yes I do Daff, because that's my heaven. I spent a lot of time on Earth on my own with no one to talk to and no one noticing me shall we say.' He stood up and walked to the window and looked in the direction of the bridge.

'You know when I spoke to you, last week at the bridge?' He didn't wait for her to answer. 'You were the first person to converse with me in over six months, that's why I picked you.'

'Really? But I hardly said anything to you. In fact, I think I just shouted at you the whole time.' She felt sorry for him at the thought of no one ever speaking to him.

'But you spoke to me, Daff. You noticed me. People try their best not to see the homeless guy and those that do, don't want to talk to you. They throw you some money and they feel good for doing that. But that good feeling is often a self-congratulatory emotion as opposed to embracing the person they are helping. Even the individual who throws a pound doesn't notice the person beneath the rags and dirt.' He turned back and looked at Grace who was watching and listening intently.

'I'm guilty of all of that,' whispered Grace. She felt ashamed.

'Daff, we all have. I wasn't born homeless you know,' he sat back down next to her.

'Where are your family, Crowley? Surely, they should know that you are gone. Would you like me to visit….'

'No!' he interrupted. 'Daff, this is the one thing I must insist that you do not interfere with. Please!' Not only did he become cross, he seemed to have sobered up a little.

'But you are lying in a morgue somewhere with a bloody address label hanging off your toe probably with John Doe written on it,' she said.

'I do hope not. John Doe. Do I look like a John Doe?' he stood and walked over to a mirror that hung over Grace's fire and admired himself from various angles. He then tried an impression, 'I always thought of myself as a bit of a Jimmy Stewart ma'am.' Grace looked up at him.

'Is that supposed to be James Stewart?'

He adopted the voice again, 'Why, yes ma'am.'

'You sound more like Kenneth Williams.' Crowley pretended to look hurt.

'John Doe it is then,' he said in his normal voice. They sat in silence for a while. They were both thinking of Crowley and his big toe peeking from a crisp white sheet with the incorrectly named label swinging. Grace didn't feel right leaving it there and decided to risk another telling off.

'Look, is it okay then if I send a letter or made a call to the police station and just gave them your name?' He went to protest but she raised her hand to show him she hadn't finished yet. 'I'll do it anonymously so no one can trace anything. That way the police can at least find some record on you and if they trace any family then it's up to them whether they want you or not.'

Crowley sat for a moment clearly mulling over her suggestion. He wasn't sure what his sister would do if she ever found out he was dead. She may just leave him and say it wasn't him and continue with her life. But he did wonder if she did take the body would she be glad to say goodbye. Would she be glad he was dead? All he knew was that there was a time when they did get on and if she thought of those moments then surely she would want to collect his body and give him a decent burial. If the tables were turned he knew he would have her back in a heartbeat.

'Okay,' he said blankly. 'But don't give them any of your details. You're already tied to the case and you don't want them raising questions as to how all of a sudden you know who I am,' he instructed.

'I won't. I promise,' she paused thinking how best to do it. 'So your first name is?'

'My full name is Hugh Phillip George Crowley and up until nine years ago De Mondford Hall was my home.' Crowley felt as if he had confessed.

'De Mondford Hall? The De Mondford Hall?' Grace was surprised.

'Unless there are two then I suppose it must be 'the'

one,' he said.

'I knew you were posh but De Mondford Hall, bloody hell.' Grace noticed that Crowley's mood had become sombre. She wanted to ask more but decided not to push it as it clearly was a sensitive subject with him.

'I'll pop a letter in the post to the police then, an anonymous letter, mind. Hopefully, they'll be able to change that tag on your foot, eh?' She looked at him but he was still clearly lost in his own thoughts. 'You don't look much like a John anyway.' Grace was trying to lighten the mood and Crowley noticed she was trying to make an effort.

'Yes, well, we'll see,' he paused for a moment then decided it was best to be off. 'I'll make a move now. Leave you to your supper.' He cast the chicken a look of contempt. Grace noticed the look.

'We can't all be at parties drinking champagne with Marilyn Monroe can we? Some of us have a bit of living to do,' and she playfully poked him on the arm.

'I have a game of poker planned for this evening with some of the boys and a lovely bottle of Macallan Lalique single malt to accompany us,' he said.

'Can I just ask before you go?' she said. He waited for her. 'Can no one else see you?' she asked.

'That seems to be the way. I thought I might be able to have fun with this. Especially in lingerie departments,' he sniggered to himself, 'but it seems that the only way I shall see any lovely ladies in their frillies is if you go in there. I'm attached to you and you only.'

'So you can only appear to me, then? I thought you would be able to rattle your chains anywhere you liked. Are you sure you're in heaven?' And they both started to laugh.

'Daff, I'm sure we are going to have some fun as we

ride along on this rollercoaster of ambiguity. But my dear, we would have so much more fun if you had a little refreshment in the house. A nice red wine would be such a treat,' he beamed at her.

'I'm sure it would but I think you get saturated enough before you come here,' she scolded.

'Well, on that note, I'm definitely off. I'll come and see you tomorrow at some point.' Grace went to interrupt but he predicted what she was about to say. 'I know, not in your work. I have to say Daff, your job looks extremely dull. Why don't you do something else? A vet maybe, so you could sort out your horse-dog's feet. Or a lasso trainer, so we could see if you could actually swing a cat in this tiny lounge of yours.' He stood and looked around the room. It was indeed tiny. It could only house one couch, an armchair, a small table and the TV and if you could swing a cat in there it would have to be a kitten, being swung by a child.

'Hey, it might not be De Mondford Hall but it's a palace to me,' she protested.

'I'm sorry Daff, I didn't mean to be a snob,' he said apologetically.

'Oh, don't worry about it. I'm used to it with my mother. She'd make you look like Fagin,' she exclaimed.

'Well, I really must go before my 62-year-old malt becomes 63.'

He stood up, saluted her and walked to the kitchen. Her eyes followed him to the kitchen and then she stood to watch him go but she was too late; he had gone.

CHAPTER 7

The following day Grace compiled the letter in her lunch hour. She had decided to print it and pop it into the post. That way the police wouldn't be able to tell it was her who had sent it. She drew some puzzled glances when she put her gloves on to put the paper in the printer and retrieve the document. She'd recently seen a programme that said they could lift fingerprints from anything so she wasn't taking any chances. She told people she was currently suffering from bad circulation and her hands were cold which was easy to get away with as Bob would only put the heating up when he was cold. Seeing as he wasn't in the office today and sat in his own mansion with his underfloor heating the workforce was notably layered up.

The whole letter writing exercise made her feel slightly uneasy and only for the SpongeBob SquarePants motif on the back of her knitted gloves she felt less like a criminal. She re-read the letter again.

Dear DC Kelly:

The body recently found in Pelsby is that of Hugh
Philip George Crowley of De Mondford Hall,
Somerset.

Yours truly.

Grace was satisfied that there was nothing in the letter
to expose her. The letter barely said anything anyway but
the police would at least be able to get things moving in
the right direction. She supposed that the police probably
wouldn't be bothered who told them if they could trace a
family member. It wasn't as if it was a murder case.

Still with her gloves on she sealed it in an envelope and
told Ellen she was popping out for five minutes. Even
though the police station was a five minute walk from her
office, Grace decided to still post it via Royal Mail. Satisfied
there wasn't any DNA or fingerprints on the letter or that
she had been followed from the office she dropped it in
the mailbox on the high street and returned to work. As
she got in the lift she realised how ridiculous she must have
looked in her red woollen gloves and how she had over
dramatized the whole exercise. She also decided that she
really needed more in her life if this was exciting to her.
With or without the added unnecessary drama she hoped
they would be able to give Crowley to a family member.

At the end of the day, Grace left the office with Sean as
he had offered to give her a lift and an opinion on the car
she was looking at. The garage was only ten minutes away
in Sean's car and on the way they discussed François.

'So Sean, is Frank still in your flat then?' she enquired.

'He's at work tonight and for the next three nights so I

won't see him until the weekend.' Sean sounded very disappointed.

'What's he do again?' asked Grace.

'Something to do with human logistics. He's quite vague about it all. I reckon he could work for the government in like a top secret department or something. What ya reckon?' He looked at Grace.

Grace thought he was joking at first but then looking at Sean's face she could see that he was deadly serious. This was typical Sean. He could not believe that anyone's existence was as dull as his so imagined that everyone had an exhilarating life. He once went on a blind date with someone who described themselves as a Ringer. Sean admitted that while he was in the taxi going back to his date's apartment for a cup of coffee he thought that his date had a look of Noel Edmonds and was probably working as a lookalike. He clearly thought that in the business they described themselves as Ringers. Sean was quite mortified to reveal to Grace the next day, that his date's apartment was a shrine to Tolkien's Lord of the Rings. The flat was covered in LOTR memorabilia. Every surface was covered in knickknacks, pictures, ornaments and some serious fan pieces including a Gauntlet of Sauron which housed his date's signet rings, a full sized Sméagol that sat crossed legged on top of the guy's washing machine and a cat called Arwen. After drinking his coffee from a glass goblet and reassessing that his date looked more like Chewbacca from Star Wars than Noel, he made a hasty exit with an 'it's not going to work' and 'it's most definitely you not me'. And Sean's silver lining? He watched the films and discovered Viggo Mortensen.

'Well, I am sure as he gets to know you more Frank will tell you what his top secret job is,' Grace rolled her eyes but Sean did not notice.

'Sean?' asked Grace, 'what do you know about De Mondford Hall?'

'That big posh pile out in the sticks?' he asked.

'Yeah,' she replied.

'Our Julie had her wedding there. Well flash it was.'

'Your cousin?' asked Grace.

'Yeah, remember I asked you to be my plus one but it was that time you had glandular fever?' Grace quickly recalled when she had stayed in bed for six days straight and had the voice of a hissing snake.

'I remember now. I forgot they do weddings there.'

'Why?' asked Sean.

'Oh, I erm… my dad is thinking of going there for some do. I was just wondering about the history of the place that's all,' she lied.

'God knows Grace, I've no idea. It probably belongs to the National Trust or someone like that. They're the only ones that have enough money to keep those places going. Mind you, our Julie's wedding cost a pretty packet so anyone could be making money from it,' he assumed. Grace decided to do a bit of homework on the internet later. Maybe, she could get some back story to Crowley without having to ask him.

'Here we go.' Sean spotted the garage and pulled in to the forecourt. Even though it was dark the floodlights made it easy for her to spot the car she was interested in.

'Here it is.' Grace pointed to the red Vauxhall Astra and waited for Sean to follow.

'She's tidy,' said Sean, opening the car door. He immediately jumped in the front seat and started to pretend he was driving somewhere.

'Oi, shift you! It's me that's buying it.' As Sean got out

of the car, the showroom manager was making his way over. He was about sixty, fairly tubby and wore a full length wool coat that reminded Grace of a football manager.

'Hello, my dear,' he said in a friendly tone. 'Miss Hammond?'

'Yes, I take it you are the gentleman I spoke to about the Astra,' she couldn't recall his name and felt slightly embarrassed.

'Barry Nuttall, at your service.' He extended his hand and as Grace took his he raised hers to his mouth and kissed it. Sean quickly turned his back on the scene and judging by his bobbing shoulders was enjoying the scene immensely.

Grace quickly released her hand, 'the car then?' She wanted to move with this quickly, maybe even leave.

'She's a little beauty this one.' Barry caressed the roof of the car like it was a cat.

'She's got air con, alloy wheels – very much in demand these days,' Barry clearly thought the benefit of an alloy wheel needed emphasising. 'Central locking, parking sensors, cruise control, seats, Bluetooth – whatever that is, somewhere to plug your phone in, the lot,' bragged Barry.

'She's very nice. Can I take her for a spin?' Grace asked.

'Of course, let me just get a plate and the keys.' Barry scooted off a lot more enthusiastically than when he walked over. Sean turned to Grace,

'Did he say 'seats'?' and they both tried unsuccessfully to supress their laughter.

'Fucking hell Gracey, you gotta buy this. Forget the fact it's got electric everything and cruise control and alloys, it's got seats man. It's the epitome of luxury. I'm sick of squatting in mine like I'm taking a shit. I need to upgrade to these beauties called chairs.' He poked his hand through the open door and stroked the head rest of the passenger seat. Grace was openly laughing now at Sean's campness.

Barry, swaddled in his coat, quickly ran over and Grace noticed that he would have been quicker if he had simply undone the last button or lost a stone.

'Okay then, let me pop these on.' Barry attached the trade plates and then passed the keys to Grace.

'You can drive to the end of this road and then you'll reach a roundabout. You can swing her back here from there,' he instructed.

Grace and Sean piled into the car and marvelled at the dashboard when she started the engine.

'Oh it's all twinkly like a Christmas tree,' said Grace excited. She drove off the forecourt under the beady eye of Barry and once she was out of his sight she started to relax a bit.

'She drives nice,' said Grace.

'You going to buy it then?' asked Sean.

'What ya reckon?'

'If it was me I'd buy it,' said Sean as he stroked the dashboard in front of him.

They reached the roundabout as Barry said and as she drove back to the garage she decided she would indeed buy the car. She thought about her dad and would he be pleased with her choice. She decided that not only would her dad be pleased but her mum would probably approve as well. All she needed was a nice deep dog bed on the back seat for Flynn and it would be perfect.

They pulled into the forecourt where Barry was locking up some of his cars and he waved her to a spot where she could leave the car. He eagerly approached Grace to ask her opinion.

'Well, what do you think my dear?' he asked.

'She's lovely, so let's talk price? Ten thousand is it?' Grace asked as she shut the door on the car.

'It is indeed.' Barry was simply waiting for her to commit.

'Tell him nine,' said Crowley. Grace looked and Crowley was stood next to Sean. Crowley crooked his finger and signalled for her to come over. Grace raised her eyebrows and then casually walked over to Crowley who was now squatting by the back wheel.

'Down here,' he gestured. Grace silently bent down and Crowley pointed to the tyres.

'These tyres are as baldy as Harry Hill. Look!' Grace looked at all the tyres and noticed that Barry was becoming fidgety.

'They're not cheap either Grace. If you are running to Cornwall and back you need decent tyres,' said Crowley.

'You all right, Grace?' asked Sean. Grace turned to Barry who seemed less confident now.

'Right Barry, here's the thing. The tyres are barely legal from what I can see. So I'll give you a choice. Either you take nine grand and I'll sort the tyres myself or I'll give you nine seven when you replace all the tyres with a brand new set of Pirellis.' Grace stared at him.

'Pirellis! On this! That will cost me about six hundred quid!' Barry was clearly stunned but Grace simply shrugged her shoulders.

'I don't think I could do that my dear.' Barry clearly had been surprised by her offer but Sean was more surprised by her tyre knowledge.

'Tell him you are overlooking the fact that the seal is going on the back window,' said Crowley.

'Is it?' shouted Grace and Crowley glared at her.

'Is it what, my dear?' asked Barry. Grace realised she had answered Crowley who only she could see.

'Is it both deals you are rejecting?' Grace tried to recover herself.

'It's not that bad. Probably won't go for years. But judging how well he has sealed his body into that coat I doubt he has a clue,' Crowley exclaimed.

'I don't see how I can shake on either of them,' said Barry.

'Even though I am overlooking the fact the seal is going on the back window.' Sean, now more confused, went to the back window and started to scrutinise the seal. He hadn't even seen Grace give it a glance. Barry walked over and joined Sean in the Seal Investigation Programme and Grace joined them. She pointed to the area that Crowley nodded to and confidently told Barry that the seal was on its last legs but she would go to the expense of getting it replaced. Sean joined in with the banter and gave a worrying look to the seal and made an audible sharp intake of breath. Sean knew more about mascara than he did about cars but Grace was appreciative of the added drama. Barry was clearly mulling over the offers and Grace stayed silent. She felt a bit nervous now and wasn't sure if she had pushed Barry a little too far.

'Okay, nine seven and I'll replace the tyres,' agreed Barry, clearly defeated and slightly confused by the whole negotiation process. 'Come with me and we can sort out the paperwork and arrange when you want to collect her.'

He trundled off to his office and Sean and Grace gave a silent victorious look to one another. As Sean walked into the office, Grace turned and gave Crowley a wink and mouthed a thank you to him. Crowley seemed very pleased with himself as he disappeared.

'I was going to keep that car and give it to my good lady wife,' said Barry.

'Fucking hell, Arfur Daley ain't dead is he?' whispered Sean to Grace. Barry had clearly heard the comment and gave Sean a dirty look while he sat down at his desk.

Grace gave Barry all her particulars and settled on the weekend for her to collect the car. She finally had a car, she thought and thanks to her dad she had a car that was really nice and thanks to Crowley she had settled on a great deal.

On the way home with Sean, Grace enthused about all the things she could do now she had her own motor. No more taxis or cadging lifts or smelly trains to Cornwall.

'Don't think Arfur was too pleased you noticing the tyres. And what was all that about the seal? All I could see was a bit coming away. Is that what you meant?' Sean was clearly impressed with Grace's eye.

'Staying in and watching Top Gear teaches you a thing or two,' said Grace. Sean laughed and agreed with her that it was a good programme and confessed that even he himself found it strange that he fancied the faceless Stig.

Sean drove Grace all the way back to Pelsby and she promised him a treat of pizza and wine the coming Friday as a thank you. She also knew that she could get a lift off him on the Saturday back to the garage to collect her car.

When she walked in to the cottage she was initially surprised to see the lights on but then remembered that Tom was servicing her boiler and had let himself in.

'Hello,' Grace called out as she slipped out of her shoes at the foot of the stairs.

'Just in here,' Tom's voice called from under the stairs. Grace found him squatting and squirting something into the skeleton of her boiler.

'So that's what's under the shiny cover eh?' she said.

'Good day in work?' he asked.

'Oh, it was all right. Hey, I bought a car you know,' she said excitedly. He stopped what he was doing and gave her his attention. 'Vauxhall Astra. Shiny red. Loads of gizmos on it. Probably won't use half of them.' Tom was smiling at Grace, clearly happy for her. 'You fancy a brew?' she offered.

'Okay, yeah. I should only be another five minutes,' said Tom.

Grace walked into the kitchen to put the kettle on and found Crowley sat on her worktop, smiling like a Cheshire Cat.

'What're you doing here?' she mouthed.

'I'm just looking out for you Daff, that's all.' Crowley nodded his head towards Tom. 'Anyway, it looks like he's using lots of tools and spraying various aerosols and turning the taps on and then turning them off. He's very professional,' Crowley started to laugh. Grace put her finger to her lips to indicate to Crowley to be quiet.

'He can't bloody hear me!' shouted Crowley at the top of his voice. Grace scowled at him.

'Tea or coffee?'

'Coffee please, Grace,' replied Tom. He shuffled his way out from under the stairs and started to pack his gear away in his tool box. Grace occasionally glanced at him in his t-shirt and tried to act casual but all the while she tried to imagine him without his top. Crowley spotted her and looked back at Tom who clearly had no idea he was being lusted over.

'Watch you don't burn your hands on that kettle, Daff. You can't look at two things at the same time,' said Crowley. Grace stared at him, looked at Tom and when she was confident that Tom wasn't looking she mouthed an obscenity to Crowley.

'Charming,' whispered Crowley.

Grace walked back into the tiny lounge and set Tom's coffee on the table next to her tea with the presumption he would join her on the sofa. Once he was all packed up and replaced the cover on the boiler he sat down and started to sip his drink.

'So, what time did you get here then?' asked Grace.

'About an hour ago, everything looked okay by the way,' he assured Grace.

'Great. Well, I can give you my dad's details or I can tell him to phone you if you like and he can sort the bill with you,' reminded Grace.

'Oh it's fine Grace, don't worry.' Tom was slightly embarrassed at telling her there was no charge.

'Oh no, Tom. You can't do that. My dad's expecting a bill anyway. Oh please, you must let him pay something,' insisted Grace.

'It's mates' rates.' Tom tried to be casual but could see she wasn't entirely comfortable with him not charging anything.

'I'll not use you again. Then I'll end up with some bloody cowboy, that tells me I have to replace all the pipes and drains and stuff, and then me or my dad will be ripped off, and then I'll have to redecorate because the cowboy took all the pipes out of the walls, and then I'll find out that the pipes are made from kitchen roll tubes, and then I'll drown in my bed when they start to leak, all because you wouldn't charge me for a serviced boiler,' she was smiling at Tom. 'You won't be able to sleep at night knowing that my drowning could have been prevented.'

'A touch dramatic, Daff,' shouted Crowley from the

kitchen.

'Well, seeing as I'm not sure you that have your five metre swimming badge, then I'll send a bill to your Dad. Just text me his address later, no rush.' Tom was smirking as he raised the cups to his lips.

While they finished their tea and coffee, Grace told Tom about the deal she had just made on the car and Tom agreed that it sounded like she had bought it for a good price.

'I can take you if you like. On Saturday, to collect the car,' offered Tom.

'Oh thanks, but Sean who came with me tonight is staying here on Friday so he will be able to take me as he lives in Lanson anyway. But thanks.' Tom shrugged his shoulders.

'Tell you what,' she said, 'if you are about next week will you join me in The Blacky for tea? My treat.' Tom looked a bit taken aback. 'I don't mean like a date! I mean as mates. Like a thank you for sorting me out. I mean the boiler out! If you want. If you're free. If not don't worry. But I'd like to, if you want to…I'll be in there anyway…but it's up to you….'

'PULL UP, PULL UP!' shouted Crowley. Grace stopped talking and took a deep breath and slowly started again.

'I just mean I would like to buy you your tea, as a thank you,' Grace finally said.

'I'd like that Grace. I just have to look at my diary at home and see where some of my jobs are next week. I don't want to say I'll meet you and then find out I have a job the other side of the county, that's all,' explained Tom. Grace was relieved.

'Oh yes, that's fine. I'm free any day.' said Grace.

'She will need two days' notice, Tom. She has legs hairier than Bigfoot and roots like trailer trash,' shouted Crowley.

Tom stood up. 'I'd best be off.' Grace stood and watched him walk into the kitchen to put his cup in the sink. Grace peered into the kitchen after him and Crowley was still sat on the worktop swinging his legs.

'See ya, Flynn.' Tom bent down and gave Flynn a scratch on top of his head. He walked back in and picked up his tool box, grabbed his coat off the floor and Grace opened the front door and said she would text her dad's address to him.

Once Tom had left she walked back into the kitchen where Crowley was waiting.

'I suppose you found all that very amusing didn't you?' said Grace. She walked over to the sink and began washing the cups.

'I did, especially the part when you were failing to make it clear that you have no designs on him,' he replied.

'I don't,' Grace insisted but briefly indulged in a daydream where Tom had kissed her goodbye before he left. She noticed that Crowley was looking around the kitchen.

'What're you looking for?' asked Grace.

'I don't suppose you have a nice little Chianti anywhere?'

'I'm not bloody Oddbins, you know,' she scolded.

'Come on Daff, we need to celebrate you buying a car,' and he gave her a playful nudge.

'There might be some Shiraz beside the fridge,' she said with a smile. Crowley immediately jumped down from the worktop and found the bottle. He started opening cupboards and found some glasses. He set them on the table in the lounge and came back and started opening drawers. Grace was now drying the cups and then opened the drawer in front of her waist, found a corkscrew and handed it to Crowley who in turn smiled gratefully and took himself and the corkscrew to the lounge. Once she was finished, Grace joined Crowley who was sat on the couch waiting patiently for her.

'Don't you think this is all a bit weird?' asked Grace.

'Only if we think about it, my dear.' Crowley was tearing at the foil at the neck of the wine bottle. Grace stared and marvelled at how normal Crowley looked, how normal he acted and how he could open a bottle of wine with the skill of a Semillon.

'Who'd have thought, a ghost drinking wine?' said Grace as Crowley poured the glasses.

'Who'd have thought I'd drink a £3.99 bottle of plonk?' Crowley raised his glass and Grace followed suit. They clinked their glasses and both took a deep gulp.

'It was £4.99 actually,' corrected Grace in amusement. Crowley winced with his swallow.

'It has an interesting aftertaste, don't you think?' he mused, 'it reminds me of a rather disturbing Coq au Vin I once consumed.' Crowley's lip curled at the thought.

'Well, that's made of red wine, isn't it? So there you go.'

'Yes, my dear. A chicken may taste of the wine but a wine should never taste of the chicken!'

Grace peered inside the glass and began to analyse the aftertaste. It was red wine to her.

'Well, if you don't bloody like it, don't drink it. I bought it for me not you and now you're bloody moaning.' Grace started to sulk.

'It's growing on me,' lied Crowley and started to make himself comfortable on the sofa.

'Anyway, can I just say thank you for helping me with the car before? That was really good of you to spot the tyres and stuff,' she said gratefully.

'Quite all right, my dear. To be honest though it wasn't my idea to 'pop down' so to speak. It was Steve's,' admitted Crowley.

'Steve?'

'McQueen. You have heard of Steve McQueen, have you not?'

'Yes! I have watched telly at Christmas! Great Escape and Bullitt and all that.' Grace was becoming excited. 'So you spoke to Steve McQueen? About me? What did he say?' Grace was eager to hear all what Steve McQueen had said about her.

'About you? Not a lot. But I couldn't shut him up about cars. I sat there for what felt like days with him talking about his Porches and his Jags. Anyway, he owned a Jag XKSS and said he went through tyres like a child goes through candy and said I should check them.' Grace stared at him with an incredulous look.

'What?' he asked.

'Of all the things you could have spoken to Steve McQueen about, you talked about tyres?' Grace was astonished.

'It wasn't my idea! I just happened to mention you and the car and he went off like a bottle of Veuve Clicquot telling me about a Mini Copper he once owned. Probably thought I'd be interested because I'm British. Do you know he painted it brown, Daff? A Mini Cooper in brown! Green is perfect. Red, white are on the borders of acceptability. But brown! I only stayed for your sake,' he turned to Grace awaiting her gratitude.

'Really?' she said sarcastically, 'and what was your water

through this 'conversation of torment'?'

'A lovely bottle of Hirsch Reserve Bourbon,' smiled Crowley.

'Sounds expensive,' drawled Grace. 'So you sat and listened to Steve McQueen for my sake? Well, thank you very much and I'm sorry that he bored you and I hope that me and the bourbon were worth it,' Grace pretended to be gracious.

'The bourbon was definitely worth it,' he mocked, 'I was rescued by James Dean who engaged with Steve about cars and helped finish the bottle. Only for him, was I allowed to take my leave without me appearing rude to my first guest.'

'Good 'ole Jimmy Dean, eh? If you're stuck with a bore you can count on Jimmy Dean to take up the slack,' Grace started to giggle and she raised her glass to Crowley for him to cheers her again.

'Do you have anything to eat, Daff? I'm starving. I had a salad with a wonderful screenwriter called John earlier but I have to admit I was still hungry when I finished. Salad to me is something that should make the rest of your meal look appealing. It shouldn't be a meal.'

Grace, impressed with this diet advice, said she was going to follow that mantra for the rest of her life but explained that she didn't have much in. She thought she might have a car by now so had been scavenging what she could out of the cupboards before she did a big shop at the supermarket. She suggested a pizza being delivered and Crowley became very excited at the thought as he had never had a pizza before.

'What? Never?' Grace was dumbfounded that anyone in this day and age had never eaten pizza. Even Mrs Mortimer craved a Hawaiian now and again. Crowley shook his head and Grace immediately retrieved a menu from a kitchen drawer and thrust it in his face for him to make a choice.

'I'll have whatever you normally get.' He was clearly confused by the vast selection so Grace called the takeaway and asked for a large mega meaty to be delivered as soon as possible. She noticed that Crowley had made light work of the wine and told him to stay put while she ran to Nell's for another bottle.

As she ran to the shop she couldn't help but look at the bridge just beyond. The man she had spoken to there on Friday was now on her couch, tucking into wine, waiting for pizza and was dead. But for some bizarre reason it was starting to feel quite normal. She walked into the shop, enquired after Nell and Roger, bought a bottle of Merlot and ran back to the cottage to find Crowley still in the place where she left him only this time he had the telly on.

She put the bottle on the table, whereby he immediately inspected it in silence, and then she ran upstairs to get changed. By the time she had hung her clothes back up, there was a knock at the door from the pizza delivery man.

Crowley sat forward on the couch in anticipation and Flynn was on his hind legs doing a doggy salsa dance, sniffing and stretching toward the box in Grace's hands. She sat back in the spot that she had vacated earlier and opened the lid and watched Crowley's face. She noted he seemed pleased with the contents.

'Tuck in then,' she instructed. Crowley tore a large slice away from the perfect circle and took a large bite. He immediately closed his eyes and started to chew slowly.

'Nice?' Grace craned her head around to see his expression more.

'Daff, I think this might be my heaven now.' Grace

laughed as he continued to chew slowly.

They sat largely in silence while they ate their pizza, drank the wine and watched some telly. Crowley found *I'm a Celebrity, Get Me Out of Here* very entertaining and gave a critique of Ant & Dec fit for The Guardian.

Grace started to clear the box away and Crowley took the hint and realised that she had work the next day so he should leave.

'I'll be off now, Daff,' said Crowley.

'I've had a nice night, all be told,' she said.

'Don't forget to text Tom,' he reminded.

'Oh God, yes,' she started looking around the room for the phone. She hadn't called her dad either to say she had bought a car.

'He's quite sweet on you, I think,' he said.

'Tom? Don't be daft. He's just a friend from the village, that's all. Anyway, he's out of my league,' Grace muttered and Crowley shot her a look.

'Out of your league?! My dear, what a low opinion you have of yourself. Who has contributed to this negative evaluation of yourself? Tell me and I shall rattle my chains in their face until they die of shock.' She looked at him and wanted to hug him. 'You are beautiful. Even with your red wine Ronald MacDonald stained lips.' They both laughed and Grace started to rub the corners of her mouth.

'Good night, Daff,' and he kissed her on the top of her head and walked into the kitchen behind her. She didn't turn around but immediately picked up the glasses from the coffee table and walked into the empty kitchen to wash them. She let Flynn out for his final wee and while she waited, she texted Tom with her dad's address and also sent a text to her dad to say she bought a car and would call him in the morning from the office.

She also decided the next day she would play Miss Marple and see what she could dig up on her phantom friend.

CHAPTER 8

The next day in the office was developing into a slow one so Grace decided to take advantage of some free time and with no Bill in his office, to start looking at some of Crowley's past. She entered all the obvious terms into a search engine and it didn't take too much digging before a story had started to develop and some of Grace's questions were answered.

De Mondford Hall was built in 1575 and had been expanded from one century to the next. The Crowley family had lived at the Hall from the 17th century until 9 years ago when it was bought by The Harton Group, a global hospitality company, at auction. The previous owner, who sold De Mondford Hall, was the last in line of the Crowley's, Hugh Crowley. His sister, Sarah, had married the Earl of Granchester 22 years ago and she and her family lived in Hyden Hall in Scotland.

Grace was surprised to learn that Crowley had a sister. When she thought of his family she never imagined he had siblings. She continued to read the history of De Mondford Hall and it concluded that due to increasing debts and a fairly devastating fire caused by old electrical wiring to the southern wing of the Hall, Hugh Crowley auctioned the house off. The Harton Group had bought it and after a multi-million restoration De Mondford Hall, was now a five star luxury hotel and spa. It was also a hotspot for celebrity weddings, high profile charity functions and featured frequently in magazines read by the upper classes.

Grace continued to search the web for more information and found a page dedicated to Crowley. The article read as if he was still alive but from various dates, Grace calculated that he was 60 years old when he died. But the Crowley that visited her only looked in his late forties. He had been married to Jennifer, according to the site. He didn't meet her until he was 40 years old and she was ten years his junior. Jennifer had come to the Hall applying for a job to help manage the house and had married Crowley within 2 years and had given him a son called Max, a year after. Grace was shocked to learn he was a father. He had never mentioned either of them. Where were they? Max should be around 12 years old by now. How did a man have all this and end up dead on the river bank in Pelsby?

It didn't take long for Grace to find out that Jennifer and Max were travelling back from Lady Granchester's house after a visit in Scotland when it was reported that Jennifer's car had hit black ice, skidded off the road and had rolled numerous times near the Pass of Drumochter. The crash had been witnessed but even with prompt assistance Jennifer and three year old Max were both dead before they were cut from the car.

Grace couldn't read anymore and told Ellen that she was going to the toilet. In the cubicle, Grace cried. She tried to tell herself that she was being silly as she didn't know any of these people. But it had upset her that she had read this on the internet which had been written in a cold, unemotional and impersonal manner. She now knew Crowley and in the few days that she had known him she cared about him. They were linked in some spiritual way and she was the only person on Earth that knew of his semi existence. Why hadn't he chosen his sister though for his positive deed, or any of her children? Why did Crowley choose a complete stranger from Wales who now lived in Pelsby? And why didn't he want his sister to know of his death? Why didn't he suggest she send an anonymous letter to Lady Sarah and not the police?

Once she had pulled herself together, she cleaned up her face and went back to her desk. She had so many questions; she wanted to see if there was anything else she could find. But there was little after that. All she could see was that the house had been sold and Hugh Crowley had filed for bankruptcy a few months after the sale and then the trail ran cold.

Grace sat at her desk and stared blankly at her computer screen for a few minutes when she decided she wanted to call home and speak to her parents. She needed to tell her dad that she had bought a car but she also wanted to talk to her mum; maybe it had something to do with the news she had just read and wanted some maternal comfort. Grace thought for a moment and could not recall a moment when she ever felt like this; her mother was as affectionate as Miss Hannigan.

'Ellen, I'm just going into Bill's office to make a call. I think it might get a little heated so it's probably best if some of the staff don't hear me,' lied Grace.

She called her parents and when she got through it was her mum who picked up the phone.

'3548,' the voice said in a clipped tone.

'Hey Mum, it's only me.'

'Grace, darling, how are you? You don't normally call during the day? Are you not in work?' enquired Penny.

'I'm in Bill's office. He's out today, probably playing golf. I just called for a chat as my work's up to date and I remembered that you and Daddy are at your dance class tonight.'

'Grace, my feet are still recovering from last week. When I got home and took off my shoes they resembled sausages sticking out of a jar of jam. Your father has the grace and movement of the Tin Man, before the oil!' moaned Penny.

'He must be improving by now. You've been going for months,' said Grace.

'I don't expect him to be dancing like Lionel Blair, but I would like to be able to wear a pair of pretty shoes the following day.'

'Mum?'

'Yes.'

'Do you ever worry about being alone?' Grace asked.

'Why? Has your father said something? I know you and he have secrets but if there's somethings he's not telling...'

'No! Nothing like that!' Grace tried to reassure her mum. 'I just meant in general. Dad may go before you, and me and Gethin are hardly around the corner so I just wondered if it was something you ever thought of,' Grace asked.

'Well, I hadn't until this cheery little conversation. Seriously, Grace where is all this coming from?' Penny was slightly uneasy with where this conversation was going.

'It's nothing really. Just me being morbid,' Grace changed the subject. 'I bought a car, by the way.'

'You did buy something decent and normal?' Penny asked.

'I bought a van and Sean is painting it like the Mystery Machine from Scooby Doo as we speak. It's even got windows in it so I'm going to take the curtains off my back bedroom window and put them on, that way I can get changed at the services without people seeing me.' Grace left it hanging. The silence from her mum was almost palpable.

'Is Sean good at painting?' Penny squeaked.

'Not really Mum, but you couldn't say that to him. You know how sensitive he can be. It doesn't matter if it looks bad as I won't be able to see it from the inside. He's just painting the outside...all over.' Grace clapped her hand over the mouth of the phone so Penny could not hear her trying to muffle a laugh.

'Will you be coming to Cornwall in the...erm...van?' Penny sounded like she was about to start crying.

'Oh God, yeah Mum. I've got him on it now so it should be dry by the weekend when I come over and see you. But what isn't dry, well I am sure I can just dry with a towel.' Grace was starting to sweat with trying to stifle her own giggling.

'Well, I'm sure when you come up Daddy will offer any advice about it.' Grace knew what this meant and could imagine the conversation when she put the phone down.

'Dai, you must tell Grace when she comes up in that van that it is totally unsuitable for a young woman to drive. Tell her that she must get the thing resprayed. Tell her that we will pay for it. Tell her that if she doesn't do it that it may be best she gets the train. Tell her that she will be too tired doing the drive. Tell her that she's a raving lunatic. Tell her if she pulls up on the drive in the van that I'm dead so she might as well go home'

'Mum, I'm pulling your leg.'

'What?' Penny's voice was so high that it was only audible to dogs.

'I'm kidding you. I have bought a very sensible Vauxhall Astra. I collect it on Saturday, so I've took Monday off work and I'm going to drive up Saturday afternoon. I'll stay until Monday. How does that sound?'

'What colour is the Astra painted?' Grace burst out laughing. Only her mum could miss the point of her daughter coming to visit but still only manage to focus on the fact she may still turn up in a car that will draw negative attention. As long as she could still show her face at dance class, yoga and her art club then all was well in Penny's World.

'It's red, Mum. A nice, boring sensible red. Like a classy Chanel lipstick. Okay?' Grace reassured her mum.

'Oh Grace, you are naughty giving your mother a heart attack like that. Jokes like that at my age are not funny,' scolded Penny.

'Yes they are, Mum. I'm not trying to kill you. I just think it's funny when your voice goes that high. I sometimes wait for all your best crystal to start shattering in the cabinet,' giggled Grace.

'Oh, I wouldn't be happy with that dear. Some of my pieces are over 50 years old.' And Penny was back in the room, thought Grace.

'Yes, it's Grace,' Penny was clearly talking to Dai in the background.

'Darling, Daddy is here and wants to talk to you. I'm pleased you are coming up this weekend. Can I ask...will you be bringing your dog?' asked Penny flatly.

'Dad said it was okay but if you don't want him to

come...'

'Of course, the dog...I mean Flynn, is welcome. So he is coming then?'

'Yes,' said Grace.

'Fine. Fine. Yes, fine.' Penny was trying to convince herself that all was okay. She was not aware that Dai had already given Grace the heads up on the ultimatum that he had given Penny with regard to Flynn.

'He'll be good. He just stays in his basket and then he can sleep in my room when I go to bed. He doesn't like sleeping on his own. And neither do I for that matter.'

'Well, you only have yourself to blame for that,' Penny muttered.

'So, is Dad there then? I'd best speak to him before I head back into the office.' Grace had reached her tolerance level with her mum. Once dogs and men are mentioned Grace could almost hear the bell of a boxer's ring declaring the end of the round. Grace always threw in the towel when the imaginary bell went off.

'I'll see you Saturday then Darling, bye.' Grace could hear the phone being passed to Dai and as usual it was accompanied by a faint whisper.

'Hello, Gracey darling,' Dai said brightly.

'Hey Dad, I won't keep you long as I'm in work. I only called to say I bought the lovely red Astra. I sent you a link on email so you could look at it online. Did you see it?' Grace asked.

'I did. You sound pleased. As long as you are happy with it,' said Dai.

'I am. I got a good deal as well. I managed to get a whole new set of tyres on her and another £300 knocked off,' boasted Grace.

'Well done, Darling. How superb! So I gather you and

Flynn will be arriving Saturday, yes?' asked Dai.

'Are you sure her nerves can handle it, Dad?' Grace whispered.

'We are so looking forward to seeing you, Flynn and your new car,' impressed Dai. Penny was clearly still stood by Dai.

'Okay, I hear you, Dad. I'd best go and find some proper work to do. I'll text you as soon as I set off but hopefully I should be at yours around tea time,' said Grace.

'I look forward to it,' her dad said gently.

'Dad?'

'Yes, dear?'

'I love you and I'm always here if you ever need me,' she said softly.

'I know that, dear.'

'And Dad...thank you again for the car.'

'You're welcome. Love you, Gracey darling.'

She felt better once she put down the phone. Maybe it was just the simple connection both verbally and emotionally but she knew she felt better for speaking to both of them. The revelations about Crowley had shaken Grace and it heightened a sense of loneliness inside her that she simply needed to feel some familiarity.

Grace loved her parents in different ways and learned a lot from both of them. For all her mum's faults she knew her mum loved her dearly. A lot of her mum's frustration came from Grace's lack of ambition in life and Grace could understand that. To raise a child and try to instil an attitude of self-worth and the belief that they can achieve anything must have a silent and disappointed aftertaste for the parent when the child achieves nothing in their life of note. Grace knew that she had achieved very little especially compared to Gethin. Her dad had a far more relaxed approach to her life, past, present and future. His attitude was a relief from her mum's but sometimes Grace questioned his laid-back attitude. Was it a lack of interest or even a lack of understanding of how his daughter ticked? The one thing however, she knew both her parents were united on and that was the lack of man in her life which in turn meant waiting longer for grandchildren in their eyes.

Grace wasn't even sure if she wanted children. Flynn was sometimes enough of a dependant for her and the frustrations that came with him made her question if she was fit to look after children, if she found a dog a challenge. Grace knew she had to move forward with her life but had no idea what direction to take or even where to start. She thought moving to Pelsby would give birth to a new Grace. But it didn't. The old Grace moved to Pelsby together with her old clothes and old albums of Red Hot Chilli Peppers and Oasis. Eventually, the old attitude moved to Pelsby as well. The one that says, 'I'll start when…..' Only her four walls had changed and her mum and dad were replaced with a suspect mixed species dog.

Had Crowley achieved all he wanted to? He had suffered terribly in the sixty years on Earth but he also had some privileges not known to all, an advantaged upbringing, wealth and social status. But above all else, he had a family. A wife and son that were cruelly taken from him, but he had had them for a few short years. Was Crowley being punished in some way? Was he given the love of these two people to subject him to suffering later on for sins known only to him? But surely if Crowley had been a bad man then he wouldn't be in his semi heaven. Surely he would be damned. Maybe, he asked for forgiveness and that's all it took? Forgiveness is absolution. Grace could not believe that Crowley had been wicked enough to warrant his family being taken from him. She hadn't known him that long but she found it hard to believe that evil people ate pizza and gave advice on tyres.

With a sigh of relief, Sean and Grace left the office on Friday night. They both bathed in that lovely feeling as they put on their coats and looked forward to their weekend. Sean was staying in Grace's house that night and Grace was to treat him to booze and a takeaway for running her to the garage earlier in the week and Sean was also to take her again the following day to collect the new car.

'You gonna be all right driving to Cornwall, just like that?' asked Sean as they went down in the office lift.

'Why wouldn't I be? I'll have Flynn with me,' replied Grace.

'Yeah, but how's that dog at car repairs? What if the car breaks down on the way? Is he gonna pull out a baseball cap and a monkey wrench? It's not like you know what to do, is it? Maybe, you should tell your mum and dad that you'll come next week and tootle around in it for a bit,' Sean suggested.

'I can't, they're so looking forward to me coming and 'sides, I can't live on old Snack a Jacks and tubes of creamy cheese any longer. I'm starving!'

They walked out of the building and onto the street still giggling at Grace's delayed big shop when they heard someone shout.

'Sean!'

It came from a man who was stood at the edge of the kerb clearly waiting for Sean to finish work.

'François!' Sean squealed and bounded over like an excited school child. Grace gave her friend's latest squeeze a quick once over while she approached him more slowly than Sean did. Grace was surprised to see that the man was considerably older than Sean. Grace guessed around fifteen years older. He was short, around 5' 6", balding and grey. But even from afar Grace could detect his slight frame was filled with confidence.

Sean was excited to finally introduce Grace to the love of his life

'Grace, this is François!' Sean stretched out his arms and presented him like a prize from a 1980's game show. Sean had missed his calling; he had managed to make François look slightly more attractive.

'Bonjour François, je suis très heureux de vous rencontrer enfin,' Grace outstretched her hand to shake his and noted his expression had not changed with her greeting.

'Grace, Grace, Grace, let us not put poor Sean to a disadvantage,' François smiled and shook Grace's hand.

'What did she say?' Sean said excitedly. Grace continued to look at François and waited for him to answer his newly found beau. But he remained silent and continued to smile at her.

'I just said I was pleased to finally meet him,' Grace turned to Sean and smiled. Sean was beaming. He had not seen the invisible exposure of his new boyfriend. Grace's heart grew heavy for her friend. 'Strike one', Grace thought.

'So, why are you here? I thought you were going to work,' Sean asked.

'I am,' François looked over at Grace and he shifted slightly on his feet. She could tell whatever the reason was for him being here he did not want to share with Grace.

'Sean, give me the car keys and I'll bring the car around.

148

You two can talk in private,' suggested Grace.

Sean quickly looked at Grace and then at François who didn't protest at her leaving. He rummaged in his coat and produced his keys and muttered that he would see her in a bit.

'Au revoir, Grace.' François's accent had clearly been taught by the cast of 'Allo 'Allo.

'Yeah, bye,' Grace's disdain was not lost on him.

Grace walked to the car and felt so sorry for Sean. He had less luck than her when it came to men. 'At least I've given up,' she thought. 'What's the point of putting yourself out there if all you're going to get are phoneys and heartbreak?'

By the time she drove the car around the block and reached the kerb where she left them, Sean was standing on his own waiting for her. Grace got out and climbed back into the passenger seat to let Sean drive to Pelsby.

'Everything all right?' asked Grace as they moved into the stream of commuter traffic.

'Yes, the cashpoint was broke by the apartment so he just asked me for some money until tomorrow when he can get some money out of the bank,' Sean idly replied while looking in all his mirrors. The drive out of Lanson at this time of night could be sometimes challenging.

'Do they have a cashpoint in Pelsby?' asked Sean.

'Nell has one in the shop,' replied Grace. 'Anyway, you don't need any money I'm paying for tonight.'

'I still need some money for cigarettes. You're not buying me them. Or are you?' he asked jokingly.

'No, I'm not! We have to go to Nell's anyway, to get the booze,' said Grace. She looked at Sean, who seemed perfectly happy at just being fleeced for £50. Grace had been with Sean at lunchtime when he took the money out to see him over the weekend. He had clearly given François the lot if he needed money to buy cigarettes. 'Strike two', thought Grace.

On the way home, Sean asked Grace what she thought of François. Grace played it cool and said that it was hard for her to make a judgment seeing as she had only been in his company for thirty seconds. But in those thirty seconds she knew he was as French as a Yorkshire pudding and either had financial issues or broken legs if he couldn't walk up the road to find another cashpoint. Grace plumped for the another option, he was just a con artist. She also knew that François had realised she knew he wasn't what he claimed to be. She changed the subject quickly as she was uncomfortable lying to her friend. After talking about their commitments for the weekend ahead they decided to get a curry but not too much drink. Grace made it clear that she didn't want to be driving the new car with a hangover so would be restricting herself to two glasses of wine. They decided to only buy one bottle between them to remove any temptation of drinking more.

'You're doing me a favour, Grace. Have you seen how puffy my face is lately? I look like Elvis during the 'Vegas Years'. I need to detox myself before I end up on one of those bad documentaries on Sky or something.' Sean glanced in the rear view mirror and looked at himself with disgust.

They drove home talking about all the various diets they had attempted throughout their lives and concluded that they had no willpower. Unless a diet allowed you to drink as much as you wanted, then there was no point in starting it in the first place.

They spent the evening gossiping about people they knew well and making bitchy presumptions about the people they didn't. Grace resisted exposing François to Sean as he showed her various photographs on his phone. She wanted to scream at him that he was a fool when he became excited at the idea of going on holiday with him, but she didn't. If Sean's past history was anything to go by then there would be no need for Grace to intervene to show Sean what a charlatan François was. It would come out eventually, it always did and if it didn't, surely Sean would realise he was far too short.

After their fill of takeaway and a couple of wines they both started to fall asleep and decided to call it a night. Grace loved it when Sean slept over, she felt like she was a kid again. Within fifteen minutes Grace, Sean and Flynn were all curled up in one bed and each snoring gently.

The next day, after they had washed, dressed and cleaned up, they packed the car with Grace's things for the weekend at her parents' house. Grace let Flynn have a quick run-around before he jumped at the back of Sean's car. She admitted to Sean that she was excited about driving the car but dreading arriving at her parents' house with the dog.

'I don't blame you; I love Flynn, don't get me wrong, but he is funny looking. Don't be taking him out for no walks in the street. Your mum will have kittens. Mind you, they'll keep the dog company,' squawked Sean.

CHAPTER 9

They pulled into the garage and both saw the car straight away. It was clearly parked ready for collection and Grace became excited again. Sean parked his own car and said he would wait with Flynn while she found Barry.

Barry wasn't in and Grace was relieved when a young lady called Meg informed her that she would serve her. Meg turned out to be one of life's greatest gossips and revealed that Barry was off with depression as his wife had left him a couple of days earlier after thirty years of marriage. Grace wondered if Barry not giving Mrs Barry the Astra had anything to do with it but it turned out that Mrs Barry's full service history had been exposed and it wasn't Mr Barry who was doing the servicing but Mr Barry's rival from Virgo Motors. To add salt to the wounds, Tony Virgo picked her up from the marital home when she left Barry in a Mercedes Roadster that Barry had traded with him three months before. Apparently, Mrs Barry had admired the car when he first acquired it. She seemed very impressed with the leather interior and how roomy it was in the back. It all made sense to Mr Barry now.

Grace feigned slight interest while Meg processed all the relevant paperwork and imagined Barry sat at home crying while still encased in his football manager's coat. Once everyone was happy, Meg handed the keys over and wished Grace all the best and thanked her for her custom.

Grace walked out of the showroom and waved the key in Sean's direction. He immediately jumped out of his car and bounded over. He seemed just as excited as Grace as he helped shift her holdall, Flynn's bed and a plastic bag with Flynn's bowls and food to Grace's boot. She thanked Sean for dropping her off and said her goodbyes with a promise of a lunch when she was back in the office on Tuesday.

She waited for Sean to leave the forecourt before she set off herself. Her phone was bluetooth'ed to the car and she had her sat nav in her phone ready to go. She looked behind and Flynn was standing on his hind legs looking out of the window. He also seemed excited and sensed he was going on an adventure.

'Don't get too excited Flynn, you'll remember my mum when you see her. Now lay down so we can go, eh?' she instructed. Flynn did as he was bid and curled up in his bed that was laid on the back seat.

The drive to Cornwall was one of the most pleasant journeys she had ever had. The car was lovely to drive, she had her tunes and Flynn gently snored the whole way. She marvelled at the changing scenery before her and wondered how people settled into various areas that she drove through. She also noted that nearly every town she passed had a Chinese takeaway. 'How do the Chinese find all these tiny villages and towns? What makes them decide to settle in these places and open up a takeaway?' It was hard enough for her to find them by accident with a sat nav.

She arrived at her parents' house at tea time as predicted and as she pulled up onto the large gravel driveway she marvelled at how beautiful the house was. One thing was for sure, she did enjoy the house when she visited and she made a note of maybe house sitting when her parents next went on holiday.

As she gently woke Flynn, the front door opened and her parents came out and made their way towards her car. They both looked excited to see her and it made Grace relax a bit as she climbed out of the driver's seat.

'Gracey darling,' her dad said as he stretched out his arms for an embrace. He squeezed her and then pushed her away pleasingly so he could look at her.

'Oh, you're here at last.' Her relieved mum pulled Grace towards her and gave her a huge hug. 'Was the drive okay? You must be tired. Come in, come in, the kettle's just boiled,' she then whispered, 'unless you would like a cheeky little wine?' Grace smiled at her appreciatively. Penny started to walk Grace into the house and shouted behind her for Dai to collect Grace's bag. Just as Penny was about to step into the house Flynn shot by her feet like a ferret and ran into the hall.

'Oh, dear God!' shouted Penny. Grace unhooked herself from Penny's grasp and bent down to pat Flynn.

'He's just excited, that's all. He'll settle down in a minute. I promise.' Grace tried to reassure her mum that this was not Flynn's normal behaviour as they walked in to the open plan kitchen. Dai closed the front door and appeared with Grace's holdall and the plastic bag. He told Grace he would put her bag in her room while she immediately retrieved Flynn's water bowl from the plastic bag to fill.

'Where can I set this down, Mum?' asked Grace. Penny walked towards the end of the kitchen units and pointed to an area on the floor where a small rug had been lain down.

'I bought this little rug and thought his bowls could go on here. The rug will stop the bowls scraping all over the slate and I can easily just wash the rug,' said Penny. Grace was appreciative. She was clearly trying to make them both feel at home even though she knew the rug would be straight in the bin before Grace had reached fourth gear on their departure.

'That's a good idea. Here you go, Flynn.' Grace set the bowl on the tiny cream rug and Flynn immediately started to lap.

Grace stood and looked around the ground floor of the house while her mum went to the huge American fridge to find a bottle of wine. The front door opened into a short hall which then opened into a large open-plan space. Straight ahead was a glass staircase that climbed against a full length glass wall. To the right of the stairs, the kitchen started. It was a beautiful dove grey kitchen they had designed and shipped from Germany. Each cupboard was curved, creating a soft scallop effect against the back wall and a huge island dominated the centre in front. Beyond the kitchen, the large living room opened out with glass walls to the left and right. Ahead was an open fire and either side of this were cleverly concealed doors to her dad's den and her mum's sitting room. The ceiling was vaulted over the lounge but due to the use of reclaimed wood throughout, the room was still cosy, especially when the fire was lit. Through the expanse of glass was the sea and miles and miles of curving beach. Grace walked to the window and drank in the view. It truly was a beautiful place to build a house.

She stood for a while and could hear her mum rummaging in the kitchen and her dad opening and then closing the front door again. He appeared with Flynn's bed and Flynn trotting beside him waiting for him to set it down.

'How about here, Flynn?' Dai asked the dog as he placed the bed in front of the unlit fire. 'It'll be warm here later.' Dai gave the top of Flynn's head a little scratch as an appreciative Flynn curled himself up in the basket. Dai walked over to Grace who was still standing at the window watching the sea.

'A foxtrot today, if I'm not mistaken,' Dai said as he stood beside Grace. The sea indeed was fairly gentle.

'Wine?' her mum said over her shoulder and as Grace turned, she took the glass with thanks. 'Let's sit,' Penny instructed.

They all sat down on the cream couches and Grace gave them a blow by blow account of her journey to see them and how the car had performed and had been a pleasure to drive. She also told them about how Flynn had been in the car and had stayed settled the whole way. During the conversation Grace could see her mum was still nervous with Flynn being in the room.

'If he wants the toilet, he will say won't he?' Penny asked.

'Yes, Mum. He's very civilised and even insists on Andrex,' Grace joked.

'Must be the dog on the advert thing,' said her dad joining in the leg-pulling.

'Here we go. Little and Large joking again,' Penny said sarcastically taking a sip of her wine.

'What do you do with him when you want to go out? I

mean, I know that you don't go out that much.'

'Here we go', thought Grace.

'But when you do go out, where does the dog go?' asked Penny.

'Well, he just stays in the house. As long as he has a wee before you go anywhere then he can hold on for a few hours. But if I'm going somewhere and I think he won't be able to last, then Mrs Mortimer will pop in and let him out.'

'Do you think he will be good if we go out this evening? I thought we could go to the new seafood restaurant that's opened by the harbour,' said Penny.

'What a splendid idea!' said Dai.

'I'll need to let him have a run but apart from that he should be fine,' said Grace.

They all agreed that they were pretty hungry so Grace fetched her coat and shoes and decided to walk along the beach with Flynn before she got ready. Dai decided to join them while Penny stayed in to use the shower first.

The beach was deserted and there wasn't another soul as far as the eye could see. Even in the summer the end of the beach where the house stood was always quiet as there was nothing around in the area. Most bathers or walkers tended to use the busier end where some beachside shops and cafés could be found. An odd walker would venture this far but only to walk past and admire the Hammond residence, Breeze Point. As they walked along, Grace wondered if her dad could tell her anymore about De Mondford Hall.

'Dad, do you know anything about De Mondford Hall or the family that used to live there?' asked Grace.

'De Mondford Hall? De Mondford Hall.' Dai was trying to remember. 'Ah, that place in Somerset. Yes, your mother and I went to a charity function there about four years ago. It was for terminally ill children, as I recall. Why do you ask?' said Dai.

'They think the body found in Pelsby last week had something to do with the place and I just wondered if you knew anything about who used to live there,' lied Grace.

'Well, not much, Darling. I heard the last of the family drank all the money away and he lost the house because of it. I think it might have been the same fellow who lost his wife in an accident of some sort. Do you think the body could be him?' asked Dai. 'If he did lose his wife then is it any wonder he drank?' Dai supposed.

'I think he may have lost a child as well,' revealed Grace.

'Well then, it's no wonder he drank. The thought of losing your mother and my children would drive me insane and I'm sure that drink would help me on my way. What's losing bricks and mortar compared to your family?'

They were soon back and Grace went to her room. After a wash she changed into a simple black dress that even her mum could not fault. She even put on some tights and a smart pair of stilettos to polish the look. When she looked in the mirror, she realised that she didn't look too bad and thought she should make an effort a bit more. As she reached the bottom of the stairs she was greeted by compliments from both her parents on her appearance.

Her dad decided he wanted to drive so they all piled into his plush seven series BMW and set off to the harbour. The car smelled of leather and her mum's Coco Chanel perfume and from the back where Grace was sat, she could see her mum and dad holding hands on top of the gear stick. It warmed Grace to see.

The restaurant wasn't far and when they entered, Grace was surprised at how basic the décor was. The walls were exposed brick and only featured simple wall lighting. The tub chairs were of plush brown velvet and the table was adorned with simple white linen and an orchid. Grace thought the place was lovely and they were seated in the window overlooking the yachts in the harbour.

Grace admired the view for a moment and as her parents settled in, she noticed Crowley was sat in the fourth spare chair next to her mum. She widened her eyes to him and he burst out laughing. He clearly wanted to surprise her.

'Good evening, my name is Carl and I will be your waiter this evening, can I get you anything while you look at the menu?' the young waiter enquired.

'Why don't we have four Dubonnets as an aperitif?' Crowley requested. Grace just stared at him while her parents perused the menu.

'Shall we just go straight in with a wine?' Dai asked.

'You choose, Darling,' Penny instructed without looking up.

'Okay, can we have a bottle of your Moorduc Estate Chardonnay please, to start?' Dai passed the wine menu back to Carl.

'How can you pick a wine without choosing your food first?' Crowley shook his head.

'We are probably having fish,' Grace said through gritted teeth.

'Indeed we should,' said Dai. 'I have heard the sea bass is exceptional.' Grace raised her eyes from the menu and could see Crowley was very merry and seemed to be checking out her mum.

'You didn't tell me your mother was a redhead. I do love a redhead.' Crowley was pretending to moon over Penny.

'You said,' said Grace.

'Did I, Darling?' Dai looked at Grace, 'I don't remember. But I quite like the look of the Dover sole,'

'An excellent choice, Mr Hammond. One that will go perfectly well with the wine that you adventurously pre-ordered. Carl, where are my Dubonnets?' shouted Crowley across the restaurant.

Crowley pretended to blow kisses to Penny while they all ordered their meal. Dai poured out three large glasses of wine and then raised his glass to make a toast. Crowley jokingly looked around on the table and on the floor for his glass.

'How rude, Dai. Just when I thought we were becoming friends,' Crowley shrugged his shoulders.

'To the two most wonderful women in the world.' Penny blushed as if it was the first time he had ever said it and Grace, for a moment, felt special until she clocked Crowley licking his lips and announcing that Penny was a 'fine filly'.

'I see where you get your good looks from, Daff. Your mum is...mmmm,' he exhaled while looking at her dreamily. 'I have to say though, you have scrubbed up exceptionally well tonight. I nearly couldn't find you.'

'Are you okay, Gracey darling? You seem preoccupied,' asked Dai.

'You're not worrying about Flynn are you and the damage he may be doing in the house,' Penny asked fretfully.

'You left Flynn in the house?' shouted Crowley. 'You'll have gaps in the floor like the London Underground from where he has been dragging his feet. The dog can hold three ton of dirt under each claw. He has feet like a raptor.' Crowley started swiping the air and tried to make dinosaur noises to an oblivious audience.

As the food started to arrive, Crowley watched all the dishes being set down and looked disappointed that each one was not being placed before him.

'I'm going! As Groucho Marx once said, I've had a marvellous night but this wasn't it.'

'I think this evening is going to be wonderful from here on in,' snarled Grace at Crowley. He took the hint, saluted and then disappeared.

'I agree,' said Penny and they all started tucking into their meal. Grace realised she had lost her appetite with Crowley's visit. Her nerves had obviously supressed her hunger. She knew no one could see him but the whole appearing thing still took some getting used to.

The rest of the meal went without a further visit, though she wished he was there as a distraction when her mum started grilling her about a boyfriend. Penny would not accept that Grace was happy that there was no one in her life. Grace admitted that she wasn't unhappy or happy about it. She just simply accepted it for now, but semi agreed with her parents that she would get out more and not just with Sean who was clearly putting any potential men off, whether he was gay or not.

Grace was glad when she returned to her parents' house. She was glad to see that Flynn had not moved or disturbed anything since they had left. Her mum's head was like a meerkat looking around and inspecting floors. Grace immediately opened a large glass sliding door in the lounge and let Flynn run out onto the decking and jump onto the sand. He didn't stay out long. He knew this time of night was simply a toilet break and nothing more than that. He was hoping his master was staying in as he had missed her today and he was also missing home.

'If you don't mind, I'm going to go straight up,' announced Grace.

'Not at all my dear, you must be tired after the drive. Is there anything I can get you before you go up?' asked Penny.

Grace told her mum she needed nothing else, kissed her parents good night, collected Flynn's basket from the floor and instructed Flynn to follow her. He trotted beside her up the stairs and waited for her lead. Once they were in the bedroom, Grace relaxed and was glad to be on her own for a bit. She rooted in the bag and pulled out a large blanket that she had packed for Flynn. Her mum would go nuts if she knew that the dog was on the bed so Grace packed a blanket to throw over the top of the quilt.

'Sneaky aren't I?' Grace smiled at Flynn as she spread it out.

Once she settled in bed, Flynn jumped up and curled at the bottom by her feet. She listened for the shut of her parents' bedroom door and then waited another five minutes.

'Crowley?' she whispered in the semi darkness. She waited for a bit, and then called again but a bit louder but still nothing.

'Crowley, I know you can hear me! Put that bloody drink down and come here and talk to me for a minute,' she whispered more forcefully. She felt the bed depress and then could see him sat on the end of the bed, his face was clearly visible in the moonlight.

'You raaaannnnng,' he moaned like a zombified butler.

'Finally! I wondered if you were ever going to turn up. What the bloody hell was all that about before?' she asked.

'It was only a bit of fun, Daff,' he protested. 'Have I come down here for you to bloody nag me?'

'Sorry, no.'

'Is there a war on?' Crowley asked looking around in an exaggerated manner. 'Why are we sat in the dark?'

'I don't want my parents coming in and telling me to turn the light off,' whispered Grace.

'Do parents still do that? My parents' favourite was 'shut the bloody door' and 'stop kicking Brennan'.

'Was Brennan your dog?' asked Grace.

'No, our footman,' said Crowley casually.

'Oh,' Grace entertained the thought for a moment and then shook her head.

'What have you been up to today then? Partying as usual, eh?' Grace asked.

'You don't normally want to hear my stories. You okay, Daff?' Crowley enquired.

'Yes, I'm fine. I just want to talk for a little bit. Did you honestly come down before just to wind me up or was there something you wanted to tell me?'

'If you mean am I any further on about the good deed then no, there is nothing I can tell you and yes, I did come down to amuse myself and meet your parents in an indirect way,' he admitted.

'Tell me then, what have you been up to? Come up here and lie down if you like.' Grace settled further in the bed and Crowley moved up the bed and lay on top of the covers beside her in the moonlit darkness.

'Well today, I have spent most of the day conversing with Abraham Lincoln. Fascinating man, Daff. He won't move on and he regularly haunts the White House giving serving Presidents subliminal messages on key policies. He was telling me that even though he is regarded as an intelligent president he was extremely forgetful. Kept all his notes, letters and even bills in his hat.' Crowley tapped the top of his head. 'Can you imagine? I asked him how he felt about a black President in the White House. He admitted at his disbelief and never thought the day would come. He said he was particularly thrilled that Obama had used his bible when he was inaugurated. I didn't know that, did you Daff?'

'Uh uh,' mumbled Grace. Her face was buried into the pillow.

'And did you know he's related to Tom Hanks? Distant cousins or something. He said he thought most of Tom's work was brilliant but wasn't sure about the film The Money Pit. I had to tell him that I doubted Tom was sure about The Money Pit either but compared to Joe Vs The Volcano, it probably felt positively Shakespearean.' Crowley chuckled to himself. 'He's a big man though Daff.' Crowley continued to whisper. 'His feet are a size 14! I told him I think your dog is one of his direct descendants but he said he doesn't remember fornicating with anything that looked like it needed a shave more than him so that's still up for debate,' he chuckled.

The room was silent and Crowley stayed quiet for a moment and realised Grace was gently snoring.

'You asleep, Daff?' The room stayed silent but Crowley was comfortable and continued to converse with his sleeping friend.

'Lovely house this, I have to say.' She still didn't respond and he didn't expect her to. 'I am trying Daff, believe me. I know you must be annoyed with me turning up here in varying states of inebriation but you would too if you were 'up there'. The company is marvellous but I know it's not where I'm supposed to be. Where that is I'm not sure; I haven't belonged anywhere in such a long time.'

Crowley stayed silent and immersed himself in thoughts

of family gone and the unknown of the future.

'I'll see you soon Daff, night night.' As usual, he kissed her on top of her head and disappeared.

The calm continued all night until her mobile phone woke her. When Grace grabbed her phone she was too late, she had missed the call.

She had missed eight calls previous to that.

CHAPTER 10

Penny and Dai were already up and were sitting in silence at the breakfast bar drinking coffee and reading the papers when they heard Grace get up. The noise from her bedroom reverberated through the whole house and Dai looked at Penny.

'I didn't realise this house carried the noise so much,' declared Dai.

''I didn't realise that Nellie might have been a better choice in name for her,' said Penny as she picked up her coffee cup to top it up from the coffee machine.

Grace was bounding down the stairs with Flynn at her heel, hair as wild as weeds and her holdall half zipped in her hand. Penny noted that her daughter's face was white and it reminded her of the time Grace had sat her first GCSE. She had filed out of the assembly hall of her school and looked like she had just been told she had an hour to live, give or take.

'What is it, Darling?' Penny said concerned. Grace was looking around the room, her eyes were wild.

'Have you seen my car keys?' asked Grace still not

making eye contact with her parents.

Dai jumped from the bar stool and placed his hands on his daughter's shoulders, 'Gracey, darling, what is it?' he sought for her gaze.

'Mrs Mortimer,' Grace mumbled, 'she's been taken to hospital in the night. They think she's had a stroke!' Grace immediately started to sob but then tried to compose herself quickly. 'I have to go.'

'What? Now?' bellowed Penny.

'Big Mick said she's asking for me.' Grace moved away from her dad and started to look for her keys again. Penny became more concerned for her daughter and the state she was in. There was no doubt that the girl was going to leave. Penny knew that when Grace put her mind to something there was nothing that would stop her. She mulled through the options and then realised she had no choice.

'Grace, you can't drive in that state. It's too far. I'll take you,' offered Penny. Grace and Dai swung round to see if she was being serious.

'But Mum…'

'I insist. We can take your car back and your father can collect me later or I'll get the train back. But you are not driving by yourself!' Grace, without warning, began to sob on the spot. She had never known her mum to be this maternal and she now wasn't sure if she was crying about her mum or about Mrs Mortimer. Either way she had to agree, she wasn't sure if she would be able to drive sensibly in the state she was in. Penny walked over to Grace, gave her a hug and then cupped Grace's face in her hands.

'Go and wash your face, brush your teeth and hair, while Daddy packs the car and I'll get you a drink,' instructed Penny. Grace stared at her blankly. 'Go on!' Penny shooed her back upstairs.

Penny turned to Dai who looked slightly shocked and unable to speak. He seemed to be waiting for his instructions.

'Can you pack the car, Darling? Get the dog's bowls and pop them in a bag. I'll make her a chamomile tea. When you've done that could you put the dog in the car as well? I think she had his little bed on the back seat when she arrived. Right, where's my phone?' Penny started to hunt for her mobile.

'Are you sure about this, Dear? I can take her home,' said Dai.

'And what if the old lady dies?' Penny snapped. 'No, she'll need me. I'll be fine. You forget the amount of times I had to drive from Wales to London to spend some time with you.'

Dai recalled the numerous times his wife would travel across the country to accompany him to some boring engagement invariably on a Friday night in London and then drive back to Wales on her own the following day.

'You're right; she will need you if anything happens. I'll wait on your call later,' Dai hung his head. 'I do hope her old friend is okay. She talks about her fondly.'

'She should be hanging around people of her own age….' Penny dropped her voice, 'preferably men!', she tutted.

Penny started to make the tea and Dai busied himself loading up his daughter's car. As Penny stirred the tea, she was interrupted with Grace coming back downstairs looking slightly tidier than before. Dai walked back into the house and called Flynn over to pack him up at the back of the car.

'I'll take that,' said Dai as he pulled the holdall from Grace's hand.

'Drink this and take these,' Penny, with an insistent look, passed the chamomile tea together with 2 paracetamol for her daughter to take. 'In case you get a headache. Just a couple of mouthfuls and then we can go,' said Penny softly.

Grace drank the hot tea and was grateful for the tablets as her head was pounding, she just hadn't noticed. She watched her dad through the open front door as he closed the boot on her car and knocked on the back window to excite Flynn.

'Are you sure about this, Mum?' Grace felt a little guilty at dragging her away.

'Of course, I'm sure. Now, do you know where we are going? I take it you want to go straight to the hospital and not to Pelsby,' said Penny tying a scarf around her neck.

'She's in St Bernadette's. I told Big Mick that I would go straight there,' said Grace.

'Well, let's be off then.' Penny scurried to the hall table and picked up her bag and stepped outside where Dai was waiting. She passed the phone to him for him to set up the sat nav for St Bernadette's and after she kissed Dai goodbye, they were soon on the road back toward the hospital.

Most of the journey was in silence. Penny was thinking about getting to the hospital on time. She knew Mrs Mortimer was 82 and if she had had a stroke, it was unlikely she would recover fully, if at all.

Grace was thinking how Mrs Mortimer would cope if she had had a stroke. Would she be able to come home? The thought of her dying would creep up on her but Grace would shoo it away. She refused to think of her friend dying. She could still go on for another twenty years. Grace would start to feel more emotional at the thought of the old lady asking for her. Grace knew they were close but they never talked about it. Mrs Mortimer wasn't the type to discuss feelings and Grace knew that if she ever brought it up then Mrs Mortimer would chase her out of the house and swear at her up the street. It didn't need to be said though; she knew Mrs Mortimer loved her and that was enough.

Grace was grateful that her mum did not speak much in the car. Flynn was also quiet as he sensed something was wrong with his master. He jumped on her lap and stayed still for the rest of the journey.

The sat nav took them straight to the hospital and they soon found a space in the car park. They had no choice but to leave Flynn in his basket on the back seat and Grace assured him she would be back in an hour as he settled in his basket, curling up in his usual position.

'I have to say, Grace, Flynn is a very good dog. Funny looking but good,' said Penny with a wry smile. Grace looked at her mum and smirked at her softening opinion.

They headed straight for 'O' Wing lift as per Big Mick's instruction. Grace started to become very nervous. She had no idea what to expect when she arrived. Mick hadn't phoned since telling her to come and she'd been too frightened to call in case there had been any changes. If there had been changes she wasn't sure she would be able to cope with hearing them on the M5.

They stepped from the lift and immediately Grace could see the top of Big Mick's head through a partition glassed seating area. As she approached, Mick looked up and relief swept across his face when he saw her. She immediately embraced him and he muttered a hello to Penny.

'What happened, then?' asked Grace.

'She called me in the night to say she had fell over going

to the toilet. She couldn't get herself back up and wanted to know if I could pop in and get her back in the bed like. Patsy came with me. I'm glad she did, Grace. Jesus, she was in a right state on the floor. I don't know what I would have done if Pats hadn't been there. You could tell from looking at her that something was wrong straight away,' Mick moved closer to Grace and whispered, 'she'd had an accident, not making the toilet, you know.' Grace just nodded. 'Anyway, Pats cleaned her up while we waited for an ambulance. I thought I should just bring her in the car but Patsy said she might have broken something and we would have made it worse if we moved her. Oh, Grace, she was in pain. Broke me heart to see her like that. Pats went with her in the ambulance and she said she just kept asking for you. She was swearing at the paramedic and kept asking where you were.'

Grace started to feel guilty. Why did she go to her parents' this weekend of all weekends?

'She's in a side ward. I'll take you to her.'

He started to move down a corridor and both women silently followed. 'She marked you down as next of kin so they are waiting for you. I said you were on your way.'

They arrived at a large Reception area and a nurse looked up and immediately replaced the handset to the phone.

'Hi, my name is Grace Hammond. I'm here to see Kate Mortimer,' said Grace nervously.

'Ah, Miss Hammond, I was just trying to phone you again. I left a couple of messages on your answerphone,' said the kindly-faced nurse. Grace could not remember her phone ringing while travelling to the hospital and then she recollected her phone was in the holdall which was in the boot.

'I'm sorry; I didn't have my phone on me. Is everything all right?' Mild panic was setting in. What if she was too late?

'I'll take you to see her. She has been asking for you,' the nurse looked at Mick and Penny. 'I'm afraid I can only let Miss Hammond see her at this moment.' Mick bowed his head in agreement and then looked at Penny.

'Fancy a cup of tea, downstairs?' asked Mick. Penny nodded and looked at Grace. Penny's face said a million things. *Be brave. Don't cry. Be prepared. I love you.* Grace watched them turn and walk away while the nurse walked on a bit further to a door and looked at Grace expectantly.

'Is she awake?' asked Grace.

'She's drifting in and out. We had to put her on morphine so she could cope with the pain.' The nurse opened the door and Grace took a deep breath and followed her.

Mrs Mortimer was in a small room and the sun was streaming in making it much brighter than it should have felt. There was a cabinet to one side of the bed and a large chair to the other and the room smelled of hand sanitiser and boiled potatoes. Grace gasped at how tiny her friend looked in the bed. She had the frame of a child and had barely disturbed the covers with her being. The nurse moved to one side of the bed and bent over the patient to tell her Grace had arrived. The old lady stirred and opened her eyes and fixed her gaze on Grace. The nurse smiled at Grace and silently left the room.

She stood for a moment and then tiptoed toward the woman who was still staring at her. Grace pulled the chair closer to the bed and sought the old lady's hand to hold.

'You know this room smells of school dinners,' murmured Grace. Mrs Mortimer turned her head in

Grace's direction and smiled.

'Fucking stinks, doesn't it?' croaked the old lady. Grace wanted to cry.

'Don't start crying. I need to talk to you,' she insisted. Grace stayed silent. Mrs Mortimer collected her thoughts, her bravery and knew that as soon as she said what she had to say then her friendship with this lovely woman would never be the same. She looked at Grace and took a breath.

'Grace…I didn't have a stroke,' the relief that Grace felt was very short lived, 'I've got lung cancer.' Mrs Mortimer couldn't believe she was having to tell her best friend this. She had kept it from her for some time now. The doctor had sent her for further tests as her cough was getting worse and he was worried when she started to show other symptoms. She had taken a bus on her own to get the results and was not shocked when they delivered the news. They seemed more shocked when she said she didn't want any treatment. What was the point? She felt as old as Father Time and was as lonely as the man on the moon since Mort was taken from her. She had taken a taxi back home from the hospital and thought about who she should tell. Obviously, she would need to tell Grace and see if she would take Benji in. But the thought of telling her friend made her start to cry at the back of the taxi and once she started she couldn't stop. The taxi driver enquired after her and she had growled at him to mind his own business and to do his job.

She knew that Grace was fond of her and would miss her and she realised that she was more afraid of telling Grace than she was of actually dying. She welcomed death because death brought her love.

And now here she was telling her. She had no choice now and she regretted not telling her in Primrose Cottage with a cup of Grace's lovely tea in her hand instead of telling her from a hospital bed with a bag of her urine hanging off the rail.

'How long have you known? Because you have known before all of this happened, haven't you?' Grace felt frustrated.

'You try telling someone you love that you're dying. Even when you can't stand them most of the time,' coughed Mrs Mortimer. Grace stood up, reacting to her cough. She looked at the patient, not sure what to do.

'Sit down,' the old lady waved her gently to the chair, 'I've been coughing for what feels like a goddamn lifetime. Don't start looking worried now.' Mrs Mortimer controlled her coughing to a clearing throat action and then her breathing returned to normal.

'Listen to me, Grace; I have all my papers in the armoire in the lounge in case anything happens to me. There's also a note in there addressed to you. It only asks if you will have Benji for me when I go?' she turned expectantly at Grace.

'You're not going! You hear me, woman?' Grace started to fill up again. She bowed her head and looked at her feet. She didn't want Mrs Mortimer to see her tears. 'Seriously, how long have you known?'

'Four months.'

'Four months? And you couldn't tell me. How have you been getting your treatment?' asked Grace.   The woman stayed silent and looked at Grace.

'Tell me you have been getting some treatment?' Again the woman said nothing. Grace jumped from the chair and started to pace backwards and forwards at the foot of the bed.

'You stupid sod! Why would you not have treatment?

Is that why you didn't tell me because you knew I would haul your arse up here for your appointments? You should have told me! You should have said something!' Grace couldn't hold back the tears and she didn't care. 'All that time I've been coming to yours drinking bloody tea and you've sat there! Smoking your head off, knowing that you were going to die and you said nothing! You had no right! You should have told me. I'm you're bloody friend and that's what you're supposed to tell your mates. You don't sit there and keep bloody secrets like that from them. I suppose you went on your own to get the results, eh? And I was probably sat at home eating fucking pizza or getting a bollocking off my boss for doing nothing and all the time you are in here getting told you have lung cancer! And you said nothing!' Grace was bordering on hysteria and she knew she had to calm down. The old lady watched Grace walk out of the room and slam the door.

Grace stood outside the room and felt like her world was crumbling around her. She had no idea until now just how much she truly loved this woman. Grace placed the palms of her hands against the door and started to try and control her tears and her breathing. Once she calmed herself down she wiped her face and opened the door again.

Mrs Mortimer was still awake and her expression did not change when Grace entered the room.

'Sorry,' whispered Grace. The old lady smiled and Grace walked back to the chair and sat down.

'Will you take Benji for me?'

'Of course.'

'There's a list of people in my papers you need to contact and there is also a list of the things I want for my funeral.' Grace hung her head.

'Yes, I know it's fucking morbid but I'm trusting you girl,' she squeezed Grace's hand. 'Please, Grace.'

'I'm sorry, whatever you want. Just tell me and I'll do it. No more secrets.'

Mrs Mortimer turned her head and looked at the ceiling. She stared for a long time and eventually said, 'Promise me you'll stay with me.'

'I won't leave you, I promise,' Grace gently raised Mrs Mortimer's hand and kissed the back of it. Mrs Mortimer closed her eyes and in a short time her breathing suggested she was sleeping. Grace stayed still and studied her friend's face. The face was lined but was as soft as a peach and the long eyelashes that rested on her cheek told you that she was beautiful. The hand she held was light as air but the age clearly showed in the creped skin mottled with liver spots and bumpy veins.

She sat for a while until the door opened and the familiar nurse told her that her mum was back outside. Mrs Mortimer did not stir as she left the room. Big Mick was also stood outside waiting.

'How is she?' asked Mick immediately.

'Oh Mick, it wasn't a stroke. She has lung cancer,' cried Grace.

'Oh dear God.' Mick was visibly shocked.

'Apparently, she's known for four bloody months. Can you believe it?' said Grace through her tears. Penny walked over to Grace and gave her a hug. Grace wiped her tears and tried to compose herself.

'Mick, can you do me a favour? Would you be able to take Flynn for me for a bit? He's no trouble…' Mick raised his hand to shush her.

'I'll take Flynn and I'd best get Benji too. They're no bother. Patsy will be glad to have them,' said Mick.

'Oh God, Benji. I forgot about him. He'll be fretting for her,' sniffed Grace.

'Your mum said that Flynn was in your car. New car, eh?' Grace nodded weakly. 'Well, I'll fetch him and his bits and bobs out of your car and he can come home with me. Your mum said she can run me back to the pub. Patsy took the car back earlier while I waited for you,' explained Big Mick.

'Darling, why don't you come back with me? I'm sure Mrs Mortimer will be asleep for most of the day,' suggested Penny.

'No Mum, I'm staying here. I said I wouldn't leave her,' Grace said flatly.

'Okay,' replied Penny. They stood to collect their thoughts.

'I'll take Mick back to his pub and I'll pass Flynn's things over to him. Can I bring anything back for you from your cottage?' asked Penny. Grace thought for a moment.

'I don't need anything but she will,' Grace started to make a mental list. 'Can you go with Mick when you collect Benji and pick up some stuff for her? In her bedside cabinet are her clean nighties. Her underwear is in the top drawer of the big chest of drawers. Her dressing gown is on the door but I'm not sure if it will be clean. Take the one hanging in my bathroom, that's clean. She'll need her toothbrush and a couple of towels. Oh, and there's some Ponds cream on her dressing table, she likes that. And soap, she likes Lily of the Valley. She might have some in the bathroom, if not you'll need to run to Nell's, she'll have some in. Do you think she will need her slippers? Best bring them in case.' Grace tried to sound hopeful. 'Put them all in the holdall I brought to yours, Mum.'

'I'll need to write all that down!' Penny started

rummaging in her bag for her pen and notebook and started scribbling like an excited journalist as soon as she found them.

'I take it you have keys to her cottage, Mick?' asked Grace.

'I had to kick her back door panel in and Patsy climbed through to let me in. I had no choice,' shrugged Mick.

'What's covering the hole?' squeaked Penny.

'The telly,' said Mick flatly. Penny and Grace both rolled their eyes.

'It was the only thing big enough to block the hole! What the hell do you want me to do at three in the morning? I'll sort it as soon as I get the dogs settled in the pub,' Mick promised.

'Right then, there are some keys behind the clock on my mantelpiece, keep hold of them.' Big Mick nodded at the instruction. 'And Mum, there's a picture on her mantelpiece of a man by a plane and there's another one of Benji further along. Can you put them both in the bag for her?' Penny returned to scribbling on her pad.

'I think that's it for now, except my phone. Can you bring my phone back with you Mum and if I need anything else is it okay if I ask you or Patsy to bring them for her?' Grace asked Mick.

'Of course,' he stepped forward and gave Grace a hug. She looked diminutive in his arms.

'Right well, you'd best be off. Poor Flynn will be dying for a wee no doubt. Probably already ruined my new car,' joked Grace feebly.

They each in turn gave Grace a kiss and left her with confidence that they would do as she asked. Grace walked over to the Reception area to the nice nurse she saw earlier.

'Can I have a word please?' asked Grace.

'Yes, of course.' The nurse left her station and joined Grace and waited for her to speak.

'I just wanna know how she really is?' Grace asked flatly.

'The doctor is just on the open ward. They'll be able to explain everything to you. They won't be a minute. They're just with the last patient now and then Mrs Mortimer is next. Why don't you wait in the lounge and I'll send someone in to see you.' Grace looked apprehensive at the suggestion. 'I promise it'll only be a few minutes.'

Grace thanked the nurse and walked slowly to the door marked 'Lounge' to wait for the doctor. Grace entered the room and saw that it was furnished with a small couch, a couple of armchairs and a coffee table littered with curly cornered magazines. Grace sat down and waited for the doctor. She sat listening intently to the noises outside and read the covers of the magazines and wondered who believed you could 'lose a stone in a week'.

CHAPTER 11

She heard her friend's door open in the corridor and shut and hoped it was the doctor looking at her. After what felt like an age, the door to the lounge opened and in came the doctor. To Grace's surprise she was female and Grace was comforted by that.

'Hello, Miss Hammond. I'm Dr Alison Rimmer. Mrs Mortimer is my patient.' She offered her hand for Grace to shake and Grace reciprocated. 'I understand you are her next of kin.' The doctor tapped on her iPad as she checked the information.

'I'm not family, I'm just a friend really. We're close like, but not related. I didn't know she marked me down as her next of kin until earlier. She never told me. Funny isn't it, how you find out?' Grace realised she wasn't letting the doctor speak. 'I'm sorry, I'm babbling.'

'Well, just because you are not related doesn't mean that you are not family. That's what I say, anyway.' The doctor smiled and hoped it would help Grace relax.

'Miss Hammond, I wish I had good news but I'm sure you have gathered that we are nearly at the end of the road with our lovely Mrs Mortimer.'

'I've only just found out that she has lung cancer,' whispered Grace.

The doctor looked at Grace and set her iPad down on top of the magazines. Situations like this were rare but not unusual.

'Miss Hammond, Mrs Mortimer is now at stage four and has refused treatment. We can only offer further palliative care.' Doctor Rimmer paused and studied Grace. She wasn't reacting at all, which wasn't strange when someone was in shock. She went back to her iPad, 'May I ask, do you live with her?'

'No, I'm her neighbour. I look in on her most days,' replied Grace.

'So, you haven't noticed if her appetite has waned at all?' asked the doctor.

'Not really, but when I am with her we mainly drink tea to be honest. I have noticed that she seemed less energetic. She would take her dog out and be really tired afterward and I suppose she has lost a bit of weight but I just put that down to her being frail looking. I mean she is 82 after all,' said Grace.

'And a heavy smoker by all accounts,' said the doctor. Grace just nodded as if it was her that had just been caught smoking, having a sneaky fag behind the bike sheds.

'Miss Hammond, your friend doesn't have long, a few days at best. She is on morphine to help with her pain.'

'Sorry, I don't understand. How can she be dying? Surely she has longer? I mean she was only diagnosed four months ago,' insisted Grace.

'When she saw her GP, she was already in considerable pain then. Even at that stage our options probably would have been the same. But we may have been able to slow any growth down, but she insisted on refusing treatment. We have upped her painkillers progressively and I understand she is on oxygen at home.' She continued to read from her notes. 'Sarah, her community nurse has said she still continues to smoke.'

'Well, what's the bloody point of giving up now?' Grace barked.

'No point probably at this stage, but I didn't say that,' she said with a smile.

'I didn't know she was having a community nurse come round.'

'It seems to be that there are a lot of things that she has kept from you. Her notes do say actually that she has no family and lives on her own,' the doctor continued to look at the iPad for more information. 'She also has a home help that comes in each day. Where you aware of that?' asked Dr Rimmer.

'No,' whispered Grace. Grace started to think there was so much she didn't know about her friend and felt hurt that she had not confided in her so she could help. She had never noticed there was anything different and any changes she had seen she had simply put down to old age and her being a cranky Yank.

'I need to continue with my rounds. If you have any questions just ask one of the staff or I can speak to you when I next see Mrs Mortimer. I think you may need to speak to her and discuss a few things.' Dr Rimmer stood up and smiled at Grace.

'Can I bring her home?'

'If that's what she wants we can arrange it but only if someone is with her all the time,' she advised.

'I'll be staying with her. All the time I mean,' assured Grace.

'Do you work?'

'I do, but I can take a leave of absence. It's fine,' Grace could feel her throat closing. 'I want to do this. Just tell me what I need to do.'

'We need to speak to Mrs Mortimer and make sure she is happy with this and then we need to make some calls about your support.'

Grace just nodded and the doctor gave her a gentle pat on the shoulder.

'Like I said, go and speak to her and see what she thinks. I'll speak to you later and we can see what needs to be arranged.'

Doctor Rimmer left the lounge with Grace standing in the middle of the stark, empty room feeling shell-shocked. She needed to convince Mrs Mortimer that she would look after her and try and get her out of this hospital.

Grace made her way back to Mrs Mortimer's room and as she sat down, the old lady stirred and woke.

'Hey,' said Grace gently. The old lady looked at Grace's face. The doctor had obviously spoken to her and even though Grace looked upset she knew it was a face she could trust.

'So how long have I got, kid?' Her voice was coarse and gravelly.

'They don't know, do they?' Grace tried to sound upbeat. 'You'll probably go on for years yet.

'You always were a shit liar, Grace. You know how I know when you're lying. Your voice goes up like a novice drag queen. What did the goddamn doc say?' she growled.

'She said...' Grace swallowed her tears. 'She said...if you want to....you could go home, but only if I move in with you. You know for a bit. Help you go the toilet and get your food and stuff.' Grace was looking at the ceiling trying to keep the tears from rolling down her face.

'I don't need you to wipe my shit!' Mrs Mortimer started coughing and Grace shot up and grabbed some tissues for her to cough into. Once it started to subside she fell back into the pillow.

'Look Grace, you ain't coming to the cottage and that's final,' she barked. Grace was slightly stunned but then started to feel angry with her. There was no way she was leaving her in here and there was no way she was going home on her own.

'Look lady, you've bossed me around for the last three years and I've took your abuse and your shit and your crap and nearly every bloody day I sit in your house stinking of fags. I don't want to bloody come and wipe your shit as you say but someone has to look after Benji!'

Mrs Mortimer's eyes grew slightly wider as she thought about her beloved dog. Grace stayed silent and let the old lady muster over her outburst.

Mrs Mortimer knew she needed someone and she knew this was the end. When she imagined herself dying, she never imagined she would die in a soulless room in a bed where a million other people had took their last breath. She was being offered to be cared for by her best friend and she would be surrounded by all her things and, of course, her much-loved dog. She turned her head and looked at Grace. Her darling Grace that had indeed took a lot from her over the years and yet she still came back with tea and kisses.

'You ain't being no carer, okay? We are gonna be like roomies?' insisted Mrs Mortimer.

'Okay,' sniffed Grace.

'Like Betty Grable and Lauren Bacall in How to Marry a Millionaire. You seen that film?' Grace nodded and smiled. 'You think Nell would make a Marilyn Monroe?'

They both started to giggle. Mrs Mortimer started to mull over the practicalities of it all. With Grace in the spare room next to hers would be a comfort on its own after last night's upset. She could also get rid of Elsa, her horrible home help who stank of fish and had dirty fingernails.

'What about your job, Grace?' asked Mrs Mortimer.

'Don't worry. I can get a leave of absence and I've got a bit put away and everything will be fine.' Grace was trying to convince herself more than her friend. But even if Bill wouldn't grant her leave she would simply walk out of the job. Life was too short. Crowley had taught her that in the few days she had known him.

'When the doctor comes, I need you tell her that you want to come home and I need to tell them that I will be taking care of you. As well as the community nurse and the home help,' Grace dropped that in. Mrs Mortimer turned to her with a guilty look of an adulterous wife. Grace's face did not show any sign of hurt or rejection. 'Of course, Flynn will need to come with me.'

'Of course,' she whispered softly. Grace grabbed Mrs Mortimer's hand and pressed the back of it against her cheek.

'You get some sleep now. You must be tired turning into a landlady there in your bed. I'll be here when you wake up, Mrs M,' said Grace. Mrs Mortimer turned her head away from Grace and closed her eyes.

'If we are going to be roomies you best call me Kate,' she let out a long breath. 'Or Betty.' Kate fell asleep with the smile still on her face.

In Pelsby, Penny let herself into Primrose Cottage with Big Mick behind her. It felt peculiar to be in a stranger's house. It felt more strange to Penny to be in a house that was so familiar to Grace. Big Mick soon found Benji shut in the living room and went to the kitchen to find his bowls and food. Once he had found them, he scooped up the dog into his armpit and told Penny to drop the keys back at the pub so he could come back and sort the back door.

Once he left, Penny walked around the cottage like a tentative burglar. She noted that the cottage was bigger than her daughter's and yet it seemed cosier. Maybe, that was because everywhere was littered with ornaments and pictures. Penny seemed terrified at first to disturb anything and felt very uncomfortable just being there. She retrieved the list from her bag and made her way upstairs with the empty holdall swinging at her knees. She found the old lady's bedroom immediately. She spied an oxygen tank to the side of the bed and various tablet containers on a small silver tray on the bed stand. She started to look through the drawers to find the requested items and sure enough everything was where Grace said it would be. Penny stopped for a moment and felt slightly sad that her own daughter had no idea where she kept her underwear or nightwear. She doubted if Grace knew her favourite soap was English Pear by Jo Malone or her night cream was by Estee Lauder. Should a daughter know this of her mother? Should she confide to her daughter that there was a drawer of underwear crammed with her favourite knickers? Dai always bought her lovely soft lace bras and matching knickers in the finest silk when he wanted to treat her but she was happier in a big pair of Sloggi's and she wondered if she needed to tell Grace this before she died. Should she tell Grace she preferred tights? How much do you need to tell your daughter in case you become incapacitated? Should she tell Grace about a rather thick hair that often spiralled out of her chin that she would need to pluck if she was ever struck down by a stroke?

Penny continued to pack the bag and occasionally stopped to inspect a photo. Some of the photos looked like they had been taken by a professional. Penny was impressed the way the mood had been captured in a lot of the shots. She made her way downstairs and found the two photographs that had been specifically requested of Mort and Benji and she put them in the bag with the rest of the things. Once satisfied she had everything, she locked up and stepped outside to be greeted by a gnarly and angry looking man. He seemed to try to soften when he realised that Penny was a little taken aback by his presence.

'Sorry,' he growled, 'didn't mean to frighten you.' Penny stood still and remained quiet. 'The name's Cousins. I'm from the farm, up there,' he pointed to his left. 'I take it you're her family. I erm…heard she had a fall. Is she all right?' Mr Cousins asked.

'She's in St Bernadette's. She may be in for some time. I've just come to collect some things and then take them back to the hospital for her,' Penny stepped forward to make her way to the pub. She found Mr Cousins unnerving. 'If you'll excuse me, I need to see the gentleman in the pub.' She made her way past him and started toward the pub.

'Mick?' he snarled.

'Yes, the BIG gentleman,' Penny emphasised her stature to ensure that if this Mr Cousins had any funny ideas she had a knight in shining armour at her disposal.

'Does Grace know?' he called after her as she went to continue down the street. Penny stopped and turned to look at him. He was still stood at the end of Primrose Cottage's gate. 'She lives in the end cottage on that row,' and he pointed to Grace's cottage, 'the one with the erm...white door there,' he trailed off.

'Grace is my daughter and she is with Mrs Mortimer as we speak,' Penny said. Who was this funny little man, she thought.

'Close see. They are. If you could say I was ....erm....asking after them,' he doffed an imaginary cap and then scurried off in the direction of Pool Farm.

Penny watched and concluded his demeanour was not as sinister as his appearance suggested. She turned back to the pub and made her way back to the village.

After dropping the keys into The Blacky and picking up some bits from Grace's cottage, Penny called Dai to ask him to start his journey to collect her from St Bernadette's. He seemed relieved to be able to get on the road and be with his girls.

Over the next few hours, Kate remained asleep while Grace liaised with the staff to sort out about getting her home. After they had made calls to the GP and Social Services, all parties agreed that she could go home in an ambulance as soon as they felt she was stable enough.

Grace met with a small team of nurses who saturated her with information on what to do, what not to do, signs to look for, her medications, telephone numbers and emotions and by the end, she felt utterly exhausted.

When she walked back to Kate's room, her mum was waiting for her at the bedside. Kate was still asleep and Grace noted that her mum also looked tired. Penny stood and embraced Grace and ushered her to the chair she had just vacated. She then emptied the bag to check the contents were correct and passed on all the messages she had received in her short time in the village. Grace thanked her then gave her a blow by blow account of what had been happening the last four months and that Kate was nearing the end.

'So, I'm moving in to her cottage to stay with her until...' Grace couldn't finish the sentence. Penny interrupted.

'Grace, have you thought this through? My dear, this is a huge undertaking for anyone. But why you? No offence, but you are not even family,' she said dismissively.

'This woman IS family to me!' snapped Grace. Penny looked shocked by her daughter's reaction. She didn't realise her daughter felt so strongly or passionately about this old lady.

'You know what I mean, Grace,' barked Penny.

'I might not be related to her by blood but all I know is that when I need someone to talk to, she is there. When I am sick and yes that includes bloody hangovers, she is there. When I need a favour with Flynn or the cottage or anything, she is there. She is always there and she doesn't …..she doesn't….' Grace was struggling for words and to keep the tears back.

'She doesn't want anything back,' said Crowley behind her. Grace didn't turn but the relief she felt was enormous.

'She doesn't want anything back,' repeated Grace. She stared at her mum who was lost for words and quickly dropped her eyes from Grace's gaze. Grace felt a squeeze of Crowley's hand on her shoulder and as she slowly cast her gaze over her shoulder to acknowledge him, she realised he was gone.

'I'm sorry, Grace. I know you love her very much and I think you are doing a wonderful thing,' said Penny quietly.

Grace cast her gaze back to Kate who was wide awake and staring at Grace with a smile on her face. 'Shit, I've woken her up with my shouting. How much of that did she hear? It doesn't matter anyway, I meant every word', she thought.

Grace knew she had touched a nerve and had probably hurt her mum but even still, she needed her to know just how much this woman meant to her. She wasn't just a neighbour that she popped in to see. This woman knew more about her than her own mum did. And yes, that was a shame, but that's just the way it was and it didn't matter how much Penny pouted, it didn't change the fact that this 82-year-old woman understood her better than her own mum ever would.

Grace looked down at Kate again who was still smiling.

'Who was the James Bond lookalike in the room before?' asked the old lady.

CHAPTER 12

Penny looked at the old lady dying in the bed and wondered if at the end of her life would she start to see things herself? Penny recalled that she had read somewhere that toward the end you start to regress and things that happened a long time ago can feel like they only just occurred. This woman was clearly at the end of her time and it gave Penny comfort to see that Kate was very calm and didn't seem the slightest bit confused.

However, over on Grace's side of the room, Grace was starting to sweat and she wasn't sure if it contributed to Kate's question or the fact that she hadn't put deodorant on that morning due to the panic of getting to St Bernadette's.

'What do you mean, sweetheart?' asked Grace.

'I know you saw him, Grace! You repeated what he told you to say to your mum! I might be dying but I'm not fucking deaf!' Kate barked.

Grace looked at her mum who was half perched on a windowsill looking at Mrs Mortimer with a face of pity. Penny turned to Grace with a hang-dog expression. Penny

191

clearly wasn't buying the story and as she looked at her mum she shrugged her shoulders as if to say, 'she's as batty as a fruitcake'.

Kate watched her two visitors and then started to doubt what she had seen. Maybe she thought she heard the man first. Maybe, he wasn't there. Surely the girls would have seen him too. But there was something about him and why did Grace turn when he touched her? It must be the drugs.

'Take no notice of the old broad about to die. She's high on morphine and seeing tall dark handsome men. Come to think of it, I recommend dying to anyone,' Kate giggled hoarsely. 'God, I need a Bogey.' Grace looked at her mum who looked confused and repulsed.

'A cigarette, not snot,' advised Grace. Her mum nodded and smiled with relief and then the door opened. The nurse was stood in the doorway and told Penny that Dai was waiting outside. Penny immediately ran out of the room to see him. Grace looked down at Kate who was still awake.

'You seen that doctor, kid? I gotta get outta here,' whispered Kate.

'I'm just going to pop outside and see my dad and then I'll find out what's happening, okay? I also want to phone Big Mick and see if he's sorted your door out. I won't be a tick.' Grace squeezed Kate's hand and stepped out of the room.

Her parents were stood outside and Penny was giving him an update and what had happened so far. Her dad immediately came over and embraced Grace.

'I'm so sorry, Darling; I know you are very close to her. And can I just say how commendable it is that you are going to look after her.' He cast his eye toward Penny. 'It's a very brave thing to do. I know there's nothing we can do but if you do think of anything, I'm only a short drive away.'

'Thanks, Dad,' she sighed.

'Do you think she is expecting me to go in?' he asked. The two women in unison said no and assured Dai that she was too tired anyway.

'She's started seeing things...' whispered Penny to Dai, 'men!' Dai looked at Grace with concern.

'Typical of her,' laughed Grace, 'she's moaning about the two things she's missing most. Fags and men.' They all started to wonder what two things they would ask for at the end. Grace knew it would be her bed and Flynn while her mum was deciding on champagne and a decent manicure. Her dad was still making his mind up between Sophia Loren and Ava Gardner.

Her parents decided there was no point in hanging around and would start to make the journey back to Cornwall. They figured they would stop somewhere on the way and have a light supper as it would be late by the time they reached Breeze Point. Grace thanked them profusely for all they had done for her that day, especially her mum whom she would have been lost without. She watched them leave in the lift and then walked back towards the reception desk on Mrs Mortimer's ward. A different nurse was on shift now. A huge black woman, that looked like she wasn't afraid of second helpings or diabetes, turned to face her.

'Hi,' said Grace nervously, 'I'm just wondering if any arrangements have been made for Kate Mortimer. She's in room 10. There,' pointed Grace to the door.

'I know where room 10 is!' the woman snapped in a Caribbean accent. Grace raised her eyebrows but held her tongue. The woman started clicking away at the computer.

'Okay, it looks like she will be allowed home tomorrow if she is fine through the night. It also looks like you have seen the Discharge Coordinator downstairs and they've set a few things in motion. So really, as long as she has a good night, she may be able to be discharged tomorrow.' Grace stood for a while trying to absorb the information and also realised that she was going to be spending the night here.

'I want to stay with her, is that all right?' asked Grace. The nurse seemed softer now and answered.

'You can stay, but there's only a chair in there. I can get you a foot rest so you can stretch out a bit and a pillow and some blankets,' offered the nurse. Grace was relieved that she could stay. It was unlikely she would sleep so didn't care about the chair.

'Oh, thank you. Really, that means a lot. I don't want to leave her, see,' said Grace.

'I'm just going in there now to do her obs,' she said. The large woman stood and made her way toward the room and looked at Grace for her to join her.

'You Welsh?' she asked.

'I am. But I live not far from Lanson now. You sound a long way from home as well,' said Grace.

'Born in Jamaica, lived in the States and now my gypsy blood brings me to England, the Land of Damp.' Grace laughed but the nurse looked less than happy as they walked into Kate's room. She was awake and looked surprised.

'Tell me you can see this one!' Kate croaked to Grace.

'Hallo, Mrs Mortimer. You can probably see me from the International Space Station,' the nurse chortled at her own joke, not realising the reference. 'Now, I'm Olive,' shouted the nurse in a thick Jamaican accent, 'and I'll be looking after you until the morning, okay? Can you sit up for me a bit? Lying down like that will make your cough worse.' Olive started to shift the pillows and pulled Kate lightly up the bed. When Kate lay back down, she was sitting more upright and seemed to look a little fresher.

'Am I going home yet? I need to get outta this goddamn joint. The smell of this place will kill me before the cancer,' she moaned.

'You should be able to go home tomorrow, Mrs Mortimer,' Olive yelled.

'Why the hell are you shouting, woman? Do I look deaf to you? Do I look confused in any way as to what the hell you are talking about? No, I don't! So stop bellowing down my ear! This is a hospital not a goddamn construction site!' barked Kate.

'I'm sorry, Mrs Mortimer. Not everyone is blessed with good hearing on this ward so I just shout at everyone. Apologies. Anyway, how does an American and a Welsh girl end up being friends?' Olive busied herself with the blood pressure band.

'Bad luck!' Kate snorted. She clearly wasn't impressed with Olive.

'We live in the same village...unfortunately,' Grace gazed at the old lady as if to tell her off. Olive picked up that Grace was chastising the old lady and found it amusing.

'How long you been in England, Mrs Mortimer? I used to live in New Jersey years back,' announced Olive.

'You did, huh? I went there once. Got lost, so I didn't go back again,' Kate said dismissively. 'I'm from Lenox Hill. Lived there until I left for Washington to become a photographer,' said Kate. Olive removed the blood pressure pad and started to write her chart. 'Did you like it there?' asked Kate.

'I did, but I came here for me son. Married an English girl. Lovely child has given me three beautiful grandchildren so I'll end my days here, no doubt about that,' Grace smiled at the nurse.

'Right, Mrs Mortimer, everything is okay. I'll be back in a bit to change the bag on your catheter,' she turned to look at Grace, 'I'll be back with the pillows and blankets as well.' She smiled and shut the door.

'Don't leave me with her, Grace. If she gets hungry she'll eat me,' joked the old lady.

'Don't be horrible. Anyway, a greedy cannibal wouldn't want you! You're all skin and bone.' Grace pulled the chair up to the bed again and sat down. 'She said I could stay the night. So, no farting or shouting in your sleep about how much you want to snog Frank Sinatra,' Grace laughed.

'Only if he sings Fly Me to the Moon; I ain't easy, ya know!' chortled Kate.

'Try and go back to sleep. Long night ahead of us I think. I'm just popping outside a mo. I need to phone Big Mick and see how our babies are doing, yeah? I'll be back.'

Grace left the room and headed for the lounge which was thankfully empty, to call Mick. She was relieved to hear the dogs were fine and the door panel had been replaced and she asked if someone could pop round to the cottage and put some milk in the fridge for a cuppa when they got home.

The night indeed was long and by three am. Grace decided to not bother trying to sleep. She sat and watched her friend in the soft light that came from the internal window in the room. Now and again, Grace could see Olive moving around and would occasionally hear her on the phone. Grace started to think about the few days that lay ahead and felt apprehensive as to whether she would be able to take care of her friend properly. One thing that did give her some comfort was knowing that she had great support from anyone in the village. In the dark, Grace could feel a tear running down her cheek and then her hand being held. It was Crowley. He was sat next to her on the footstool she had discarded earlier.

'I didn't call you,' she whispered.

'I know, but figured you could do with a friend right now,' he whispered back.

'I think she saw you before,' remembered Grace.

'I doubt it, my dear,' he said dismissively.

'No, honestly. She said you looked like James Bond!' Grace insisted. Crowley was a bit taken aback as he remembered he was wearing a tux with a dickie bow at the time. Surely, this old woman couldn't see him as well.

'I may need to speak to someone about that,' he mused. Grace turned to look at Kate who was sleeping soundly aided by the oxygen mask.

'They say she hasn't got long. I'm taking her home; hopefully tomorrow so she can...you know...in her own home.' They stayed silent for a moment. 'She said she's missing Benji but I think she just wants to get out for a cigarette,' smiled Grace. She continued to think about Mrs Mortimer dying.

'Will she have to do something as well, when she leaves us? I mean, like you?' asked Grace.

'Without a doubt.' Crowley sat further back on the stool and leant against the wall. 'Have you heard of a thing called fate?'

'Course I have,' replied Grace.

'Well, not all things are down to fate, some things are down to us,' he pointed upwards. 'If you hadn't missed that bus, then you would never have met the love of your life. If you hadn't bought that cat that went into the garden of your dream home, then you would never have discovered it and bought the house. Sometimes we intervene and you are not even aware we do it. But sometimes it ends up like me and you where the living are aware of it. Why is there a difference? I do not know and it doesn't seem to matter if we don't know what the deed is in the first place.' Grace mulled over what he had just said.

'Do you think your deed may have something to do with her?' asked Grace.

'We shall see,' hiccupped Crowley. Grace rolled her eyes.

'You drunk again?' she asked.

'Just a bit merry...which is a poor choice of adjective, given the current circumstances. I've just been having a quiet one with some of the boys. Nothing too boisterous,' he whispered.

Grace and Crowley talked for the next couple of hours about Mrs Mortimer and living out those winter years on your own. Grace was very careful not to poke at memories hidden in Crowley's mind of homelessness and the loss of his own family. He stayed quiet when Olive came in to attend to Kate and made no comment on her departure.

The room started to brighten up and Grace noticed that the noise outside was increasing slightly. The new day had arrived and though the night had been long she had been grateful for Crowley's company.

'Thanks for staying the last few hours. I'd have been so bored if you hadn't been here,' she said gratefully. 'I don't think 'them upstairs' had in mind you should be sitting with me with a dying old woman, somehow. We need to find out what this deed is so you can move on and be with your own loved ones and I can look after her,' muttered Grace.

'Your priority is to her. The rest will happen when it happens. We can't jig something along when we don't know what it is. And to be honest, I'm having a marvellous time in the interim so stop worrying about me.'

Kate began to stir in the bed as if she was about to wake up.

'I'll go now. Chin up for today,' Crowley gently pushed Grace's chin, 'and I shall see you later, my dear.' And he went.

'Is that you, Grace?' Kate croaked.

'I'm just here,' Grace took her hand and kissed it.

Neither of the girls were very hungry when they were offered breakfast. The potato smell had increased with the noise levels and they could only presume that the smell related to whatever they were being offered. Olive insisted that Mrs Mortimer had to eat something so they opted for a little porridge and a cup of tea. When it came, Grace had to cajole her to eat half of it even though it looked like it was only fit for wallpaper adhesive but she drank the tea without fuss.

Various doctors and nurses came in over the course of the morning to look at her notes and discuss the discharge plan. Everyone seemed happy enough for her to go home and the community nurse was scheduled to come to Primrose Cottage later that day. It was all systems go and both girls were relieved that they could get back to Pelsby.

Grace called Big Mick to tell him to leave her keys behind a plant pot so they could get in straight away without nipping to the pub first. Mick explained that he and Patsy had sorted the house and asked for Grace to call as soon as they reached the bridge in Pelsby. Grace was touched by their concern and promised she would.

The nice nurse from the day before called Steph kept them updated as the morning went on and told them to be packed and ready for the ambulance to take her home. Grace explained to Kate that she would follow in her car as it was still in the car park from when her mum had left it the day before.

'The porter will be along in a moment with a wheelchair to take you to the ambulance,' said Steph.

'There's nothing wrong with my legs!' Kate snapped.

'I know, but you need the oxygen as well and we don't want you getting out of breath now, do we? So just enjoy the ride, otherwise you can always stay here another night,' Steph looked at Kate as if she was waiting for an answer who just grumbled something under her breath.

The door swung open and the chair appeared.

'Here we go,' cried Steph. Grace looked up to see François pushing the chair. He looked at her and then recognised her immediately. He flushed and started to twitch slightly as Grace continued to stare. 'Logistical services, my arse. He's a bloody porter. What the bloody hell is he playing at?' Grace thought.

'Frank, can I give you this bag?' Steph passed Frank the overnight bag to hang off the handles of the wheelchair. He took it silently and tried not to look at Grace.

'Right Mrs M, Frank will take you down now to the ambulance bay. Now, I have given your care plan to Grace and she will give your discharge letter to your GP. I have given Grace a prescription as well and there is some other medication in a bag for you. Now let's get you in the chair.'

Frank stepped forward with the chair and assisted the nurse in getting Kate in. Grace just continued to stare. She remembered him taking money from Sean which began to wind her up again. She also remembered the way he didn't understand her smattering of French and had tried to pass it off as manners when he wouldn't answer her. She knew then he was a wind up. She also noted that his name badge said Frank and not François. Sean would be devastated. Again!

The nurse walked with them to the lift and went over some things for Grace to remember and reminded her that the community nurse would be with them later that day to discuss the care plan.

The silence in the lift was broken with Kate enthusing about being able to see Benji later and it would be good to be back in her own house and have a decent cup of tea. Frank watched the numbers on the display panel decrease until they reached the ground floor while Grace looked him up and down and wondered what the hell Sean ever saw in him. As Grace stepped out of the lift, she stopped before Frank could push her chair clear of the doors. She lifted her phone and an audible click was heard.

'You taking a fucking picture?' barked the old lady.

'I am. Just to send to folks back in Pelsby to say we are on our way,' lied Grace.

'You don't need to send a goddamn picture of me with wires hanging out everywhere. What kind of friend are you?' she growled.

They reached the ambulance bay and two kindly gentlemen took her bags and notes and as they started to load her at the back of the ambulance, Frank tried to scurry away. Grace grabbed his arm and lowered her voice.

'That's strike three, mate. Tell him or I will. I don't care what you say but you had better do it gently,' Frank mutely nodded. 'And don't even think about confessing about you being married.' Grace looked at his hand gripping the wheel chair handle and he followed her gaze to his wedding ring. 'If you don't tell him, I'll show him the photograph and believe me when I say you don't want to get on the wrong side of Sean or me and I bet your partner might have a temper as well if they saw the pictures on Sean's phone.' Frank lowered his head in shame. He couldn't even look at her and stayed silent.

'You really are one of life's little turds,' she whispered near his ear. She let go of his arm and he ran away like a sewer rat.

Grace kissed Kate goodbye and told the ambulance men she would meet them at Primrose Cottage. Grace felt awful about Sean's impending heartbreak but she couldn't stand by and watch him being fleeced week in and week out.

Once they were out of Lanson, Grace managed to manoeuvre in front of the ambulance which then happily tailed her all the way to Pelsby. She sent the text to the pub, as promised, and as she pulled into the village she could see Big Mick and Patsy running to the cottage.

Grace was pleased to see them but Kate looked disappointed when she noticed that they didn't have her beloved dog.

'Where's my Benji?' she shouted through the oxygen mask as they lowered her out of the ambulance.

'She's back at the pub. I thought you could get settled first and then we can bring him over with Flynn,' said Patsy.

Big Mick opened the cottage and allowed the paramedics to enter first. Grace followed behind and instructed them to wheel her into the lounge to the right. The paramedic stopped in the middle of the room and looked at a bewildered Grace.

'Shall we pop her in the bed?' asked the paramedic.

Mrs Mortimer's bed was where the couch used to be and the dining table had also disappeared with a single bed in its place. The room had been cleaned and it smelled lovely and fresh.

'How long was your bloody mum here for? Where's my stuff?! Where is everything?' Kate was shouting and starting to cough. Big Mick and Patsy stepped into the room and bent in front of Kate who was still in the chair.

'We can change it back if you want, Mrs Mortimer. But we thought this might be easier if we put your bedroom down here. Didn't we Pats?' Mick started to panic. Patsy looked at Mrs Mortimer and took her hand while the paramedic started to place her bags down.

'My mum was a bit poorly and we brought her bed down. She said it was the best thing we did as she still felt like she was still living and hated being cooped upstairs and forgotten about. We thought down here you would see more of Benji and the bathroom and kitchen are down here,' Patsy continued to talk in a soft tone. 'Your sofa and stuff are all in your bedroom. Nothing's been thrown out, it's just all upstairs. We left the armchair for your visitors and we've moved the dining table up into the spare room so Grace can sleep down here as well. But if you don't like it we can get everyone back to put it exactly how you want it.' Patsy was still stroking Mrs Mortimer's hand.

'Everyone?' asked Grace.

'A few of the boys from the village came to help with shifting stuff like Tom, Amos and that. Some of the women came in and cleaned up a bit as well,' revealed Mick.

There was silence while Kate looked around the room. While she didn't like it, she knew that it was for the best and it was better than the place she just left. All her photographs were still on the mantle and on the display cabinet in the window and she had to admit to herself the place did look a lot cleaner. She did however like the fact the Grace's bed was at the foot of hers and that Benji's bed was in front of the fire still.

Kate pulled the mask from her face and looked up to the paramedic.

'Well, get me in the bed then or are you auditioning for a part in Driving Miss Daisy?' Everyone breathed a silent sigh of relief as the paramedics lifted her into bed and set up her equipment to the side of it. Big Mick eventually saw them out while Patsy popped the kettle on. Grace opened the old lady's bag and found the two missing photos from her mantelpiece collection and placed them in their usual place. Patsy came scurrying back from the kitchen.

'Right, kettle's on. Grace can you put that fire on, it's a bit chilly in here, then make that tea when the kettle's boiled. I'm just going to run home and collect the dogs, won't be a tick. Mick you can come with me and get back behind the bar. I'll have no Guinness left if Amos is left much longer,' moaned Patsy.

'See ya later, Mrs Mortimer,' murmured Mick. He came towards her to give her a kiss and she noticed his hang dog face.

'For crying out loud I'm not dead yet, so save the miserable face for the bookies,' she snapped.

Mick looked embarrassed and it amused Patsy to witness someone else shouting at him. They left the cottage and Grace made a pot of tea for her and Kate. It felt a little odd to Grace knowing that she would be serving it to her in her bed where the couch should be instead of at the dining table where her bed now was.

After setting the tea down, Grace found the medication

and passed the tablets to her with a glass of water. The tablets were simply to help with the pain now. Kate was lying in the bed and looked worse than she ever had. The last few hours had obviously taken its toll on her and the oxygen mask made her look even sicker.

Once she took the tablets, she laid her head back on the pillow and fell asleep. Her tea was untouched and Grace just stood by the window drinking her own and kept a look out for Patsy to return with the dogs. She wanted to make sure that Kate wasn't disturbed.

Patsy wasn't long with the dogs and Grace shot to the door to explain the patient was asleep. Patsy understood and didn't venture into the house. She simply passed the leads over and a huge bag with various dog bowls, food, chews and a Tupperware container of homemade soup for Kate and Grace. Flynn's basket was also among all the paraphernalia. Patsy kissed Grace goodbye and told her to call if she needed anything but if not she would pop in tomorrow to look in on them both.

The dogs were very pleased to see Grace and shushed on her instruction. Grace pulled Flynn's bed from the bag and placed it in front of the fire next to Benji's. 'They're roomies too', thought Grace with a smile.

She had not long finished her tea when there was a knock on the door. It was the community nurse and as she stepped in, she introduced herself. She had a slight frame with mousy hair and a rosy complexion.

'I'm Roz. I'm Mrs Mortimer's nurse. Are you Grace?' Grace nodded and stepped aside to allow her in. 'Is she in bed?'

'She is, but she's in here now,' Grace pointed to the lounge and Roz stepped in. Grace gave Roz an account of the last 24 hours in the hospital. Roz agreed that for all concerned it would be easier to take care of Kate now the bed was downstairs.

Roz checked the old lady physically and then she read over the care plan and discussed a few points with Grace regarding her medication, diet and sanitary issues. She also told Grace to call the surgery the following morning so Kate could have a home visit from the GP. When she had finished, Roz left the cottage with Grace following.

'I understand you have been seeing her for some time,' said Grace. Roz nodded and smiled. 'I only found out yesterday...about everything.' Grace started to fill up again. Roz placed her hand gently on Grace's arm.

'Grace, I did ask her to tell you. She talks about you all the time and I felt that you two were close. I'm just glad she has told you now and you didn't find out when it was too late. I doubt she has very long at all now so you had best be prepared,' Roz gave Grace's arm a squeeze. 'At least you are with her now.' The nurse sighed, 'I would worry about her being on her own.'

Roz then opened the front door and made her way to her car which was parked outside the cottage. She put her bag in the boot and called back to Grace.

'You have my number, just call if you need anything or you are worried. But until then, I'll see you tomorrow.' Roz jumped in the car and Grace waved to her from the doorstep before shutting the door.

The afternoon turned into evening and the house remained silent. Kate had stirred a few times but had not woken properly. Grace wasn't even sure if her friend realised that Benji was back in the cottage.

Grace was hungry and remembered the soup. She must get Kate to eat something, she thought. She went to the kitchen and warmed the soup on the stove and tried to make some noise so the patient would stir and sure enough when she returned to the room with a tray carrying a steaming bowl of soup, Kate was awake.

'Hey, sleepy head,' said Grace as she set the tray down on the side table. Grace moved toward Kate and lifted the mask from her face. 'Patsy made some lovely soup for us. You feeling a little hungry?'

'No, thank you,' she croaked softly.

'You have to eat something,' said Grace. Kate smiled with a resigned look at her friend.

'No, I don't dear,' she whispered. Grace looked at her for a moment and then simply smiled back. She moved the tray to the display cabinet, pulled the armchair closer and called Benji to her lap. The dog immediately came to Grace and jumped up into Grace's arms.

'Look who's home.' Grace lifted Benji and placed him on the bed to the side of Kate's hand where she could see and touch him.

'Hello, old boy,' she said breathlessly. Benji was very quiet and allowed his master to stroke him whilst he kept still. Grace noted how subdued the dog was. It was as if he knew.

'Grace, I need to talk to you,' she croaked. Grace pulled her chair closer to the bed. Her friend's voice was so low she could hardly hear her.

'All my papers…' She took a breath.

'I know,' interrupted Grace. 'They're all in the cabinet there. You told me before, in the hospital.'

'And the numbers…of everyone?' Kate asked.

'They're all with the papers,' Grace assured Kate she knew where everything was.

'Don't worry. I'll take care of everything, I promise.' Grace was fighting back the tears and could hardly talk herself for the huge lump in her throat. The silence fell between them and Grace continued to stroke Kate's hand and Benji simultaneously.

'Grace?'

'Yes?'

The old lady turned her head and looked directly at her friend. 'I know I haven't got long left so I need you...to listen to me,' she said breathlessly. 'I want you to be happy. I want you to have...dreams and...make them come true. You're such a...beautiful young woman...even though... you don't think so. You're bigger than this place,' she gasped. 'I mean it; promise me...that you'll try.' The tears were freely rolling now, down both their faces.

'I promise.' Grace took her friend's hand and looked at her face. She could see her in the soft glow from the kitchen light, the only light lit in the cottage. She felt the old lady squeeze her hand.

'I wish Mort...met you, he would have...loved you, you know,' she murmured.

'I'm sure I would have loved him too,' replied Grace from the semi dark.

'Course ya would...he was my Mort.' Kate stopped to catch her breath again. 'He would have...treated you like...a princess,' she patted Grace's hand. 'He probably would have...run me out of town for the way I speak to you,' she tried to laugh but only a rattle could be heard. 'I don't...mean it, you know,' she croaked.

'I know you don't. That's just us isn't it?' whispered Grace.

'I always...thought of you as...my daughter,' she exhaled. 'Even though...I was too...goddamn old,' her chest rattled harder.

Grace stood up, picked up Benji and set him down. She

took the oxygen mask and placed it gently back on Kate's face.

'No more talk now, you old biddy. You get some rest. I'm going to feed the dogs and have some of Patsy's soup.' Grace picked up the tray from the cabinet and called the dogs to follow her into the kitchen. She stood in the kitchen for a while still holding the tray and tried to compose herself. All these promises and things that needed doing. The hard thing was that she had no idea what she was doing. From looking after Kate to helping Crowley or sorting the rest of her own life out. She had no idea where to start or what she wanted at the end.

Grace poured the soup back into the pan and relit the stove to warm through again. She wished she had insisted on buying Kate a microwave. The old lady refused, saying she was terrified if she stood near it, it would cook her liver. Grace chuckled at the memory of arguing with the woman who had told her to 'fuck off with your space shit'.

The dogs devoured their food and Grace felt a little guilty at neglecting them, especially Flynn. He hadn't been home since Saturday morning and was probably wondering what the hell he was doing here.

Grace reset the tray with her soup and buttered some bread then took the tray back in to the lounge to eat. Her friend was breathing noisily but looked content enough.

After she finished the soup, she placed the tray on the floor and called the dogs to her lap. They jumped and snuggled in, one on each side and all three of them fell asleep in minutes.

Back in The Blacky, Big Mick, Patsy, Amos and Tom were all discussing the Mortimer's. After reminiscing well into the evening, they all agreed that Mort was one of life's true gentlemen and he was the best match for the irascible Kate.

'I don't know how Grace has put up with her all these years. She deserves a medal,' announced Patsy from behind the bar.

'She gives it back though, Pats,' replied Mick. 'She doesn't take it from her without giving it back.'

'That's true, I suppose,' agreed Patsy. 'I hope she's all right over there, on her own. She would call, wouldn't she, if something was wrong?' she looked at her audience with an earnest look.

'I'm sure she would,' said Tom. 'But, she'll be fine. Grace is a strong lady.' Patsy turned and picked up four shot glasses and filled each one with Jack Daniels, Mrs Mortimer's favourite drink.

'Here,' she said, placing a glass in front of herself, Tom, Amos and her husband. They each picked up their glass and mirrored Patsy when she raised her own.

'May God give Kate peace and may God give Grace strength.' She knocked the drink back and the three men followed suit and took a moment of contemplation to think of their friends.

Primrose Cottage remained dark and when Grace awoke she was confused at first as to where she was. But soon the noise from the oxygen apparatus reminded her and as she stirred, the dogs jumped down and returned to their baskets. The clock on the wall said half one in the morning and she couldn't believe she had been asleep that long. She jumped up to look at her patient who was still soundly asleep even though her breathing sounded hoarser.

Grace sat for a while and started to feel lonely so she

decided to call for Crowley. Who else could she call at this time of the morning? She hated being awake and watching her friend deteriorate.

'Hello! Hello! Hello!' roared Crowley from the corner of the room.

Grace turned and could see in the filtered light from the kitchen that he was lying on her single bed on the other side of the lounge. She walked over and could tell from his breathing that he was drunk.

'On a scale of one to ten, how drunk are you?' she snapped.

'I'd say more than you but less than whatever had sex with your dog's mother,' he laughed. 'Come here, Flynn,' he called sitting up, 'let's see if we can donate your legs to a fork lift truck factory.'

'I thought you might be company for me, but I'm not so sure now!' Grace was disappointed at his inebriated state.

'How is your friend this evening?' asked Crowley as he jumped off the bed.

'She's pissed off she's not as drunk as you,' barked the old lady. Crowley and Grace looked around to Kate. She had pulled off the mask and was looking directly at the pair of them. Crowley realised she could see him and soberly turned to Grace.

'What the…' he stuttered.

CHAPTER 13

Grace and Crowley tentatively walked towards the old lady's bed who stared at them with every approaching step.

'Who are you?' she growled at Crowley. Grace was switching her gaze between Kate and Crowley. Kate was definitely looking directly at him. Crowley cleared his throat and stood up a little straighter to introduce himself.

'My name is Crowley.' He gently took her hand and kissed it softly trying to be perfectly normal. But Grace could see in his eyes that he was confused.

'Crowley?' Kate looked at Grace expectantly.

'He's a friend of mine,' assured Grace.

'Why is there...a light around you? Where's it...coming from?' she croaked.

Grace looked at Crowley. 'What light? Was this it? Was she leaving? Was this Crowley's task? How would this woman dying have anything to do with him or it having a positive effect'?

'Can you see the light, Kate?' Grace stepped closer to the bed.

'Noo....not like that. He's got a glow around him...like

he's about to…fucking Quantum Leap,' she sighed.

Grace started to panic and wasn't sure what she should do. Kate shouldn't be able to see him and yet she could. What did this mean?

'I was at the hospital the other day,' he slurred slightly. 'James Bond?'

Kate continued to stare at him trying to recollect her time in the hospital.

'I…remember,' she said at last. Crowley took her hand again and sat on the edge of her bed.

'Did you see a light then?' he asked. She continued to stare and then shook her head.

'I don't…think so,' she croaked

Grace was still rooted to the spot, trying to make sense of it all.

'What does that mean, Crowley? Why can she see you? She's not supposed to see you, is she?' Grace could feel the panic rising while Crowley just continued to look at Kate. 'Crowley! Please?'

Crowley, still holding Kate's hand and looking at her replied, 'She can see my ethereal light.'

Kate smiled at Crowley. In an instant Kate understood he was not of this world. Apart from the light, there was an energy about him. It felt warm, inviting, safe and bizarrely familiar. She felt peaceful as he held her hand and any fears she had about passing over had completely evaporated.

'It won't be long, dear,' he said soothingly. Crowley looked at Grace.

'She can see me, Daff, because it's nearly her time. She must be close if she can see my essence. She's at the periphery of the next plane.' Grace could feel dread enveloping her and felt the need to sit down. She wanted to lie down and make it all stop somehow.

'I thought I'd have more time with her,' Grace whispered. She stepped forward and stroked her friend's forehead and she looked up and smiled.

'So...how long...you been...seeing spooks?' she cackled.

'Not long. He's just here to help me do something,' Grace looked at Crowley. 'Thing is, we don't know what it is yet.' Grace continued stroking her friend. 'You're not supposed to see him. Only me, like. I'm glad you can though. I think he might be here to look after you. You must be the reason he is here.' Grace looked at Crowley who looked just as bewildered as her.

'What's your story...buster?' asked the old lady turning to her new friend.

'I died over a week ago and until I fulfil my task I can't move on,' he replied.

'Not that!' she barked. She took another lung full of air, 'I mean...YOUR story. Tell me...who you are.' She continued to stare at him and an air of resignation came across him. He placed the oxygen mask on her face and began.

'I was born in De Mondford Hall in 1955. My parents were called Richard and Georgiana...'

Crowley continued with his story of his childhood, his sister and going to school and Kate remained awake throughout his whole recollection. Grace became relaxed listening to his account and curled up in the armchair to listen. She knew some of it but not like this. This was heartfelt, warm and personal. He continued with story of meeting his wife Jennifer and the birth of his son Max and how happy they all were and you could feel his joy as he talked of them.

However, his joyous tone turned to sorrow and he began to cry as he recounted hearing the news of their deaths. Kate had remained quiet until he confessed that he had turned to drink not long after the accident.

'Who could...blame you?' she sighed.

He carried on telling her the taxes on De Mondford Hall were mounting and his father was never a great one for maintaining the house, always preferring to spend his money at the casino. The maintenance bill was rising higher than the tax bill.

'Couldn't you...get a job?' Kate croaked.

Crowley chuckled at the naïve suggestion.

'The only thing I was any good at was historical art! And what was I supposed to do with that useless skill. I knew people who worked in the arts and it pays a pittance. My dear, I needed a lottery win to cover the existing bills alone, never mind any future demands,' Crowley took a deep sigh. 'I had no money and no interest in doing anything except getting drunk.'

Crowley continued about becoming bankrupt and his estrangement from his sister, Sarah who had blamed him for losing the house and didn't understand the enormity of neglect on their father's part. She had firmly laid all the blame on his drinking and refused to speak to him once the Hall was gone.

Grace couldn't believe some of the detail he was revealing. Couldn't his sister see that this man was grief stricken over his family and the added burden of losing his ancestral home must have been enormous? She understood now why he didn't want her to contact his sister when he died. She also understood why he was homeless. His pride had prevented him from asking for help elsewhere and the drink had prevented him from caring.

He drew his story to a close with his meeting of Grace at the bridge the Friday before last, visiting her for the first time and his positive deed.

'So, were you the dead guy that I found?' croaked Kate.

'Yes, I was. And I'm very grateful that it was you who found me, so thank you,' said Crowley.

'And you're the guy…who calls her…Daff? After…the flower?' she asked.

'I am, indeed.'

Kate lay for a while and digested his story. What a sad tale in the end, she thought.

'You…need to…hurry up. Your wife…your boy…are waiting,' Kate gasped.

'I'll be with them soon enough,' he patted her hand. He turned to Grace to read her face. He had never told Grace his life story and he wondered if she was judging him about mistakes and choices that he had made.

'You okay?' she asked warmly. A smile crept across his face and he took a deep sigh.

'I am, yes. I have avoided that story for so long and now I don't know why. I feel so much better to have told you both.' He paused and looked at Grace imploringly.

'It wasn't all my fault was it?' He asked the question and he knew himself he wasn't to blame for all but he just needed someone to agree. He could have done things differently but he would have still lost his Jennifer, Max and the house.

'None of it was your fault.' She leant forward from the armchair and took his other hand and gave it a squeeze. He smiled at her appreciatively.

'I'll put the kettle on,' she said and walked to the kitchen. She could still hear Crowley and Kate talking.

'I knew...she was different...she came...for my ...parcel and looked different. I must...have been close...to the end...for a while,' she exhaled.

'My dear, this is not the end. This is just...' he paused trying to find the right thing to say, 'another floor, shall we say. You're going up and soon you will be in the penthouse,' he joked. He was still holding her hand when he asked, 'Any regrets?'

Grace, still listening from the kitchen, stopped making the tea and waited for her answer. She wasn't sure if the lady regretted anything and if she had, she had never revealed them to her.

'I regret letting Mort...convince me to see...fucking Liberace...instead of...Sinatra at...Caesars Palace...in '78.' Crowley roared laughing and Grace realised that that was typical of Kate. She continued to make the tea with a sense of relief that her friend felt she had led a contented life.

Grace walked back into the room and set the tray down on the cabinet to pour the tea. She didn't bother asking Kate if she wanted one, she had refused any offer of refreshment since eating the porridge wallpaper paste at the hospital. The woman had closed her eyes and even though her breathing sounded strained, she seemed to look peaceful.

Crowley climbed down from the bed and sat on the side table and took the tea from Grace. She, in turn, sat in the armchair and they both drank in silence. Once they were finished, Crowley announced that he needed to disappear for a short time but would come back as soon as he could.

'Do you think she will last the night?' Grace asked.

'Let's hope so. I won't be long and I'm not going for a drink. I'll be back as quick as I can.' He disappeared as soon as he set the cup down.

Grace quietly picked up the teacups and took the tray back out to the kitchen. She looked at the old clock on the wall and noted it was nearly four a.m. and even though she should have felt tired, she didn't feel sleepy. All she wanted was a drink. She began opening doors in the kitchen looking for the old lady's booze. She soon found her stash under the sink and even though the selection was small, it was not disappointing. She spied the bottle of Jack Daniels and then hesitated, thinking she would be scolded if she drank it. But Grace soon realised that this bottle would never be started or finished by her friend and she was sure she wouldn't mind her taking a measure from it.

Grace returned to the lounge and went to sit back in the armchair when she heard her friend beckon her to the bed.

'Can I get you anything?' asked Grace.

'You drinking…my…liquor?' growled Kate.

'Jeez,' thought Grace, she has a nose like a Beagle!'

'I'll buy you another bottle tomorrow, you miser,' Grace tried to pacify her with a fake and empty promise. Grace sat on the edge of the bed and stroked Kate's hand. Kate was trying to open her eyes and then Grace could see her moving her tongue in her mouth.

'Put…some on…my lips,' she croaked. Grace felt an ache in her heart. This poor woman who had lived her life in full was left with small requests for simple pleasures. Grace slowly pulled the mask away from her face and then dipped her finger in the cool brown liquid. She then stroked her wet finger across the old lady's bottom lip and left a trail of the delicious whiskey. As the old lady slowly licked her lips Crowley appeared on the other side of the bed.

'My dear,' whispered Crowley and Kate struggled to

open her eyes. 'Are you awake?' Kate slowly nodded.

'Good, because I've brought a friend,' he announced gently.

Crowley stepped aside from the bed to reveal who was behind him. In all his glory and looking about thirty-five-years-old stood Frank Sinatra. Grace looked on the scene dumbfounded and Crowley looked pleased as punch. He walked over to the other side of the bed by Grace's side while Frank, dressed in a grey suit and with Brylcreemed hair, sat on the bed and took Kate's hand.

'Can I sing you a song, beautiful lady?' he asked gently. Kate struggled to smile but you could see in her eyes she was full of joy. She simply nodded and as Frank leaned forward, he started to gently and very slowly sing, 'Fly me to the moon, let me swing among the stars...'

Grace wasn't sure how to feel but all she did know was that her friend was truly happy. She could see Kate's joyous tears rolling down into her hair and onto the pillow. Grace's tears also started to silently flow down her face and she turned to look at Crowley who was simply entranced by the scene before him. Grace, still smiling, sat in the armchair while clutching her glass and settled in to listen to this wonderful voice. Crowley sat on the arm of the chair and whispered in her ear.

'Am I forgiven, Daff, for turning up drunk?' he smiled at her.

'You are forgiven,' she whispered back and leant her head against his arm while they watched Frank sing.

When he had finished, he bent down and kissed the old lady on top of her head, slipped gently off the bed onto his feet and placed her hand back on the bed. He looked at Grace silently with a sorrowful look.

Grace looked at Frank and then slowly placed her

empty glass on the floor and stood up. The room seemed quieter than before. She walked slowly to the bed and looked at her friend. The rise and fall of her chest had stopped and the threatening rattle within her disease-ridden lungs was silent. Grace picked up her hand and allowed the tears to roll down her face. She was happy that her best friend was now with her beloved Mort and she had died with a smile on her face.

Crowley was now stood next to Frank who had each taken on the stance of a pallbearer with their hands placed in front of them. Grace thought they looked slightly comical and smiled through her tears.

'She died without one regret. Thank you both so much for doing this for her.'

Grace took a huge breath as she realised that this was not the only farewell she would be making this evening. 'I doubt I will see you again,' she said to Crowley. 'This had to be it. If anyone can die in a positive way, then this was it,' smiled Grace. 'You must have been sent here to help me cope and…I don't know…maybe see a different side to her or…make me realise just how truly lucky I was to have had her in my life.'

Grace collected her thoughts and quickly ran through the past ten days of her life. 'You've changed my whole world on…well, everything really.' Grace continued to let the tears fall. The men stayed silent and Grace turned to look back at Kate in the bed.

'Can you do me one last favour?' she cried. 'When you go back,' she began to sob, 'tell her that I love her and that I will keep my promise.'

CHAPTER 14

The funeral was well attended by everyone in the village on that bitter cold December day. Friends from Kate Mortimer's past had also come to pay their respects and had travelled from various corners of the country to see her lowered into the frost hardened hole with her husband. Grace had called everyone on Kate's list as instructed and the only notable absentee was a family member from the States. They had promised someone would be here in time for the funeral but clearly they had other commitments. Grace didn't blame them. The only family that was left out there were nephews and nieces that hardly knew their old aunt.

After the funeral, they all congregated back at The Blacky where Patsy had laid on a lovely spread that was a tongue in cheek tribute to the old lady with its Hawaiian pizza and Marmite sandwiches. Rosemary, from the bakers, had also contributed cupcakes, complete with an American fondant flag. Grace was touched by all the effort and made a mental note to send thank you cards to all who had helped.

Her parents had also come for the funeral which Grace had mixed feelings about. She felt slightly self-conscious crying in the church and worried slightly that her mum was watching and judging. Grace felt that with each tear it revealed her profound love for the old woman and in turn it illustrated an unspoken comparison. However, she was very grateful they had made the journey and they were clearly concerned over her emotional state when they arrived.

Her parents were now sat in the corner of the pub on their own not far from Mr Cousins who nodded in their direction in acknowledgement of having met before. All the usual regulars were sat in all their usual places and Grace felt unsure what she should do. She stood in the pub looking lost until she caught Tom's eye at the bar. He raised a glass at her and cocked his head for her to join him. She felt slight relief and walked over to him where he immediately passed the full glass of wine to her.

'Thanks,' she said, taking the glass appreciatively. Tom looked behind her at the occupied table in the corner.

'Are they your parents?' he asked. Grace just looked at them and nodded.

'I'd best go over. They said they are only staying for one and then getting back on the road to Cornwall.' She looked at Tom with a beseeching look. 'Come with me.'

Tom did as he was asked, picked up his drink from the bar and followed Grace to the corner table.

'Mum, Dad, this is Tom, a friend of mine from the village.' Tom offered his hand to shake and after her parents both gave him their names, he sat down to join them.

'Are you the gentleman who looked at Grace's boiler?' asked Dai.

'Er yes, yes I am,' Tom stammered.

'Very reasonable charge, I must say,' said Dai. Tom looked embarrassed and drank his pint to hide his face.

Penny sat in silence and surveyed the clientele in the room. She recognised the old man, Mr Cousins, next to her and noticed that no one spoke to him. She wasn't surprised, as he looked wretched. The lady behind the bar hadn't changed either. She was still wearing far too much make-up and clearly not wearing the correct sized clothes as her heavily lacquered hair had more give in it than the black dress the landlady had squeezed herself into, thought Penny.

The four of them continued to make small talk about the weather and how lucky they were that even though it was cold it had stayed dry for the burial. They talked about Christmas coming and did Tom have any plans to see his own family over the holidays. The inane chat continued until Dai finished his cola and Penny had drained her wine glass.

'We had best be off, Gracey darling,' announced Dai. 'The black ice out there is treacherous and there's been very heavy snow over parts of the country.' They all stood up while Dai and Penny put their coats on and collected their belongings.

'I'll walk out with you,' said Grace.

They bid everyone farewell in the pub and the noise level rose as the patrons all wished them a safe journey back. As they all stepped outside, they shivered with the biting wind and Penny realised that Grace was not wearing a coat.

'You go back inside Grace,' instructed her mum. 'The car is only over there.'

'Call me when you get home, okay?' Grace asked.

'We will.' Penny opened her arms and Grace willingly accepted the love and warmth of the farewell hug. Her dad in turn did the same and then shooed her back into The Blacky.

Grace walked back in and immediately went to the window where the buffet was laid underneath to watch them leave. She stayed there until the car disappeared over the bridge and then walked over to Tom who was now at the bar.

'I was just going to get you another drink,' he said.

'I won't bother, if you don't mind. To be honest, I think I'm just going to go home and cuddle up with my Flynn.' Grace walked over to the coat stand and retrieved her coat and discreetly folded it over her arm. 'I just want to leave,' she said quietly. Tom nodded and mouthed a goodbye before she turned and walked out of the pub.

Once she was outside, she found the cold wind refreshing and it livened up her senses. As she walked away from the pub, she found herself walking to Primrose Cottage. She felt drawn to it and wanted to be there on this sad day as she felt it might offer some comfort.

The house was dark and eerie when she entered and she walked into the lounge where it was just as she left it. The beds were still there, now made up, but Benji's bed was no longer in front of the fire as it was now at Grace's home.

Grace threw her keys down on the foot of the bed, walked to the kitchen cupboard under the sink and retrieved the bottle of Jack Daniels. The glass she had used previously was still on the draining board from where she had washed it last week so she picked it up and filled the glass to the top. Clutching the glass and tucking the bottle under her arm, she walked back to the lounge, sat in the armchair and closed her eyes while she savoured a mouthful of the old lady's liquor. She sat thinking about how everyone had rallied around to help her sort the funeral arrangements. Even Mr Cousins had offered to help. Her boss, Bill, had been particularly sympathetic and had told her to take as much time off as she wanted, thanks to Sean and Ellen. They had bolstered her cause by trying to get Bill to understand the relationship she had with Kate Mortimer, even though she was not a family member. She had told Bill she wanted one more week off after the funeral and then she would be back in.

Grace sat on the armchair and filled her glass again. While sipping her drink, she tried to formulate a plan for the next week. She wanted to go through the rest of Kate's papers tomorrow and then after that she decided to make a start with packing Primrose Cottage and reorganising the rooms back to their original state. She had no idea what was to happen to the cottage but she knew that something would be sorted by Kate. Before the house was to be handed over, she wanted some pieces to take and keep. Nothing of any value, just bits to remind her of her friend such as the teapot, a photo on the mantelpiece of them both at a summer fair and a cushion from her bed that Kate had crocheted but Grace had completed on her sewing machine.

It was starting to get dark and Grace was cold and starting to feel drunk. She realised she had best get back to the dogs and let them out. As she walked to the kitchen she thought of Crowley and hoped that he was with his wife and son. The only person that knew of his recent existence had also passed away and Grace felt comfortable with that. She would have found it difficult to make anyone believe the incredible story so what was the point of telling anyone. She knew what happened and how he had helped her and Kate in the end. Without him, her death would have been the tragic story that is common to most. But she was lucky. Her story ended with her heart full and she was serenaded into submission and she had Crowley to thank for that.

The banging on the front door snapped her back into the kitchen where she was drying the glass. Puzzled as to who would be knocking the door to an empty cottage made her presume that someone had seen her enter. It was probably Tom, so she grabbed her coat so he could walk her back to her own cottage.

However, as she opened the door she was surprised to see a stranger stood on the step. The good looking man was around 6' 2" with short blond hair, blue eyes and more noticeably was carrying a suitcase. He smiled, but Grace just looked at him waiting for him to speak.

'Are you, Grace?' he said in a fresh American accent. Grace then realised this was Kate's nephew. She had seen photographs of him and his brother in frames around Primrose Cottage. Kate would always comment on how good looking the boys were.

'Yes,' she replied and the man stepped forward and offered his hand.

'I'm, Todd. Todd Mortimer. Kate was my Aunt,' he said nervously. Silently Grace shook his hand. Todd was too late for the funeral. He was told what time the service was, they were all told last week.

'You've missed the funeral,' she said flatly. Todd pushed his hands back into the pockets of his inappropriate coat for December.

'My flight was due in this morning but then we got diverted to Birmingham because of the snow. I tried to call the only number I knew which I think is Aunt Kate's but I guess no one was here to take the calls,' he said.

'No, we were at the funeral, funnily enough,' she said sarcastically. Todd was wondering if this woman was ever going to invite him in as he was freezing. The weather back home was not as cold as this.

'Well, I erm…caught a train and then I caught another train and then I took a cab and erm…' he looked at his suitcase, 'well here I am. I know I missed the funeral and I'm real sorry but hey, I can't control the British weather and if I could I'd turn it up a few degrees as I am pretty cold standing here.' Todd was now jogging slightly on the spot in an attempt to keep warm. Grace realised that it was indeed cold and she was being rude to the stranger. He had, after all come all this way with the good intention of making the funeral.

'I'm sorry, come in, come in.' Grace stepped back into the darkness of Primrose Cottage and switched on the light in the lounge. In all its starkness it took her back to when Kate had arrived from the hospital. Todd followed behind her and was visibly taken aback by the beds in the lounge.

'Wow,' he exclaimed raising his eyebrows.

'I know, not very inviting is it. We had to bring the beds down to care for her but to be honest she only spent one night in here and then she passed.' Grace's voice trailed at the end and Todd could see that this woman cared for his Aunt. Grace looked around the room and maybe it was looking at it through Todd's eyes but she could see the room was grim. After a journey that he had just endured, it wasn't a great place to rest. She wondered if there were any rooms available in Lanson but that would mean him taking a taxi back into the town. She also thought if anyone could put him up in the village, but who would she ask? She didn't feel comfortable just putting on someone like that. Maybe it was because she was a little drunk or maybe she just didn't have the energy to argue with herself but she felt she had no choice but to at least offer an alternative. He was Kate's nephew and for some reason she felt obliged to look after him.

'It's like a hostel in here for the over nineties isn't it? Tell you what,' Grace turned and looked at Todd, 'I know we've only just met but well, you're Kate's family and I know she wouldn't want you staying here when the place is like this. If you want you can come and stay at mine. It's only up the road. It's not a palace but it's warmer than here but I'll warn you, there's only a couch to sleep on. I've slept on it and it's pretty comfortable actually. I do have a bed...but what I mean is I sleep on the couch when my parents visit and they have my bed but usually I sleep in my bed. Well, of course I would sleep in my bed...'

Todd was looking at Grace and was amazed that she went from super snappy to super chatty in less than a minute. He just kept nodding politely waiting for her to breathe in. Grace realised she was babbling again. Why did men do this to her?

'Anyway,' she told her mouth to slow down, 'the offer's there. Or you can stay here but you'll need to sleep in one of these beds.' Grace looked over her shoulder at the untouched bed she was supposed to sleep in. 'I'd erm...take that one if I were you.' Todd looked at the bed that they were standing at the foot of and realised that his aunt must have died in this bed. He looked and Grace and smiled. In a way, he felt he should refuse as she didn't know him; he could be a murderer for all she knew. But looking around the room after the arduous journey he had just completed, he felt he could convince her that he was very grateful for her hospitality.

'So, your place isn't far,' he said brightly and picked up his suitcase and walked out of the cottage. 'Shit!', thought Grace. 'I've just invited a complete bloody stranger to stay in my house. Me and my big mouth!'

Grace walked outside and found Todd waiting for her at the end of the path. They started to walk in the direction of Grace's cottage and Grace pointed to it to reassure Todd it wasn't far.

'You must be tired after that journey,' supposed Grace.

'Hmm,' replied Todd, who was clearly struggling with the cold.

'Is it always this cold? I thought England was just rainy.'

'It is pretty cold today to be honest. I s'pose in America it's warm most of the time?' asked Grace.

'We have proper winters and at night, in Ohio, it can get real cold,' replied Todd.

They continued with 'weather chat' all the way to the cottage, the universal subject that crosses over all nationalities and always invites an opinion. As they walked into the cottage, they were met by two excitable dogs who started to bark as soon as they saw Todd. He immediately bent down and started to stroke them and soon enough they were jumping to lick his face.

'The light one is Flynn. He's my dog and the dark one is Benji. He's your aunt's,' she paused for a moment, 'but I guess he's mine now.' Todd looked up at her to read her face. 'Not that I mind! She asked me to take him and to be honest I would have been upset if he had gone to someone else and so would Flynn, probably.'

Todd straightened up, still looking at Grace and thought how warm she was. Grace looked at Todd standing in her lounge. He looked even taller in her cottage and more masculine, now that he had stopped shivering.

His blonde hair was slightly wavy and his stubbled chin made him look like a model from a black and white aftershave advert. Grace realised she was staring.

'Right then,' she cast her gaze away, 'this is the lounge, of course,' and she smiled at the obvious, 'that's the kitchen through there and upstairs is the bathroom and a couple of bedrooms, except one of the bedrooms is just full of junk. There's only one toilet which is in the bathroom and erm…well that's it really,' finished Grace. Todd was still looking at her with a warm smile and when he gathered she had finished, he realised he was still looking at her. He noticed that she had one of the most beautiful smiles he had ever seen, even though she had not smiled properly. He also noticed her eyes were puffy from recent crying but he was drawn to the blueness of them.

'Can I take your coat or are you still cold? I can light a fire if you want,' suggested Grace.

'To be honest, I could do with some food. I haven't eaten for hours and my ribs are starting to show, I think,' he sniggered.

'I've got some lasagne in the freezer. Loads of neighbours have been popping in with food but between you and me a lot of them went straight into the bin. If I don't know what it is by looking at it, I tend to give it a wide berth.' Todd smiled at her confession. 'I'm not holding out much hope for the lasagne either to be honest.' Grace thought for a moment. 'Tell you what, why don't I take you over to the pub. We all went back there today after the funeral. They had some food laid out. Mind you, that's probably a bit ropey now,' said Grace.

'Ropey?' Todd raised his eyebrows with a questioning look.

'Oh, erm, like gone off a bit. It's been sat there all day,

that's if there's any left, mind. They do hot food though,' Grace suggested brightly. Todd liked the sound of that idea.

'It'll be nice to introduce you to some of her friends. She had no family there today you see,' said Grace.

'Sounds like you were family,' replied Todd. Grace looked at him and he smiled again at her. She felt like she was Kate's family and it was nice that this stranger could see that without her having to explain how she felt about the old lady. Grace just smiled at him appreciatively.

'Is it okay if I have a quick wash and change? I'll only be two minutes,' asked Todd.

'Oh, yes of course. You can get changed in my room and the bathroom is next to it. I'll take you up.' Grace walked up the stairs with Todd behind her and all she could think about was the size of her bum. She was glad she was wearing black as that might make it look a tiny bit smaller. But all of a sudden she was very conscious of her walk and then felt she was moving like a Thunderbird.

Her bedroom was thankfully in a presentable state as she had gone into a cleaning overdrive in the last week to keep her mind busy. She left Todd, went back downstairs to let the dogs out and then rooted out bits of make-up at the bottom of her handbag to make herself look a little less like a tear gas victim.

She continued to wait for her guest in the backyard as she watched the dogs. Her mind was wandering to Todd and of him getting changed in her bedroom. The only men that had ever been in there were her dad and Sean.

'Parents and gays don't count as potentials, do they dogs?' she whispered. But the dogs were completely unaware that she was imagining Todd without his top on while he rummaged in his bag for a clean one.

'Ready!' Todd interrupted her thoughts from the kitchen with his clean shirt and freshened face.

'He actually looks more lush', thought Grace and felt herself blushing.

After calling the dogs in and locking up, they crossed over the square and headed to the pub. Grace was hoping a few of the people would still be in there from the funeral today. They would love to meet Todd.

Sure enough, as she walked in, the place was more or less as she left it. Only a couple of people had left but most of the attendees to the funeral were still sitting and supping ale. Some of them stopped talking and stared at Grace and the stranger and she waited for the noise to reduce a bit more.

'Hey, everybody,' called Grace. The remaining talkers stopped and looked in her direction.

'This is Todd, he's Kate's nephew. He's just flown in from Ohio and unfortunately missed the funeral as the snow diverted him to Birmingham. So he has spent most of the day trying to get to Pelsby,' she looked at Todd who looked a little awkward. 'Anyway, it'll be nice if you come over and speak to him at some point and make him feel welcome.' Immediately, half the pub stood up on her instruction.

'Not all at once! Let the man have a drink first, eh?' Grace walked over to the bar with Todd following while everyone sat down.

'Mick, Pats, this is Todd, Mrs Mortimer's nephew from America. Todd, Mick and Patsy own the pub.' Big Mick leaned over the bar to shake Todd's hand.

'Howdy,' said Mick. Grace looked at him aghast.

'He's not a bloody cowboy home from the range. He's just come in via Birmingham,' said Grace, rolling her eyes.

Mick turned crimson and Todd smirked; he then offered his hand to Patsy. Grace judged by Patsy's giggle that she had regressed to a time when she was fifteen years old but unfortunately for her, her face had stayed over fifty.

'Hello, Todd,' tittered Patsy. Grace couldn't make up her mind if Todd was amused or scared by the Landlady and Landlord.

'What can I get you then, young man?' asked Big Mick.

'Erm…' Todd looked around the bar and couldn't make up his mind.

'What do you drink at home?' questioned Grace.

'German beer mostly,' replied Todd.

'Fine,' assured Mick, 'you two sit down and I'll bring them over. Wine, Grace?' asked Mick. Grace nodded and indicated to Todd for him to follow her. They walked through to the other side of the pub where the fire was burning and it was a bit quieter so they took a seat.

Todd began to look around the pub and was surprised that it looked like a typical English pub like he had seen on TV. He noticed the beams on the ceiling and the old worn slate floor.

'How old is this place?' asked Todd still surveying the room.

'I think it's about three hundred years old. It used to be an old coaching inn. Outside on the cobbles you can see where they're worn where the coaches would pull up. Everything in Pelsby is old though, except for a few houses round the back of the village.'

Big Mick walked through with a tray carrying a pint and a large glass of wine.

'Mick, do you think Patsy could see to Tom. He wants something hot,' Mick raised his eyebrows, 'to eat! Can he have a menu please?' Mick smiled and went off to fetch the menu. Todd picked up his glass and waited for Grace to do the same. She did as he expected and waited for him to speak.

'To my Aunt Kate, who I erm…have only come to know recently…and erm...what I know so far is, she is…I mean was…a very persuasive woman.'

'This is a funny toast', thought Grace.

'And a fine woman, and I erm...hope to...' Todd was struggling to say something that simply made sense. 'I hope to make my trip to England memorable and erm…well, that's it,' he finished quickly and started to gulp at his pint. Grace looked at him and wondered if he was suffering from jet lag or if he was he a bit stupid. 'Looks and brains. Doesn't happen'! she thought disappointingly.

'Not great with the…erm…toast thing,' he muttered. After a quick think, Grace decided not to respond as there was nothing she could say that would make him feel better.

She sipped her wine while Todd looked at the menu and decided to have a steak to which Grace emphatically shook her head.

'Believe me, Patsy's steak probably went neigh more than moo. I'd have the fish if I were you,' she whispered. Todd started laughing and finished his pint. He was about to get another one when Mr Cousins appeared with a pint for Todd and a wine for Grace. Todd looked at the old man in bewilderment. He set the tray down, placed the drinks in front of Grace and Todd and then pulled up a stool.

'Cousins, the name,' growled the old man and Todd politely shook his hand. 'I knew your aunt,' he said bluntly.

'Thanks for the drink, Mr Cousins, you didn't need to do that,' said Grace. Mr Cousins waved his hand at her dismissively.

'I knew your uncle as well, Mort. Nice man.' Mr Cousins paused and shifted on the stool. 'I keep having dreams about him lately,' he looked into the distance, beyond Todd and Grace. 'Strange, they are,' he spoke softly and looked distracted. Todd gave Grace a sideways glance who in turn met his gaze. 'Anyway, I just wanted to say your aunt was a lovely woman, one of the few in this village that would give me the time of day. A true lady she was and I am very sorry for your loss,' he barked. He jumped to his feet and touched his imaginary hat and immediately left the pub. Todd turned slowly to Grace.

'Who the hell was that?' he drawled.

'That, my dear Todd, is Mr Cousins. He owns a farm at the top of the road and he happens to own my cottage as well. He's a funny bugger to be honest but your Aunt Kate had a lot of time for him. Some people in the village reckon he's a paedo,' Todd winced but remained fascinated. 'They also say that he used to pick up hitchhikers off the road and take them to the farm. But they don't reckon his intentions were good once they were up there. There's even some that say he murdered them,' whispered Grace. Todd's eyes were now like saucers.

'Seriously?' he asked.

'I don't believe it, mind. I think he's just a cantankerous old goat who smells of manure. He is a bit odd but I can't see your aunt entertaining him if he was a kiddie-fiddler. All I know is she used to say to me, (Grace attempted an American accent) 'there's a lot of horse shit around this village and some have bigger spades than others'.'

Todd began to laugh, 'I don't know what's worse. Your story or your impression of Aunt Kate,' and he continued to laugh.

'It wasn't that bad, was it?' she said still laughing.

'Oh yes, it was bad. Like Dick Van Dyke bad,' he teased. They started laughing again and clinked their glasses and took a long swallow.

During the course of the evening, various patrons came over and offered their condolences to Todd who felt awkward receiving sympathy about a woman he hardly knew. All these people that approached him seemed to know her very well as they each had a story to share about her. He was genuinely interested and wished he had made more of an effort at keeping in touch with her. He could only remember a few things of her from when he was a kid, but he could remember that she was funny and there was a lot of laughter in the house when she and his Uncle Mort came to the ranch.

Grace was grateful that various friends had come over and spoke to Todd. The only person who had left the pub without acknowledging them was a loner from the village called Ian. Ian had led a tragic life similar to Crowley's. His wife had died from cancer a few years back and his stepdaughter had been murdered a few years later. Since then, his only friend was drink and he kept himself to himself. He had not come to the funeral but then again he didn't know Kate that well. Today was one of the few days where he had left the pub early no doubt, to catch Nell's for more drink before she shut the shop. Even though he had led a sad life Ian had a bad temper and could start a fight over very little, so everybody avoided him. Grace was glad he had not come over or mixed with anyone today of all days.

At ten o'clock, Grace decided that they should call it a night as they were both getting pretty drunk. She told Todd she was impressed as they had been drinking for six hours solid and had not bought a round in. Even Big Mick had refused to take money for the meals.

They weaved their way back to the cottage giggling about the various characters that Todd had met that night and he concluded that Pelsby was the strangest place he had ever been in and he was including New York in that criteria. Grace asked him about New York and she confessed that since she met Kate she had always wanted to go.

'I'm moving there when I go back home. You should come and I'll show you the sights,' he slurred.

Once they were in the cottage, Todd slumped on to the couch and realised he was very drunk. It seemed to be a regular state of his the last week or two. His host looked perfectly sober and he marvelled at how good she looked.

'I'm drunk, Grace,' he bellowed, 'are you drunk, Grace? Cos you don't look it,' he drunkenly smiled, 'you look just as good as you did when we went out,' he closed his eyes, 'you look fantastic.' Grace could feel herself blushing and tried to act more sober. Todd was feeling incredibly comfy and overwhelmingly tired. 'I hope she leaves me alone tonight,' he whispered.

Grace quickly went from feeling flattered to insulted. 'What a fucking cheek'! thought Grace. She stomped upstairs and found a quilt and a pillow and clomped back down again. He had now slid horizontally on the couch so his top half was lying down but his feet were still on the floor. Even though she felt like throwing the bedding at him and leaving him to it, Grace shoved the pillow under his head and lifted his legs so he was lying down completely.

'Leave you alone! Believe me, you're not that bloody irresistible!' and she flung the quilt over him and walked away in disgust. The dogs followed her as she wobbled up the stairs to bed and after slamming the door, the house became peaceful again.

The next morning, Grace woke to a clattering downstairs. She remembered she had a house guest and quickly recalled the end of the night and wondered if he had remembered anything at all. She sat up in bed and to her relief felt surprisingly okay. Flynn and Benji jumped from the bed and wagged their tails at her as if to say 'good morning' and she rewarded them with a smile.

After tidying herself up a bit in the bathroom she ventured downstairs to make some coffee for her and her guest but was surprised to see Todd already stirring at two cups.

'Morning,' he said brightly and offered her a cup. 'I'm not sure if you drink coffee or how you take it.' Grace took the cup, thanked him and walked to the armchair to drink it. Grace felt uncomfortable and wasn't sure what to say to him. She was still smarting over his comment last night and felt insulted that he thought she was some uncontrollable nymphomaniac.

Todd picked up that Grace wasn't the same as she was yesterday and though he didn't know her he felt that she was annoyed with him. He was trying to remember if he had said something to her last night but his mind was blank from leaving the pub until he woke this morning.

'Thanks for letting me crash on your sofa last night,' he tried to sound normal hoping she would warm up.

'I said you could,' she said flatly, still looking at her cup.

'I feel fine this morning,' he said still trying to sound upbeat. 'I should drink English beer more often,' he joked.

'It was German.'

'Oh yeah,' he replied. The silence fell between them. Grace wasn't sure if she should say something but then concluded there was no point as he would be leaving as soon as he had sorted Primrose Cottage. Todd couldn't stand the silence any longer.

'So…um…today, I need to go to my aunt's cottage and find something.' Grace shot him a glance and tried to control her temper.

'What do you need to find? I probably know where it is,' Grace snapped. Todd decided that he didn't need to put up with her cranky mood, as lovely as she was. He stood up, took his cup to the kitchen and poured the coffee down the drain and came back into the lounge behind her to fetch his coat.

'Can I have the keys to my aunt's house please?' He stood and waited for her to respond, to which Grace jumped to her feet and turned to face him.

'I'm not giving you the keys, just like that!' shouted Grace. Todd sighed and realised that he had a fight on his hands.

'Look lady, no offence, but she was my family and there's something I need to get from her house.' Grace was about to interrupt but Todd raised his hand to stop her. 'Now I don't want to stand here and argue with you. You've woken up in a bad mood and I don't know if this is normal for you but I don't need to watch the show. So you can either get dressed and come with me or you can just give me the keys, let me get what I need to get and then I can be outta here.'

Grace started to slowly walk towards him and in a low voice said, 'Oh, I'll be coming with you, you can bet on that! And for your information,' her voice started to increasingly raise, 'I'm only in a mood like this when I kindly offer my place to stay to someone that thinks they are so bloody desirable that I wouldn't be able to last the night without trying to get a grip of them!' she shouted.

Todd started to feel nervous as he desperately tried to remember what he said last night. He had clearly upset her but simply couldn't recall what he had said.

'Grace, look, if I said something last night that was maybe…um…inappropriate, then I'm real sorry. But I can't remember anything after leaving that pub last night,' he confessed.

'So, you don't remember asking me to leave you alone?' she asked cynically.

'No! I don't! Are you sure I said that? You didn't mishear something?' He couldn't believe he would say something so direct unless she was coming on to him. 'Were you hitting on me?' he asked with a smirk.

'You arrogant bastard,' she hissed. 'You parked yourself on my couch and as clear as day said, "I hope she leaves me alone tonight". And no, I hadn't hit on you and do you know why?! Because you're a smarmy, egotistical Yank, that's why!' Grace was close to him and even though she was angry she felt she just wanted to kiss him. They stood practically nose to nose and they could feel each other's breath on their faces.

Todd couldn't remember saying it but he knew it had to be true. It was a line he had thought before but had not said it out loud. There was no point in trying to explain to Grace what he meant as she would never believe him and he wasn't sure that he believed most of it himself. He just knew that if he went to the cottage and found what he needed, then he wasn't going mad.

'Well, this smarmy, egotistical Yank is still waiting for you to get dressed,' he said blandly.

She swooped away from him and he felt awful as she marched upstairs to get ready and started banging around.

There was a moment in the pub yesterday when he had fleetingly entertained the idea of keeping in touch with Grace. There was something about her and it wasn't just because she was beautiful, warm and funny. He didn't know what it was, but he had never felt this comfortable with a woman as much as he felt with her, even when she was cross.

He walked to the kitchen and opened the back door to let the dogs out while he waited for her. He told himself that he hadn't known Grace forty-eight hours ago and once he was back home then he would be able to forget her and put this down to a sad visit to England.

Twenty minutes later she appeared at the open back door. She was dressed in jeans, a black t-shirt and a close fitting black jacket with a fur collar. She was wriggling her hands into a pair of black leather gloves as she called the dogs back into the cottage.

'Thanks for letting them out,' she said reluctantly and walked to the front door to leave. He silently followed her outside to the street and remained quiet while they walked to Primrose Cottage.

Once in, Grace immediately opened a lounge window to let some fresh air in. She wasn't sure if she had done it as the room needed airing or if it was a habit that was hard to break.

'Right, what is it you are looking for?' she asked. 'I thought she had sent everything to you in that parcel.' She really did know everything, thought Todd.

'She sent over some photographs, my grandpa's pocket watch and just some other bits and bobs. But I erm… have to find a black briefcase that belonged to my Uncle Mort.' Grace noticed he seemed nervous and he glanced up the staircase. 'Is there a wardrobe upstairs?' he asked.

'There's a big one in her room but I don't think there's a case in there. There are just some clothes and shoes. She got rid of Mort's stuff years ago I think.'

'Is it okay if we go up and just check? Please?' Grace was sure there wasn't a briefcase up there but agreed that there was no harm in checking.

The bedroom felt strange when she entered. The settee from downstairs was pushed up against the wall but Kate's nightstands where still in the same place where they had always lived but now there was a huge void between them where the bed once was. On the opposite wall from the settee was a huge wardrobe that had been in the house for as long as Grace could recall. It was a huge, ornate, old fashioned piece of furniture that had a mirror inlaid in the centre panel. Todd immediately walked over to the piece and opened up the doors. After a quick glance, he crouched down and started taking the contents out that were laid on the bottom shelf. He had completely emptied it and still not found the briefcase. He stepped back and saw a shelf above the hanging rail.

'They're just shoes and bags up there,' she exclaimed.

'Tell him to look anyway,' said the voice behind her. As Grace turned in disbelief she was face to face with Crowley who then put his finger on his lips to indicate to her not to say anything. She turned her head back to Todd who hadn't noticed or heard Crowley.

'Maybe, move all the stuff, it might still be up there,' suggested Grace. When Grace turned back, Crowley had disappeared, leaving her reeling. She thought his deed was done. He was supposed to have moved on. 'What the hell is going on', she thought. She wanted to run from the cottage so she could call Crowley back but something told her that Todd's mission was important.

She watched Todd as he silently began looking around the room. He spotted the night stands, walked over to the nearest one, placed all the items that had been sitting on top of it onto the floor and then carried it over to use as a stool. Grace stepped forward and as she started taking the items from Todd that he passed down, she continued to look out to the landing. Todd spotted her and wondered what she was looking for.

'What's the matter?' he asked bluntly. Grace looked at him and he glanced at the landing to give her a hint.

'Oh, nothing, I just thought I heard someone that's all, old houses and that,' she lied. 'Can you see anything up there?'

Todd pulled the last few bags down and sure enough a black briefcase was pushed to the back. He slid it out gently, then jumped off the nightstand onto the floor and while still clutching the case he sat on the settee. He couldn't believe it was actually there. It hadn't been a dream. How the hell would he have known where to look for it if he hadn't been told? Grace looked at Todd's face and realised he looked shocked. She tentatively stepped forward and slowly sat next to him on the couch while Todd continued to stroke the contours of the case with his finger.

'Todd? Todd, are you okay?' she asked gently. He carried on looking at the case and started to smile slightly. 'How did you know that that was there?' asked Grace. Todd was still staring at the case. It was a simple looking gentlemen's briefcase in black leather with brass-looking locks that had become tarnished with age. She decided to probe further.

'Do you know what's in it?' asked Grace. Todd chuckled more to himself.

'Grace, if I told you, you'd never believe me,' he said with resignation.

Grace thought for a moment about all what she had experienced in the last month and quickly concluded that there was nothing that he could say that would shock her. She may be surprised, but never shocked. She also, for some reason, knew that whatever he said, it would be the truth.

'Try me!' And she put her hand on top of his which pulled him slightly out of his trance-like state.

Todd looked at Grace and believed that she would listen to him and not make him feel like he was going mad. He trusted her and fleetingly hoped that she might be able to make sense of it all.

'I don't know even where to start,' said Todd.

'Try somewhere in between being born and you jumping on a plane yesterday...or was it the day before...I'm not sure which.' Grace was trying to be light hearted.

Todd carried on staring at the case still on his lap.

'Okay, here goes. As you know, I received a parcel from my aunt a few weeks back. Like I said there were a few bits in there, jewellery, old photos and stuff. Anyway, she said in her note that there was some more bits in her attic but it was bulky stuff and she wasn't sure if I wanted it, but if I did it would be nice if I came over and visited and collected it seeing as I hadn't seen her in years. But she also said that if I didn't want to come to England then one day she would leave it to me or my brother, in a will.' Grace remained silent. She remembered the parcel that she posted to Todd and never asked Mrs Mortimer about the contents but she was clearly sorting things out as she knew she was dying. Todd continued.

'To be honest, I was thinking about maybe coming over to England to see her and even my brother Beau was thinking about coming too. But with me in the middle of moving to New York and Beau taking care of the ranch we figured we could sort another time, you know.' Todd began to feel guilty at how dismissive he and his brother had been to the old lady. 'Anyway, the next thing I know I get a call from Beau to say that she had died.'

'It was me that called your brother,' Grace said softly. Todd briefly looked at her and smiled.

'So he said, the old lady had died and one of us was going to have to go to England, which meant me. Beau couldn't go. He's got his family and the ranch and…God, I don't know. So I said I couldn't go. Hell, I was only moving across the country, setting up a new apartment and starting my new job that I had waited so long for. But hey, what's that compared to Beau's responsibilities?' Grace noted the sarcastic tone and realised that there were some issues between the brothers but she knew that was a conversation for another day. Todd was hesitating and started to gently shake his head.

'You're not going to believe this,' he muttered. Grace gave his hand an encouraging squeeze and smiled as he took a deep breath.

'I was at the ranch last week, in the stables and I was helping some of the hands to clear the boxes. It was their break and they always go to a little area away from the stables to kick back for a bit. Anyway, I stayed and carried on. But I knew someone was behind me and I thought maybe Milo or one of the guys had come back and when I turned around,' he paused and smirked, 'she was there.' Todd looked directly at Grace, 'My Aunt Kate was stood there…in the stable…as clear as you or me and she was looking right at me.'

Grace made an audible gasp. 'I know, right!' chuckled Todd. 'Man, I hardly recognised her. She was about thirty-years-old and looked like a photo my dad used to have of her and my uncle years back. She was beautiful, you know.'

Grace's body was prickling all over. She couldn't believe he was saying this. How could this happen to someone else that she knew?! Did Crowley know? Why was he here before? She thought everything was finished and all she had to do was grieve for her friend and sort her life out as she promised. But this felt more complicated than it ever had.

'I was just standing there! Looking at her and the guys outside didn't even notice her at all. I thought I was dreaming. She just smiled and said that I was a good boy and she and my Uncle Mort were so proud of me for giving the ranch to Beau even though I was the eldest.' He paused for a moment and swallowed. 'Then she started asking me questions. I mean, does that happen in a dream? I didn't think so, but she was asking me stuff about the parcel and the stuff in the attic,' he said.

'What's in the attic?' questioned Grace.

'I dunno. But she said, "I didn't tell Grace about the will and she needs to know. You need to tell her and you have to go into the attic. You'll like it".'

'Like what?' asked Grace. Todd shrugged his shoulders.

'She said that there was a copy of the will in her wardrobe in England and I was to find it. She said I had to come. It was like she knew I had made my mind up not to go. You know the strange thing? Towards the end, when she was talking, the guys walked back in and didn't see her. I mean she was there, right there in front of me and they couldn't see her. I looked at the guys and then when I looked back…well, she was gone,' he laughed quietly, 'just gone.' Todd put the case on the floor and placed both his hands on his face and started to rub and then gave a loud frustrated growl.

'I don't know about you, but I need a drink; wait here,' said Grace.

She bound downstairs and headed straight for the under sink cupboard. She then poured the dregs of the Jack Daniels in one glass and then some Scotch that she had found in another glass and went straight back upstairs.

As she walked in, Todd looked defeated and very tired. He had clearly not been handling this well at all.

'JD or Scotch? Take your pick,' offered Grace. Todd took the nearest glass and waited for Grace to sit next to him again. He tapped her glass and took a large mouthful.

'So, that's when you decided to come to England?' she said softly.

'God, I wish,' he took another drink. 'Grace, I got so wasted that night you wouldn't believe. I was like some crazy drunk and then convinced myself that I had imagined it all. I mean even if she was a ghost, then the hands would have seen her, right? I went to bed that night, drunker than a Texan, but then she woke me. She was shaking me and swearing at me to wake up telling me to book the goddamn ticket.'

Grace's eyes immediately filled as she knew they were her words.

'She came back the following two nights. Screaming like a banshee saying she wasn't going away until I did this. She was scary, man! I even said to her what happened to that lovely aunt that I remembered when I was a kid and then she slapped me! Told me that I had to go to England to see if I could find my balls at least.'

Grace burst out laughing. She thought it was bad enough that Crowley turned up drunk each time he visited, but poor Todd had to deal with Kate's temper and a mild beating to boot.

'Then Beau was saying that it didn't look good that no one from home was going to the funeral and we should call you and tell you. And then he said your name, he said Grace! Then it hit me. It was real, her visits, her talking to me, her messages, everything. So, I booked the flight and you know the rest.' He took another gulp of his drink and looked at Grace. His deep blue eyes looked almost childlike as he searched Grace's face for judgement.

'Crazy, huh?' sighed Todd. Grace had an overwhelming feeling of wanting to put her arms around him and tell him that it wasn't crazy. She wanted to tell him all what she had experienced in the last few weeks but she wasn't sure if he could handle it right now.

Grace bent down, groped for the briefcase handle and pulled it back up onto Todd's lap.

'Look, she was right about the case, so let's see what's in here, eh?' They both sat for a moment staring at the briefcase. They both knew that it contained a will but what was in that, they didn't know.

Todd fumbled at the worn mottled clasps then simultaneously pushed each button. A loud crack emanated from each of them and then Todd slowly lifted the lid.

Inside was a heap of papers, some of them dating back to the fifties but nothing of any consequence. Then sure enough, they found a white envelope that looked almost pristine compared to the rest of the contents. Todd passed the envelope to Grace who immediately shook her head.

'She wanted you to find it, so you need to be the one to

open it,' she insisted.

Todd gently opened the envelope, pulled out the documents and unfolded the paper to read. The first page was headed Gerard & Daniels who were obviously Mrs Mortimer's solicitors. The letter had simply stated that enclosed was a copy of the will that she had recently drawn up in their office. The letter was dated 7 months ago.

'You think it's okay if we read it?' whispered Grace.

'Hey, I didn't come all this way thinking I was as mad as Dr Frankenstein just to rearrange somebody's wardrobe.'

CHAPTER 15

Stepping into the office of Gerard & Daniels Solicitors in Lanson was like hopping back to the 1960's. The office was furnished with huge antique wooden desks, battered leather chairs and old metal filing cabinets dotted around the room. Even some of the secretaries looked like they may have handled Henry VIII's divorce. The only clues that illustrated modern times were the computers on the desks and a few magazines set on a coffee table in the waiting area.

Grace and Todd took a seat as instructed by one of the staff and silently surveyed their surroundings.

'Is anything in this town modern?' whispered Todd. Grace looked over and smiled.

'Miss Hammond? Mr Mortimer?' An elderly gentleman stood expectantly in front of them and waited for them to acknowledge him. He was very short and thin and looked to be in his mid-sixties. His brown tweed suit was shabby and looked like it might have fitted better thirty years ago when he had bought it. His face was heavily lined and jowly and reminded Grace of a Bassett Hound that used to live back home in Wales. Under his arm he carried a manila coloured folder bursting with paper while his other hand was stuffed into his sagging jacket pocket.

'Yes, that's us,' declared Todd and he and Grace stood. The man smiled, nodded and gesticulated to them to follow him into an office that was set within the larger open floor.

Once they were in, they took a seat and watched the man try and clear a space on his desk to set his folder down. Every surface in his office was covered in similar looking folders of varying thicknesses.

'Got yourself a little fire hazard here,' joked Todd. He looked at Grace who didn't smile and then at the solicitor who found it less amusing. Todd lowered his eyes, slunk slightly in the chair and decided to keep his mouth shut.

'I don't like computers,' snapped the solicitor. He continued to move skittishly around the room trying to tidy a work area. He had a nervous disposition which made Grace feel uncomfortable, as he scurried around the room like a sniffing ferret. Eventually, he sat down and seemed almost out of breath.

'I'm Mr Gerard, Kate Mortimer's solicitor. Thank you for coming in today,' he said. 'Before I start, may I offer my deep condolences. I felt very privileged to have called Kate and Mort friends of mine.' He paused to reflect and then continued. 'Now, I understand you have already seen a copy of the will that was in Mrs Mortimer's personal effects?' he asked. Todd and Grace nodded.

'We wouldn't normally do it like this. We tend just to contact those named in the will but seeing as you are from overseas, Mr Mortimer; it is probably more convenient just to tie it all up now, so to speak. Okay, well I will just run through this quickly and then I have a few things I need to go over with you.' Mr Gerard opened his file and turned a few pages over until he came to the will. He silently read a few points and then continued.

'So, as you know already Miss Hammond you have been appointed as executor of the will as well as myself. As we discussed on the phone, between us we can satisfy all of Mrs Mortimer's wishes. There is some provision for Alice Barker, a cousin I believe, in Canada whom I will be speaking to in the morning. There is also a lump sum left for Beau Mortimer and yourself Todd. However, she has noted in the will that there are items located in the attic of Primrose Cottage, Pelsby that belonged to your Grandfather, Jake Mortimer Sr., which you can keep or dispose of at your discretion. She says here these items are boxed and marked for your attention. Have you investigated the attic at all, Mr Mortimer?' enquired the solicitor.

'No, not yet. We couldn't be sure that this will was her final will and that her wishes in the copy we found were her final ones. We thought it best to wait to hear what you had to say before we…well, did anything,' said Todd.

Grace was shifting in her chair. She didn't want to think of anything, she just wanted to listen to what the old man had to say.

'I suggest you investigate the area as soon as and if there are any problems you will need to bring them to my attention or Miss Hammond's. So…' he continued to read, 'apart from the marked items in the property, all other effects are to be included in the inheritance of Primrose Cottage to Grace Hammond.'

Grace was still silent and felt slightly detached from the present scene. She wasn't sure how to feel. She would flit from feeling grateful for the inheritance, then sad at the circumstances, then scared of owning her own home, then not wanting to live there, then excited at a new start, then remembering her friend was gone. She just wasn't sure if she should be happy or sad. Her life at the moment felt alien to her. Nothing felt familiar. Todd was still staying on her couch and she had not returned to work yet. Even taking Benji for a walk now felt strange. Through all this she had struggled and was finding it hard to even talk some days. She felt if she had to talk then she had to think and right now she didn't even want to think. She had not seen Crowley since they had found the will and she had made a point when walking the dogs of asking Crowley not to see or contact her until she was ready.

'Grace?' Todd's voice was drifting into her thoughts.

'Sorry, I was…erm…' she trailed off.

'Miss Hammond, I will transfer the deeds but you will need to contact Land Registry and the Local Council about council tax until such time you decide what you would like to do with Primrose Cottage,' said Mr Gerard.

'I'll sort it,' she whispered.

'Now, there's nothing else really I need to do. I'll make all the relevant transfers to you and your brother and Miss Barker. All the other items noted in the will I can take care of.' He pulled some paper from the file, 'I just need your signature on a couple of things.'

Mr Gerard presented them with various documents to sign and then quickly concluded the business in hand. He wished Todd a safe journey and advised Grace that he would be in touch to finalise a few things.

Once they were out on the street, Grace was grateful for the fresh air and clean light of the day. As they headed back to the car, she turned her phone back on and it immediately started bleeping with various messages. They were all from Sean.

'You're a popular bunny, aren't you?' joked Todd.

'It's just my mate Sean. He's nursing a broken heart after his boyfriend chucked him. It was for the best though, turned out he was married. He just wants to meet and offload probably,' grumbled Grace.

'Why don't you meet him? Go to the pub or something?' suggested Todd as they climbed into the car.

'I'm not in the mood,' she moaned.

'You gotta get out, Grace. You can't stay cooped up,'

'Why don't you mind your own bloody business?' Grace snapped. Todd was taken aback. He had not seen this outburst coming. Normally, there were little warning signs. He went to say something but thought best not to while she was driving.

The journey home was in complete silence. Todd decided when they got back to the cottage he was going to The Blacky to finalise his flight back home. He needed to look in the attic of Primrose Cottage as well and collect the box, but he really wanted Grace to be with him when he did that. Hopefully, she would be more agreeable later.

Once they were back in Pelsby, Todd grabbed a couple of things from his bag and went to go straight back out. Grace spotted him putting his passport in the inside pocket of his khaki jacket.

'You going out?' she asked softly.

'Yeah, I'm…erm…going to the pub. I need to sort a few things out,' he went to open the door.

'What things?' Grace asked.

'Um..well, I need to sort about going home. I'm not needed here anymore and you need some…um…space,' he muttered.

'Space? What do I need space for?' Todd noted that

she sounded like she was challenging him. He knew this tone already and wasn't sure if he had the energy to fight with her. He stepped towards her and tried to sound sympathetic.

'I just mean, we all need to get back to normal.'

But that was just it. What was normal anymore? She didn't know. The only person that understood her at the moment was Todd and now he was going too and all she could feel was anger.

'What the hell is NORMAL?!' Grace screamed.

'Hey! I ain't got time for another scene from The Shining!' shouted Todd.

'Then GO! I don't know why you are still here anyway! Oh, actually I do, you still need to get your booty from the attic. Well, go and get it then! The will's real, you don't need to wait,' she barked.

'Why are you being such a bitch?' Todd hissed. Grace knew she was but she didn't care she wanted to fight.

'You come over here, acting like you knew her. You didn't know her! You didn't give a shit about her. I was the one who went in every day. I was the one who made sure she had food in the cupboard. I was the one that made sure she took Benji out just so she would get some exercise. I was the one who would listen to her stories of Mort and home and you! You! The last time she saw you, what were you, fifteen? No one knew her like I did. She was a bloody cow! Goin' on all the time about me having a bloke and having no life. Always saying about how I looked and how I should be jumping on any man that sat within a mile of me!' Grace was pacing around the room like a mad animal. Todd was still at the door.

'Do you know she'd slag everyone in this village? Everyone! After all that they did for her, right up to the end. They were all good to her and she was as nice as pie to their bloody faces, but not to mine, oh no. I got it with both barrels! She would go on about my life and all the time she knew she was dying and couldn't fucking tell me!! Months of talking crap and she didn't tell me! And then the best, oh this is the best by a long shot, she comes to you! Tells you what needs to be done. Not me! I get the drunk! I get the Lord fucking Snooty visiting me who's too pissed to figure out what he needs to do and in the meantime I just have to put up with him 'popping in'.' She illustrated speech marks in the air to Todd who was now wondering who the hell she was talking about.

'She couldn't come to me, could she? Now, I've only got her bloody dog to feed and walk and pick up its shit. But I suppose that's better than the shit I used to take from her! So yeah, Todd, you go the pub and leave me with normal, eh?'

All of a sudden there was a strange sense of relief. He was glad she had said all that. He knew that she didn't mean any of it but he was glad she said it. She needed to say it all. She had become more and more quiet with each passing day and he felt like he was living with a ticking bomb. He had previously hoped that she would explode long after he had gone home. But now, he was relieved that she had done it with him.

Grace was now standing still in the middle of the living room and was staring at him. Her eyes were puffy and even though her lips were in a tight line he could see her bottom lip was starting to tremble. He silently walked towards her, opened his arms and drew her close.

Grace willingly sank against him and started to cry. It was a cry she had never experienced before. She buried herself into his chest and uncontrollably let out a wail. And as he held her tighter, the harder she cried.

'I didn't mean it,' she sobbed into his chest.

'I know,' he whispered and kissed the top of her head under his chin.

'She wasn't always mean,' she pulled away and looked at Todd. 'I loved her and I'm glad she went to you. I'm sorry.' She began to cry again and as she put her head back against him, he pulled her close and started to stroke her hair.

'I just don't know what to do with myself,' she sniffed. 'But you're right, you have to go home and I need to start sorting myself out.'

She pulled away from him and walked to the kitchen to blow her nose. She felt awful for saying those things. She just felt angry and needed to vent.

Todd followed her into the kitchen where she had her back to him and he gently placed his hands on her shoulders and whispered into her ear.

'I want you to go upstairs and wash your face while I make us a coffee. Then I want you to come back down and talk to me. Properly! Okay?' He pushed her shoulders around so she was facing him and looked at her so he could see her acknowledge him.

'Okay,' she sniffed.

Ten minutes later Grace returned to the lounge to find Todd waiting for her on the sofa with two steaming cups on the table in front of him. She sat down next to him and he picked up a cup and passed it to her. He watched her while she took a sip.

'Grace, when I told you about seeing my aunt, you didn't...um...seem fazed at all. I mean, well, most people would be kinda freaked about that, but not you.' Todd continued to read her face and noted that she had not changed expression at all. 'Grace, who is this Lord Snooty?' he eventually asked.

Grace took another sip from the coffee cup. This was it. This was when she would tell him. She knew that he would believe her but she was never sure if the day would come when she would tell him. Why would she need to? It was clear now that Crowley's deed did not have anything to do with any of the Mortimer's. She placed the cup on the table and turned to Todd.

'I'm having a similar experience to what you had with your aunt,' she said eventually.

Todd felt shocked and became very conscious of his reactions. Grace had been wonderful listening to him when he revealed his story and felt he must do the same. He put his own cup down and took her hand into his.

'Tell me,' he asked softly.

'Mine's a stranger. Well, not now, but he was when he first came to see me.' Grace explained about the bridge, Mrs Mortimer finding him dead and then his first visit.

'He comes every now and again and I can call him if I need him. He can hear me,' she explained.

'Do you call him?' asked Todd.

'I do. Well, I did. He would keep me company when your aunt was asleep,' Grace let out a huge sigh. 'All I know is that he has to do a deed. Something that has a positive effect and until it's done then he can't move on. He's in some sort of limbo, I think. His family have moved on but he can't until he does what he needs to do.'

'So, what is it he needs to do, then?' he probed.

'That's the thing, we don't know. I thought it was to do with your aunt and making her cross over but it couldn't have been as I saw him in Primrose Cottage the day we found the briefcase,' Grace shrugged.

'So what's he said since then?'

'I haven't seen him. I told him that I didn't want to see him just yet.' Todd raised his eyebrows in surprise.

'I know. I know. But with everything else that I've had to deal with this week I just couldn't cope with him as well. He likes a drink, does Crowley.' Todd again raised his eyebrows. 'Oh, he's okay. He's a merry drunk shall we say. It's just me being judgemental I s'pose. He's a good man.'

They were both quiet for a while and Grace continued to finish her coffee while Todd digested this new chapter of the story.

'Man, I can't believe this,' he said in an incredulous tone, 'I mean, I was never into anything paranormal or supernatural. Then all of this happens, to us. I mean, why us?' asked Todd.

'Crowley said no one can move on until they leave a positive mark on something or someone. He said a lot of people are not even aware that 'they' are intervening. He said that's when people call it fate. But some people, like you and me receive messages. We're not gifted we're just…well…more involved I guess. I don't know,' Grace sighed. Todd was deep in thought and then looked at Grace.

'My mum said that she was once hanging sheets on the line and a gust of wind snatched the sheet out of her hand before she had a chance to peg it. She said the next thing was she could see me running towards the pond on the ranch. I was only about three years old and I didn't understand that the pond was pretty dangerous. She got to me in time before I fell in. But she always said if the wind hadn't whipped the sheet then I probably wouldn't be here today. Do you think maybe that was some kind of intervention from someone she maybe knew?' he questioned.

'I think that's the kind of thing that Crowley meant,' concluded Grace.

'Wow,' he whispered. He looked at Grace who smiled at him and chuckled.

'So now you see why I wasn't shocked at all. I have my own little Casper,' she joked.

'Grace, you need to talk to this guy. He may be drinking with presidents and film stars but he still needs to be with his family. At least I know my aunt and uncle are together now but you need to help him do what he needs to do and get him to move on. I know your head is messed up at the minute but it ain't gonna get any easier with this still not finished.'

Grace nodded. She knew he was right. 'Look, I know me being here is stalling things and as much as I would like to stay a lot longer I can't. I'm going over to The Blacky and sort out my flight home. In the meantime, I want you to call your guy and talk to him and get things back on track. I'll be an hour and then I'll bring some groceries back and we can have something to eat after we have been to the attic in Primrose Cottage. Okay?' smiled Todd.

'Okay,' agreed Grace, 'thanks for listening, Todd. I feel so much better now and I'm really sorry about before, shooting my mouth off like that. Kate was like my mum, grandma and best friend all rolled into one. I just miss her that's all,' Grace admitted.

Eventually, Todd gathered up his things again while Grace took the cups to the kitchen and shouted that she would see him later then returned back to the lounge ready for her next gentleman. She wondered if Crowley would be annoyed at all at not being able to come and see her. After all, as Todd said, she had delayed his moving on and she now felt very selfish. Nervously, she called out.

'Look Crowley, before you come and see me I just want you to know that I'm sorry for being selfish and I didn't mean to keep you away and I'm sorry that you have been stuck in wherever you are and…' she was struggling, 'well, I'm just sorry, that's all,' she trailed off, ready to call him.

'It's okay, Daff,' she turned and he was sat to her left on the couch. 'There's nothing to forgive,' Crowley said gently and smiled at her.

Grace was relieved to see that he seemed perfectly happy. She didn't even care that he was a bit squiffy.

'Hey, Crowley,' she smiled.

'Hey, Daff,' he shifted on the sofa to make himself more comfortable. 'We have a lot to talk about, you and I,' he stated. 'I think maybe I should start,' he offered.

'Okay,' said Grace apprehensively.

'First, let me relieve you of that bottle of Peach Schnapps that I spied on one of my last visits here.' He jumped off the couch and walked to the kitchen, 'I'm sure you're never going to drink it,' he shouted from the kitchen as he pulled the bottle from the cupboard and inspected the label, 'seeing as this should have been drunk when Prince Charles got married,' he returned to the room with the bottle and two glasses, 'to his first wife!' he chuckled.

He poured two glasses and settled himself back onto the sofa.

'Take a drink, Daff. You're going to need it,' he said. Grace became worried about what Crowley was about to say.

'What is it?'

'Do you remember some time ago I told you about a fellow who I would drink with at a few soirees that had not moved on since he arrived in 2005?' Grace looked at him blankly.

'I told you, my dear. Remember I said he wouldn't complete his task as he was waiting to have a drink with his wife at one of our wonderful parties?' offered Crowley.

'Oh, yes,' she remembered thinking at how romantic it was that he would wait.

'The man, is Jake Mortimer Jr…it's Mort!' he declared.

'What?! Kate's Mort?' cried Grace.

'The very one!' Crowley waited for Grace to digest this before moving on.

'Kate is still with us and so is Mort,' he added.

'Why haven't they moved on? Kate's task has been fulfilled. We found the will,' Grace was confused.

'Indeed it has. But she will not leave until Mort's task is done.'

'So what's Mort's task? Why hasn't he done it?'

'He's tried but the person he selected will not listen or at best doesn't believe or understand that what he is being asked to do is real. So the thing is Grace, we need your help.'

Grace shot him a glance. She sincerely hoped that the help didn't involve her having to explain any paranormal influences or ghostly association. But even if it did she knew she would have to try and help the Mortimer's, especially Kate.

'Mort's task was something he was asked to do while he was still alive. The thing is, he died before he had a chance to complete his request so he has taken the task with him,' Crowley revealed. Grace's mind was swimming with it all, trying to compute what little she knew about passing over and the new detail she was now learning. As some of it started to slip into place she realised something.

'So, are you telling me that when Mort was alive he was

given a deed to fulfil but didn't and then he didn't want to do it when he died because he's been at one of your parties waiting for ten years for his wife to join him so they can be there together before moving on?'

Crowley went to continue, but Grace stopped him, 'So, does that mean that the person who asked Mort to do the task has also been waiting for over ten years before they can move on?' asked Grace. Crowley smiled as Grace finally understood what was happening.

'So who was Mort supposed to help?' questioned Grace.

'Mr Cousins, from Pool Farm, my dear. Mr Jacob Cousins. His daughter is with Kate and Mort as we speak,' revealed Crowley.

CHAPTER 16

Grace reached for the Peach Schnapps and knocked the drink back in one huge gulp, much to Crowley's amusement.

'My dear, you could give Dean Martin a run for his money.' Grace poured herself another drink. She didn't even like Schnapps.

'Old Mr Cousins, from up the road you mean?' asked Grace. Crowley nodded. 'He hasn't got a daughter. I mean, he never had one. He's always been on his own. Surely, if he had had a daughter then I would have heard by now. Someone in the village would have said. He's never been married has he?' asked Grace.

'No, he's never been married,' confirmed Crowley. Grace took a sip from her glass.

'Does he know he has a daughter? Jesus, does he know she is dead?' shot Grace.

'Daff, they need your help,' he said softly. Grace concluded that she had to tell Mr Cousins that he had a dead daughter. 'How in the hell do you tell someone that?' she thought.

'Don't ask me to tell him that he has a daughter and that she's dead. I'm sorry Crowley but that's too much to ask. I mean, I have no proof or anything. He won't believe me! You don't know this man. There are people in the village that reckon he's a murderer and you want me to go up there and tell him that! I can't! I won't.' Grace was starting to become hysterical. 'Oh, my God! Did he kill his daughter? Is that what this is about? Oh fuck!'

Grace stood up and started to pace backwards and forwards in front of Crowley. Was this Crowley's deed? Did she have to do this so he could be with his wife and son?

'Is this your task Crowley? Is this the thing that means you can move on?' she asked.

Crowley stood up and stopped Grace from moving by taking her hands gently into his. He looked at her with an earnest look and waited for her to calm down.

'I don't think this is anything to do with us,' Grace lowered her head in relief, 'but my dear, these are your friends. They need your help. The wanting to move on is so great with all three of them that they are…how can I explain it?' Crowley sought for the words. 'Have you ever been to a party and decided you need to go home, so you call a cab?' asked Crowley. Grace nodded. 'It's like they've had enough of the party and are waiting for the cab. They can't enjoy themselves anymore as they know it's their time to go. But when they call the cab company, the driver can't hear the address. So they keep trying but the cab driver is now ignoring the calls. Does that make any sense?' he looked at her imploringly.

'I guess,' Grace muttered.

'They need you to see Mr Cousins. They need you to tell him that his dreams are real. That's all they want you to do. I promise,' assured Crowley.

'I don't have to mention that he has a dead daughter?' she whispered.

'No. That's not necessary.' Grace walked back to the sofa and Crowley joined her and they both sat down.

'If I do this, does that mean they can all move on? Even if he doesn't believe me?' she asked.

'He'll believe you, Daff. Trust me.' Crowley seemed so self-assured and so she did trust him.

'Kate's nephew is still staying with me. He's just over at The Blacky sorting his flight out. Is it okay if I tell him? I wouldn't mind him coming with me, you see. We have to go to Kate's place later and then we could go from there. The sooner I do this the better, for all concerned I think.'

'I'm sure they would be happy to know that Todd accompanied you,' he said. 'You like Todd, don't you?'

'I do. I like having him here. I feel…' she paused and took a breath, 'I feel like he's someone I might have had, you know, a chance with, maybe.' Grace felt awkward but wanted to tell someone how she felt.

'What about Tom? Do you not like him?' probed Crowley.

'Tom! Well, I do like Tom but not like this. Tom is lovely and all but I don't know. I sometimes think I like Tom simply because there's no one else in Pelsby and he's nice but that's just it. He's nice.'

'And Todd?' asked Crowley.

'Todd is like no one I've ever met before. But then again I've not met that many men to be honest. Don't get me wrong, I've had boyfriends, but they've just been a bit of fun. But Todd…' Grace thought for a moment, 'Todd is the first man that I've been bothered about them saying goodbye.'

Crowley felt a pang of jealousy. Not about Todd, but never again experiencing that pang of want. He was lucky enough to have had it with Jennifer and, apart from being in love itself, it was an extremely powerful feeling. Grace jumped up from the couch and walked to the kitchen to fetch herself a glass of water and to relieve the atmosphere in the room.

'Anyway,' she continued, 'he does have to say goodbye. He has a new job in an architects' firm in New York and I have just inherited Primrose Cottage. So, that's that. He probably has a girlfriend in America anyway,' she muttered.

'You don't know?' Crowley asked.

'Why do I need to know? None of my business,' she retorted.

Crowley stood to join Grace and he could tell that she didn't want to talk about men anymore. He so wanted to shake her and ask her to look in the mirror and see the beautiful person that she was. He was constantly surprised that she thought herself plain and boring. But he suspected that Todd thought the same as he and found Grace to be a truly wonderful being.

'Well, my dear. Whatever you decide to do with your life is entirely up to you. You know more than most that every man dies, but not every man really lives.'

'Braveheart?' Grace asked in an incredulous tone.

'You've seen it?'

'Yep.'

'Damn! I wanted to say something profound so you thought I was intense,' he said disappointingly.

'Oh, believe me, talking to a ghost and being asked to see a potential murderer by a gang of spirits in a heavenly party room is a pretty intense day,' she chuckled. 'But I do know what you are trying to say.'

'I'll be off then. Good luck, Daff. We're all counting on you.'

Grace, now alone, walked to the lounge window and looked beyond Flower Cottages towards Pool Farm. She had no idea how to do what she had been asked. She only hoped that Todd would come up with some bright idea.

It wasn't long before Todd returned and updated her on his flights.

'My flight is Saturday, so you are stuck with me another three days, I'm afraid.' Grace was trying to judge his face about how he felt about going home.

'I can run you to Heathrow, if you like?' offered Grace. Todd looked slightly awkward but accepted her offer. It was clear that the atmosphere had changed between them and they both felt very self-conscious.

'Well, I have a few things to tell you as well,' Grace announced trying to change the mood.

'Yeah? You spoke to Crowley?' asked Todd. He was disappointed that she didn't seem that upset about him going. Why should she, he supposed.

Grace relayed the whole tale to Todd about his aunt and uncle and the fact they were still stuck until they could help. Todd couldn't believe what had happened in the short time that he had been away and realised that Grace wouldn't be that bothered about him going. She clearly had a lot on her plate and his departure was simply something she just needed to add to the list.

'So, I was wondering if you would come to Pool Farm with me. Say no if you want to but I thought maybe we could go after we have been to Primrose Cottage or before or whatever you prefer. If you'll come, I mean. You don't have to though. Actually, forget I asked. I'll go on my own…'

'I'll come,' he said reassuringly. Grace let out a huge sigh of relief.

'Thank you,' she sighed.

'Let's do Pool Farm first then the cottage so I can bring the things straight home. I mean here!' he corrected quickly.

'Okay. Right then, I'll get my jacket,' said Grace. The awkwardness had come back. 'Three days of this', Grace thought. 'I need to keep busy'.

They were soon outside and heading to Pool Farm and trying to ignore the change between them. Grace's thoughts were flitting from visiting Mr Cousins and the time she had to say goodbye at Heathrow. Both were equally dreadful.

'I've no idea what I'm going to say to this bloke,' admitted Grace.

'We just say what we need to say and have to trust Crowley that he will understand what the hell we are talking about,' said Todd.

They decided that it was best if Grace did the talking seeing as Mr Cousins knew her and Todd would interject if things went awry. Grace pointed up ahead to the old farmhouse and revealed to Todd that Mr Cousins owned a lot of land in Pelsby.

They soon arrived at the house and thought it best to try knocking there first before investigating the outhouses for him. The house was typical of the area in grey stone and the front door had been painted red in years gone by and was looking worse for wear. As Todd knocked on the door, Grace was aware that she was starting to sweat. As she was trying to decide how to start, the front door shot open by Mr Cousins who was now squinting at them through his gnarly face.

'Grace,' he growled, 'problem with the cottage?' Mr Cousins gave Todd a deliberate once over and then waited for Grace to answer.

'Not quite, Mr Cousins,' Grace gave Todd a sideward glance. 'Is it okay if we come in a moment?' Grace tried to smile in the hope that it would make Mr Cousins more hospitable. The old man contemplated for a moment and looked at Todd again. For Grace to come to Pool Farm must mean that it was important but how Todd fitted in, he couldn't quite muster. Silently he stepped aside and pointed for them to go through into the house.

They all trotted to the back where the kitchen could be found. It was a large square room with shabby cupboards to one wall, a huge black range to another and a large battered kitchen table set in the middle. It was surprisingly tidy and clean and Grace waited for Mr Cousins to settle somewhere before speaking. Todd took the lead and pulled a chair to sit and the others soon silently followed.

'What's this about then?' Mr Cousins looked uncomfortable. Grace again looked at Todd who then gave her a reassuring smile and nodded for her to start.

'Well, I'm not sure where to start really, cos whatever way I put it it's going to sound odd, so here goes.' Grace took a deep breath and pressed her palms together.

'Have you been having dreams about Mort, Todd's uncle?'

Mr Cousins looked at them in turn like he was watching a tennis match while Grace and Todd remained silent awaiting a reaction. He suddenly stood up and leant over the table on his fists.

'What the hell are you talking about?' he shouted.

'Trust me', Grace remembering Crowley's words. 'Now what?' She could feel panic rising.

'Could you answer the question please, sir?' asked Todd locking Cousins' gaze.

'I told you the other day that I was,' he barked, 'in the pub.' His breathing was becoming louder and faster and Grace could tell the old man was frightened.

'Mr Cousins, please, won't you sit down?' asked Grace softly. He continued to look and then submitted to her request and slowly sat back down at the table. He started to fidget with his hands and turned his gaze to them.

'I think you know that they're not dreams don't you?' said Grace. The old man slowly looked at Grace and his face relaxed a little as he realised she knew something and could maybe make sense of it all.

'Todd and I have been experiencing similar things and I've also had a message, for you.' Grace waited for him to digest what she was saying before continuing.

'I've been told to tell you that you must do what you've been asked. Kate and Mort...well...they're kind of stuck, shall we say. They can't move on until you do what you need to do. Now we don't know what that is and we don't need to know, I've just been asked to tell you to stop ignoring the message and do what's being asked.' Mr Cousins continued to look at his hands. 'Does any of this make sense to you?' she asked.

Todd and Grace looked at the old man who seemed to be lost in his own thoughts. They sat for a while and just as Grace decided to leave him, Mr Cousins spoke.

'I had a daughter,' he whispered. 'She'd be twenty-seven now.' Grace felt relief that he knew about the girl. As she looked at the old man she could see he wanted to tell her more. Grace and Todd stayed silent and waited for him to speak.

'Her mum, Linda, lived in the village since she was little.

We grew up together really. We weren't close or anything like that. She got married and that was that. Anyway, one day I found her, crying she was, walking along the path of the high field. So, I asked her if she wanted to come to the house for a cup of tea and sort herself out and that, and she did. Turns out, her husband was a bit handy with her, if you get my drift.' He looked at Grace who tried to give a reassuring smile for him to continue.

'She came a lot after that. Said she felt safe here. Sometimes I would be out in the fields and I could see the smoke coming from the chimney and I would know she had let herself in.' Mr Cousins became lost again in his thoughts for a moment.

'I fell in love with her and I thought she loved me and then one day she told me she was staying with him and she was pregnant, wanted to make a go of it now they had a baby on the way. Said he'd calmed down and knowing that he was gonna be a dad had changed him. But it didn't,' he said with disgust.

'Anyway, she had a little girl, Jane she called her and I stayed away,' he paused for a moment. 'Then a few years later, Linda found out she had cancer. Nothing they could do for her. It was your Aunt Kate, who told me,' he looked at Todd. 'Kate knew straight away that I was hiding something. So I told her. Eight years of being quiet and I just told her the lot. She was good to me, Kate,' he smiled at Todd.

'Linda didn't have long left and she sent Jane along with a note for me to come and see her as he was out, said she wanted to speak to me. I went of course; I wanted to see her before she was gone.'

Mr Cousins turned and looked at Grace. His eyes were wet and becoming red.

'Jane was mine, not his, she was my daughter and he knew. He had always known apparently. The child didn't of course. Linda wanted me to keep an eye on her as she was growing up but never to say who I really was. She just said she wanted me to try and get close to Jane. Then she asked me to forgive her.' He became silent again.

'And did you?' asked Grace. Mr Cousins nodded, bent his head and then started to cry. Grace spied some kitchen roll and went to fetch it. She tore some off and passed it to him. He took it silently and wiped his face.

'I watched Jane grow up. I used to like seeing her play in the school playground but then I had to stop as people started to talk,' he growled. 'I couldn't say why I was really there could I? Stupid thing to do looking back on it now. Anyway, her dad was drinking. He always liked a drink but he was drinking more and more and as the years went by Jane started to go off the rails a bit, hanging around in Lanson with gangs of boys. The police were always bringing her home. I tried speaking to her but...well, I was just some old codger wasn't I? Then one night she turned up on my doorstep. Her and her dad had had a huge row and he told her.'

'About you?' asked Todd.

'She knew everything, about me and her mum and that I was her real dad. She hated me. She was screaming at me saying it was all my fault that her life was shit. Sorry for swearing,' he added. 'She was so angry and then left. I didn't see her for a few days and then Kate told me that she had run away and her dad couldn't care less. I was worried sick and tried to get him to help find her but he didn't care, told me it was none of my business. He just wanted to drink,' he snorted.

'So, about a year later, she called, out the blue, like. She said she just wanted me to know that she was okay and to let her stepdad know. I asked her to come home but she said no. She was living in a bedsit with some friends in London and was working in a bookstore. Anyway, she called a few more times and I started putting money in a post office account for her so she wasn't going short. I kept asking her to come home but she wouldn't at first. I begged her and then I thought she wouldn't want to come back to him and she wouldn't want to live with me so I bought the cottage. Your cottage,' he looked at Grace. 'I thought if she had her own place then that would tempt her back to Pelsby, but it didn't. Then about a year later she called to say that the bookstore had closed down and she was coming back,' he paused again trying to assemble his thoughts.

'It was your Aunt Kate, who told me,' the old man's voice started to quaver. 'Jane was trying to hitchhike back from London. A man picked her up…and they erm… found her at the side of the road on the Downs. Excuse me,' Mr Cousins shot up and left the kitchen leaving Todd and Grace at the table feeling shell shocked. Todd began to whisper.

'You didn't know any of this?' he asked.

'No, not a thing. My God, he's been called a paedophile all his life and he was only up there so he could look at his little girl playing. Jesus Christ! I moved from Wales to come to a nice sleepy village, but this place has more secrets than the sodding CIA.' Todd snorted and then quickly composed himself as Mr Cousins walked back into the room. He sat back down and looked at them both. He clearly had been crying.

'Sorry about that,' he said gruffly.

'Look, maybe we should go now and leave you alone

for a bit?' suggested Grace. Mr Cousins shot Grace a fearful look and in a moment Grace could see a different man. There was a vulnerability that she had never seen before and a deep sense of loneliness.

'Can I ask what it is that my uncle wants you to do?' questioned Todd. Mr Cousins sat back in his chair and recalled all the various forms of Mort's visits. They were always short and concise and the same.

'He said I have to see Ian and ask him for Jane's diary.'

Todd looked at Grace with a confused look and Grace mirrored the sentiment.

'Sorry, Ian? Who's Ian?' asked Grace.

'Ian Baldwin. He's Jane's stepdad,' revealed Cousins. Grace realised who he meant, the town drunk and general thug. The last time she had seen him was in The Blacky, the day of Kate's funeral. Grace turned to Todd.

'He's a bloke from the village. He still lives here. He was in the pub the day you arrived. He was sat at the table near the door,' said Grace. Todd could vaguely remember a man leaving the pub who was extremely drunk. He was the only person who had not introduced themselves that day.

'What's in the diary?' probed Todd.

'I've no idea and I doubt it will make that much difference to me. I don't want to go anywhere near that cretin,' he spat. Grace threw Todd a concerned glance and felt she had no choice but to reveal more.

'Mr Cousins, there's something else I need to tell you. You see, Jane is with Mort and Kate.' The old man stared at Grace. He went to speak but nothing came out. 'They all need to move on. But they can't, until you do what you've been asked.' Grace was starting to sound desperate. Mr Cousins stood back up and turned to look out of the kitchen window over the sink. Todd stood up and walked over to him.

'Listen man, I don't know you and you don't know me, hell I hardly knew my aunt and uncle but all I know is we gotta do this and we can do it together. This is one thing that you can do for her that will make a difference. And it's the right thing to do. Now, Kate and Mort, they can't leave her and I doubt they would if they could and you said it, you said my aunt was good to you, so you owe her as well. I know it's hard, hell, we all feel like we've been chewed and spat out these last couple o' weeks but this is something good that you can do. And if I know my uncle, he's never gonna stop asking.' Cousins lowered his head in thought.

'If you can't do it for us, or for my aunt and uncle, or even for your daughter, then do it for Linda.' The old man looked at Todd to understand. 'Linda's waiting for her little girl on the other side.'

Mr Cousins turned to look back out of the window.

'What the hell do I say to him?' he growled.

'You just say that you know that there is a diary that belonged to your daughter and you want it and if he refuses, then I'll step in.' Grace raised her eyebrows. 'Now, let's go,' Todd said persuasively.

'What? Now? Just like that?' Cousins asked mockingly.

'Unless you got a better idea or something more important to do?' scoffed Todd. Both men turned to look at Grace waiting for her opinion on the plan. Grace had been listening and thinking back to all the times she had seen Ian Baldwin. She was also thinking about how this secret had never come out. If anyone farted in the village, it was a hot topic for at least a day.

'There's a reason that he has never said that Jane is your

daughter. Reasons probably best kept to him. So I say we have nothing to lose. What's the worst thing that could happen? He calls the police? Well, we can just deal with that if it happens, which I doubt. Todd's right, let's just go round there and tell him what we want and if he says no then…well, we just deal with that at the time won't we? And I'd rather take on Ian bloody Baldwin than having all of them sat 'up there' saying what a bunch of poofs we all are.'

Grace sprung to her feet with new found vigour and stared at Cousins for him to jump on the 'Save The Day Train'. He broke out into a grin, slammed his hands on the draining board and marched out of the kitchen.

'Right! Let's do this,' he shouted from the hall. 'Come on then, before I change my mind!' Grace and Todd looked at each other and started to laugh as they quickly followed the old man outside to the lane. He was already striding toward the village and pulling on his coat as Todd and Grace ran to catch him up. The three of them walked in silence past the Flower Cottages, through the village past The Blacky, towards the newer houses of Pelsby. Grace wondered if Ian would actually be in or if he would still be in the pub. They were soon walking up Ian's path.

'Right, Mr Cousins, do you want to do to the talking or should me or Todd say something?' Grace was feeling nervous now.

'It's my problem and she's my daughter. I'll deal with it.' He turned to Todd, 'You,' he stabbed his finger towards Todd's chest, 'if he gets rough, you have my full permission to knock him out,' he ordered. Todd wanted to say that surely any judgement of knocking people out was up to him but he didn't want the old man to lose his nerve so while trying to supress a smile, Todd nodded.

Mr Cousins banged on the door like an impatient rent man and before long, a very drunken Ian opened the door.

'Believe me Ian, I got better things to do than be knocking on your door at any time of my life but I will make today the only exception,' snarled Cousins.

Ian was wavering slightly and was gripping the door to steady himself.

'What the hell do you want?' Ian hissed.

'I want to see Jane's bedroom. There's something in there that belongs to me!' He went to push pass but Ian staggered forward and blocked him

'Everything in this house belongs to me! You might own half the fucking village but not this bit or anything in it. So sod off back to your farm and wait for another hitchhiker to come and murder them, you paedo.'

Without hesitation, Todd was shoving Ian back into the house by the collar of his polo shirt and pushing him into a chair in the lounge. Grace and Cousins stepped in and watched Todd.

'You sir, are gonna sit here and behave like a good little boy while my friends go upstairs and try and find one of Jane's books,' Todd turned to look at them and without hesitation Grace and Cousins bounded up the stairs. 'Now you can sit nice for the next five minutes and we'll be gone before your gin's gotten warm or you can fight me and spend a few days in hospital where the only alcohol you'll be getting is the kind they'll be rubbing on your cuts.' Todd still had hold of Ian's shirt but could feel him physically slump into submission.

Cousins and Grace walked into Jane's room. It looked untouched since she left only for a few things on the bed that had been discarded since her death. They both scanned the room and haphazardly started to open drawers. Then the search became more frantic, looking under beds and behind furniture. The room wasn't large and soon they were losing their optimism. Grace walked over to a built in wardrobe and spotted a brown box on the floor. As she pulled it out she noticed that it had been posted by Hampshire Police.

'Mr Cousins?' Grace slid the box out and onto the floor so he could look at it as well.

'You think it'll be in here?' he whispered.

'If she was keeping a diary, then it's likely that she had it on her when she was coming back,' offered Grace. Mr Cousins understood and nodded his head silently. He began to peel off the tape and slowly opened the box. Inside was a rucksack with various personal things. A toothbrush, underwear, an old magazine and some money. There was also a large hold-all that held clothes, some electrical items, an old battered pink bunny and make-up but there was no sign of a diary. Mr Cousins looked defeated and sat on the floor looking around the room. Grace could see grief creeping into his face.

'If I was Jane, where would I hide a diary'? Grace thought as she stared at the contents of the hold-all. Grace noticed the bunny was the kind of bunny that children used to keep their pyjamas in. As she reached to pull him out, she realised that it was heavy and his belly distended with something hard inside. Cousins watched Grace slowly unzip the back of the bunny and pull out a small book covered in stickers and sticky tape. She looked at it for a moment and then passed it straight into Mr Cousins' shaking hands who took it tentatively. He opened the book at some random page and silently read its contents as the tears ran down his face.

'I think we should go,' Grace said.

Mr Cousins, still gripping the diary, pulled himself from the floor and stuffed the rabbit into one pocket and the diary into another then followed Grace down the stairs. Grace stopped in the hall to speak to Todd but Cousins walked straight out onto the street. Grace nodded to Todd with a half-smile who was still standing over Ian.

'See, that wasn't hard, was it? The old man got what he wanted and you don't have to check in to the local hospital. Everyone's a winner,' Todd began to walk out. 'Enjoy the rest of your life Ian, if you can remember any of it.' Todd slammed the door behind him and saw Grace and Mr Cousins up ahead waiting for him.

'You guys find the diary?' Todd asked when he reached him.

'We did,' said Grace. 'Mr Cousins just wants to go home now, on his own. I said we would walk him as far as Primrose Cottage.'

They walked through the village again back towards Pool Farm and once they reached Primrose Cottage, they all stopped. Mr Cousins stared at his feet and shifted his weight from one to the other.

'Well, I guess this is where I say thank you. To both of you. I erm...' he started to stammer.

'It's okay, I know. Been an emotional day today hasn't it? You go on home and if you need anything then you know where I am? I mean it,' said Grace.

Mr Cousins touched his imaginary hat to say goodbye, turned and walked back up the lane to his farm. Grace and Todd watched him for a moment and saw, as he was in the distance, him pull the pink bunny from his pocket and press to his face.

Grace turned and looked at Todd and gave out a big sigh.

'You think he's gonna be okay?' asked Todd.

'He'll be no worse off than before. I don't know whether to feel sorry for him or to be glad for him. What a day, eh? And you, acting all masculine, I was impressed,' she sniggered. Todd blushed slightly then turned to look at Primrose Cottage.

'Well, the day's not over yet. Let's see what's in this attic then?' They both shuffled to the cottage and felt slightly raw with what had just happened. Grace was trying to make sense of it all and Todd was finding that this constant state of amazement was now being the norm.

Once in the cottage, they headed straight upstairs and found the door to the attic on the landing ceiling. Fortunately, for them, as they pulled the door a loft ladder was attached which slid with surprising ease onto the floor.

'I hope there is electric up there. We forgot to bring a flashlight.' Todd climbed the stairs and disappeared through the hole. Grace remained at the bottom as she listened to Todd shuffling around. In unison to a light turning on, she heard Todd give a triumphant cheer.

'Come on up,' he shouted.

Grace climbed the ladder and emerged into a fairly small attic space. It was surprisingly tidy and only for a couple of pieces of old furniture the whole attic was bursting with ordered boxes. Todd offered Grace his hand as he gently pulled her onto her feet to stand in the room itself.

'Christ, look at all these boxes. What's in them all?' asked Grace.

'Look, these ones have my name on,' informed Todd.

Grace walked over and there were two fairly large boxes with Todd's name printed in large letters. Todd pulled the first one open like an excited child on Christmas Day. He peered inside but Grace couldn't see.

'Oh, wow,' grinned Todd.

'What is it?' asked Grace. Todd reached in the box and pulled out a huge leather saddle.

'A saddle?' Grace was surprised.

'This is not just any saddle, this is my Grandpa Jake's saddle,' Todd was slowly inspecting it with a look of awe across his face. 'This is a genuine R.T. Frazier saddle!' Grace continued to look at him with a blank expression.

'Jeez, Grace. This is a piece of American history. I knew it had been passed to Uncle Mort but I figured he must have sold it.' Todd stroked the metal horn and then gave the seat a rub with the sleeve of his jacket to buff the leather which already had a surprising shine to it.

'See here,' Todd pointed to a stamp in the leather, 'Frazier, see?' Grace could see the stamp and smiled to look slightly interested.

'What will you do with it?' asked Grace. Todd silently looked at the saddle and continued to stroke it contours and gently polish various areas. A sad look came across his face.

'This should be Beau's. He has the ranch now, so it should go to him, really.'

'It's marked for you though,' pointed out Grace.

'Yeah I know, but this saddle belongs on a ranch, not a wall in a New York apartment. My aunt may have thought the ranch was coming to me with me being older than Beau.' he sighed. He quickly recalled the hard conversation he had had with his dad, Paul, about not wanting the ranch as he wanted to be an architect. His dad had been disappointed but knew it was for the best. Beau's blood ran with stallions and he made John Wayne look like Laura Ingalls.

Todd set the saddle back and turned his attention to the other box. Once opened, it revealed photographs, hundreds of them of the ranch in years gone by. There were all old black and white photos of previous generations of Mortimer's. Todd became animated again as he flicked through the contents and passed them to Grace narrating who was who in the picture. Grace marvelled at how artistic the pictures were especially the ones of the ranch hands that illustrated true life on the land.

'All these must have been taken by my Aunt Kate. She always had this old camera swinging around her neck. It was like something from biblical times,' laughed Todd. 'She would hold it about here,' and he pointed to his midriff, 'look down into it and click.'

They continued to root through the box and came across pictures of Todd and Beau having a food fight and then more pictures of them crying after being scolded for the mess. How Kate had captured the animation of life was breath-taking.

'I didn't realise she was this good. I knew she was a photographer for the American Embassy and that, but I had no idea that she was this good. I remember her taking pictures when I first knew her. I asked her about her taking pictures and she said that once Mort was gone she found it hard to see life anymore, which is so sad when you see these pictures.' Grace felt an overwhelming wave of sadness and wanted to cry for her friend but she swallowed the choking lump in her throat and stood to scan the other boxes in the attic to distract and compose herself.

'What do you think are in these ones then? I s'pose these are all mine seeing as they are not marked.' Todd stood up and walked beside her to a tower of boxes standing four deep high.

'Listen,' Grace said, 'if there's anything in these boxes or even the cottage that you want, then take it please. I only wanted a cushion that we made together and her teapot and I've ended up with the cottage, so honestly, take anything you want. Even the cushion seeing as you haven't got a saddle to sit on anymore,' joked Grace.

Todd was standing very close to Grace and they silently became aware of each other's physical presence. She couldn't see him as he was standing slightly behind her but she knew he was staring at her. She could feel her heart starting to quicken so she started to babble.

'Okay, shall we take one of these boxes down and have a look at what's inside. I'm not sure how to do this. Shall we open one each and see if there's anything you might want to take back or shall I just leave you up here and you can have a mooch yourself. Mind you looking at the amount of boxes you might have to delay your flight, which I'm not saying you should, unless you want to, I just mean there's a lot of stuff to get through isn't there?' Grace was frantically trying to think of more things to say.

'Let's just open a couple of these boxes and see what's inside,' Todd said calmly trying to slow Grace down.

He pulled the top box and placed it on the floor and tore at the tape. Inside were more black and white photographs, mainly of buildings. As he began to leaf through Grace pulled another box down and quickly opened it to also find more photographs of black and white images of buildings.

'What do you think all this is for?' asked Grace.

'I'm not sure,' said Todd distractedly as he continued to look at the photographs. Grace could see he was absorbed in looking at the contents of his box and dismissing the one she just opened. She pulled another to investigate.

Again, she found more photos of buildings. There were some of people, mainly black people and a few shots of The Lincoln Memorial.

'Hey, did you know that Tom Hanks is a distant cousin to Abraham Lincoln?' asked Grace passing the photograph to Todd. Todd took the photograph, studied it and passed it back without saying a word. He then looked in Grace's box that she first opened and then moved to the second one that was still at her feet.

'Can you put that photograph back in the box where you found it?' he asked still rifling through.

'Sure,' said Grace slowly, 'Todd, are you okay? What are all these photos about?'

'Grace, would you mind if I stayed here for a while. I just want to go through some more of the boxes,' asked Todd.

Even though he seemed distracted Grace noticed an excited glint in his eye.

'Yeah, okay. Do you want me to stay?'

'Erm...' Todd looked awkward. He clearly wanted to be on his own but was struggling to say it and Grace could see.

'Tell you what, why don't you stay here and have a root through all this stuff. I'm just going to see Mr Cousins again and make sure he's okay. I'll meet you back home later and you can tell me if you have found any hidden treasure,' suggested Grace.

Todd was grateful that she recognised he needed to be on his own and thought she was wonderful for acting on it. The awkwardness came back so Grace turned on her heel and walked to the hatch in the floor. As she descended she smiled at Todd and left him standing amongst all the boxes.

She thought of Todd all the way to Pool Farm. She wondered if he was sad about the saddle but then realised that they thought the saddle was lost and even though he wouldn't have it personally, he would have a sense of happiness knowing that it was intended for him. She wondered if he would ever tell his brother that detail.

The smoke was billowing from the farmhouse and Grace supposed that Mr Cousins was inside so went straight there. She wasn't at the door long when he answered it and invited her in. He walked straight into his lounge and stood with his back to the fire.

'I only called to see if you were all right?' You left in such a hurry before,' she said. Grace spied the diary on the armchair, together with the pink rabbit. Mr Cousins noticed her gaze and looked on them also.

'Can you stop for a bit?' he quietly asked. He clearly wanted someone to talk to and Grace felt relieved that he wanted some company.

'Why don't you sit yourself back down? I'll make us some tea,' he went to protest. 'It's no trouble,' insisted Grace.

Grace soon found her way around the old man's kitchen and set a tray with teacups, sugar, milk and a pot of tea and carried the load back to the lounge where Mr Cousins pulled a table in front of the fire for her to place it. Grace poured the tea and sat herself down in the old shabby armchair opposite Mr Cousins in front of the fire. Even though the room was slightly grubby, it was decidedly tidy. The furniture was old and worn and the walls had a film of soot disguising its original colour which she suspected had once been pale green. Threadbare rugs covered the old slate floor that ran throughout the farmhouse and the one beneath her feet was scorched in parts from the spitting fire.

'Are you glad you went, in the end?' asked Grace.

'I am,' he whimpered. He started to sniff and produced a handkerchief from his sleeve and wiped his eyes and nose.

'Here,' and he passed the diary to her. Grace slowly took the book and watched the old man's face. He sat back into his chair and stared at the fire. As she leafed through the pages she could see that the diary was in letter form and all the letters were to her mother. The dates confirmed that the diary was written after her mother's passing. Grace thumbed the book to the last entry.

Dear Mum,

I called Dad last night and I'm going back to Pelsby. I told him about Carters closing down which means I have no job so I can't stay in the bedsit. Jack's been an arse and said I can only stay if I put up my share of the rent. I know Dad's been putting that money away for me but I'm trying to save it. I've had an idea. I want to do an apprenticeship, maybe in agriculture so I can help him with Pool Farm. I hope he thinks it's a good idea. If he does then I can use the money for driving lessons. I've not told Ian. There's no point. He doesn't care and he's still drinking and I don't want him in my life. I know Dad's not liked much in the village but that's only because people don't understand him. So I'm going to change all that, I hope. I feel like it's time to do something with my life and losing my job has kind of done me a favour. Is it you looking down on me and helping me? I hope so. I hope me and Dad can get along though. I've never said it to him but I do love him. He's been the only one that has been bothered about me even after all the horrible stuff I said. I'm going to ask him if I can live in the farmhouse with him. I don't want to live in a cottage on my own and I keep thinking that Ian will just turn up and cause trouble. Do you think he will mind? Maybe if I just tell him it's for a bit and then try and win him over with my Pot Noodle recipes (ha ha). Anyway Jack's got a mate who can take me some of the way back to Pelsby and then I'm going to hitchhike the rest. The start of my new adventure which I need to start now by packing. I'll write soon and let you know how I get on with Dad and what he says.

Wish me luck and stay by my side.
Love you, Mum.

Jane xxx

Grace closed the diary. She didn't want to and couldn't read anymore. The whole entry was full of hope that was never allowed to flourish and even though the page that followed was blank it still read full of tragedy.

'Have you read all of it?' asked Grace quietly.

'No, just bits. Did you read the last one?' he looked at Grace as she nodded. The old man carried on looking at the flames and Grace followed suit sipping her tea. Grace sat there for nearly an hour, just her and the old man looking at the fire and soon she became aware that it was getting dark.

'Mr Cousins, I'd best be off,' she said softly. He stirred from his trance and placed his tea cup on the table that had been resting on his lap.

'Before you go Grace, I just want to say thank you. For everything,' he shifted to his feet and Grace stood up as well. 'You won't say anything to anyone. I mean in the village. About Mort and that,' he urged.

'Of course I won't,' assured Grace. He took her hands into his.

'You're a good girl, Grace. Kate always said you were a diamond, she loved you dearly. I'll miss her, that's for sure.' He was still holding on to her hands.

'I've not had much love in my life, Grace, only Linda. And until today I didn't know that Jane cared,' his voice was faltering and he was trying his best to keep his emotions in check. 'But she loved me, Grace. She loved me.' He started to cry and Grace enveloped him into her arms and held him tight while he cried.

Grace also wept. This poor old man had been labelled the worst of any human trait and none of it was true. Quite the opposite; he watched his child from afar and made no demands due to his love of Linda. His charity to hitchhikers also made sense now. He obviously wanted to make sure they were safe for some of their journey. Grace was overwhelmed with guilt and shame at the thought of contributing to the lies, rumours and unkindness this man had endured.

Mr Cousins calmed himself and pulled away from Grace's embrace and retrieved his handkerchief from earlier.

'You be off now then, my girl,' and he started to shoo her toward the door. Grace turned to him before he closed the front door.

'I'll pop in over the next couple of days. Todd leaves on Saturday; no doubt he'll want to say goodbye to you.'

Mr Cousins touched his imaginary hat, smiled and then shut the door.

Grace's mind was whirring with the detail of the day as she walked back home. With Todd telling her he was leaving, to Mr Cousins, the diary, Ian Baldwin's, plus all the boxes in the attic of Primrose Cottage, Grace felt she needed to sleep for a week.

She was glad to come home and find Flynn and Benji happy to see her. They felt like the only familiar thing to her all day and she plonked herself on the couch and beckoned the dogs to jump up and join her.

'Bloody hell dogs, what a day! Can you believe old Cousins is a dad, eh Flynn? There's hope for you to get your leg over yet, me laddo,' she laughed and scratched both dogs vigorously on top of their heads.

As soon as she started to relax and settle down with the dogs for a nap, Todd burst through the door. Grace sat up with a start. Todd looked like he had run all the way from Primrose Cottage.

'Grace, the attic! It's full of her photographs. It's full of history. Everything is in there! It's incredible! The stuff, and there's so much of it!'

CHAPTER 17

'What the hell are you talking about, Todd?' Grace was confused. Todd sat beside her on the couch.

'Grace, there's a ton of stuff up there, all old photographs. Every box is full of them. But Grace, the pictures, there's photos of buildings in New York, Washington, California, God knows where else. But there are a lot of pictures of buildings that don't even exist anymore. She has pictures of buildings being demolished and then more of them rebuilding. The visual documentary of it all is so stunningly detailed. There's a lot of photographs of people as well and the artistry in them is incredible; her sense of light and her awareness of the environment is extraordinary,' Todd gushed.

'How many photographs do you think there is?' asked Grace.

'Thousands, it's gotta be in the thousands!'

'Well, what do I do with them all?' Grace felt confused by his enthusiasm and a little ignorant as well.

'I'm not sure yet. But I reckon some of the architectural photographs might sell,' offered Todd.

'What? You think they might be worth some money?' Grace was amazed.

'I dunno, I wanna call my new boss back in New York. The guy's been in architecture since the dawn of time and if anyone can offer some advice, then I reckon he's a good place to start. What do you think?' asked Todd.

'To be honest Todd, I've no idea what to think. I'll be guided by you,' Grace shrugged her shoulders.

Todd could sense that Grace had not grasped the enormity of the find. Why should she, he questioned. What did she know about architecture or even the USA for that matter? If the photographs had contained images of places in England, would he have enthused as much as he was now? He doubted it. Todd briefly toyed with the idea of maybe leaving the find to the confines of the attic but then he remembered the pictures he had seen of the old Hotel Astor and the UN Headquarters being built. If he was getting excited about the images after only being in the industry for a few short years then he imagined that other people would be interested in seeing them also. Besides, it wouldn't do any harm just to make a call and see what reaction he got from someone else.

Todd looked at the clock and calculated that it was only lunchtime in New York so would call his boss straight away. He ran up the stairs leaving Grace still on the couch with the dogs feeling a little dumbfounded. What was she supposed to do with thousands of photos? Who would want to buy them? How would she sell them?

She could hear Todd talking to someone on the phone so walked to the kitchen to put the kettle on. Without even realising it, she called for Crowley and he soon appeared walking in from the lounge.

'Darling Daff, you called?' he stretched his arms out to

embrace her, which she ignored.

'Todd's upstairs,' she whispered.

'Oh,' he mouthed.

'Have Kate, Mort and Jane gone then?' she asked.

'They have. Jane went first. Then Mort took Kate onto the dance floor and well, it was beautiful,' he sniffed but mainly for effect.

'How did they go? What happens?' she was genuinely interested.

'Well, it's quite hard to explain.' Crowley pondered for a while. He felt it was like trying to explain colours to a blind person. 'It's like their being becomes energy I suppose. Then you see a million sparkles of light and they seem to shine so bright but only for a millisecond and then they fade.' He paused for a moment as he continued to recall. 'But you are left with a feeling that I really can't explain.'

'Oh, please try,' insisted Grace. Crowley sighed at Grace's tenacity.

'The only way I can describe it is that it's like every emotion you ever felt in your life you feel, just for a moment,' he explained.

'But that's good, right?' asked Grace.

'Yes, Daff. It's good,' assured Crowley.

'Is that all you wanted, my dear? I had a very good hand with Wild Bill Hicock which is a rarity with him. Never mind,' he sighed.

'Todd's leaving Saturday,' she blurted out.

'Is he?' Crowley looked genuinely sorry for her. 'And what happens next?' he asked cocking his head to one side.

'Nothing, only he's found a load of photographs in Kate's attic, thousands of them of buildings and stuff. I'm no photographer but the ones I did see are lovely. Anyway, he seems to think that this is a big find. He's on the phone to New York to his new boss in the architect's office. He wants his opinion. He thinks he can sell them,' said Grace.

'He thinks you can sell them. They are your photographs, I believe,' pushed Crowley.

'What do I want with them? I've no idea what to do with them!' She whispered louder.

'I may need to come and look at them myself I think. Promise me you will call for me when you are next at the cottage?' he raised an expectant eyebrow.

'Okay, if you think it will do any good,' she promised.

Grace could hear Todd coming to the end of his call, so she motioned to Crowley it was time for him to go.

'Did they seem happy, when they left though, Mort and Kate?' she asked quickly.

'Like a couple of five-year-olds in Disney Land,' he smiled.

'What did they dance to?'

'Etta sang "At Last". It was wonderful,' he said softly.

Todd appeared at the bottom of the stairs and Crowley was gone. He hadn't noticed Grace's guest. He was looking at a piece of paper with scribbled writing all over it.

'What did he say then?' asked Grace bringing herself back to normality.

'He sounded stoked. Said he wished he was here so he could go through it all. But the main thing he was saying is that we have to find out exactly what's in the boxes. No one will look at them in the condition they are in,' said Todd.

'What? You telling me that they'll all need framing?' she squealed.

'Nooo,' snorted Todd, 'it all needs cataloguing. It's still

a huge job. It could take months. Each picture will need a code and the code needs to be recorded somewhere that tells us the detail of the photograph. The thing is, Aunt Kate has done half the job already,' said Todd.

'How do you mean?' asked Grace.

'Well, the ones I looked at have on the back of each photo says what the picture is and she has even put the date. The ones she has taken of people don't have a name but it still says where she took it and the date.' Todd looked expectantly at Grace and waited for her enthusiasm to kick in.

'Todd, I'm not going to lie. I don't know anything about photography or buildings or architecture or light or anything like that. I'm not sure what to say or even do. If you hadn't been there in the attic, I probably would have just binned all the boxes and turned the attic into a sex den,' she joked.

Todd walked over to Grace and placed his hands on her shoulders and looked deeply into her eyes.

'Grace, this could be huge,' he said slowly.

'Really?' she felt breathless slightly. He nodded and kept her gaze. They stood looking at each other unable to move and then Grace lowered her eyes. It felt too intense. She couldn't allow herself to feel any more for him; after all he was leaving soon.

Todd let his arms fall to his side. It was becoming harder to be around her. Sometimes he felt it was hard to breathe. In a knee jerk reaction he said,

'I'm going to stay at Primrose Cottage until I leave,' he said reluctantly.

'Oh,' she was taken by surprise.

'If I stay there then I can make a start on sorting the boxes,' he turned to walk away and then stopped again.

'Grace, look, I've just realised this is your property. I've just railroaded you into...I dunno...something. But if you wanna leave it, then I understand. Maybe, you wanna think about it?'

'It's okay,' she muttered.

'No really, I can steam in like a freight train and then realise that I left people on the platform,' he smiled, 'but at the very least the cottage needs things putting back, so I can do that for you,' he offered.

'Sure, that will help. So will you stay there until Saturday?' she asked.

'Probably best. There's plenty to do,' he replied awkwardly. He scratched the back of his head and headed for the stairs.

Grace turned and looked out of the kitchen window. She hadn't seen that one coming. She knew it was her fault. She felt a longing when she was near him and he had clearly picked up on it and it had frightened him off or he was miffed that she wasn't enthusiastic about the photos.

In a way, she was glad he was leaving her cottage. The tension was rising and they were both now aware of it. Maybe this way, after a few days apart they could say goodbye without the pressure. Grace hoped a little time apart might also give her a reality check and realise that her feelings for Todd were nothing more than a fleeting crush.

Todd reluctantly packed his bag. He didn't have much to pack, all be told. Still, he took his time. Even though he hadn't meant to say it, it was probably for the best that he stayed in Primrose Cottage for the next two nights. Today was almost over, then there was only tomorrow and then he was gone the next. He wondered if he would ever come back to Pelsby. He wondered if Grace would realise the treasure that she had inherited. It might not be worth anything but how do you make someone realise that this was art that needed to be shared if they didn't see it as art in the first place.

If she couldn't see what she possessed then there was no reason for him to come back, he concluded. Grace was completely out of his reach and he started to chastise himself for allowing his feelings to get carried away. He had never fallen for someone where it was one-sided and it was starting to hurt. Being around her was confusing for both of them and with all that she had to contend with recently he was just adding fuel to the fire.

He zipped up his bag and slipped on his jacket and made his way down the stairs where he found Grace still in the kitchen where he left her.

'Look, I'll be busy tonight and will crack on with the boxes tomorrow. But seeing as tomorrow is my last night, can I take you out to dinner?'

Even though he mumbled towards the end of his question, Grace's heart leapt and she broke into a huge smile.

'Yeah,' she was nodding her head emphatically, 'erm...dinner? The only posh restaurant around here is the Italian up the road. I've never been, to be honest, so I don't know what it's like. But my mum and dad went last time they stayed and raved about it. And it's in all the magazines and that. They come from all over as well.' Grace took a breath, 'Sorry, I'm babbling...again. I'll book a table for us at eight o'clock. Is that okay?' she asked.

'That's fine. I'll not call for you, I'll meet you in there if you don't mind?' he asked.

'Oh, okay, if you like,' Grace thought that was odd. She made a mental note to be late as she didn't want to be sat at a table on her own like she was waiting to score something.

'It's on the row of shops past the monument in the square; it's called Prosecco,' she instructed.

'Tomorrow at eight then,' he smiled then immediately turned and walked out shouting goodbye to Flynn and Benji.

The cottage felt empty all of a sudden and she found it disconcerting. She started wandering around from room to room looking for things to do then realised there was nothing to do. She decided to do what all girls do in times like this, buy some wine and have a bath.

After putting her coat on, she beckoned the dogs to join her as she walked to Nell's. The village felt very different as she walked to the shop. She wasn't sure if it was because there was no Mrs Mortimer or that Todd was in Primrose Cottage or even the fact that she knew more about Mr Cousins and Ian Baldwin. It could have been simply that she had Benji with her as well as Flynn.

A degree of familiarity came back when she entered Nell's. Nell was shuffling around the shop trying to find places for goods in places where they would fit on the shelf as opposed to the goods being in the place where people would naturally look for them. No one batted an eye anymore that deodorant could be found with other slender cans that included furniture polish and synthetic squirty cream.

Nell enquired after her and Benji and asked if she would be moving into Primrose Cottage to which Grace said she wasn't sure what her plans were yet. Grace passed her love onto Roger and left the shop with her bottle of white and a family pack of M & M's.

Once Grace was home, she set up all she needed in the bathroom and decided to also use the time to make some phone calls. She plunged herself into the bath, watched her skin turn to a rosy pink which reminded her of Angel Delight. Not that she had ever had Angel Delight; her mum said, 'why would you buy Angel Delight when you can have panna cotta from Waitrose'.

After calling her parents and booking the table at the restaurant for tomorrow, she dialled Sean's number. She felt she had neglected him lately and even though she was going through a difficult time herself she still felt she should have been more attentive to her friend's needs.

'Hi,' said Sean. Grace found it difficult to judge his demeanour.

'Hey Sean, how are you?' Grace tried to keep her tone flat.

'I'm okay Grace, just been worried about you. Everyone's been asking about you in work. You still coming back next week? I feel like you have been off since forever. We have so much to catch up on. Charles and Di's divorce, was she pregnant to Dodi and the poor choice of millinery in some of the younger Royals,' he joked.

Grace burst out laughing. Sean was clearly fine with her recent neglect and was simply missing her. She realised in that moment how much she was missing him too.

'I'll be back next week. I spoke to Bill the other day and told him for definite.'

'Are you in the bath? It sounds dead echoy,' asked Sean.

'I am. I need to sort myself out...I have a date tomorrow,' revealed Grace.

'What?! Who? Where? How? Oh my God, you didn't kop off at the funeral did you?' gasped Sean.

'No! I didn't and to be honest with you it's not a proper date. It's more of a farewell dinner with Kate's nephew,

299

Todd,' said Grace.

'And?' pushed Sean.

'And…he's flying back to America on Saturday and he said he wants to take me out before he goes.'

'And?'

'And nothing. That's it!' Grace barked.

'Come off it Grace, you're in the bath twenty-four hours before your date and you're saying nothing. Time for Sean interrogation,' he adopted the voice of a quiz show host.

'Sean, really…'

'Shush,' he interrupted.

'Question number one,' Sean was unaware that Grace was rolling her eyes and smiling in amusement at the same time. 'And remember the rules Miss Hammond, only yes or no answers. Question number one, have you imagined him with his clothes off?'

Grace sighed down the phone. 'Yes,' she replied. Sean was silently punching the air on the other end of the phone. He tried compose himself again.

'Question number two.'

'How many questions are there?' asked Grace.

'I'm asking the questions, now be quiet,' he retorted.

'Have you kissed him yet?'

'No.'

'Have you wanted to?'

'Yes'

'Does he like you?'

'Not like that.'

'How do you know?'

'He moved out today to stay in his aunt's until he leaves. I think he has picked up on the fact that I like him.'

'Mmmmm,' pondered Sean.

'What's 'mmmm'?'

'Do you have something decent to wear tomorrow?'

'There's a couple of things.'

'So he's not there tomorrow day?' asked Sean

'Nope, there's a…' Grace wasn't sure how to describe all the photos in the attic just yet so decided to leave it for now, 'a few things he needs to sort in the cottage before he leaves and he said he will move some furniture and beds around for me as well.'

'Well, isn't he just missing a cape and a pair of shiny, red boots,' joked Sean.

Grace was imagining Todd in a Superman outfit while Sean's imagination and suit was being filled with Ryan Gosling.

'Right Grace, I'm throwing a sicky tomorrow and I'm coming over to do your hair and makeup,' said Sean. Grace thought for a moment. On one hand she would be grateful for his help as Sean's beautifying skills were incredible but on the other she shouldn't be encouraging him to throw a sicky. She quickly weighed up how many dates she had been on recently and how many times she had actually been on one with someone she really liked.

'Okay,' squealed Grace, 'shall we? Oh, sod it, let's do it. I want to look my best. Even if he doesn't fancy me, I want him to see that I'm not frumpy all the time.'

'You bloody annoy me, Grace. You talk about yourself like you would only fit in on a Jeremy Kyle show. The amount of times I have walked into a pub or a club and I can see them looking at you and you just don't see it!'

'Okay Sean,' Grace was trying to shut him up. She had heard all this before but didn't believe it. Sean picked up on her exasperated tone so dropped the subject.

'I'll call Bill in the morning and tell him a tale, then I'll be over yours around lunch time. Wash your hair tonight, not tomorrow. No more carbs until your meal and even then I wouldn't advise it,' suggested Sean.

'What about wine and M & M's? It's my tea tonight,' Grace said in amusement.

'Jeez Grace, no wonder you're like a stick. You don't eat properly. I'll pick up some bits in Lanson tonight for us tomorrow. Best go tonight in case I get seen tomorrow. Oh, this is so exciting. I wish I could go and discreetly spy on you from a corner.'

'Discreetly?! You're about as discreet as George Michael in a public loo,' she snorted.

Sean was still giggling as he gave his final instructions to Grace on de-fuzzing her entire body and then bid her goodbye.

'Love you Sean, see you tomorrow.'

'Love you too. Bye Grace, bye.'

Grace felt much better after talking to her parents and Sean and after clamouring out of the bath she poured herself one more wine before taking herself off to bed.

In Primrose Cottage, Todd had finally moved all the furniture back into the correct rooms by ten that evening. He wasn't sure it was all in the right place but he used the carpet shading and various dents in the floor to judge where pieces went. Grace could always move stuff around if she wanted but at least the heavy lifting was done.

He didn't feel comfortable sleeping in his aunt's bed after Grace's comment, so he decided to sleep in the spare room. The whole cottage had warmed up now and he felt more comfortable as he sat up in bed. He had brought some boxes down from the attic and was perusing through them while he listened to Marvin Gaye singing from his phone.

The box he was currently looking through was filled with photographs from New York taken in 1947 and 1948, according to his aunt's notes on the back. Some showed streets completely buried in snow; the snow looked to be at least two feet thick. Todd could tell that some of the photos had been taken from a high rise building and the aerial shots illustrated the vastness and impact it had on the city. There were no people in the shots and the only signs of life in some of them were the smoking chimneys and mounds of snow that had once been snowmen. Todd correctly assumed they were photos of the Great Blizzard. It was still talked about when he was younger about how ill-prepared people had been and the panic that people felt as they found themselves cut off from supplies and sources of heat.

More photographs showed children playing, clearly when it was thawing. Todd marvelled at how the images were taken and the subjects seemed unaware of her taking pictures. The box also included more architectural images. There were pictures taken in 1948 of a newly built Idlewild Airport which later became JFK. He admired the winged roof that reminded him of a gliding bird and wondered if people thought the design slightly futuristic in its day.

Todd started to feel tired and tidied up the photographs into a neat order and placed them back into the box. There was one more box that he was intrigued by as it didn't feel as if it contained photographs. He swung his legs out of the bed and stooped over the box as he tore off the tape. As he revealed the contents, a hundred memories of his aunt flooded his mind as he gently lifted out her old Rolleiflex camera. Todd recalled that she would always have it swinging from her neck and would click away. Most of what she had taken of the family, Todd had never seen and he wondered if he would find any of them in the boxes he was still yet to investigate. He climbed back under the cover still clutching the camera and recalled Christmas, birthdays and simple visits where she would turn up with his Uncle Mort, a suitcase and her camera.

He leant over the bed and placed the camera gently back into the box and made a mental note to tell Grace that it needed a more suitable case to protect it. He continued to think about Grace well into the night until sleep finally enveloped him.

The next day, Grace was up early. She had taken the dogs for a walk towards Pool Farm and checked that Mr Cousins was okay. She also went to Nell's to pick up a blank card to write Todd a thank you note for all his help the last few days. She planned to give it to him at the airport before she said goodbye.

Sean was on her doorstep by eleven carrying a multitude of bags and a vanity case which contained his 'tools' as he called them. He had looked on Grace's make-up brush set in disgust once and couldn't believe she could look as good as she did with brushes that were 'only fit for flicking flies off window sills'.

Over lunch, Sean regaled her with more detail on his break-up with François.

'He actually said he thought I could do better than him and you know what Grace? I probably could. Caught him out a few times telling a few jackanories as well. He reckoned he'd been all over the world but when I would ask him about places he'd been to he'd come out with some shit like, 'I don't want to tell you and ruin the experience when we do it together'. He said he'd been to Jamaica and when I said I had and what did he think of the Falls, he said they looked bigger in Superman 2!'

'They're Niagara Falls in Superman 2,' said Grace.

'Exactly! Not bloody Ocho Rios Falls which were the ones I was talking about. I doubt he was even French and do you know what? When I showed a picture of him to Ellen in the office she reckons she saw him working as a porter in the hospital. Said she saw someone like him in the lift with her when she was taking her mum to get her piles sorted out.'

Grace winced at the thought of piles and Sean misunderstood.

'I know! A bloody porter!'

Grace was glad that Frank had dumped Sean for obvious reasons and Sean didn't seem to be any worse for wear for it. She was also glad that most of the truth had come out without her having to say anything or even pass an opinion.

Once lunch was finished, they made their way upstairs where Sean started to lay everything on the bed. Rollers, grips, tongs, cans with various contents, brushes and enough make-up to rival any counter in a department store.

'Bloody hell Sean, you don't wear all that make-up do you?' asked Grace.

'Don't be daft. I've started doing make-up for the family and some girls in work. I love it. I'd love to do a proper make-up course but all the decent ones are so expensive. I've started trying to save but as soon as I have any money in the bank I find myself in Ted Baker trying on shirts,' he bit his lip in guilt.

'Right, let's sort this barnet out of yours. What you thinking?' asked Sean, clearly looking for direction.

'Oh, erm...I dunno. I just want to look half human,' she admitted.

'We can do better than that. Mind you,' he was stood

behind her teasing her hair over her cheeks, 'I'll have to be careful with how it sits on your face. You've lost a bit of weight since I saw you last and it's not like you needed to either. Still grief, it's a terrible thing but for fat people it has some great side effects.'

Grace looked at herself in the mirror while Sean gathered his tools. She hadn't looked at herself properly lately and she could see herself that she had lost a little weight.

After rollering her within an inch of her life, he slathered on a face mask and started working on her nails. Grace was very much enjoying all the fuss and she felt totally relaxed as Sean was obviously in his element.

'I've been dying to give you a proper make-over for ages,' he confessed. 'Not that you look bad kid, it's just...well you don't exactly polish your potential shall we say?'

Once, he had finished with her nails, he instructed her to stay still and relax while he popped out to have a cigarette. Grace did as she was bid and heard Sean open the front door.

As Sean was outside he wondered how Grace could live in such a small village. It had its positives, he supposed, such as community spirit. But he also knew that keeping a secret in places like this was hard and if you didn't fit in then you were fucked, basically.

Sean noticed a tall good looking man staring at him as he walked past the house. He had never seen him before and wondered if he had recently moved to the village or was visiting someone. Sean tried his best to give a flirtatious smile but then noticed that the man was clearly scowling at him. Sean pulled a face in disgust, stamped on his discarded cigarette to put it out and muttered 'homophobe' under his breath as he slammed the front door.

'I don't know how you live here Grace,' he sniffed as he walked back into the room.

Grace was far too relaxed to even open her eyes when she asked him what happened.

'Okay, I admit I may have been a bit camp with holding my fag, but I only smiled at him and he gave me such a dirty look,' Sean moaned.

'What did he look like?' asked Grace, still with her eyes closed feeling like she was ready to fall asleep.

'Blonde, cute, jaw like a Davidoff model, tight fitting khaki jacket…' Sean started to daydream about him. Grace opened her eyes and looked at Sean.

'Jeans, brown boots, jacket totally inappropriate for December?'

'Erm, yeah, I s'pose so. Who is it?'

'Todd.'

Sean stared at Grace for a moment while he digested his thoughts.

'Fuckin' hell girl, we got a lot of work to do,' he said finally.

To say she had been pulled from pillar to post, by seven-thirty Grace felt amazing. Her hair was so thick and wavy Sean joked that it was making him sea sick just looking at it. Her make-up was immaculate and yet she looked like she hardly had any on.

'Your talents are wasted Sean, they truly are,' she said, admiring herself.

'What time is he picking you up?' he asked.

'He's not. He asked me to meet him there,' she said quietly.

'Why? What the hell is that all about?' Sean was taken

aback by Todd's request.

'Don't ask me. Maybe it's an American thing. I plan to turn up late so I don't look like a hooker,' said Grace. Sean burst out laughing.

'Listen girl, no hooker ever looked like that,' he waved his hand in her direction, 'and certainly no hooker ever had a meal in Prosecco.' He continued to giggle to himself.

'Right, let's see what you're wearing,' he bawled.

Grace walked to the wardrobe as if a book was on her head. She was terrified in case her hair moved at all. She wanted it to stay as perfect as possible. She gingerly pulled out the black dress she wore when she went to the seafood restaurant with her mum and dad. She clocked Sean's still expectant face so pulled out a pale green tea dress. It was a little flimsy for this time of year but with a pashmina she could probably get away with it. She looked at Sean's face who sat in silence with a disappointed look.

'What?' barked Grace.

'Seriously, Grace? He's only seen you in black since you buried his aunty and unless Prosecco are hosting a 'Let's Remember the War Night' you are not wearing that,' he jabbed the floral tea dress.

'I thought I looked pretty in that,' she mumbled.

'I've not worked all fucking day so you can go out looking like the Queen Mum,' he snapped. 'Move out of the way and let's have a dig in here.' He started swiping at the hangers and dragging the clothes from one side of the wardrobe to the other still muttering under his breath about how she could have a wardrobe that only Sue Ryder would be interested in. He finally found a cream dress that caught his eye and as he pulled it out for a better look, he gasped.

'Is this a Halston?' he stroked the dress.

'I think so,' said Grace unimpressed. 'My mum bought it for herself and then said it made her look like mutton dressed as lamb so gave it to me. But it doesn't fit me. Shame, because it's nice isn't it?' she sighed.

'Grace, please try it on! I reckon you could well get into this,' Sean was already taking it off the hanger without even waiting for Grace to agree.

The dress was a simple cream halter neck that was fitted all over with an asymmetrical split from mid shin to just above the knee and behind was completely backless. Sean zipped the side of the dress with ease and stood back to look at her like a proud Father of the Bride.

'I think I'm gonna cry, Grace. You are my greatest creation,' he joked dramatically.

Grace had to admit that her reflection was pleasing and the dress looked better on her than it did on her mum. For the first time in a very long time, she actually felt beautiful. As she smoothed out imaginary wrinkles in the dress, Sean was taking pictures like David Bailey. She then completed getting dressed with nude shoes and a bag to match.

'If you weren't gay Sean, would you want me?' she pouted.

'I'm on the turn already kid,' he laughed.

It was quarter to eight and Grace was starting to feel nervous. She began to pace around the lounge and started to wring her hands. Sean clocked the signs and grabbed her hands.

'Grace, stop it. Remember, it's not a date, it's a farewell thingy. And you don't fancy him anyway, he's just good looking. And he's practically family.' Grace raised an eyebrow. 'I'm trying to help here,' he protested.

Grace had an idea.

'Could you do me a favour? In case it all goes a bit pear-shaped tonight and I'm home early, would you mind running to Nell's and getting a bottle of wine?' she asked.

'Good idea, Batman. I'll go now before you go.'

Sean quickly grabbed his coat from the banister, threw on his shoes and headed out of the door.

As soon as he was gone, she shouted. 'Crowley, are you there? Quick, I've only got a couple of minutes!' she shouted. She waited a moment and then heard him behind her. She turned to look at him. He was clearly tipsy when she first looked at him but then she noticed his expression change when he looked at her.

'I'm meeting Todd in a bit. Sean sorted me out. I just want a man's opinion before I go, that's all. I'm so bloody nervous. Anyway, Sean will be back in a minute. I've sent him out for a bottle of wine, see, so I could get you here.' Grace realised she was babbling, but Crowley's silence was making her more nervous. Maybe this was a bad idea, she thought.

'My goodness, Daff,' he said softly, 'you would not look out of place in Heaven. You look like an angel, my dear.'

Grace was relieved and relaxed a bit. His opinion mattered to her. She wasn't sure if it was because he was refined, or a man or that she simply respected his opinion but either way she was glad she called him.

Crowley always thought she was beautiful and would often talk about her 'up there' about how wonderful she was and yet she didn't see it. He suspected that tonight though, maybe she did.

'Now, seeing as I'm practically like a father to you I feel I should impart some advice.' He walked over to Grace and took her hands into his.

'Try not to let that beautiful mouth of yours move faster than your brain.' Grace began to laugh. 'Try not to get annoyed at everything you disagree with. Just accept that people have a different opinion to you. But most of all relax and accept all the compliments that he will no doubt bestow on you gracefully. Live up to your name, dear child.'

'What? Daff?' she joked. Crowley sniggered and blushed at the same time. They were interrupted by Sean knocking on the door.

'I need to get that. Thank you so much for coming down and calming me down a bit.'

'My pleasure, now I shall want all the details when I see you next. Well, not all the details. You can edit and embellish as you see fit.' The door banged again and Grace started to make her way to the door. Crowley blew her a kiss and then disappeared.

Grace opened the door and Sean announced that it was time for her to go and to grab her pashmina as 'it's fucking Baltic' as he put it. She grabbed the wrap, gave herself one more quick once over and stepped outside to join Sean. She no longer felt nervous and found it amusing that Sean's nerves were obviously starting to wobble.

'I got two bottles, Grace. I'll have a little one while I'm waiting for you. He'd better be there. You okay?' he garbled.

'You know what Sean? I'm fine. I think I've realised that it doesn't matter whether he likes me or not. He's going tomorrow and I'll probably never see him again. I'm glad I met him though,' she said acceptingly.

'Bloody hell Grace, you're so calm. What's happened to you? God, I need a fag!' he moaned.

'Well have one then,' she said.

'Next to a Halston! Are you mad?' he squealed. Grace giggled as they continued to walk to the restaurant.

It was after eight o'clock when they arrived and Grace thanked Sean again for all his help.

'Now listen, my little Cinderella, Yanks love to pay so don't argue with him about going Dutch. Don't let your mouth run away with you, don't touch your hair and keep that lip gloss topped up after every course. And if you're not back by midnight I'll presume you've turned into a slag and you're back in Primrose Cottage giving it a bit of Yee'ha!'

Grace started to laugh again and then quickly tried to compose herself. Sean leant in for a kiss and then left her as he instinctively knew she would want him to leave.

CHAPTER 18

As Grace walked in she quickly scanned the room but couldn't see him. The restaurant was a small 'L' shape and very elegant. The walls were papered in a mustard low sheen paper that glistened here and there with the concealed lighting. The far wall was exposed with the grey stone seen throughout the village. The ceiling was painted in a similar soft grey and clever coving from the wall that did not meet the ceiling housed more concealed lighting. All the tables were dressed in grey and white linen while the glassware was subtly decorated with gold. No wonder her parents loved this place, she thought.

A pretty lady, the Maître D, approached her with a broad smile and gentle voice and politely greeted her. Grace offered her name while the lady checked her on her tablet.

'Your dining partner has already arrived,' she said brightly. 'May I take your wrap before I take you to your table?'

'Oh, yes please,' said Grace. She still couldn't see Todd. The lady placed the wrap on a padded hanger and placed it in a concealed wardrobe in the wall and then smiled at Grace to instruct her to follow. As they walked around the corner into part of the 'L', there he was, sipping a Jack Daniels in a black suit and white shirt that was unbuttoned to 'just the right place'. Grace had never seen anyone so handsome in all her life. His hair was sexily ruffled where he had been nervously running his hands through it and even with his faint scar he did indeed have a jawline like a Davidoff model.

He spied her as she walked around the corner. He knew she was beautiful but she had simply taken his breath away when he saw her. Her dress was skimming all over her body and as she walked she flashed her legs through the split in the dress. He instinctively stood up to greet her and the lady noted his manners and wished that she was dining with him. As Todd stood, he noticed that nearly all the men were watching Grace.

'Grace,' was all he could muster with a half stunned smile. Grace wasn't stupid, she knew that he was shocked by how she looked and she knew that he liked what he saw.

'Hey, Todd.' Grace sat down at the table for two and then asked the Maître D for a small vodka and tonic.

They sat for a moment drinking each other in. The awkwardness was still there but this time it felt different and seemed acceptable.

'You look amazing,' he whispered. She went to protest and then remembered Crowley's advice.

'Thank you. You look good too,' she took a breath. 'Do you like the restaurant?'

'It ain't no Denny's, that's for sure,' he said softly, still staring at her.

Grace's drink arrived and Todd enquired about what wine they should order. He admitted that he wasn't a big wine drinker.

'A friend once said to me that you shouldn't order wine until you know what you are eating. But seeing as my wine knowledge is taught by Nell's shop, then I guess I'm not much use either,' she confessed.

'Then let's just buy some champagne and opt for the Signature Menu which takes out all the hassle?' suggested Todd, and snapped the wine menu shut.

A few moments later, a waiter appeared and Todd gave the order.

'Are we celebrating anything this evening?' the waiter enquired. Todd gave a gentle laugh.

'We sure are, but you would need to pull up a chair if I told you,' Todd joked.

The waiter gave a confused smile and hoped it was true that Americans gave good tips as he walked away.

Grace enquired after Todd's day to which he told her about emptying the attic. He had pulled all the boxes down and they were now in his aunt's bedroom and the smallest bedroom also. He updated her briefly what was in the boxes as he had now managed to open them all. He told her about finding the Rolleiflex camera and suggested she find a case for it as it was probably about seventy-years-old. He also asked if she would mind if he took some of the prints with him back to New York to show Elliott, his boss and some that he had found of the family.

'Crowley said he would also like to look at the pictures, if that's okay?' asked Grace.

'Sure! They're your pictures, Grace. I'm glad you think they may be…erm…interesting,' stuttered Todd.

'I know what you mean. I'm not as enthusiastic as you but maybe I can learn to appreciate what is in all the boxes.'

They continued to talk until the first course came. As

the waiter walked away after serving them, Todd looked at his plate and then looked at Grace's which looked exactly the same.

'Please tell me this is some sort of canapé?' Todd raised his eyebrows in hope.

'I think this is the first course,' she whispered back over the table. Todd tried to nod in an enthusiastic manner and Grace found him amusing.

The meal continued in a similar fashion and each course was either the same size or smaller and Todd found it hard not to expel a loud groan with each course served. Grace's laugh became more obvious with each serving as well. She enjoyed his reactions more than the lovely food.

Todd leaned over the table, 'seriously, would it kill them to put maybe a potato on the side. And I mean a real potato not potato that's been painted on the plate with a brush,' he half joked and half moaned.

'I think they call this a dining experience as opposed to filling your face,' she whispered suppressing a laugh.

'Ooooh...' he tried to look impressed but failed miserably. 'Shall we get some more champagne?' he asked. Grace nodded.

By the fifth course, they were both pretty squiffy and Todd was no longer being discreet about his opinion on the portion sizes which Grace thought was hilarious.

'This is Iron Age pork, served with fermented carrots and baby squid,' the waiter proudly announced as he placed the plate in front of Todd.

'Excuse me, waiter,' the waiter turned. 'Could I have the squid's mum instead?' Grace roared laughing and the waiter suppressed a chuckle. 'Hey, don't tell the chef, man, that I trashed his food. It's real nice,' he mouthed a loud whisper, 'I just need more of it.' The waiter thought the whole scene was funny and shook his head to illustrate he would keep his mouth shut. He was glad he was given this table.

With the last course, which was a macaroon, the waiter discreetly placed a Jack Daniels and another vodka on the table with a whisper and a wink that it may fill them up a little bit more.

Grace and Todd were starting to feel quite drunk and Grace became aware that she still hadn't been to the toilet. She was scared if she stood up, the sexy illusion would be shattered if she walked like a pissed giraffe.

She excused herself from the table and Todd watched her walk to the ladies'. His gaze flitted from her bare back to her backside until she disappeared. He then saw a man watching her, who then noticed Todd watching him. The man turned embarrassed, back to his wife who had also noticed and was not pleased, judging by the thinness of her lips.

Grace was soon back and when the meal was finished, they decided to get the bill and leave. Once the bill was presented, Grace couldn't help herself but to offer some contribution to the bill.

'Are you kidding me?' Todd looked at Grace's face and then realised she was serious. 'Erm, no Grace. I'll get this. I asked you to dinner, remember? 'Pay the goddamn bill'. Who's been taking you out recently?' Todd raised the bill wallet to his waiter to indicate he wanted to pay.

'Talking of which? Who was the guy at your place today?' Todd tried to sound casual but Grace waited for him to look at her before she answered.

'My friend, Sean,' she said flatly, watching his reaction.

'Your friend?' he asked, still trying to sound casual.

'My gay friend. I told you about him the other day. He

317

came over to help me...erm...sort some personal things out,' Grace stammered slightly.

Todd's face broke out into a smile. He had been wondering all day who the good looking man was smoking on her step. He didn't seem Grace's type, not that he knew what her type was, but as he thought about it her friend was a bit feminine.

Once the bill was paid, Grace retrieved her wrap and they made their way outside and started to walk in the direction of Grace's cottage. She wondered if Todd was expecting to come in for a night cap.

'So tomorrow,' he said, 'what time are we leaving for the airport?' That brought Grace back down to earth with a bump.

'I reckon about eleven in the morning. That should give us plenty of time.' Grace felt like the wind had been snatched from her sails and soon enough they were approaching the start of Grace's path. She noticed the light was still on in the lounge and there was an occasional flicker which suggested the TV was on and Sean was still up.

'I'd invite you in but my friend Sean is still here. Unless, you want to come in and meet him of course,' Grace offered. Todd looked over the cottage and reluctantly declined. He wasn't sure if it was appropriate now to even ask her back to Primrose Cottage seeing as he had already walked her home.

'I had a wonderful evening, Todd. Haven't laughed that much in ages,' she admitted.

'Me neither,' he sighed. He continued to look at her. She looked even more beautiful in the street light. Grace was aware that it was that time when no one knew what to do next. Do you go in for a kiss or shake hands or give a gentle hug? As much as she wanted to kiss him properly she knew that it would only have two outcomes. One, being that he would recoil as soon as she leaned in, or two being a kiss that she wouldn't be able to stop giving. In the end, Grace stepped forward and kissed him gently on the cheek, said goodnight and walked up the path. She opened the front door and waved to a disappointed Todd who then put his hands in his trousers pockets, smiled and started to walk back towards the village.

Grace walked in to find Sean spread out on the couch with the dogs laying on his legs and a glass of wine in his hand.

'Oh God, Sean…'

Sean sat up suddenly, sending the dogs in different directions and waited for her to speak again.

'…I've only gone and fell in love with him,' she moaned.

'You silly cow,' he hissed.

.

CHAPTER 19

The airport was busy, busier than Grace expected. She realised that Christmas was not too far away and everyone was probably spending it somewhere more exciting and warmer than England.

The car journey had been quiet most of the way. Todd had given her an update on what he had done and the photographs he had taken to show Elliott. He was stiff in his conversation when he suggested he could give her number to anyone that may be interested in them and she could deal with them direct. She agreed that was probably best until she had some advice herself on what to do with them.

In the terminal, she stood near the entrance and watched him check in at the British Airways desk and then once he was through she started to walk towards him. They both reached the security gate at the same time and Grace realised that she could not go any further.

They both stood awkwardly for a moment and then Grace started rummaging in her bag and produced the card that she had written the night before.

'I wrote a little note for you,' she said quietly. He took it and looked at the envelope. 'Don't open it now. You can read it later on the plane or when you get to New York, maybe,' she suggested.

He slipped his rucksack from his shoulder, opened a side zip and pulled out a similar looking card.

'Great minds, huh,' as he offered the card. She smiled, took the card and put it in her bag as he did the same.

'Well, I guess this is it,' she said reluctantly.

'I guess,' he whispered, staring at her. His eyes were sad and his jaw was clenched.

'Well, have a safe journey and if you are ever in England again, please come and visit won't you?' She was trying her best to sound bright but she knew her face was contradicting her. She knew she had to leave now.

'Sure,' he shifted on his feet. 'Thanks for the lift and you too have a safe journey home,' he croaked. She couldn't take any more and had to go.

'Bye, Todd.' She leaned forward, closed her eyes and kissed him tenderly on his cheek and at the same time quietly smelled him. He smelled warm and smoky and she wanted to bottle the smell and take it home. She turned away quickly and was already walking to the exit when, from behind, she heard him say goodbye to her. The tears were starting to well up in her eyes and she could feel her throat closing over. She needed to get out into the fresh air.

Just as she reached for the door she felt a sharp tug on her arm and was being pulled away. She briefly caught Todd's face before she felt his lips on hers kissing her hungrily. She felt him drop his bag and then his hands were cupping her face as she kissed him back. 'This is real! This is real' she was saying in her head as she savoured the kiss. She could feel her tears running down her face as Todd slowed his kisses and stopped to look at her. He was still cupping her face and was flooded with joy when he saw her tears and her smile.

'I couldn't say goodbye like that,' he said softly. She could feel his breath on her face as they nearly were nose to nose. 'I've wanted to do that since the day I met you,' he confessed. He was searching her face to see how she felt. He could feel it, he was sure, but he wanted her to say it.

'I didn't think you liked me all that much,' she sniffed. 'I wish you would stay,' she whispered. As soon as she said that, he pulled her quickly into his arms and squeezed her. He closed his eyes and relished her feeling so close as he knew it was to be brief.

'I have to go,' he said softly. Todd loosened his hug and kissed her again. Her heart was pounding in her chest. He then picked up his rucksack, threw it over his shoulder and then gently stroked her cheek. Todd smiled and without another word turned and walked to the security gate until Grace watched him disappear.

She walked outside and felt completely dazed as she made her way to her car. Once she was in the car she tried to compute what the hell had just happened in the last ten minutes. What did this mean now? Was this just an honest goodbye? Was this the start of something? How could there be something when they lived thousands of miles apart? Would she ever see him again? Should she have kissed him? The last question was the big one. It had changed everything. She never knew that he felt the same as her. She briefly chastised herself for wasting the last few days when they could have been spent with him. But surely that would have made things worse. It's one thing to kiss someone goodbye but then to admit that you have feelings for someone is a whole new ball game. But surely that kiss had exposed how she felt anyway, she thought.

She needed to get back home as soon as she could. Being in the airport was making her feel even more strange and she felt she could only sort things in her head properly in her own environment, that being with the dogs or even in The Blacky.

Her head was cloudy most of the way home and she wondered if Crowley would be able to find her in a moving car. She called for him and it wasn't long before he was in the back seat.

'Daff, Daff, Daff,' he sighed, 'I fear you are going to shout at me.' Grace was straining her head to see him in the mirror.

'Why are you back there? I'm not a bloody chauffeur, get your arse up the front,' she shouted.

No sooner had she asked, he was there, very, very drunk.

'Jesus Christ, Crowley, how much have you had to drink?' she looked on in slight disgust.

'Since when?' he slurred.

'Huh?' said Grace confused.

'Since I was last sober…I can't remember. You're asking me to count the drinks over years and years and years…'

'Okay, never mind,' she said reluctantly. 'I'm not sure I want to talk to you when you're this bad.'

'I'm fine. I'm fine,' he tried to sit up and look more sober. 'Where the hell are we and where the devil are we going?' he burbled.

'We're on the motorway. That's why there are lots of cars around me,' she said sarcastically, 'and I'm going back to Pelsby. I've just dropped Todd off at the airport.'

Crowley wobbled his head in Grace's direction and screwed up his eyes to study her face.

'You've been crying,' his voice softened with concern. 'What happened, my dear?'

'What's the point in telling you? You're not going to remember what I said,' she moaned.

'Do I need to?' he asked. Grace thought for a moment. Crowley wasn't being rude he was simply saying that it was about her, not him.

'He kissed me,' she turned to look at Crowley, 'properly. Like on the lips and everything.' She turned back to look at the road.

'And?'

'I don't know. What am I supposed to do now?' she snapped.

'What would you like to do?' he asked flatly.

'I dunno,' she pouted.

'Come on Daff, apart from a million cars on the motorway whose drivers are all listening to trashy music or stuffing their faces with confectionery, it's just you and me. What would you like to do?'

'Really? I'd like to jump on a plane and follow him to New York and stay there forever. But that only happens in the movies, it doesn't happen in real life does it?'

'Why not?'

'Because it doesn't!' she yelled.

Silence fell between them. She wanted to talk to him, but not in this state. They drove for a few miles with Crowley staring out of the window. Grace felt it was rude to ask him to leave after calling for him so she merely hoped he would fall asleep, that's if ghosts fell asleep, she wasn't sure.

'I think I'll go,' he muttered, 'the silence is deafening.' Grace continued to look at the road.

'You can't blame me for being a bit tipsy. I didn't know you were going to call did I?' he said accusingly and then disappeared.

Grace felt guilty. Again she had called him down and again had a go at him for being drunk. She was not his wife or daughter or sister, so she had no right to chastise him about his behaviour.

She realised the silence was indeed deafening so put on the radio.

"Love is in the air, everywhere I look around..." Oh God, no, she thought and immediately pushed a button for another station.

"It's up to you, New York, New Yooooorrkk…"

Grace stared at the radio and started to laugh.

'Okay, Crowley. If that's you, then very funny,' she shouted to the air. He didn't come, but she knew why and she knew it was his way of giving his opinion.

'Sober up a bit and come and see me later, eh?' she called.

Grace arrived home late afternoon and as she pulled up at the back of the cottage she remembered his card was still in her bag. She also wondered if he had read hers yet. If she knew then what she knew now she may have written a lot more. She reached to the back seat for her bag and retrieved the card. Still sat in the car, she slowly tore open the envelope and pulled out the card. To her surprise, the front of the card was illustrated with a daffodil.

Grace,

By the time you read this, I will be long gone but the thing is I'm not sure for how long, I guess that's up to you. We have just had our meal and I've been the pub. To say I have enjoyed my time in England seems the wrong thing to say seeing as my aunt just died, but I have. My whole world had changed a couple of weeks ago, even before I met you with all the ghost stuff. But to find someone that not only believed me but had also experienced the same thing has got to be some kind of sign, hasn't it? I hope your Crowley finds peace soon. Grace, I can tell you now because I doubt I will see you again. But I have fallen for you and I don't want you thinking this is some kind of holiday crush thing because it isn't. You are the most beautiful, funny, selfless and frustrating person I have ever met. I accept I may never see you again but I want you to know that I will never forget you. I leave with two wishes. The first one is I hope you have a happy future and you find someone that deserves you. The second one is that I wish I could kiss you, even if it was just once.

You have touched my heart.
Todd x

PS. I'll get Elliott to call about the photographs.

PPS. I bought the card and the lady in the village shop said the daffodil on the front is your nation's flower! Strange!

Grace read the card three times before she closed it. Had she really been that blind that she couldn't see that he felt the same way?

Todd thought he would feel happy about returning to New York, but he wasn't. He looked out of the cabin window and into the clouds. He thought of England, his Aunt Kate visiting him, her photographs but most of all he thought of Grace. He wondered if she had read his note and how she had reacted. He wished he had said more but he didn't know until he left her how she felt.

He asked the steward for a drink and when he returned with it Todd pulled out Grace's card that he had moved to his seat pocket earlier.

Dear Todd,

I just wanted to say thank you for all the help and support you have given me over the last few days. It's been a tough time for me losing Kate and you have helped me enormously. I'm not going to lie, I really hope I see you again. I'll need all the help I can get with sorting these photographs; I think you and I make a good team. Even if nothing happens with them maybe I could send them over to Ohio and come and visit you and bring the camera. Just an idea. Anyway, I hope you settle to life in New York. You must be so excited with your new job and new life. I wish you all the happiness in the world and hope you have a great Christmas.

I'll miss you.
Grace
xxx

He closed the card and looked at the photograph on the front of two dogs. He wondered who the dogs reminded her of. Him and her, Mort and Kate or was it simply Flynn and Benji. Her card felt like it had been written by a different person to the one he had kissed goodbye. But he could read between the lines and could feel that she wanted to see him again and that was all that mattered right now, except for a couple of more drinks, maybe.

After Grace had let the dogs out for a run she locked them back up and walked to Primrose Cottage to see how the cottage had been left.

All the boxes were where Todd said they were and various notes had been stuck to the side of boxes already indicating the contents. However, there were two boxes that he had placed on the dining table downstairs. She opened the first one to reveal the Rolleiflex camera and as Grace gently lifted it from the box she marvelled at not only how old the camera was but how many images Kate must have captured on this one piece of equipment. The camera was a sturdy oblong shape and featured twin lenses to the face. To view the image, Grace discovered you had to look at a window on the top and a mirror would reflect the image captured in the top lens. She recalled that Kate would often talk of her photography but not of her passion for it and seeing the cottage filled with her work it clearly had gone beyond passion. It looked obsessive.

She placed the camera back in the box and started to investigate the contents of the other one. There were only a few photographs in this one but as soon as she started to look at them she began to feel emotional.

The images were of last year's Summer Fair in the village. Mrs Mortimer didn't attend that day. Looking back she had been complaining of a chest infection and Grace felt a flood of rawness rush through her body. She wondered if Kate suspected or even knew then.

The box contained photos of everyone in the village. They had clearly been taken from a bedroom at the front of Primrose Cottage. Grace tried to imagine her friend sat at the window with a camera in one hand and a cigarette in the other. However, to Grace's surprise a lot of the photographs contained her and the thing that startled her was the fact she looked wonderful in all of them. Most were black and white but some of the wider shots of the whole fair were in colour. Big Mick, Patsy, Tom and even Mr Cousins had all been captured laughing and some of the images seemed to be revealing personalities that she didn't know existed. It seemed that the box contained at least one shot of everyone who had turned up that day and judging by the photos it looked like the whole village had attended.

While she sat there going through them she heard Crowley come into the room from the hall. He looked far more sober than he did a few hours before and looked a little smarter too.

'Hello Daff, sorry about before,' he murmured.

'I should be used to it by now,' she sighed. 'Here, look at these.' She threw some photos on the table near an empty dining chair and Crowley eagerly stepped forward and took a seat.

He looked through the photos in silence and smiled at some of the shots of Grace.

'You said there were more?' he asked.

'Follow me.' Grace led him upstairs and showed him the two bedrooms that housed the boxes.

'My God!' he whispered under his breath.

Grace and Crowley began to open the boxes and study the contents. With each box opening Crowley seemed to get more and more excited.

'And she never told you about all these?' he asked still sifting through piles.

'Nothing. So what do you think then? Any good? I mean proper good like Todd says, not just that they're nice,' she questioned.

'They're more than good, Daff. These are incredible. In her architectural photos, her attention to light and shadow reminds me of works by Eugène Atget and Jack Boucher,' he said with a grin. 'Did you say Todd was speaking to someone about these?'

'His boss, Elliott, he's an architect. He seemed excited as well when Todd told him about them. He's taken some of them to New York with him to show Elliott. What do you think I should do with them?' she probed.

'My dear, you must exhibit them. These shouldn't be in boxes!' Crowley was beginning to shout with excitement. 'But first they all need sorting properly and that could take some time,' he said scanning the room.

'Todd said I need to catalogue them. But I'm not being funny, how the hell do I put on an exhibition?' she cried.

'Daff, there are people who do that sort of thing…for a fee…which won't be cheap, even if you did it yourself,' he mused. 'But I agree with Todd, you have to catalogue them properly even if you were to sell them as a job lot. The buyer would still need to know the complete detail of the contents.' Crowley walked from one bedroom to another, occasionally shouting in euphoria at his next find.

'Daff, can I ask you a huge favour?' Grace raised an eyebrow; he no doubt wanted a drink of some sort. 'Would you mind awfully, staying here tonight? I want to stay and continue with the sterling work that Todd had clearly started. And if you don't mind, bring that computer with you, that way we can start getting it all recorded somewhere.'

'This really is a big deal, isn't it?' she said.

'It's not only a big deal, it's a big job. Cataloguing all this is going to be a mammoth task. Do you know anyone that would be willing to help you?' he suggested.

'Not really, everyone I know works full time. People would only be able to help at weekends and I'm not so sure that they would want to give up their precious free time to sit in an old lady's cottage and read numbers,' she groaned.

'Well, if that's the case then I guess it's down to me and you then. Maybe this is my good deed,' he guessed. Grace looked at him and he seemed to have quickly resigned himself to the fact that this was it. It had to be, she thought. If he wasn't here, then she probably would have said to Todd that she would be freighting the boxes to Ohio.

Grace and Crowley made a plan. She was to collect the dogs and some essentials for an overnight stay and he was to come back in an hour.

Once the dogs, computer, food and wine had all been packed into a small wheeled case she walked back to Primrose Cottage ready for her hard night's work.

They decided after some deliberation on how to catalogue the detail and where to save it. Crowley was also quick to point out that they would need a good quality scanner of some sort to digitise the images. Grace said she would speak to her dad about that as he had some contacts and may be able to come across a good one that was cheap.

Grace made a start on inputting the data onto her computer that Todd had already referenced while Crowley continued with the referencing of the boxes that Todd had not managed to complete. They took various breaks to discuss what had been found. Crowley was excited at finding pictures of the old Hollywood sign in a dilapidated state and said he never knew that at one time it had been missing an 'O'.

Grace made a long call to her parents. She explained more about Kate's past and her professional career as a photographer for the USDA. She then went on to reveal what her inheritance had included and now the huge library of photographs belonged to her also. She relayed Todd's reaction and that he was conferring with an architect in New York about some of the shots. She went on to explain that she also had a friend who felt that the photographs should be exhibited and the laborious task ahead of cataloguing all the photographs. She then concluded the whole tale with a request of a scanner and if her dad knew anybody. He said he did and would be back in touch soon and not long after she hung up the phone went again and she presumed it was her dad calling her back.

'Hey Dad, did you forget something?' she asked returning to the computer.

'It's me,' said the American voice.

'Todd,' she exhaled, 'you okay?' He paused for a moment.

'I just wanna come back,' he admitted. Grace felt her chest tighten and her heart leapt.

'You're just tired; you couldn't have been home long. It'll seem different tomorrow,' she said trying to placate him.

'It won't. I'm sat in a beautiful apartment looking out over the whole of the city. I've got a great job that I start Monday with a fantastic boss but all I want is you,' his voice sounded as if it was breaking.

Even though Todd did indeed feel tired he had never felt more alive. In the first time in his life he felt that he was physically aching for someone.

'Todd, I wanted to say so much more in my card but…well…you know,' she stammered.

'I went to the pub after I left you. I wanted to talk to people that you talk to so I could still feel close to you. I know it sounds crazy but I can't seem to think straight or know what I'm supposed to do from one minute to the next. But God, Grace, they all love you in that village. They all said it will be a sad day when you leave, as if it's a foregone conclusion. Patsy guessed how I feel about you, she's a good woman,' he said.

'Why? What did you say to Patsy?' asked Grace.

'Don't laugh, okay?' he giggled slightly, 'promise me?'

'I promise.'

'Okay,' he paused, 'I used to have this stupid dream since I was a kid. I watched way too many movies on the ranch.' He waited for Grace to respond.

'Yeah,' she was intrigued as to where this was going.

'Well, I had this dream that I would walk into a bar or restaurant and the love of my life would be sitting there waiting for me, like in a Humphrey Bogart or Cary Grant movie, which is why I asked you to meet me in Prosecco. But you were late and I thought, 'what an idiot, this ain't the movies',' he giggled nervously. 'But then you walked in. God...did you walk in. You looked incredible,' he confessed.

Grace was taken aback by the whole story but now it made sense as to why he wouldn't collect her from the house. She was also recalling his face as she walked in and she knew at the time that he was happy and that made her happy. She looked around the bedroom in which she was standing and could see his handwriting everywhere. It made her miss him more.

'I never thought I'd ever be lost for words,' chuckled Grace, 'but I think for the first time in my life, I actually am.' Todd was laughing down the end of the phone. 'Just promise me one thing, eh?' she asked.

'What's that, baby?' he whispered.

'Promise me that we will see each other soon and I mean proper soon, not real soon or sooner rather than later or as just plain ole soon. I mean proper soon,' she emphasised.

'I promise. Proper soon,' he impersonated her Welsh accent.

'Now get some sleep and call me tomorrow and I'll tell you what you've been missing,' she teased.

'I know already. Bye, baby.'

'Bye.'

Grace was still clutching the phone to her chest when Crowley walked in.

'I take it our ranchhand has arrived in the big city.'

Grace nodded. 'And he's missing you already.' Grace continued to nod, 'and he wants you now more than ever,' Crowley ended on a dramatic tone.

'Hey you, word on the town is I'm a bit of a catch. But I'm also a slave driver. So get back to work and stop listening at doors,' she joked.

They continued to work well into the early hours when Grace had to call it a night. Crowley agreed and even though they had been hard at it, they had barely made a dent.

The next day, as Grace made her morning tea, Crowley arrived for another day's work, only this time he came with a bottle of red in each pocket. He patted each pocket in turn.

'This one is for stimulation and this one is for motivation,' he chuckled.

They continued to work until lunchtime until they heard a knock at the door. Grace was surprised that anyone would be calling but she was more surprised to see her father on the doorstep.

'Dad?!' said Grace, surprised.

CHAPTER 20

'Gracey, darling.' Dai and his daughter embraced as Crowley looked on from the top of the stairs. Dai admitted he was so intrigued as to the contents of the boxes that he couldn't wait to see them so jumped in the car first thing and headed straight for Pelsby.

After a quick cup of tea, Grace took him on a tour of all the boxes and the work that she and Crowley had done so far. Grace had to tell her dad that Crowley lived out of town and was currently attending to other needs. Crowley was actually sat on the floor in the spare bedroom hiding his bottle and glass under the bed in case Dai stumbled across it.

As Dai started to root through the boxes, he exclaimed that he was impressed with the quality of the photographs and picked on some particular images of the 'March on Washington' in '63 which featured not only Dr. Martin Luther King but Kate had also managed to capture A. Philip Randolph and Bayard Rustin who had organised the march, Sammy Davis Jr, Charlton Heston and numerous other celebrities. Grace, however, was more impressed with the pictures of the crowd and the way Kate had succeeded to capture the look of hope in the audience faces as they stood entranced listening to what is now the most famous speech ever made.

'Gracey, one scanner for this lot will take forever. You need at least three, probably more,' he said surveying the room.

'What's the point of having three when there's only me who will be using it?' she grumbled.

'Well, can't your mother and I help?' he asked. Grace was surprised.

'Really?' she sounded astounded.

'Why not? It's not like we have anything that is as important as this. Your mother and I could come for a few days each week and stay here or in your cottage,' he suggested. Grace caught Crowley in the hall nodding emphatically. She wasn't sure if he was excited at the thought of having help or the fact that her mum would be here.

'Well, if you or Mum don't mind then I'm not going to object,' she shrugged gratefully.

'Excellent! I'm going to call Edward who has his own IT equipment company. You met him once at the house, bad Christmas jumpers and a touch of halitosis, but a gent nonetheless. He'll need to put any machines in the lounge; he can't be humping them up those narrow stairs. Is there any way we could have some of the men from the village to put the furniture somewhere?' he asked.

'I'll see Big Mick. Don't worry I'll get it sorted,' she promised.

Dai soon got into the stride of cataloguing and she left him and unknown to Dai, Crowley, in Primrose Cottage while she ran to The Blacky.

Big Mick was behind the bar as usual and she asked if she could have a quiet word with him for ten minutes. He lifted the hatch and took her into the kitchen at the back where two bar stools where pushed against the wall. He pulled one over for her to sit and he did the same for himself. Patsy walked in and looked confused and Grace asked her to stay so she could explain all to both of them.

She more or less told the same story to them as she had to her dad, only this time explaining that they needed the room and could they help her move the furniture somewhere. Big Mick said he was happy to move furniture but he couldn't offer anywhere to store the big items such as the table and the suite. But then Patsy suggested Pool Farm and said if they had some plastic sheeting they could even store it in one of Mr Cousins's barns if he didn't mind. Grace was sure that he would store the items and she asked Big Mick to ask a couple of people in the pub if they would help while she ran to Pool Farm to ask about storage.

Grace was soon outside and ran past the Flower Cottages and headed up to Pool Farm. Mr Cousins was shutting the gate to the field when he spied Grace and broke out into a smile. He was always pleased to see her now. As he invited her in Grace again repeated what had happened lately about the photographs and the ideas that they had but nothing could move forward until all the images were scanned and catalogued. She asked about storage which he said he would gladly give.

'My friend had the idea of holding an exhibition, maybe. He said there are people who can organise it but it costs a lot of money. So maybe I will look about doing some of it myself,' she said.

'And how are you going to do that with a full time job, lady?' he growled.

Grace felt deflated and Mr Cousins felt guilty for supressing her enthusiasm.

'We'll think of something,' he said with a wink. 'Now let me change these shoes and I'll come back to Kate's with you. Sorry, I mean your house now,' he smiled.

Within an hour, Primrose Cottage was overrun with half the village. Patsy was passing a box and newspaper to people as they walked up the path with instructions to wrap all knickknacks carefully and to take straight to the top barn at Pool Farm. Grace walked over to Patsy and marvelled at how she could organise everything so quickly.

'Come on, admit it. You sorted the Beijing Olympics, didn't you?' Grace nudged a giggling Patsy and walked back into the house.

Within an hour and a half most of the cottage had been cleared except for the bedroom furniture and a couple of dining chairs and they all made their way back into the empty lounge on Grace's instruction.

At least twenty people stood and waited for her to speak.

'I just want to say thank you to you all, you've been amazing as usual. But I would like to say a particular big thank you to our village landlady, Patsy and Mr Cousins who has kindly let me store all of Kate's things at Pool Farm. If you don't know why we have done this I know Mick and Patsy will be happy to tell you. But I want to add that this has been a huge favour to me. Now, there's a drink waiting for you all back at The Blacky,' she finished.

Smiling faces started to file back out of the cottage and Grace asked Big Mick to make a note of how much she owed him to which he shook his head at.

'Listen Grace,' said Patsy, 'I'm not good with computers but I could help with the coding. It can't be that much different to stock coding. I can come in during the day after the lunchtime trade when it's quiet,' she offered.

Grace was becoming overwhelmed by all the offers of support. She accepted Patsy's offer and passed her a spare key to the cottage so she could let herself in and out in case her parents were not around. Dai looked pleased that he had another member in his midweek team and also thanked Mick and Patsy for all their help.

Once they had gone, Grace insisted that Dai leave as well. The day had certainly flown so her dad agreed and promised to be back tomorrow afternoon to let Edward in to deliver the scanners which he had manged to get.

When she shut the door, Crowley was sat on the top of the stairs with an outstretched arm holding a glass of wine in her direction. She slowly trudged her way up and gratefully took the glass to which she took a large mouthful and sat on a lower step.

'How does it taste, my dear?' asked Crowley.

'Heavenly,' she giggled.

The following two weeks for Grace seemed to be an endless spinning wheel of her job, data inputting, organising all the data, sorting help and keys for the cottage, walking the dogs as well as Christmas shopping. She had managed to recruit Sean to scan at the weekends and Tom also helped the weekend team when he wasn't spending time with his new girlfriend Zoe, the pretty Maître D from Prosecco.

Todd had called every day and Grace would keep him up to date on how far they were getting and that it wouldn't be much longer until all the images would be scanned. They talked about how Elliott knew someone who would be happy to look at the images once they were all catalogued and would be happy to set up a meeting. Grace promised that the scanning project would be completed before Christmas Day and so in the New Year they could have some preliminary discussions.

They also talked about Christmas. Todd was spending the holidays with Beau and his family at the ranch in Ohio and Grace was going to her parents' for a couple of days which she was looking forward to. Her mum was far more relaxed these past few weeks even though she had been busy with heading over to Pelsby three days a week, sometimes four. Grace also tried to make Todd understand how incredible it was that her mum now managed to fit in a walk with the dogs each day and would often turn up with treats and new toys for Flynn and Benji.

Their wanting of each other had not waned since their separation and they talked about trying to set up a meeting with Elliott's contact for the end of January. Grace had even gone as far as letting Bill know that it was likely she would be off for at least a week before the end of February.

With a final flourish in Christmas week and with help from practically everyone she knew at some point, the cataloguing was finished by 22nd December and the scanners were gone by the 23rd. Dai, at his insistence, had settled the bill with Edward and Big Mick had asked all who had helped to come to a closed pub on the evening of the 23rd to celebrate the end of the job and to thank everyone. No doubt it was Patsy's suggestion, thought Grace, who also thought it was a wonderful idea when Patsy said it was also to remember Kate.

The 23rd turned out to be one of the busiest days she had ever had. She had started at five in the morning to complete the cataloguing and taping up the last of the boxes. She had also changed the linen on the bed at

Primrose Cottage as her parents were staying in the cottage tonight after the party. She was then in work by nine for half the day and then returned back to Pelsby with Sean who was coming to The Blacky too later that evening. He had insisted on bringing all his tools again to give Grace another well-deserved pampering even though they calculated they only probably had about an hour and a half to get ready.

She fired some emails in the afternoon to Todd and Elliott of particular pictures they asked for. They included a wide selection of the building of the UN Headquarters in New York around 1950 and shots of the Singer Building. She then text Todd to say she would be out with friends from the village in The Blacky and would text some snaps of the night over to him.

After a quick walk with the dogs and the wrapping of some final presents she was ready to be pampered at Sean's insistence. Grace had already told Sean that she would be wearing the Halston dress again that night seeing as no one in the village had seen her in it apart from Tom's new girlfriend to which Sean agreed was a good idea. Once, they were both made up and Sean was happy with his results, he produced a beautiful gift wrapped box for Grace.

'I know it's not Christmas for another two days but I'm not gonna see your face when you open it so I want you to open it now,' Sean squealed. Grace was surprised and excited and wondered at the timing of the gift giving. But with Sean, who was about to wet himself with excitement or chew the bottom lip off himself, she opened the lid and beyond the tissue paper she saw a flash of red. As she drew the garment out of the box, a deep red cat suit uncurled all the way to the floor. The top half was strapless with a deep frill from the shoulders to the waist and the material felt exquisite, then she spied the Stella McCartney label.

'Stella bloody McCartney?!' shouted Grace.

'Before you do your nut, listen. It didn't cost me as much as you think. It ain't no Ricki Lake, it's proper Ian Beale. I just bought it in one of those posh dress agency shops. Anyway, I saw it and thought of you and thought you'd look amazing in it,' Sean was trying to read Grace's face as she stared at the suit. 'Fuckin' 'ell Grace, it's not like someone died in it,' he sounded hurt.

'Oh God, Sean, I love it. It's too much that's all. But I absolutely love it,' she squealed and ran to Sean to hug him.

'Do you think it's a bit posh for The Blacky though?' she asked pressing the suit against her body.

'No, I bleeding don't!' he snapped. 'Patsy's gone all out because your mum said she 'might just throw on some old Vivienne Westwood dress' and I bet Tom's new bird won't be sporting Primarni so get the thing on and be quick about it, we can't be late. Big Mick wants to start his speech at seven-thirty sharp so we've got ten minutes,' he ordered.

Without any delay Grace wriggled herself into the jumpsuit while Sean threw a pink shirt on and his slate grey trousers. Once they were dressed, they stood in front of Grace's mirrored wardrobe and admired themselves.

'I've never been out with anyone who was better looking than me before,' said Sean looking at Grace in the mirror, 'and I'm glad to say that that record will still stand tonight,' laughed Sean.

'You're such a troll, Sean,' she said hitting him on the shoulder with her bag. They were still laughing when they walked into the pub and set down the presents that they had brought to be opened later. Grace and Sean were one of the last to arrive and everyone seemed relieved that they were finally there. All the girls starting cooing over Grace's new outfit and Sean reaped the compliments as if they were being slathered on him.

The last to arrive were Tom and Zoe who apologised for being last and they soon made their way along the long table that Patsy had set up to accommodate all seventeen of them in the main bar of the pub.

Grace sat between Sean and her mum who quickly asked if the dogs were okay. Grace couldn't believe how quickly she had changed in the last few months. She had gone from Cruella De Vil to Barbara Woodhouse in the space of two weeks.

As Grace was talking, she noticed that Crowley was sat at the bar on a stool. She had asked him earlier if he could come for the speeches as he was a part of the team as well and she was pleased that he had made it. He mouthed the word stunning to her and looked incredibly happy to be a part of the proceedings, albeit invisible and without a drink.

'Ladies and gentlemen,' shouted Mick from the head of the table, 'I just want to say a few words before we start the beautiful meal that my lovely wife has been slaving over all day in the kitchen, which has meant that she's not been nagging me so thank you all for that.' The table started laughing and looked in Patsy's direction at the other end of the table.

'You keep laughing Michael and there'll be no dessert,' threatened Patsy. Big Mick patted his large belly covered in a straining shirt.

'I could do with missing it anyway,' he joked.

'I didn't mean that kind of dessert,' she said sarcastically. This was met with a roar of laughter and the whole table shifted its gaze to Big Mick. Grace caught him wink at his wife and then beam as he looked around the table.

'It's been a funny month hasn't it? A sad month to start with the loss of our cantankerous and opinionated but beautiful Kate Mortimer but what an ending, eh? We have all proved this month just what a special village Pelsby is. And I know some people aren't from round here, but whether you were born here or not or live here or not, this place…well, it pulls you in. It's not just the lovely buildings or countryside that surrounds us, it's the fact that anyone who comes here is automatically part of the Pelsby family. It's as simple as that and I think the past two weeks have shown that this family knows how to pull together. Now everyone here has done their bit in helping Grace try and get an exhibition of Kate's work off the ground. I don't know how she's going to do it but all I do know is that if there's a way then she'll figure it out and she has all of our help and support.' The table all nodded and looked at Grace.

Big Mick continued, 'Everyone who has been on the start of this journey is here now at the table apart from two people. Grace has asked me to mention that she would like to thank her friend Hugh Crowley who unfortunately none of us have met but Grace has talked of him often. She said if you could meet him you would no doubt love him as she does. So before I finish, Grace would like me to make the first toast to Crowley.'

They all raised their glasses in a haphazard way but Grace's was in the direction of the bar as they said in unison, 'to Crowley.'

Grace could see that Crowley was clearly starting to cry and he quickly began mopping tears from his face. No one noticed that Grace was staring at the bar at her wonderful friend.

'The only other notable absentee is of course, Todd.'

Grace was snapped back into the room with the mere mention of his name. 'Todd, as you all know is Kate's nephew and when he was here a few weeks ago he had been with Grace when they found all the photographs. He had also started the massive task of cataloguing it all and made Grace realise just how special these photographs are. Now, I spoke to Todd recently who said he would always be upset that he missed his aunt's funeral and he also said that he made a promise to himself to make sure he would always be at anything he was expected to be at, or invited to. So I invited him to this evening.'

Big Mick stepped aside and from the darkened snug at the end of the pub appeared Todd. A cheer went up throughout the pub but Todd stood still in his crisp white shirt and jeans and stared at Grace. The whole table was cheering and clapping and looking at Grace. 'Is he really here'? she thought. She looked around the table and everyone was still clapping and she even saw Crowley on his feet clapping too. The clapping soon died down and Todd was still stood looking at Grace as he broke into a huge smile.

'Gotta kiss for a cowboy?' he drawled.

Grace jumped to her feet ran around the table to where Todd met her half way and they were soon showering kisses on each other. Another cheer went up to which Big Mick shouted that it was now time to get the party started. Todd pulled Grace back into the semi darkness of the snug while people helped themselves to drinks and to help Patsy bring the first courses through.

She felt Todd pull her near until his nose touched hers. 'Merry Christmas, baby,' and then he kissed her long and hungrily. She felt as if she was melting with his kiss, his smell and his touch. She only stopped when she heard someone politely coughing. As she pulled away Crowley was stood a couple of feet behind Todd.

'Why did you pull away?' he whispered.

'Crowley is behind you,' she said quietly. Todd spun but could see only darkness.

'I'll go now, Daff. I don't think I can take any more of this emotion without a decent Dom Perignon in one hand and the lovely Rita Hayworth in the other,' he sniggered.

'You and the redheads, eh?' said Grace. Todd watched her eyes to where she was looking, but he still couldn't see Crowley.

'You have made me feel truly loved this evening, my darling and I want to thank you. I haven't felt this good in years. Now, I presume you will not need my services for at least 24 hours so until then have a night that's as wonderful as you look.'

'Good night, Crowley,' she whispered.

'Good night. Oh and by the way, I love you too, Daff.'

Grace cast her gaze back to Todd.

'Has he gone?' he asked.

Grace nodded and as her mouth smiled Todd started to kiss her again.

They were soon bullied back to the table by Dai and they squeezed a chair in between her and her mum so Todd could join them. Grace looked at Sean who started to fan his face and pout at his appreciation of Todd's looks.

'It's a good job you gave me my present early,' she said out of the side of her mouth.

'That was no coincidence, girl.' Grace looked at him and Sean started to laugh.

'We all knew he was coming, even your mum and dad.' Grace went to speak. 'And another thing, darlin', I'm bunking in with Penny and Dai in the spare room at

Primrose Cottage so you got that big empty bed all to yourself. Handy that, eh?' Sean started to laugh and hollered a 'Yee-ha!' above the singing of Slade in the background.

Grace looked around the table. Everyone was talking and laughing and her mum and dad were clearly interrogating Todd who didn't seem to mind at all as he stroked Grace's leg under the table.

The meal was splendid and Patsy was pleased that there were plenty of empty plates. Everyone was starting to get tipsy so Grace decided that it was time to hand out a few presents. Sean helped her hand out the identical sized presents around the table. The only ones not to receive something were her mum, dad, Todd and Sean. Big Mick and Patsy had the largest pile of all. Grace stood back at the head of the table and spoke.

'Before you open them, I want you to know that these presents are really from Kate. As with all things with Mrs Mortimer, she liked starting stuff but hated finishing it,' Grace thought of the cushion they made together, 'Mick and Pats, some of yours are presents to the village and seeing as you two are the heart of it I thought they would be best to come here.' Grace nodded at them to start opening. They were overwhelmed to see framed pictures of the Summer Fair from the previous summer and after passing them around the table promised Grace that they would be hung on the walls of the pub for all to see.

Everyone opened their presents to find a framed picture that Kate had taken of them and they were all stunned by the beauty of each shot. These too were being passed around and Grace was satisfied that everyone was happy with their gift.

'What a beautiful idea for presents, Gracey,' said Dai.

She made her way back to her seat and as she sat down Mr Cousins got to his feet. The whole table went quiet again and looked at him waiting for him to speak. He quietly pulled out an envelope from his breast pocket and handed it over to Grace. The whole table remained quiet while Grace took the envelope nervously smiling at Mr Cousins. Grace looked at Todd who seemed just as perplexed as her.

'Shall I open it now?' she asked the old man.

'If you would,' he growled.

Grace began to open the envelope which enclosed a letter of some sort. As she opened the letter the table noticed her face becoming crestfallen and the mood around the table began to feel more sombre.

'Is this a joke?' she asked quietly.

'No, joke!' he barked.

'What is it?' asked Big Mick starting to frown.

'An eviction notice. He's throwing me out!'

CHAPTER 21

The whole table went stony silent and exchanged their gaze from Mr Cousins and back to Grace. Grace felt numb and kept reading the notice. After all the help she had given Mr Cousins lately she felt truly let down.

'What the hell?' hissed Todd, staring at the old man.

'I'm selling up. The farm as well,' there was an audible intake of breath. 'Got a sister in Jersey and she's asked me to stay with her for a bit. Not sure when I'll be going yet.'

Grace could still not look at him. She just wanted to go home and start packing so she could move into Primrose Cottage right away.

'Who you selling to?' barked Big Mick.

'I'm in talks with Deeres University. Seems they might want it so kids can learn farming,' Mr Cousins was looking at Grace, hoping she made the connection. She raised her eyes and looked at him and could see the earnest look in his face. Of course, she realised that this was all about Jane and her unfulfilled dream.

'They said that they are interested in taking the cottage as well. Seems sometimes the students might need to stay overnight for lambing and things while the tutors stay at the farmhouse.' Patsy was now on her feet and her mouth was in a taut thin line.

'Well, that's all well and good. But could you not have told Grace properly? I mean, come on, your timing's a bit shit!' she snapped.

'Patsy, please? Listen.' Mr Cousins turned back to Grace.

'Grace, there's things I want to say but I'm not going to say them here and you know why. But all of you,' he glanced around the table, 'should know that this young lady changed my life a few weeks ago and I can't repay her because what she did has no price. I'm selling up for me, yes. But I'm also selling up for you as well.' He reached in his pocket and pulled another envelope and handed it over. You could hear a pin drop in the room and Grace could hear Todd's breathing getting more and more strained.

As she pulled out the envelope and read the contents she jumped to her feet like an electric current had shot through her backside.

'No way! I'm not taking this!' Grace started trying to pass the piece of paper back and Mr Cousins gently pushed her hand away.

Todd stood up as well and looked at the paper.

'A hundred grand!' he roared.

'Jesus Christ,' whispered Big Mick, 'what the hell did she do?'

'Well, whatever she did she must have been fucking amazing!' Patsy whispered back.

'Mr Cousins, really, I can't take this…'

'You will and I'm not arguing at Christmas. It's only half of what the cottage is worth anyway. The money is for Kate's exhibition not for you buying purses and things,' he croaked. Grace looked at Todd who started to beam.

'You two know why I bought that cottage and that…well it never happened. But this'll be good,' his bottom lip was starting to shake. 'Please take it, Grace. You'll make an old man very, very happy if you do.' Grace could hear sniffing and realised that Sean was in floods of tears at the table.

'Come here, you old goat,' she cried. Mr Cousins burst into a smile and started to push past people still seated so he could reach Grace to embrace her and then they moved into the darkness of the snug.

'The eviction notice isn't real by the way,' he said softly, 'I called one of the kids I took in a while back and he told me how to do it over the phone.' Mr Cousins seemed quite proud that he had managed to make a realistic looking notice. 'But I presumed you would want to move into Primrose anyway with it being a lot bigger.'

'I don't know what to say. I was blown away when my dad gave me some money to buy a car! Are you sure though?'

'Yep!' he said firmly. 'When you are back from your parents' after Christmas come and see me and we'll talk more.' He rubbed the tops of her arms and then walked back into the pub to join everyone at the table.

The rest of the night disappeared into a haze of wine, spirits and beer. Grace had managed to get Mr Cousins to his feet for a dance to Last Christmas by Wham and she even had a heart to heart with Tom who admitted that he used to fancy her but since he met Zoe he was really happy. Grace was happy to for him. She liked Tom a lot but never felt that what was between them amounted to nothing more than a fleeting daydream and a serviced boiler.

Todd and Grace were some of the last to leave. Sean

helped Penny carry a very drunk Dai back to Primrose Cottage who sang 'Parapapapum...' on a continuous loop as it was the only lyric he knew from Little Drummer Boy.

Once Grace and Todd were back in her cottage, Todd retrieved his suitcase which he left earlier by the back door and pulled it into the kitchen.

'So you just thought I'd let you stay here did you?' asked Grace with a smile.

'Hey, Big Mick offered me a couch in The Blacky. Patsy even offered me the bed and said Big Mick could go on the couch but that's an adventure I don't think I have the stomach for,' he slipped his arms around her waist.

'You want me to leave?' he breathed. Grace shook her head and started to kiss him. He pulled her against him and he could feel the contours of her body and her quickening breath. Within a few seconds she was holding his hand, leading him up the stairs and then shutting the bedroom door.

Outside in the street the world was dimly lit and cold and all was silent until a 'Yee-ha' and a bout of giggling was heard.

Christmas went by in a flash at Breeze Point and Todd commented on how relaxed it all felt. He told stories of Christmases at the ranch and how it usually ended up with the men fired up on whisky ready to take each other on.

They all decided on Boxing Day to take the dogs for a walk along the beach and shake off some of the previous day's indulgences. Dai and Penny walked on ahead with the Flynn and Benji happily running beside them. Penny would occasionally throw a ball and if they fetched, she would give them a treat.

'I was talking to Elliott last night,' said Todd. He zipped

up his coat further up to his chin and grabbed Grace's hand.

'He wasn't working Christmas Day was he?' asked Grace.

'No. He just called to say Merry Christmas and...' he trailed off for a moment.

'And what?'

'He told me he put all the hard copy shots that I took with me to New York and some from the scanning work you guys did and uploaded them to 500px: and Flickr. Seems everyone is going nuts for them, Grace. People are asking is there any more and can they buy prints or if there are any galleries showing Kate's work?' Todd was trying to control his excitement. 'The pictures have gone viral! Everyone is talking about them,' said Todd excitedly. Grace's mind was starting to whir with all the things that they had to do. The whole idea was starting to feel more tangible now.

'We need to make a plan,' suggested Grace, 'we need to start talking to some influential people and see what needs to be done next.' Grace started trying to make a mental list. 'We need to see what kind of galleries in New York show work similar to Kate's. We also need to see about costings and who is supposed to do what. I've already enquired to the Copyright Service and I also spoke to Kate's solicitor to make sure that the contents of all the boxes definitely belong to me, which they do. Did Elliott get any further with that gallery owner he was going to speak to?' asked Grace. Todd was looking at his feet as he kicked the sand and Grace could feel he was anxious.

'Grace,' he stopped and looked at her, 'come back with me. We need you in New York,' his voice dropped to a whisper, 'I need you in New York. You can't do all this work from the other side of the Atlantic. We could get all the photos shipped over and put in storage while we try and launch the exhibition.' He studied her face and she looked slightly taken aback, scared even. 'You don't need to answer now, but at least think about it.' He wanted her to make a decision without him pressuring her.

They started to walk on again, 'You were coming anyway in a couple of months. I just thought you could come back with me for a couple of weeks so we can see what needs to be done even with work visas and stuff. Maybe talk to your mom and dad and see what they think.' Todd tried to smile encouragingly at the end.

Grace silently nodded and they continued to walk along the sand with their own thoughts. Grace would be lying if she said it hadn't already crossed her mind to go back with Todd. She had dismissed the idea as she had already made loose arrangements about leaving in a month but the more she thought about it the more she realised that there was no reason for her not to leave the day after tomorrow with Todd. However, she was aware that she was currently experiencing the best sex she had ever had so thought it best to maybe talk to her parents and make sure it was her head talking and not something else.

The walk certainly cleared her mind and while walking back they all caught up with each other. Penny asked Grace if she would help her finish the pie she had started with the Christmas leftovers and Dai asked Todd if he could give him a hand with removing the tracked ladder in the library as it was sticking.

Back at the house, Grace and Penny could hear the men doing very little work in the library and could only hear the clinking of glasses on the tray and Dai revealing to Todd as to how he liked to describe the sea as a ballroom dance.

Penny gave a smiling tut, thought of Gethin and then back to Grace.

'He's a lovely man, Grace. I wonder if your father would have crossed the Atlantic to be with me at Christmas in the early days,' she muttered as she rolled out the pastry. 'Go back with him Grace,' she said softly still rolling. Grace noticed that it was paper thin and her mum was obviously more absorbed in her thoughts than cooking.

'He just asked me to go back with him when we were walking, but I said I wanted to talk to you and Dad first. I want to go…but I'm scared. I know nothing about photography or galleries and to be honest, I hardly know Todd,' she sighed. Her mum immediately stopped rolling, picked up the two glasses of wine that she had poured earlier and passed one to Grace.

'None of us, not even Todd's boss Elliott knows about how to exhibit this work! But all I do know is that there is no one left who knows that woman as much as you did and only you can make this work for her and do her work justice. And who the hell is counting how many days, weeks or months you have known Todd? All I know is that when he looks at you he sees no one else and he is always looking at you. And I've never seen you this happy, ever! Grace, darling, you are one of the bravest people I know. I would never have moved to the other side of the country on my own. I would never have lived on my own. I would never have done what you did in a million years because I've always been scared and now I regret it. I thought it was being adventurous building this house. But what did I do? Bought some new wellington boots when it was a building site and meandered around the Farrow and Ball showroom. I did nothing Grace because I was too scared. Be like Kate Mortimer and grab life 'by the

goddamn reins' and ride life until you are out of breath.'
Penny raised her glass and looked at her daughter's
beautiful teary face.

'To Kate?' suggested Grace.

'NO! To you, darling. To my Grace,' and she clinked
her glass before Grace could argue.

For the first time in her life not only did she have her
mum's approval but she also had her admiration. A state
that she had never envisaged as she always thought her
mum was disappointed in her. How wrong Grace had
been. Kate's death had robbed her of her friend but on
reflection it had given so much to her as well.

Todd never raised the subject of her returning with him
for the rest of the day and even when they went to bed
Grace thought he may ask again, but he didn't. She
appreciated he didn't pressure her and they carried on with
the happy festivities for the rest of the evening.

The next day after breakfast Dai and Todd began to
pack Grace's car for their journey back to Pelsby. Todd
was leaving for New York the following day so Grace's
parents wished him a safe journey home and after kisses
and handshakes Todd climbed into the car with the dogs
and waited for Grace.

Grace embraced her mum and dad in the hall and
thanked them for the lovely Christmas that they had given
them but it was clear they just wanted to know if Grace
had made up her mind. She told them of her plans and
after some whispering they walked Grace to the car and
watched her climb in.

'I'll call you when I'm home,' Grace said as her mum
tapped the back window to wave to the dogs.

As soon as they were on the motorway, Grace told
Todd she needed to make a phone call. She was on a

speakerphone and the ringing of a phone reverberated throughout the car.

'Moore Haulage,' said the receptionist's voice.

'Hey Tina, it's Grace. Is Bill in?' she shouted.

'Oh Grace, he is. I'll put you through.' Todd gave a sideways glance to Grace and silently hoped.

'Hello Grace,' came Bill's voice on the line.

'Hi Bill. Good Christmas?' Grace tried to sound pleasant.

'No, it bloody wasn't! Maggie is sending all her presents back for one reason or another. The oven broke down on the day so we all had fish salad for Christmas lunch, then my daughter announces she's getting married, so that's gonna cost me an arm and a leg, then West Ham got beat yesterday and now you are calling me to tell me no doubt, that you're not coming back! Aren't you?' he snapped. Grace took a deep breath.

'I am Bill,' Grace looked at Todd who was lighting up the car with his smile. 'I'm going to New York, hopefully tomorrow. I need to get this exhibition off the ground. I know this is leaving you in the shit Bill but if I don't do this, I'll regret it and then end up blaming you and then I'll probably have to kneecap you or something to make me feel better. Then Maggie will be after me so I'll probably have to kill her and your daughter as well as her wedding will be ruined. So maybe instead of having a total blood bath it might be best if I just went to America. What do you think?'

Todd was silently laughing and shaking his head as he looked out of the window. There was more silence in the car and Grace started to worry.

'You still there, Bill? Don't tell me you're dead already?'

'I'm still here, you Welsh idiot. How can I tell you that

I'm dead?' Todd and Grace looked at each other with a wide-eyed knowing look.

'Grace, I knew this was going to happen. Why do you think I kept the temp on?'

'Because she has great legs,' snorted Grace.

'Yes, there's that, but also because we all knew this was coming. There was more chance of Julian Dicks and Billy Bonds smiling at each other than you coming back here. So when are you leaving?'

'I'm going to try and get on Todd's flight tomorrow. If not it'll be as soon as really. Look Bill, I'm sorry to leave like this. You've been so good to me, especially the last couple of months. And I know I should have given you notice but this thing is taking on a speed of its own and I need to catch up,' she said.

'Grace, believe it or not our Maggie and Tara were on their laptops yesterday looking at your friend's work. It was on the internet or something. Even those two pair of dozy articles said the pictures were good.' Grace and Todd smiled at each other. 'Grace, if it doesn't work out and you want to come back then just call me, I mean it, you're a good girl. Just don't come back with a weird accent like Catherine Zeta Jones, you hear me?' Bill laughed and Grace joined in. After, a heartfelt goodbye, Grace ended the call and waited for Todd to speak.

'So you're coming to New York, huh?' he asked trying to sound uninterested.

'I might,' teased Grace.

'And ummm…where you gonna be staying?'

'I have a gorgeous bloke over there that will show me the sights, introduce me to all his wonderful friends and shower me with kisses on demand,' she joked.

'The bloke sounds like a douche,' said Todd.

'You think? You might be right. Maybe I should just stay in a hotel then and steer clear of him.'

'But then again, you could maybe give him a couple of weeks, see if he ends up being as cool as me,' Todd threw his head to one side and pretended he was trying to look cool.

'Mr Whippy isn't as cool as you,' mocked Grace.

'Mr Whippy?' Todd raised his eyebrows.

'A contender, he will always be a contender,' laughed Grace.

Todd called the airline and managed to get Grace on his flight and then called Elliott to tell him Grace was coming back with him. A pleased Elliott said he would arrange a meeting with Charles Mackenzie within a couple of days.

Todd explained that Charles Mackenzie was the director of an art gallery in New York. His exhibitions in the past had a similar feel to Kate's so the gallery already had a particular demographic that Kate's work needed to attract. Charles was also a friend to Elliott, in as much as they played golf together and were often seen at the same charity functions.

Once they were home and settled, Grace called her parents and asked if they could sort air freighting the boxes over. Her dad was very aware of the collection and she could trust him to make all the necessary arrangements. They discussed the costs and how to control spending. Grace also gave him Sean's number to see if Sean could help with haulage and to liaise with Bill about the best people to speak to about transporting the boxes.

Grace then called Sean to give him the heads up and to break the news that she had left her job and was leaving for New York for a couple of weeks to see what needed to be done. Sean was squealing down the phone with excitement at her news and said he wanted to help as much as he could.

As soon as she sat down to relax with a wine, the phone went again. It was her mum.

'Grace, darling, what's happening with the dogs?'

'I was going to book them into the kennels, failing that I was going to ask Mr Cousins could he keep them on the farm until I come back,' mused Grace.

'In all that mud! Flynn's feet couldn't cope! I'll drive down in the morning with Daddy and I'll bring them back to Breeze Point. If that's okay with you?' she asked in hope.

'Mum, that would be brilliant. They love the beach and I think they feel quite at home with you,' sniggered Grace.

'If you don't mind Grace, I'll buy some new beds for them. I saw some fabulous ones in Padstow the other week and they will go well with the palette of the house and they look very comfortable Grace,' she added.

'It's up to you Mum, spoil them all you want. They're your dogs while I'm away. Just don't be putting stupid clothes on them and making them look like they should be on a cheap talent show,' laughed Grace.

With the dogs sorted, Grace felt she was truly ready to go and take on the art world. With a wine in her hand she tapped away at her laptop and opened the sites where Elliott and Todd has posted some of Kate's pictures. She was staggered by some of the lovely comments left on Flickr. and felt encouraged that she was doing the right thing. She also noted the photographs that were generating the most discussion and started to make a list of the images she felt should be exhibited. Todd offered his opinion on works to be included that he felt would be attractive to not only people who were interested in architecture but also the general public who were interested in American history.

Once she was finished with delegating jobs and prioritising, she then made a start with packing. She agonised over what to take as she had no idea she would be doing this 48 hours ago. She managed to throw a few outfits in the case and pacified herself with the fact that she was not visiting a third world country and anything she needed she was sure to be able to get there.

Todd was impressed with her efficiency and more impressed that her passport photo didn't look like she was a prisoner or a corpse. He wondered for a moment about how he would feel about her when he was in his own territory but then realised she would be even more attractive being British amongst the New Yorkers. Some New Yorkers thought it was novel that he was from Ohio so listening to his Welsh girlfriend would impress a fair few.

Later that night when Grace was sure that Todd was asleep, she crept down the stairs and quietly called for Crowley. He soon appeared and looked pleased to see Grace.

Grace sat beside him and told him all her news of the last few days and that she had decided to go back to New York with Todd to try and launch the exhibition.

'What I'm concerned about is will you be able to still find me in America?' she asked.

'Only if you wear a huge ten gallon hat, like JR Ewing. Then I want you to go to Times Square and kick your legs like a Nazi signing "New York, New York, it's a wonderful town". I might be able to home in on you when you are taken downtown to the nearest police precinct for looking and acting like a complete and utter moron. My homing signals need something very obvious you see.'

'How about a pair of jeans and a t-shirt on West 42nd?'

'Yeah, that should do it,' he said disappointingly.

'I need you there with me. I know it sounds daft and I know that Todd has been great but at least I know you are on my side. And I promise as soon as this is all sorted and I'm back in Pelsby we start to really find out about your deed and get you moved on.' assured Grace. Crowley nodded in agreement.

'I can't wait to see New York, Daff. I haven't been since 1980 when MOMA held a Picasso exhibition.' He sat further back into the sofa and made himself comfortable, 'It had been a few years since finishing my degree in Art History. Felt it might reignite my passion, which it certainly did. Only my father soon dampened my spirits on my return.' Grace looked at him quizzically.

'I was to run the estate like all the generations before me and that was that,' he sighed.

'Well, he didn't even let you manage that after the shit he left you in,' Grace snapped.

'Our paths are already set my dear,' he said.

'Really?' Grace mulled over his revelation. 'So it doesn't matter what I do, I will always end up doing what is predetermined?' she asked. This was news to her.

'More or less. There are things that may happen that can steer you away from the path and that's kind of why 'we',' he pointed upwards, 'exist. There's still an element of choice and variation but essentially the path will always lead to the same place,' he finished.

'And there was me thinking that everything was down to me and any deviations were whether I allowed them or not,' Grace sounded disappointed and Crowley could see. He didn't want her thinking that she had no influence on her life whatsoever.

'Daff, you do have influence and that can enhance the outcome that is inevitable,' he said. Grace looked more confused.

'Okay, let's say you want to buy some flowers for your mum. You go to the shop and there is the most beautiful bouquet you've ever seen and all for the price of £20. Next to it is a much smaller bouquet and the heads are already beginning to wilt but that's only £1. So do you get the cheap one that will no doubt bring a smile to your dear mother's face and, in turn, you are happy as you still have £19 change in your pocket? Or do you buy the large bunch which will have your mum gasping for breath and on the phone to all her friends about what a wonderful daughter you are?' asked Crowley.

'The second one, definitely. I wouldn't buy flowers for a pound!' she sniffed.

'It doesn't matter. The fact is the end is still the same which is to buy the flowers. Your choice will make the path differ but the end is still the same. Does that make you understand?'

Grace thought for a moment and while she did understand she tried and failed to recognise the predetermined points of her own life; she realised she didn't want to know either. However, it did make her wonder why Crowley was destined to end up on the streets. She was sure that Crowley would have questioned it at some point as well. She thought about how much had happened in the last few weeks and wondered if all that was part of the path.

'Well, I don't want to know what my path is. I want to live my life in blissful ignorance. Which will be hard now knowing what I know about what happens when I go,' she babbled.

'Daff, go and get some sleep dear. You have a busy few days coming up and you need some rest so you can take on the world,' he winked. 'I'll be at your side whenever you want me, my dear.'

'Thank you Crowley, you're the best.'

CHAPTER 22

When Grace arrived in Todd's apartment, she felt absolutely exhausted and excited at the same time. She dropped her case and walked over to the huge floor to ceiling windows that had a breathtaking view that stretched for miles.

Todd's apartment was on the 47th floor and from here she could see the Hudson River and the Statue of Liberty in the distance. But her eye was drawn to the Empire State Building. She couldn't wait for it to become dark.

The apartment was small and sparsely furnished. A deep amber maple floor ran throughout the lounge and into the kitchen located at the end of the long room. All the sofas and tables were arranged towards the window, clearly to enjoy the view.

Todd returned from moving the cases to the bedroom and walked over to Grace who was still looking out. He slipped his arms around her and nuzzled into her neck from behind.

'You have no idea how many times I looked out of this window and thought of you and wished you were here.

And here you are.' He spun her round and kissed her gently. Grace couldn't believe she was here but she kept telling herself that she was here for a reason and as much as she was falling for Todd, he was not the reason.

They planned to have a lie down and then grab something to eat later. But later came around four in the morning the following day. They both were clearly wiped out and stayed asleep for hours.

They had something to eat in the apartment and then after a leisurely morning they got themselves ready to head over to Todd's office to meet Elliott. Grace was feeling very nervous. She had no idea what to expect and if anyone started to challenge her on anything arty, she knew she would be exposed as a total charlatan.

They jumped into a cab on West 42nd Street which took them to 5th and dropped them outside an unassuming building. They entered and took a lift to the tenth floor which opened out onto a sign that read Elliott Benson Architect. Todd's position was to assist Senior Designers as he had not long qualified but he hoped to make an impression in his first year.

As they walked through the office, everyone stopped and asked how Todd's vacation had been in England. They all seemed very friendly but Grace could see they were all giving her the once over like a new contestant on the X-Factor. She immediately felt self-conscious about what she was wearing. She wasn't sure what was good enough for Bill Moore Haulage was going to cut it with Elliott Benson and his trend-setting, effervescent and fabulous looking team.

Todd led the way to a glass office at the end of an open plan floor not too dissimilar to Bill's. Only this one was cleaner, brighter and everyone looked like they were on happy pills. Bill's office stank of old smoke, booze, sweat and toast for some reason.

A tall black man in his fifties who looked like he worked out, stood up as he could see them approaching through the glass and quickly made his way to the door before they reached it. He opened the door as wide as his smile to greet them.

'Todd! Great to see you, man. I didn't expect you this early. My God, you must be Grace,' then he threw his arms around her. 'Todd said you were fine but he didn't say just how beautiful you were,' he laughed, beckoned them in further and then shut the door. 'What can I get you to drink, Grace? I got some English tea brought in for you or you could have coffee or juice or hell, whatever you want,' he laughed again.

Grace wasn't sure if he was really happy or really nervous. All she did know was she liked Elliott instantly. His brown eyes were warm and his dazzling smile was furnished with a trim moustache.

'Well, seeing as you went to so much trouble, may I have a cup of tea please?' she asked.

'*May I have a cup of tea?* I just love that accent! It's like Downton Abbey has landed in my office,' Elliott chortled. Grace didn't like to point out that she was not even English, never mind posh but who was she to destroy the illusion; she instantly felt very English, something she had never felt in her life and wondered if she should give it the Maggie Smith's or the Julie Andrew's.

Elliott called to a girl outside and asked her for some drinks and to get them something to eat, then they all sat on an 'L' shaped couch in Elliott's office and talked of the journey and the decision to come straight away. Elliott agreed that the whole idea was taking a life of its own and someone needed to steer it. He admitted that he had no experience in the art world but the architectural photographs in Kate's collection were something that should be seen by a wider audience. He agreed with Todd's initial sentiment that some of the photographs were little pieces of American history. Grace revealed her initial obliviousness to the find and confessed that she was influenced greatly by friends, family and of course, Todd. Elliott divulged that he had been making enquiries regarding a working visa for Grace which seemed to be fairly straight-forward if they had Elliott's assistance.

'Leave that to me, we can get all of that sorted. I have some papers that I need you to fill in Grace and then we can get the ball rolling with that one.'

Grace brought Elliott up to speed as to the shipping of the boxes that her dad was taking control of. Elliott explained that they had another wing to the floor that they never used but was there for future expansion of the office. But until then, if that ever came to fruition, they could use the space to store all the photographs.

'I've set up a meeting with Charles Mackenzie at his gallery for tomorrow. He only knows we want to discuss some art with him. I thought it was best for Grace to do the hard sell,' suggested Elliott. He went on to explain that Charles was a good pick as he had galleries all over the States including California and Washington, places that Kate had taken pictures.

Grace could feel a rise of panic in her at the sheer enormity of the task ahead and how much she was to be relied upon. Her garbled thoughts were interrupted by a knock on the door which Elliott immediately attended to. A petite Chinese girl pushed a trolley into the office and left silently. The trolley was groaning with pastries, cakes, fruits, yoghurts, juice and toasted items such as bagels and muffins.

'Come on kids, help yourself. We've got a long morning ahead of us.' Elliott beckoned them to the trolley and they each took a plate and looked at the food like it was a birthday party. Grace then looked at each of the men in turn as they piled their plates and realised that both of them, in their own way, would look after her and support her in her decisions.

They spent the morning compiling a slide show of all the photographs they wanted to impress Charles with. They included some of Washington's Union Station, the Lafayette Square Opera House and the old Cellar Door Club. Elliott admitted that he had been so impressed with a photograph of Nina Simone leaving the Cellar Door Club, he had had it made into a framed poster and hung in his study at home already.

The California section included shots of the Whizzer Roller Coaster still under construction at the Great American Theme Park. Then they decided to include further photographs of the crowd when the park opened including happy images of children and photos of tired looking parents, the emotion totally relatable in both groups. There were also numerous photos from 1976 of the first outing of Space Shuttle Enterprise in Palmdale. She had even managed to get some natural shots of the cast of Star Trek while they watched the event.

Grace started to feel very relaxed with Elliott and Todd and could tell they completely respected her opinion on what she wanted to show to Charles. Seeing as she wasn't very arty, she simply put it down to being a girl and simply knowing when something looked right. Todd was making notes as to why she wanted to include certain images, so her presentation was more or less complete by the time they had finished with constructing the slide show.

Once they were all completed, they assigned themselves a role. Grace was to lead with who Kate was and how the photographs were discovered. Todd was to lead with the impact of social media and why they thought Charles should be included in the project, while Elliott was to talk figures and general responsibilities of getting the exhibition off the ground.

Once they were all happy with what they were to do the following day, they all said goodbye and agreed to meet in a restaurant before the meeting. Outside in the street, Grace looked at Todd and felt slightly dazed by the morning's work.

'Todd, I feel nervous. What if I mess up? What if the fella can't understand my accent? I've never felt so Welsh in all my life and English at the same time. I don't know how to talk, never mind what to bleeding say. What if I get all the names of the buildings wrong, or say something is in New York when actually it's in Timbuk-bloody-tu?! What if we don't have enough money? Everything here looks so expensive. Shit!'

'You finished?' asked Todd. He put his arms around her waist and pulled her close. 'You are not on trial, it's a presentation and I know you have done plenty of them before in your old job. We are a generation that grew up listening to Sylvester Stallone, Arnie Schwarzenegger and Penelope Cruz, so you will be fine. Just talk as if you were walking in the park, not racing down a freeway.'

'I babble, I know I babble.' They started to walk down the street hand-in-hand.

'Come on, let me show you a bit of my new home town,' offered Todd.

Grace and Todd spent the rest of the day and evening taking in some of the tourist sites. They grabbed some dinner in Loeb Boathouse Restaurant in Central Park before jet lag finally beat them into submission and they headed home.

Grace's sleep was more off than on as she worried about the following day which was soon upon her. She climbed out of bed, leaving a sleeping Todd and quietly made herself a cup of tea. She sat in one of the huge armchairs and looked at the sun rise up over the New York skyline. She thought of Kate and Crowley and how without them she would never have been here.

Todd soon joined her and they quietly talked of Kate and her talent. They talked about how belligerent she could be and yet very easy to love. They then sat in silence until the dawn had fully broken. Grace would occasionally glance over to her right where Todd was sat and marvel at how handsome he was and how lucky she was to have him in her life. She allowed herself for a moment to daydream of growing old with him but then quickly dismissed it as silly, ambitious and naive.

They quietly got themselves ready and while Todd thought of Grace, she thought of Crowley and her guilt at neglecting him. She thought of his wife and son still patiently waiting for him to cross over and all the while she was swanning around America dealing with her own life. It wasn't fair on Crowley but she wasn't sure what she could do about it when the deed was still unknown. How the man had not had a positive effect on her already was beyond her. He had helped to change her life immeasurably.

Grace still felt quiet as they waited in the restaurant for Elliott. Todd had picked up that Grace was reserved but simply put that down to nerves. Elliott walked in not long after them and joined them in the plush red-leathered booth.

'I'll have a scotch,' he said to the waitress when she seated him.

'I'll have JD and the lady will have a glass of Pinot,' added Todd.

Grace could see that Elliott was jittery. He offered Grace some advice and she was relieved to hear that Charles was actually English. As she listened to Elliott, she realised that he was talking to calm himself down more than her. Todd seemed the most relaxed and mostly watched Grace.

The time eventually came for them to leave and they made their way to the next block where the gallery was. Huge glass smoked windows dominated the façade which hinted at what was inside and enticing one to enter. As they walked in, a tall blonde lady dressed in a severe white trouser suit greeted them in a cool and somewhat aloof manner. Elliott introduced the party while the lady gave them a disdainful look. She nodded and asked them to follow her.

The gallery was minimal with its white walls and white flooring. The only colour to be found was in the artwork upon the walls. Grace had to admit to herself that the gallery did showcase each piece to its full potential with clever lighting and themed grouping. She also noted that even though it was early, the gallery had a fair amount of customers already.

They walked up an open glass staircase to a mezzanine level which opened out into a lounge area. This area was clearly for staff, judging by the rope that had to be unclipped at the top of the staircase. To the left, Grace could see a fairly large boardroom through its glass windows. The blonde asked them to wait a moment while she walked towards the boardroom and Grace thought she reminded her of a giraffe.

Grace slowly broke away from Todd and Elliott and pretended to be pacing the room and once out of ear shot, called Crowley. He soon arrived in front of her and she immediately placed her finger on her lips. He looked behind her and could see Todd and Elliott deep in conversation.

'Who's that with Todd?' he whispered.

'Elliott,' she mouthed. He nodded.

'Mr Mackenzie will see you now,' said the blonde giraffe.

'Jesus Christ! Was she weaned on Baby Bio?' snorted Crowley.

They all walked into the boardroom, including Crowley as Charles Mackenzie stood to greet them. He was fairly tall and in his late fifties with a hint of a tan. His blond hair was floppy and was obviously grown to a length to hide his receding hairline. He wore a cream linen suit with a pale blue shirt beneath; to Grace he looked quintessentially British.

'Elliott!' Charles shook Elliott's hand and then turned to Todd. 'Todd, I take it,' and shook his. 'And you must be Grace?' he smiled at her which Grace found slightly creepy.

'It's great to finally meet you, Charles,' said Grace extending her hand. Grace noted that he shook it but his smile dropped a little.

'Charles Mackenzie. Well, I never. So this is where you got to,' said Crowley. Grace looked up at Crowley who was stood against the wall staring at their host.

'So, how can I help?' asked Charles in an accent similar

to Crowley's. Todd and Elliott turned to Grace. She quickly looked at Crowley. 'How did he know him'? she thought.

'Tell him the story of Kate,' Crowley whispered.

Grace did as she was instructed and gave Charles a brief biography of her friend. She told him of her life, her loves and eventually her death. She then went on to explain about the find in Primrose Cottage and then passed him an edited list of what the body of work included.

Todd rose to his feet and asked for the use of the projector and while he set it up, Elliott continued to explain the media reaction her photographs had received and that there was an audience for Kate's work. He ran through statistics of how many people were following, tweeting and sharing the links to her work, all of which were impressive.

'How exciting for you,' he said dismissively and turned his attention to Todd who was now ready to show some images of Kate's work. Todd ran through some of the historical photographs of lost architecture and landmarks in New York, California and Washington. Todd would particularly enthuse about Beaux Arts style with its symmetry, balustrades and cartouches. He clicked through to the razing of the Ritz-Carlton and the Murray Hill Hotel and raved about the vibrancy that Kate had found in the demise of an old building. He continued more with images of the remains of the Seven Buildings in Washington, the first residential structures in the city, and the photographs that catalogued the incorporation of the facades into a modern day building.

Once Todd was finished, he turned the lights back on and saw that Charles's expression still had not changed.

'So, why have you come to me?' he asked flatly.

'Well,' said Elliott, 'your reputation in this field is unsurpassable,' he chuckled nervously. 'With your galleries in these key cities we think you are the best to exhibit this wonderful body of work. You have already shown architectural work as well as the street art that she has in the collection...'

'Oh, so you want to show these in my galleries?' he interrupted.

Elliott looked at Todd and then back at Charles with a confused look.

'Well, why else would you think we were here?' Elliott smiled.

'I simply thought you just wanted some friendly advice,' he muttered, leaning back in his chair. 'I can't show this,' he laughed and threw his papers across the table.

'Why not?' asked Todd.

'You want me to launch an exhibition on a nobody. No one has heard of this Kate Mortimer. Just some old biddy who got bored traipsing after her one-dimensional husband, no doubt.' Todd's jaw became clenched and his eyes turned steely. 'I admit her work shows a sense of warmth and even a sense of humour. Her framing is superb and I particularly like the way her shadow alters the emotion of her art. But that's it! Nothing special and to exhibit posthumously on somebody's work that we don't know is such a risk. We don't know if we are interpreting her art in the way she would have liked and more to the point why did she never exhibit her work before? No, I'm sorry but this is not something that I can exhibit.' He continued to sit back in his chair and looked slightly bored.

'There's an audience for this, Charles. She wasn't your run of the mill photographer taking fifty cent pictures for the family mantle. This woman had talent!' insisted Elliott.

'Well, good luck, that's all I can say. I can certainly offer you some basic advice but it's not something I can give a lot of time to.' They all picked up on the hint that basically said: 'don't bother me'. He finished with a look that questioned why were they still sitting there?

Elliott and Todd stood up and started to tidy their things to put back into various cases. Grace felt slightly stunned that all their efforts were simply disregarded and the whole idea was dismissed in the space of an hour. Grace noticed that Crowley was clenching his jaw and could see that he was angry. He marched around the table and told Grace to ask where the bathroom was and he would meet her in there.

They all reluctantly shook Charles's hand and muttered their goodbyes. Grace noted that Charles not only seemed happy but slightly victorious as well. 'The smug bastard', she thought.

Once out of the boardroom, Grace made her way to the other side of the mezzanine to the toilet. Crowley was in there waiting for her and once Grace was satisfied they were alone she began by saying she just wanted to jump on a plane and head back to Pelsby. Crowley scooped Grace into his arms briefly and then instructed her to go back in and make another appointment for just her and Charles. Grace looked at him confused.

'I know Charles from way back. We studied historical art together at university. I'll tell you a little story about him later. But for now I want you to go back and tell him you want to see him later today,' instructed Crowley.

'He won't see me. You saw what he was like. I'm not even sure I would want him to exhibit Kate's work anyway,' she sulked.

'Daff, you need him. Let's not forget he has galleries in

all the key cities you need to exhibit in. His reasons for not wanting to show her work are valid and you will no doubt come across the same excuses with other galleries but we need him, so put your feelings aside and think like a business woman. Now go back in there and tell him you know the Crowley's and more importantly my sister, Sarah,' he insisted.

'Sarah? Why? What?' asked Grace.

'Trust me. I'll reveal all later. Now just do it,' she stared at him blankly. 'Go on!' he pushed.

Grace took a deep breath and left the ladies' toilet. She could see over the balcony that Elliott and Todd were outside on the pavement waiting for her and ahead of her was Charles shutting the boardroom door behind him.

'Charles, may I have a word?' Grace marched over to a surprised looking man. He clearly thought she had already gone.

'I'd like another appointment to see you later today, just you and I?' she asked.

'I'm sorry Grace, but I have an appointment already for the end of the day. I'm not sure there is anything further for us to discuss, even without your entourage,' he chuckled to himself and started to walk away from her.

'It won't take long,' she caught up with his stride. 'We don't have to talk about Kate's work. We could maybe talk about the Crowley's.' She threw it out there, not knowing why or even if the bait was juicy enough for him to bite.

He stopped and turned to her.

'Of De Mondford Hall? And how the hell would you know them?' he sneered.

'Hugh and I are…were good friends.'

'Yes, I heard he died…on the streets. Is that where you knew him from?'

'I was a friend of the family. Especially Sarah, she and I were very close,' lied Grace.

'Still are,' pushed Crowley.

'Still are as a matter of fact. Wait 'til I tell her that I finally met Charles Mackenzie,' Grace smiled and hoped she was pulling it off whatever 'it' was. Grace could see that Charles became slightly agitated and was looking around to see if anyone was around.

'Meet me at six back here,' he snapped and quickly walked away.

Grace looked at Crowley who continued to stare at Charles until he disappeared. He then turned to Grace and gave a gentle smile.

'What the hell was that all about?'

'Go for a walk somewhere later. No Todd! Just you. Can I suggest Central Park? And bring a phone, okay?' he took her hands.

'Don't make me look an idiot Crowley, I mean it. I'm really trusting you on this.'

He smiled and disappeared. Grace then walked back down the glass stairs and joined the men outside.

'You okay?' asked Todd, looking relieved.

'I'm meeting Charles later at four,' she lied taking into account she needed to see Crowley beforehand. 'I want to have one last go on my own. A bit of flirting and flattery might help and I can't do either with the Chuckle Brothers watching me. I've come all this way and I want more than a poxy hour with him,' she barked.

Todd looked at Elliott who shrugged his shoulders.

'I dunno, Grace.' Todd didn't like the idea of her turning on the charm to influence the creep.

'We need him Todd, it's as simple as that. And all I know is I don't want to get on that plane back to England wishing I'd tried something more.' She stared at both of them and Todd could see her determination.

'If you're sure,' said Todd. They had nothing to lose that they felt they hadn't already lost. He had to trust her.

'I'm not so sure he's gonna change his mind,' said Elliott in an exasperated tone and started to march down the street.

'And if he doesn't?' asked Todd, 'then what do we do?'

'We can approach another gallery or even a cultural centre in New York and hope that if it's a success we can ride on that with galleries in Washington and LA or San Francisco maybe.' Even though they were in a state of shock at the abrupt dismissal, they were trying to formulate a Plan B. Grace noticed that Elliott was shaking his head the farther they walked down the street and then he stopped suddenly.

'Man, he knew why we went there today! All that bullshit about asking for advice, sorry Grace. But he just sat there like he was the fucking President and bullshitted us! Why in hell would Grace come all this way from England? To listen to his invaluable advice? On what?! How to be fucking rude to people? How to waste our mother-fucking time?! I'm sorry Grace but he ain't nothing but a dumb English asshole with bad fucking hair, man.' He eventually ran out of steam.

'I'm not English, I'm Welsh and he does have bad fucking hair,' said Grace with a smile. Elliott looked up, caught her eye and then burst out laughing. He scooped her into his arms and continued to laugh. Grace pulled away slightly and looked up at him.

'Trust me; I might have a trick or two up my sleeve. It's not just Richard Burton and Anthony Hopkins who can put on a good performance you know.' Elliott let go of

Grace and they all started to walk down the street again.

'If he says no, you gonna eat his brains Grace?' Elliott asked with a wry smile.

CHAPTER 23

Grace had managed to persuade Todd to let her go on her own to the meeting. He was insisting he would take her and simply wait for her in the restaurant that they had been in earlier with Elliott, but Grace convinced him that she wanted to see a bit of New York on her own and felt that being a bit independent would give her more courage by the time she got there.

In Central Park, it was starting to get dark and the temperature was dropping as well. Grace made her way to the Wollman Ice Rink in the park and found an empty bench. She then pulled out the phone and called for Crowley.

'My oh my Daff, this is a treat,' Crowley who was now beside her beamed at the skaters. They sat for a moment and watched the swishing and whooshing of the skaters, all of whom seemed very competent. The last time Grace went to an ice rink in Wales it looked like a blood bath with split lips, bust up chins and limbs hanging at awkward angles.

'What's the story then?' Grace didn't have the phone to

her ear yet. She was simply staring straight ahead.

Crowley began his story and Grace continued to stare straight ahead for most of it. Occasionally, she would look in Crowley's direction to see his reaction or to even offer her own. Once he had finished, he let out a long sigh.

'The whole thing didn't help my relationship with my sister. But then again I doubt a million dollar psychiatrist could have helped Sarah and me.'

'Do you think this will help?' asked Grace, now placing the phone to her ears. Crowley simply shrugged his shoulders.

'Worth a bash eh, Daff?' Grace looked at her watch and realised she needed to make a move to make the meeting on time.

'Will you stay with me?' asked Grace.

'Of course I will,' he patted her knee.

They made their way to the street and hailed a taxi to take them back to the gallery. Crowley sat in the taxi and watched the neon world go by while Grace mulled over her thoughts.

'Thanks for not drinking, by the way. I noticed that you haven't been drunk much lately,' said Grace.

'I haven't felt like drinking much to be honest. Must be coming down with something,' he turned and looked at Grace. 'Hope it doesn't kill me,' he smiled.

The taxi stopped in front of the gallery and they both climbed out and entered the building. Grace noticed the giraffe had gone and a small man that reminded her of a ferret had replaced her. He seemed more welcoming than the giraffe. Grace introduced herself to the ferret who seemed pleased to be able to show her up the stairs to where Charles had taken his usual seat in the boardroom.

Charles stood as she entered the room but his welcome

was a lot colder than it had been earlier in the day. There was no handshake or refreshments laid out and certainly no smile, not even a creepy one. She took a seat next to him and decided she didn't need to follow suit. She had the upper hand and she was going to take control, so she smiled at him and in an instant she could feel the power shift in her favour.

'So what's all this about Sarah Crowley,' he growled.

'She still has the ring you know,' said Grace. Charles lowered his gaze. 'She told me everything about that night.' His eyes darted to Grace's face in panic. 'The party at her home, her arriving back early to catch you with, who was it again? Oh yes, your cousin Seb.' Charles screwed his eyes up at the memory. 'I mean if you had simply been caught sleeping with him then it wouldn't be too bad. Or even watching a bit of porn? But cream cakes? Bit unusual to say the least.' Charles remained silent and stared at the table.

'It's funny how the world can tolerate a bit of buggery but throw in an éclair or a choux bun and people become very judgemental.' Grace stood up and started to walk slowly around the very long table. Crowley was stood in the corner silently enjoying the spectacle.

'You've clearly made an effort to project a squeaky clean image. Heard you play golf with the mayor and have quite a high profile with the movers and shakers of the city. Am I right?' Charles looked at her with a nervous glance. The corner of his mouth was twitching like he was ready to break into an Elvis impression.

'What do you want, Grace?' he whispered. Grace paused for what felt like a long time. She knew exactly what she wanted but she wanted Charles to stew in his 'worst case scenario', then it was more likely she would get what she wanted. She continued to walk around the table, pretending she was mulling over what she wanted.

'I want six weeks in this gallery for an exhibition in the summer. I'm not going to push it with your other ones until we have proven that there is not only an audience for Kate's work but there is a profit there. I want to have full control of what goes in and I want your full support in launching this as you would give to any other exhibitor. I want you to liaise with Elliott and Todd in my absence and give them the respect you should have shown the Crowley family years ago. If you don't, I'm sure you remember the camera that Seb used that night. Well, Sarah still has the negatives.' The colour drained from his face and he instantly aged ten years. 'Do I make myself clear?' she hissed.

'Crystal.'

'So, do we have an agreement?'

He let out a long sigh. 'Agreed.'

He lowered his head again and felt shame but he couldn't figure out what it was specifically that made him feel so bad. Was it his behaviour to Sarah Crowley or was it simply that his past had finally caught up with him?

'You have all our contact details so I would appreciate a call in the next day or two with dates we can launch the exhibition. I take it that won't be a problem?' she asked.

'Can I have the negatives once the exhibition has started?' he asked.

'I'll see. I was thinking I might keep hold of them until the other exhibitions are launched. But if this one is as successful as I think it will be, then we might have other galleries biting off our hand to exhibit with them so they can have a piece of the pie,' she smiled, 'pardon the pun.'

'Now, if you'll excuse me, I have a lot of work to do

now we have finally agreed to work together.' Grace grabbed her coat and she started to put it on in a casual manner. She felt like Alexis Colby in Dynasty. She made her way to the door and looked over to where Charles was still sitting.

'By the way, I don't want that giraffe you call an assistant working when the exhibition is on. I will bring my own greeter if you don't mind.' He looked up and went to protest and Grace quickly interrupted him.

'You must have been picking out the strawberry seeds for weeks,' she sniggered and his mouth promptly closed. Grace's exit was accompanied by a huge roar of laughter from Crowley.

Once they were outside, Grace started to walk down the street. Her legs were shaking slightly from the huge adrenalin rush she was feeling. Crowley was still beside her.

'You were wonderful in there. My God, you were terrifying!' he began to laugh again.

'I want to hug you so much,' she said, 'but everyone will think I'm nuts. But I want you to know that I am hugging you with all my heart. I can't believe I've just pulled that off. I feel I could do anything!' She screamed and some people in the street started staring at her. They continued to talk about how well it had gone and how subservient Charles had become. They carried on talking about launching the exhibition until they reached Todd's apartment when she realised they had walked a few miles.

She said goodbye to Crowley and insisted that he have a drink to celebrate. He understood she needed to get back to Todd and tell him the good news.

She knocked at the door of his apartment and the door was opened mid-knock. His brow was furrowed and she saw the relief flood his face as soon as he saw her.

'You okay?' he asked pulling her in. 'I was worried.'

She slipped off her coat and passed it to him.

'I'm fine. I just need a wine and a comfy chair. I suggest you get the same, I have a story to tell you.' He raised an eyebrow but did as he was bid.

Once they were settled in their chairs, Grace explained that when she went to the ladies' after their morning meeting it was at Crowley's insistence. She explained it was his idea to meet later in the day and that he had some information for her on Charles.

'Information? What kind of information?' asked Todd.

'Well, it seems that Charles and Crowley were friends in university, they were studying the same degree in art history. Anyway, Charles's family were a bit strange so he would always spend the holidays with the Crowley's in De Mondford Hall. This went on for a few years and I suppose because of all the time that he was spending at the Hall, Crowley's sister, Sarah, fell in love with him. Well, old Mr & Mrs Crowley already saw Charles as a son so they thought it was a great idea when Charles proposed. Crowley said Sarah was besotted with him. She would mope around the house when he went back to uni and literally counted the weeks until the next break in term.

But Crowley said he started to see a different side to Charles especially when he was doing a bit of cocaine. Crowley said Charles liked to go to the seedier side of the city once everyone had called it a night. He tried to tell him to sort himself out but Charles insisted he was just having a bit of fun before he got married. Crowley said that the rumours had started to increase about him sleeping with other people and his drug habit was getting worse as well. Anyway, one weekend Crowley decided to have a party at the Hall for his twenty-first. Sarah was staying with friends and was due back before the party started but the trains were off because of a severe gale so she couldn't get back. Charles turned up with his cousin Seb and Crowley said it was weird the way he wouldn't let Seb out of his sight all night. He said they were cosying up on the couch and getting a little too close. Crowley said he became distracted with other guests and didn't notice that Charles and Seb had disappeared until Sarah turned up at the Hall. She had managed to get a lift from one of her friends as she was determined to see Charles. When they realised he wasn't with people at the party they looked for him in his bedroom and when Sarah and Crowley walked in, they found Charles and Seb. The whole bed and floor was covered in black bin liners and Charles was tied upright to the four poster bed and was completely bollock naked! Seb was also naked and was taking pictures of Charles who was covered in cream, jam and chocolate from a cake throwing frenzy. It turned out that Seb wasn't his cousin but was some rent boy that Charles had picked up in Soho and just brought to the party for a laugh!

So, poor Sarah was absolutely devastated that her fiancé was at best a bisexual with a fetish for cream cakes being thrown at him! Crowley managed to get the camera from the rent boy and told the pair of them to get dressed and get out. That was the last Crowley saw of Charles. He didn't even finish his uni course; Crowley reckoned that Charles must have thought that Crowley had gone back and told everyone, but he didn't to save Sarah's feelings. Apparently, Sarah blamed Crowley for it. Saying how could he have let Charles bring someone in like that and when he tried to explain that they were the kind of people Charles was hanging around with, she blamed Crowley further saying what kind of man lets his mate go to seedy bars and pick up men.'

'Fuck,' added Todd.

'So I went to the gallery tonight and pretended that I not only knew Sarah and his whole sorry tale, but that there were still pictures from the camera that Crowley snatched from the rent boy.' Grace added.

'And is there?' pushed Todd.

'No, he ripped the film out of the camera as soon as he left the room as he didn't want the images relating back to his sister. But Charles doesn't know that, does he?'

'So what now?'

'I've told Charles that we want a six week exhibition in his New York gallery in the summer and if we prove ourselves, we have the option of Washington and California. By that time we might have other galleries interested anyway so we will have to see. He's agreed to all the conditions that I asked which was that he was to liaise with you and Elliott and to work with you in the manner he would work with anybody else.'

A smile started to creep across Todd's face.

'Are you fucking kiddin' me?' he drawled. Grace shook her head with a beaming smile. 'Grace, you are unbelievable! THANK YOU, CROWLEY!' he bellowed at the top of his voice.

CHAPTER 24

As Grace walked into her cottage in Pelsby, she felt like she couldn't walk another step. The flight back from New York had been delayed for hours due to the weather and she had managed to find a seat on the plane that had a snorer on one side, a kicking kid behind her and a couple who argued most of the way back about something that had been left in the hotel. She knew that Todd would be pacing the floor so decided as soon as she had put her case upstairs, put the kettle on and fired up the boiler she would call him.

The house felt very different without the dogs. The cottage felt different too. She wasn't sure if it was because she knew that she wouldn't be there for much longer due to Mr Cousins selling or the fact that she felt like a different person now. She would never have believed that the Grace of six months ago would have been on this incredible journey and she was centre to it all. She called Todd who seemed very relieved to finally hear her voice.

'It's strange being back here you know,' she declared.

'It must be. Bet it feels warmer than here though?' Todd

asked.

'I was sat here before thinking about my life six months ago and my life now. I feel like I've been on such a journey,' she said.

'Hey, it's not over yet. We still gotta lot of work to do,' he sighed.

'I know and I can't wait either. I'll be back as soon as the visa is sorted and then you'll be sick of me,' she joked. 'I feel like I should do something here in the summer maybe. At the summer fair? I'm not sure what, but I just want to somehow say thank you to everyone properly. There are so many people I need to thank. I need to contact Deeres University as well and see about offering a scholarship in Jane's name. I think that will be the best way to thank Mr Cousins and use some of his money well.'

'To offer a kid an opportunity like that is a great way to honour her memory,' agreed Todd.

'And then there's Crowley, how do I thank him? I mean I would never have got the exhibition in that gallery if it wasn't...' she stopped mid-sentence.

'If it wasn't what, Grace?' pushed Todd.

'If it wasn't for him,' she whispered. She jumped off the armchair and with a mild panic finished her call, 'Todd I have to go. I'll call you back later, I promise.' Then she hung up. Her breath was quickening and she stood in the middle of her lounge and called for him. She waited for a few moments but it felt like an age and eventually Crowley appeared at the window with his back to her.

'This was the deed, wasn't it?' she croaked. He stayed on the spot but turned to look at her. He had a look of resignation.

'It was my dear, Daff,' he said softly.

'So why are you not with Jennifer and Max?' She was

struggling to keep her voice steady.

'I asked 'up there' if I could wait until you returned to Pelsby,' he turned and looked back out of the window toward the bridge.

'We met in Pelsby, I died in Pelsby so it only seemed fitting that I say goodbye to you, in Pelsby. It's funny how such an unassuming little village could have such a profound effect on a person,' he mused.

'It was the gallery wasn't it? With Charles? That was your deed,' Grace pushed. She was shifting her weight from one foot to another and starting to wring her hands. 'All the other things that I thought were your deed I could have done without you. But this was the one thing that I couldn't have done. This was the positive effect. It wasn't about a positive contribution; it was about making a change that only you could do. And that was it. Am I right?'

'I believe so,' he said.

'And you have been waiting for me to come home so you could say goodbye? You could have been with them nearly a fortnight ago.' He turned and looked at her.

'My dear, there are some goodbyes that I regret saying. There are some that have been denied to me and there are some I simply should have done earlier in my life. This was one that I didn't want to get wrong,' his voice was starting to shake.

'Is this really goodbye?' Grace could hardly see Crowley through the tears welling up in her eyes.

'I'm afraid it is, Daff,' sniffed Crowley. Grace ran into his arms and held on to him.

'How am I supposed to do all this without you? I know you were never going to be here forever but it always seemed to be another day. I can't believe that today is the day,' she cried. 'Is this like the taxi thing? Are you simply waiting now to leave the party?'

'Yes,' he whispered into her hair.

'But there's so much to do still. What if I get stuck or Charles starts being an arse? What if this isn't it and we've got it wrong?' Grace could feel a slight chuckle from him in his arms. 'This is 'it' though and I'm babbling. I know this is for the best and you will finally be with them,' she moaned.

'I can smell her perfume, Daff. She is so near,' he confessed. Grace loosened her grip on Crowley but still kept him in her arms. She looked up at him. He looked different, peaceful somehow.

'Then go to them and tell them the story about how Grace met a ghost and how she fell in love with him and how she will always think of him until the day she dies when she will see him again,' Grace's tears were flowing and Crowley gently wiped her face.

'I shall, Daff. I'll be there when the time comes. To say you've been like a daughter to me is such a terrible cliché. You are more than that, you are part of my soul and so you will always be with me. My dearest darling, please always feel my love for you,' he croaked.

'I will.' They stared at each other for a long time absorbing all their memories and love for each other. He eventually began to smile at her and she knew the time had come.

'Goodbye Crowley,' she cried.

Her arms fell to her sides when he disappeared and she dropped to the floor and sobbed.

CHAPTER 25
The Summer

Grace stood over the road in the blazing sunshine to check the external images of the gallery. She was happy with the photos she had selected for the vinyl promotional banners that hung and gently flapped in the breeze. She had picked images of New York buildings but had cropped certain areas of particular photographs to suggest and entice people into the gallery. She was more than pleased with the final details of The Big Shot Exhibition. She had plumped for the name not only for its photographic references but also Kate used the term to describe people in a slightly derogatory manner and yet everyone knew that deep down Kate was the only Big Shot in town.

She ran over the road, dodging cars and yellow cabs and stepped inside the gallery. Todd was working with the electricians, Elliott was in the glass boardroom with Charles and numerous other people were keeping busy with cleaning or moving furniture around.

Grace was glad to see Sean at the far end telling a team of waiters what he expected of them and to keep everyone's glass topped up and who was responsible for what food. She was glad she insisted he come over and replace the giraffe for the first few weeks. Her parents had travelled over with him and they had more or less adopted him in the last few months. His warm personality had won everyone over and the staff couldn't do enough for him; even Charles had succumbed to his raw humour which had helped brighten his dour demeanour.

Todd spied Grace had come back in and ran over to her.

'The lights on the back wall are all working now so they are just going to adjust the lamps and then that's it. How does it look outside?' he asked.

'I'm happy with it. I just hope we have enough food and drink. The phone hasn't stopped with people asking for extra tickets. I've had to say no to so many people. I just hope Charles lives up to his promise of all these high flyers that he said are coming,' she groaned.

'They'll be here. This is a hot ticket, Grace,' Todd looked around the room, 'you happy with the way it looks in here?'

Grace started to slowly walk around the gallery and looked at all the framed photos hanging on the walls.

'I just hope I've done her justice that's all,' she whispered. She stopped and looked at a picture of Kate. It hung proud in the centre of the whole collection. The black and white picture was the only one in the exhibition not to have been taken by her. In the picture, Kate was around thirty; she wore a white linen shirt and white linen pants and her blonde wavy hair was being blown to one side by the wind. The only other thing she was wearing was the Rolleiflex camera around her neck. She was laughing and Todd and Grace presumed that the picture had been taken by Mort.

They stood for a moment and gazed at the picture and Todd blindly sought her hand. He gently pulled her fingers to entwine with his own.

'I've never said it before Grace, but you know that I love you, don't you?' They both carried on looking at the picture.

'I love you too, Todd.' She turned her face to look at him and he stepped forward and kissed her.

'Now we've got work to do,' he smirked and left her standing by the picture.

She stood for a moment on her own and looked at her beautiful friend. In some ways, Grace couldn't wait to die to see what she thought of all what she had done. She had so many questions for her. She hoped that she had fulfilled the promise of making something of her life. But who would have thought then that the start of her new life would be in the city that Kate had left behind. All those endless cups of tea she had made and all those chats that they had had and never once had either of them seen this coming. Who would have thought that the advice Kate had given would have fundamentally only happened because of her? Grace chuckled at the irony of the promise she had made. Her thoughts turned to Todd. She knew she would be with him for the rest of her life and though she worried at first as to how that would happen, she no longer worried anymore. She had learned that making plans could be a futile exercise when some things are pre-destined anyway. The path to them would always differ but the end result would remain the same. So Grace had decided to simply skip along the path and see what happened as she more or less knew the ending already.

'So, you're going to marry him then?' came the voice

from her right. Her skin prickled all over. Could it be? If it was, then how? And why? She didn't dare hope but yet the voice was so familiar. She turned her head gently and there he stood in all his glory. Crowley.

'What the...' She was stunned. She hadn't seen him for nearly six months and never thought she would see him again as long as she would live.

'My dear Daff, it seems I've been promoted.' And he let out an enormous belly laugh.

ABOUT THE AUTHOR

Estelle Maher was born in the heart of Liverpool, England. After spending her teens in rural Dorset, she returned to the North of England and now resides in Wirral with her husband, 2 children and 2 dogs.

Throughout her life, Estelle has experienced lots of 'inexplicable moments' which inspired her first debut novel, Grace & The Ghost.

For more information on books by Estelle Maher:

www.estellemaher.com

T: @EstelleMaher

FB: @EstelleMaherAuthor

Coming in 2017:
Angel's Rebellion

93149985R00224

Made in the USA
Columbia, SC
06 April 2018